SEPTEMBER

DAY

LARRY
SCHWEIKART

Cover art by Jay D. Dyson

Published By:

Alpha Connections

Emmett, ID 83617

ISBN 0-9747610-8-7

Proudly produced in the United States of America

Introduction

No living American can, or should, forget 9/11. But the process of trying to place this book with a major publisher has alerted me to the fact that many indeed want to do just that. Repeatedly, my agent got rejections with the words, "It's well written, but we don't want to touch that topic." They could have added, " . . . especially from a patriotic point of view", as this book offers.

Fortunately, a friend and published author in his own right, Jeff Head, assisted me in bringing this into print. Jeff's "Dragon's Fury Series" at www.dragonsfuryseries.com, a techno-thriller about World War with China and Iran that arises out of current events, is a testimony to what self-publishing of a good book can accomplish. Jeff has served as production supervisor and as "editor" in most matters of getting this into print

I also thank Jay Dyson of www.sacredcowburgers.com, who provided the cover art.

Although it never was accepted by a major publishing house, I don't think it was for a want of trying on the part of my agent, Scott Hoffman, and I thank him for his many labors on my behalf.

Finally, my intent was never to write a "religious" fiction, but I do hope that the Christian faith of several of the characters emerges as a reflection of the One hero above all others, Jesus Christ.

Larry Schweikart
Centerville, Ohio, January 2006.

SEPTEMBER

DAY

LARRY
SCHWEIKART

Prologue

Khartoum, Sudan, May 18, 1996

The black Mercedes rocketed through the deserted, unlit streets of this old city, nearly camouflaged against the darkened buildings. Weaving almost drunkenly at times, the driver was, in fact, quite sober. He did not care if he nicked a pedestrian or two: there were more pressing issues at hand. Frantically, the car skidded around curves, negotiating the narrow roads that during the day would have been impassable, crammed as they were with merchants and beggars, bankers and imams. But it was not daytime. No cars, camels, or carts impeded him.

Ahead loomed a pothole the size of a small television, which he could not dodge. The Mercedes' right front tire slammed into it, propelling him off his seat. A Lebanese curse sprang to his lips---*Ja Harandin!*---exemplifying his capacity for swearing in six languages.

Screeching to a halt on 12 El Meshtal Street, the driver, almost as an afterthought, checked his mirrors. He swiveled his head, looking around, and concluded he was alone, sitting outside the iron gates that protected the compound home of Osama bin Laden. Checking his mirrors, Falik Malid surveyed the row of smaller "guest houses" that stretched down El Meshtal on each side where bin Laden's lieutenants lived. Tonight, they were quiet.

That's because tonight they were gone. Good. At least that much is going according to schedule.

Malid threw open the car door and burst through the gate without a key or a password. Bin Laden, obviously, was a man who had no fear of common burglars, or, apparently, foreign intelligence services.

Like bin Laden, Malid was a Saudi, born shortly after the Yom Kippur War in a village not far from Riyadh. He'd known his share of poverty, but tonight he was dressed in a western-style suit, sans tie and head covering. Aside from his stubble and a scorpion tattoo on his left wrist, Malid looked like any other Middle Eastern businessman. But under his suit rested the Glock 9 mm, which peeked out from his belt. He had only one spare clip, in his left pocket. If he needed more than that, . . . well, the battle would have been lost by that time anyway.

Walking briskly through the small courtyard, Malid smelled the fragrance of lemon trees, which were laced among the date palms in the lush vegetation surrounding bin Laden's residence. On the tiled courtyard stood several empty plastic chairs, the site of so many of bin Laden's many "business meetings" that were little more than murder planning sessions. Malid recalled the powerful messages Sharif had delivered to the infidel west and to Muslim heretics from these insignificant-looking, cheap chairs. His mouth curved into a tiny grin: *Ironic, no, that bin Laden has made "low tech," as the Americans say, his modus operandi.* Malid had witnessed these decisions first hand, and had been privileged to sit in on some of them. Privileged indeed.

Tonight, though, was not about delivering messages, but protecting the messenger.

Osama bin Laden's luxurious two-story house had pink faded walls that concealed an extravagant, if gaudy, interior, all paid for by the Bin Laden Construction Company. Although it hardly compared with Saddam Hussein's lavish palaces, the residence contrasted sharply with the poverty-ridden shacks that littered Khartoum's streets.

Now marching deliberately to the front porch, Malid slammed his open palm hard into the wooden door. *Sharif dislikes doorbells*, Malid recalled. Dogs barked their dissatisfaction from nearby neighborhoods, but Malid heard no response inside the house. Again he pounded the door. Then it opened a crack.

Peering out was Osama's servant, Talil, a short, ugly woman who cleaned the house and cooked for the family. She'd been with bin Laden as long as Malid had known him. *Whatever she lacks in beauty she makes up for in her ability to keep secrets.*

"What do you want?" Talil growled.

Normally, Malid might be polite, but there was no time now. "Out of the way. This is important . . . and no business of yours." He pushed the door open, sweeping Talil back with his free arm, then he bolted up the stairs to bin Laden's office, racing through the darkened hall without switching on a light.

Bad art deco hung on the walls---*bin Laden had no taste*, Malid sniffed. *But then, what do warriors know of art?* Climbing the stairs to the second floor office, he quickly scanned the room, peering at tables with numerous Arab-language newspapers strewn about. He was not interested in them. Without looking in the direction of bin Laden's bedroom, he began to flip through the papers, shouting over his shoulder, "Hurry! Hurry, the Mukhabarat are coming."

Returning his attention to the desk, Malid spotted what he wanted. Throwing several papers in a small metal waste basket, he extracted a small container of lighter fluid from his pocket. Once he had drenched the papers, he dug out a cigarette lighter and put the paper to flame. He then conducted another quick survey of the room, then another. Satisfied that the had sanitized the office, Malid finally felt his pulse slow. He checked the fire, which was nearly out now, having consumed the contents. Satisfied that only ashes remained, he doused the remnants with a nearby pitcher of water when a shadow dimmed the light from behind him.

Osama bin Laden's 6'6" frame filled the doorway, dressed in traditional robes, his long, thin beard prominent. He wore the light Afghan turban rather than the Arab *kafiyah*. Tonight, he was not armed, although it was not unusual to see him wander about---even in Khartoum---with his favorite AK-47 and double bandoliers. Bin Laden had watched Malid's entire arsonist display, then uttered a brief, bored sigh. He turned, and, moving with deliberation and grace, crammed his remaining clothes into a small suitcase, tossing in his cell phones (he carried several) as an after thought. Only then did he address Malid.

You're too late," he said in his characteristic monotone. "I already destroyed all the business records after you called. You managed to find a couple of duplicates, which I was getting to," said bin Laden.

And when would that be? When the Mukhabarat are pounding on the door? Malid wasn't sure whether to respond or not, then found he didn't have to. Bin Laden had already dismissed the notion that there could be any loose ends.

"The aircraft is ready?"

"It has been ready for several hours," Malid replied, still out of breath. "150 of your fighters are already aboard."

"My family?"

"All three wives, two of your sons, and your four daughters, yes, *al-Sharif*, all await you."

Bin Laden methodically continued placing items in his travel bag. "And the pilot knows his instructions."

Malid, grew agitated. *The man has no urgency.* He wiped beads of sweat from his brow.

"Of course. It has all been well planned, as you know. We must hurry. Jamaal said there isn't much time. The Mukhabarat have already started questioning people."

While Sudan's security forces were no match for the Americans or the British in their intelligence-gathering abilities, they were second to none in brutality. Even those loyal to bin Laden or the cause could be made to talk under the Mukhabarat's "gentle" questioning.

Bin Laden grabbed his suitcase and small shoulder bag, then shrugged, "Jamaal has been wrong before. The Sudanese feed him lies whenever the Americans press them for action."

Undeterred, Malid gently took bin Laden by the elbow and guided him down the stairs and gestured toward the front door. "Perhaps, *Sharif*. But can you afford to find out? Do you want to risk falling into their hands? Besides, you have been planning this move for weeks. It was only a matter of time."

For a lieutenant, the man is a master manipulator, bin Laden thought, *but he is right.* He grunted his assent, but turned and lifted his finger to Malid. "Nevertheless, I like leaving on my terms, not those of the infidels." Malid gulped, and nodded, then again pointed to the door.

The two men crossed the small courtyard, hidden from prying eyes by its eight-foot high concrete security fence and the trees, then they reached the waiting Mercedes. Without getting in, Malid jammed in the key, started the engine, and punched a button that opened the trunk, then rapidly moved to assist bin Laden. He heaved the suitcase in the trunk, while bin Laden dropped his shoulder bag in the back seat before crawling in.

"Al-Zawahiri is meeting us as planned?" bin Laden asked.

"I instructed Mahmood to contact him," said Malid, slamming the trunk, then running to the driver's side to slide behind the wheel. " I don't know his status. Regardless, we must go."

Bin Laden leaned forward and placed a firm hand on Malid's shoulder. "You haven't talked to Ayman? I will not travel without him. You know that."

You'd risk getting tortured by the Mukhabarat over your doctor? Malid adopted a pleading tone with bin Laden. "Please, we must go. Mahmood will see that Dr. al-Zawahiri meets us. You will have your physician. But we have to leave now. The Mukhabarat could be here any second." Bin Laden slowly removed his hand from Malid's shoulder, then leaned back. After seconds that seemed like an eternity, through the rear view mirror Malid saw bin Laden signal to him to go, and the Mercedes sped off toward Khartoum Civil Airport.

As the car hurtled back through the black streets, bin Laden pulled a cell phone from his pocket and hit a speed-dial number. "We have left. Clear out as much as you can from the accounts tomorrow if the Sudanese haven't already frozen them. No telling what the

Americans will intimidate the Sudanese cowards to do." He listened impatiently to the voice on the other end, then shrugged.

"Yemen. Or Afghanistan," he answered. "We have many friends. I will inform you later of our ultimate location." He snapped the cell phone shut and addressed Malid. "Closing these businesses is a blessing. They were losing money anyway. The Americans have done me a favor."

Why didn't you close them yourself? thought Malid. *You are very smart, Sharif, but I fear your overconfidence will be your undoing.*

Malid was no fool. Educated only to equivalent of a 10th grade in Saudi Arabia, he had worked for years in a friend's import business. There, he met bin Laden while filling orders for concrete and technology items for bin Laden's company. Five years ago, bin Laden brought him into the organization---after the Afghan war he had called it al-Qaeda, or "the base," and the name stuck---and his facility with numbers, combined with his common sense and his exceptional ability to maintain the strictest secrecy had vaulted him up through the ranks to be bin Laden's personal aide, not far down the pecking order from Zawahiri himself, though he often thought he was little better than bin Laden's errand boy.

Americans have a term for people like me---a "gofer"---but better a "gofer" for Allah than a lackey for the Royal Family or, worse, the Egyptians. He was loyal to his employer and to the cause, but Malid was neither blind nor uncritical. To that end, he kept his own counsel.

Bin Laden is right about one thing, he thought. *His companies were losing money. He is an excellent terrorist, but a poor businessman.* Like most al-Qaeda followers, Malid thought bin Laden was anointed---hence he always addressed him with the more respectful "*al-Sharif*," or "Enlightened One," than the "*al-khaliph*" ("leader," or "boss") used by some of the more secular al-Qaeda dogs, and certainly never as "the Contractor," as the local Afghans had dubbed him in the struggle against the Russians.

The car sped on, arriving at the Khartoum Airport, circling around back to the freight loading section, passing several old Boeing 737s and four Fokkers of Sudan Airways, all of questionable airworthiness. A tired, bored guard at the gate briefly held up one hand until he noticed a small decal of the bin Laden company on the Mercedes. Malid took no chances, moving his right hand to the Glock should it be needed. But the guard, squinting at the person in the back seat, suddenly recognized the passenger and with great deference waved the vehicle through. *Fortunate for you, my friend. The Mukhabarat must not have involved the local police forces. Either that, or no one bothered to tell this guard what was going on.* Cleared through, the Mercedes sped around the main terminal to the rear, where a large, chartered private 737 awaited, engines screaming, cabin door open, stairs extended.

Malid pulled to a stop next to the jet, whereupon he was instantly out and already had the trunk open. He quickly dug out bin Laden's bag, all the while his eyes flicking back and forth around the airport. "Do you think they are watching us?"

Bin Laden replied with a tight smile, "Of course. I'm counting on it."

Instead of boarding, however, bin Laden paced nervously near the wingtip. For the first time all night, Malid sensed that the plan may not be as brilliant as he once thought. But he had no reason not to trust bin Laden's judgment, which had proven astute on so many other occasions. Ever mystified at his employer, Malid threw the last few pieces of luggage aboard, then folded his arms and waited patiently.

As the seconds stretched to minutes, bin Laden grew more animated. "Where is he? I will not go without him. Are you sure Mahmood understood his instructions?"

Poor Mahmood, thought Malid. *As the Americans say, dung rolls downhill.* But Malid himself was becoming increasingly concerned. *All this for a doctor? Sharif is a multi-millionaire. Couldn't he just fly Zawahiri to wherever he finally relocates?*

In an attempt to speed up matters by getting bin Laden on the plane, Malid said "We don't have time for this. Ayman al-Zawahiri will be here. I will personally get him on another plane, *al-Sharif.*"

Bin Laden shot Malid an icy stare. "No! There is no debate! You were ordered to make sure he is here."

Malid knew this was *al-Sharif's* greatest weakness, even more than his occasional overconfidence or pride. The man was committed, and a gifted strategic planner---a terrorist's terrorist---and Allah knows he received special enlightenment and revelation. But there were these quirks. This same man who lived in caves and slept on rocks, who ate dung to survive, nevertheless insisted on his own private doctor. It was this type of weakness the Americans or the Jews could exploit.

Becoming more uncomfortable by the moment, Malid started imagining the Mukhabarat descending on them any second. He could see himself in their chairs, his genitals attached to electrodes wired to car batteries. Beads of sweat again appeared on his forehead. He scanned the blackness around the hangar in hopes of seeing a second car, when he detected . . . *movement?* A shape appeared, a Volvo, wheeling into sight around the terminal. Relieved, Malid looked over his shoulder at bin Laden who had resumed his stoic countenance, as though he knew it all along.

You don't fool me, Sharif. You were close to panic at the thought of being without your doctor. What else do you fear?

The Volvo lurched to a stop just a few feet in front of bin Laden. From the back seat emerged Ayman al-Zawahiri, bin Laden's personal physician. Bin Laden's relief turned to anger, as he momentarily ignored Zawahiri and glared at the driver, Mahmood. Before he could say anything, Zawahiri breathlessly bowed and said, "*Salaam, al-Sharif.*"

For a moment, bin Laden's iron gaze remained on Mahmood, then he broke into a full smile as he hugged Zawahiri. "I would not leave without you. You are aware we are not coming back?"

Zawahiri nodded. "I don't need much, wherever we go," he said, pointing to his large medical bag as Mahmood pulled the physician's suitcase from the trunk. "I am sorry we are late, *Sharif*. The family . . . . saying goodbye is difficult. It's not Mahmood's fault."

That seemed to appease bin Laden, who waved away Mahmood. "It is understandable. And the dialysis machinery will meet us?"

"As you requested. Your kidneys will be pure as the driven snow."

Bin Laden, nodded approvingly and escorted Zawahiri up the steps of the aircraft. Already the engines were warmed up. Within moments, the doors were sealed and the 737 ramped up to taxi speed.

Inside, the aircraft was full of more than 100 of bin Laden's trusted fighters and family members. He greeted a few before sitting down in row one, but left his seat belt unbuckled. Looking at Zawahiri, his eye twinkled. "Short trip," he noted. Zawahiri nodded knowingly.

No sooner had he uttered the words than a loud pop sent a shudder through the plane and it immediately sagged down and to the right. Rather than screaming, the passengers sat composed. A few flinched instinctively, but no one spoke. Those on the right could see the 737's right landing gear, now collapsed, and the plane's wingtip now churning up sparks on the taxiway as the aircraft slid to a stop.

From inside the cockpit, bin Laden heard the pilot calmly report in Arabic: "Tower, this is 17023. I have a landing gear failure. This is an emergency."

Malid and Zawahiri exchanged glances with bin Laden. They quietly rose and joined the others, who calmly exited the rubber emergency slide attached to the doorway. One by one, bin Laden's fighters and family leaped down the slide, straightened themselves, and gathered a few feet near the 737's lopsided wing. The process occurred without the slightest apparent concern over the aircraft's malfunction. Inside the tower, airport officials peered through binoculars into the darkness at the crippled aircraft. Fire vehicles---what few there are at Khartoum Civil---were already en route.

Suddenly to the right by the stalled jet, the scream of another set of engines was heard. A second 737, also with the markings of the bin Laden business group, but with no landing lights, violently set down and taxied next to the broken airplane. As it rolled to a stop, the stairway was lowered, and with clockwork efficiency the fighters and family members boarded, followed by bin Laden, Malid, and al-Zawahiri. Before the emergency crew could arrive at the first aircraft, the second raced down the runway and disappeared into the folds of the black Sudanese sky.

Looking back through his window, Malid asked "*Sharif*, you are confident the Mukhabarat had a tracker on the other aircraft?"

Bin Laden nodded. "The Americans want me, therefore the Sudanese want me. They know my plane. If they did not get me at home, they would send jets to escort us to one of their infidel bases. Do not think they would have let us fly out of the country. Now, it will be hours before they realize what has happened. By the time they figure out we are not on the ground at the Khartoum Airport, we will be over Saudi airspace and on our way to Afghanistan."

August 1996, Jefferson Memorial, Washington, D.C.

Khalid Insar, a handsome and well-dressed Pakistani-born American citizen, paced angrily around the national memorial to the author of the Great Declaration. Its light reflected off his immaculate slick-backed hair and well-trimmed thin moustache. A businessman with extensive contacts in the Middle East, Insar had hob-nobbed with American aristocracy. Photos captured President Bill Clinton greeting him like a long-lost friend at the White House. Of course, the five-digit contributions to the Democratic National Committee did not hurt, and, no doubt, the administration expected plenty more where that came from. Tonight's meeting wasn't about money, however. It was about something much more serious.

Insar did not wait long before a portly, disheveled figure emerged from the shadows and trudged up the Memorial steps. Insar had met him before, and did not particularly like Deputy National Security Advisor Dusty Brolin. Next to the impeccably-dressed Pakistani, Brolin looked both worlds---and classes---apart.

"Why in the hell do we have to meet out here, Khalid? And why at night? You working for the CIA all of a sudden?"

Insar did not appreciate the joke. "Are you people insane? You are threatening the Sudanese? They are willing to help us!"

"I don't know what you are talking about. I . . . ." Brolin stammered.

"Do you think I'm a fool? Does Clinton think that?"

"Look, Khalid, why are we meeting out here like a scene out of Watergate? What's this all about."

Insar only became more irritated with Brolin. "I hardly need to tell you anything." He produced a piece of paper from his pocket. "Do you know what a ghost letter is?" *Of course you do, you fraudulent toady. It's a letter with official backing from the U.S. government that lacks a signature or name. Plausible desirability.*

Even without looking at the letter, Brolin blanched. "Where did you get this? You aren't authorized to see this."

"Typical response from this administration---question the source, not the content. Is it true? Answer me!"

"Yes, yes, er, that is, even if it's possible that someone in the administration wrote this, it's not what you think. This does not concern you."

"Doesn't concern *me*?" Insar seethed. "You people really are arrogant. You have delivered a letter warning of *war* against the Sudanese government, without any 'official' letterhead or signatures, through back channels, so that it can be denied, and expect them to meekly comply?" *What do you know of war? Real war?*

Brolin stumbled for words. "They were harboring terrorists, for Pete's sake. This was just a little shot across their bow to tell them to stop it."

"A 'little shot across their bow?' You threatened *war*. They had already offered you Bin Laden's head on a *platter*, and you did nothing."

The revelation jolted Brolin. "How do you know we did nothing? That's not true!

Who . . . ." Perspiration beaded on Brolin's brow. "You, ah, you don't have . . . ."

"Did Minister Ali Taha offer to extradite Osama Bin Laden to us? *Did he*?"

"You don't understand," the flustered, NSA advisor answered, "I mean, yes. We . . . uh, we couldn't take him."

"What do you mean, we 'couldn't take' one of the world's most notorious terrorists when he was offered to us?"

"Look, you know that the President views this as a law enforcement matter . . . . "

"*It is war!* Are you people blind as well as arrogant?"

"Look, Khalid there is more to it than that . . . ."

Then a new reality suddenly dawned on Insar. "Oh, no." Shaking his head as he paced, Insar glared at Brolin. "They didn't offer to *give* us bin Laden---they offered to *kill* him, didn't they? They offered to kill bin Laden, give us the body to prove that it was him, and Clinton refused?"

Brolin tried to conceal his patronizing tone. "Khalid, the President would have to sign a 'finding' to allow us to kill him, or even to authorize another country to kill him on our behalf. They didn't see that as politically viable in the White House. It would have been a distraction to our . . . ."

"Politically viable?' 'A distraction?' By now the sound of Insar's screaming could be heard from far beyond the Jefferson Memorial. "The man planned the bombing of the World Trade Center! He's been involved in terrorist acts from Saudi Arabia to Yemen to my home country of Pakistan. How could this possibly be a distraction to *anything* Clinton was involved in."

"It's not like this guy's Hitler. He's a run of the mill terrorist, no worse than half the guys on the FBI's 'Most Wanted' List."

Insar rolled his eyes. "A 'run of the mill' terrorist with millions of dollars and an avowed commitment to *jihad*. Do you fail to grasp he has pledged to topple the Saudi royal family? To assassinate the president of Pakistan? He has issued a *fatwa* against our own country! He even tried to assassinate President Bush."

"Come on, Khalid," Brolin lectured. "These *jihads* and *fatwas* are a dime a dozen They don't mean anything. We get terror threats every day. As for the assassination attempt on Bush, we caught it; we stopped it. What's the big deal?"

"You people really do not have the slightest clue about Islamic extremists, do you? Do you really think this is some Arab version of the Irish Republican Army? A bunch of Klansmen in turbans? Osama bin Laden *exists* to make war on the innocent in a dozen countries, here, . . . in *my* adopted country, the United States. These are not empty threats. He will carry them out. He *has* carried them out. Have you forgotten the World Trade Center? Yes, you stopped the plot against Bush. You are one for five."

"We have those people from the WTC bombing in custody," Brolin sputtered, "and . . . ."

"Are you serious? You don't have anyone of significance in custody. You don't even have the tail of the snake, let alone its head. And here a government like Sudan, desperate to get back in your good graces, offers to kill a terrorist mastermind and you need a presidential *finding*? Why did you not at least have him captured?"

"I'll say again, the President sees this, er, sees the whole terrorist thing as a law enforcement issue." Brolin, completely disoriented, added, "We didn't think we could convict him in a court of law."

"You are at war. *We* are at war. This isn't about arresting and trying people---it's about killing them and defeating their evil organization down to the last man. This is not something for the FBI---it's an issue for the *army*."

Insar realized he had been shouting for five minutes, and composed himself. "It's an issue for *our* army. This is war." *No, it's useless. Brolin doesn't get it. Clinton sure doesn't get it.* Shaking his head, Insar pointed his finger at Brolin as he backed away. "You will regret this some day. *We* will regret it. These are killers. May Allah protect us all."

Brolin still held the ghost letter in his hand. "Khalid. Khalid! We have laws . . . . we have procedures we have to follow . . . ."

Insar dismissed Brolin with a wave of his hand, disappearing into the darkness.

PART ONE

THE PLOT

Chapter 1

Tempe, Arizona, April 1998

"With the 226th selection in the NFL draft, the Cincinnati Bengals select . . . ." On screen, ESPN's announcing crew dissected the low-round pick as the family of Arizona State University linebacker Thomas Palmer gathered around the television. This was the NFL draft's lower rounds, watched only by the football fanatics and by the family or friends of players about to be selected. All the "quality" players have been taken, and the rounds were now only five minutes long as the draft stretched into the 7th round on Sunday afternoon. It is here that running backs who are too slow, quarterbacks too short, and linebackers too light finally hear the phone ring. Yet athletes still wait for the call, because a representative from an NFL team is on the other end, offering that long-shot prize: a chance to attend at an NFL training camp and possibly win a spot on a professional football team.

Like thousands of other college football stars, Thomas Palmer waited for his call. A popular player with Sun Devil fans for his shock of long hair bursting from beneath his yellow football helmet and flowing down to his maroon jersey, Palmer had dispelled any doubt that he was a sissy: he started at linebacker, delivering punishing hits, without any trash talk. No, the hair, many thought, reflected Palmer's streak of irreverence. Anyone with that hair had to be a rebel. A Bill Walton in pads, a white Tommie Smith, an un-pierced Dennis Rodman.

ESPN's cameras cut from the analysts to rejoin Gene Washington of the NFL, who strode to the podium to announce the latest draft pick: *"With the 227th selection in the 1998 NFL draft, the Arizona Cardinals select Thomas Palmer, linebacker from Arizona State University. Detroit is on the clock."*

Cheers erupted in the Palmer household. Ann Palmer leaned over the sofa to kiss her smiling son on the cheek. David punched his brother in the shoulder. Tom, wearing a Phoenix Suns jersey ("B-A-

R-K-L-E-Y" stenciled on the back), smiled and shrugged with relief. At least he'd still be playing in front of the home crowd.

"There you are, Peabrain" David said, laughing. "Now you're making the big bucks!"

Tom smiled, but his eyes were dead serious: "I'll be the starter," he told David.

"At what? Water boy? Come on, Peabrain, you're 5' 11" and 200 pounds. I mean, I'm your bro. I support you. But you can count on one hand the number of 200-lb. linebackers in the NFL. It's great that you'll get to go to camp, but ya gotta be realistic. NFL linebackers run 230-240. You can't put on that kind of weight if you eat like John Goodman."

"Who said I'd be a linebacker? I'll convert to safety. I'll play cornerback, if I have to."

David had seen this before in his big brother, and knew Tom's resolve could move mountains. He grabbed his hand and gripped it with both of his. "I believe you will big brother. Anyway, you're close to home here, even if it is with the Cards. I kinda hoped you'd go to the Broncos or Packers, or one of the powerhouses."

"It's all good," shrugged Tom. "Weaker teams mean more opportunity. They'll be more willing to give me a chance, you watch."

Thomas Palmer, Sr., who had quietly observed this interplay between his boys, chimed in, "We're just thrilled you'll be an NFL player, son . . . ."

Keith, Tom's big brother, interrupted, " . . . because that means we get free tickets to see the Cowboys when they come to town!"

Tom bolted off the sofa, good-naturedly taking Keith down in a headlock. "Yeah, well, here is what I'll do to Emmitt Smith and Troy Aikman!"

Over their roughhousing, Ann Palmer heard the phone ringing. "That's quite enough. If you want to wrestle" (she pronounced it "rassel" in her Oklahoma twang) "go outside, draft or no draft." She lifted the thin receiver, then covering the mouthpiece, announced, "Tom, it's coach Schultz."

Bill Schultz had recruited Palmer while an assistant coach at ASU, and Tom was closer to him than any of his teammates. Still in his 30s, Schultz was a *wunderkind* who had been stolen away from Arizona State for a less imposing, but better paying, job at UNLV.

Tom gently took the receiver out of his mother's hand, all the while mouthing to Keith, *"You're dead. Dead!"* Then, to Schultz, Palmer said, "Guess you want tickets to the Cowboys game, too, huh coach?"

Schultz laughed and replied, "No, but I'll check back with you when the 49ers come to town. I gotta say, though, you were the best scholarship I ever handed out."

Palmer deflected the compliment. "Arizona State got its pound of flesh. I got you to a Rose Bowl."

"Too bad you didn't beat Ohio State. I think that hair slowed you down. Think what you could do with a buzz cut. Hey, you also had a lot of help that season, as I recall, from a guy named Plummer. Anyway, seriously, I just wanted to congratulate you. I'm off to UNLV."

"Yeah, you better get that gambling habit under control," Tom joked. Schultz, a Mormon, and one of the most moral men Palmer ever met, in fact had no vices that Palmer even knew of. Yet the man hardly led a boring life, from skiing to white water rafting, Schultz was one active dude. Palmer had read a little about the Mormons, and although he didn't share much of their theology, he respected Schultz's commitment.

"All kidding aside," Schultz responded, "I learned one lesson in coaching four years at ASU."

"And what's that?"

Proudly, Schultz answered, "Never bet against Thomas Palmer."

There was an embarrassed silence at the other end, before Schultz continued, "Anyway, good luck. Stay in touch."

"You too, coach. And thanks. I know I wasn't the easiest guy to coach sometimes. I'll miss you." Palmer hung up the phone, but stared at it for a few moments. Finally, he turned to his family, who still stood like an eager audience waiting for a speech from a political candidate. Palmer shook his head and smiled. "Do you think maybe one of you can help me get a Cardinals' playbook before training camp starts in a few months."

Tom, Sr., whispered to Ann, "He'll not only memorize the damn thing, but will find all the misspellings and rearrange their sentences." Then, as an afterthought, and to no one in particular, added, "Think they'll make him get a haircut?"

CNN, August 7, 1998

Over the video of smoking embassies and the sounds of ambulances, weeping and moaning, came the superimposed CNN announcer's voice. *"We have reports that more than 200 people are dead, and as many as 5,000 wounded. Again, truck bombs today went off outside the U.S. Embassies in Nairobi, Kenya, and Dar-es-Salaam, Tanzania. Sources have not identified those responsible . . . ."*

Nairobi, Kenya, October 1998

Colonel Wadi el-Hage sat at his desk in his first-floor apartment, busily recording his latest activities on behalf of Osama bin Laden in his personal diary. As a correspondent and secretary to *al-Sharif*, el-Hage kept track of African operations, and transmitted a weekly update via e-mail to bin Laden. This week's subject was a follow-up on the successful bombing of two American embassies two months ago.

Suddenly the door exploded, showering el-Hage with splinters, smoke, and cordite. The blast sent him flying out of his chair and knocked his diary 20 feet away. He wasn't sure that he could hear anything---later he would find out he had a punctured eardrum, and the pain in his head already blinded him. Laying sideways on the floor, however, he could see the five Kenyan soldiers in uniform burst in, accompanied by a pair of Kenyan intelligence officers dressed in civilian clothes. And Americans. There were two Americans. Before el-Hage could speak, the Kenyans hit him with TASERS, then added a few well-placed kicks before the Americans instructed the Kenyan officers to cease. As the soldiers tied el-Hage's hands behind his back with plastic cords---*my arm! My arm is broken!*---the American and Kenyan officers inspected his work space.

His diary lay wide open on the floor, covered only by a fine dust. CIA agent Cliff Harrison carefully picked it up, and after concluding that it was safe to do so, blew the dust off. By prior agreement with the Kenyans, the two agents got first crack at whatever they found in el-Hage's residence. Harrison placed the diary in a baggie, which he then dropped in his shoulder bag with any other evidence the team found. El-Hage, writhing on the floor, nearly blacked out. Not only was the pain in his ear and arm unbearable, but he looked down to see a large piece of wood, perhaps six inches long, sticking out of his knee joint. Then he screamed.

El-Hage had been under observation for weeks. There was no question of his ties to bin Laden, or to the explosions at Dar-es-Salaam and Nairobi. But to record the details of who, and where, in a diary . . . . Well, if el-Hage did not die in the interrogation that would follow, bin Laden would ensure that he never said anything else. The last thing he saw before the Kenyan soldier dragged him out of the room was the two Americans waving at him.

Harrison and Agent Lonnie Jackson were partners, a duo, nicknamed "lethal weapon" by their colleagues at the Ranch, apparently only because one was white and one black. In fact, they shared almost nothing in common with the Mel Gibson's Martin Riggs and Danny Glover's Roger Murtaugh characters in the movies. Jackson was a 42-year-old former LA cop. He might have fit the

Murtaugh role, except unlike the real-life Glover, Jackson was a lifelong Republican and put his kids through private schools in D.C. The eternally optimistic church-going Jackson was quite a contrast to the 51-year-old Harrison, who looked nothing like Mel Gibson. Already developing a paunch that protruded over his khaki slacks, Harrison could no longer even jog the Agency's minimum, and managed to escape his last two reviews only with the help of sympathetic superiors who knew his value in the field. and although he occasionally flashed an engaging smile and a certain charisma, far too often it was obscured by his pessimism and fatalistic world view. Like Martin Riggs, though, he could be crazy when energized by the whiz of bullets or the thrill of the hunt, and he had a conspiracy streak that, when properly plied with alcohol, led him into dark tales of the Bildeburgers and Freemasons.

Both agents wore colorful but dirty Hawaiian shirts and grease-stained hats---Jackson a Raiders cap, backwards, while Harrison a "crocodile hunter" bush hat---but despite the sunglasses, no one would mistake them for tourists. Their stubble and rumpled clothes might be better suited to unemployed adventurers or bush guides. Either way, it achieved their aim, which is to say that they looked far too unprofessional to be what they, in fact, were: deadly killers, and complete pros. Both spoke and read Arabic (Jackson was passable in Turkish); could forge a driver's license or passport with basic school supplies; stitch a wound with a needle and thread; or extract a confession from a hardened operative with only a pair of pliers and a screwdriver.

Harrison also hated to wait for a bunch of pencil-necked analysts in some air-conditioned office to examine the goodies. While the Kenyans continued to sweep the apartment, against all protocol, Harrison extracted the diary out of the baggie.

"Bingo," Harrison announced, thumbing through the diary. "You won't believe this."

"I bet I will," agreed Jackson. "The embassies are Bin Laden's work?"

Harrison nodded. "What was this guy thinking? He wrote it all down" *Sometimes we give these terrorists too much credit. They certainly aren't supermen. They make critical errors. Dumb mistakes, actually.* "This is the work of AQ all right, but---there's something else here that smells."

Jackson leaned over Harrison's shoulder to read for himself. "He refers to some 'joint-venture,' but doesn't say who with." He looked at Harrison, who also shook his head.

"Well, let's sweep this place, but it will be hard to top this." He turned to the Kenyan agents. "You guys know the drill. Collect any papers, computer records, physical evidence, but be careful. Watch for bombs or other booby traps. Just because we nabbed el-Hage and some items from his desk safely doesn't mean he didn't trip-wire the whole place. I'll drop off a copy of what we got at your place tomorrow."

Harrison patted the shoulder bag where he had the diary as he sifted through a few loose papers on the table. "Ya know, Lon, we've had el-Hage on tape for more than five years, and connected him to Hamas, but never to AQ or bin Laden before."

"We have now, and I don't like it. There is something bigger going on here" Jackson pointed out.

"Yah, duh. Like two burning embassies?"

"No," Jackson said grimly. "Bigger than that."

Harrison rarely saw fear in his partner's eyes, and the look he got from Jackson sent a chill down his spine.

Peshawar, Pakistan, hours later

"So, The Americans are faster than I expected. It will do them no good. We are ahead of them at every turn." Osama bin Laden spoke to Zawahiri and Malid as he walked among the mountains, unarmed, walking stick in hand.

Overconfident again, Sharif? thought Malid. "Nevertheless, Sharif, it might be best if you put yet another layer between yourself and the operations. Perhaps dispatch all future orders through a subordinate?"

Bin Laden stopped and glared at Malid. "Do you think I'm a coward who can be frightened off by these infidels?"

Malid returned his stony stare. "That is not what I meant and you know it. We should take reasonable precautions." Malid had noticed bin Laden not only getting more reckless, but more bloodthirsty in the two years since they left Sudan. He no longer spoke of the Koran, or explained his actions in terms of how it advanced the cause of the Prophet. *Indeed, aside from a few public pronouncements, he doesn't mention the Prophet at all. Blood has become its own end.*

Bin Laden looked at Zawahiri who gave him the gentlest nod. "Very well, we shall begin to route all orders through you or Ayman. Use cell phones only, and change them every month. Never accept a call from a number you do not recognize, and if a call comes in from the same unknown number more than once, destroy the phone immediately.

Both nodded, and bin Laden walked away. Although Malid had won his point, the recent embassy bombings still tore at him. In the two years after they left Sudan, Malid found it increasingly difficult to rationalize the killing of innocents, even infidel innocents. Worse, the weight of the past now sat on him even heavier because of the knowledge of what would soon happen in the future.

Is there no room in the Koran for mercy, Sharif? Do you honor the Koran any longer?

Aden, Yemen, October 12, 2000

From several hundred yards away, the Arleigh Burke-class *U.S.S. Cole* looked both serene and majestic. Without an aircraft carrier alongside to dwarf the destroyer, it was imposing, yet sleek. It sat at anchor, receiving supplies from local vendors in small boats, but the three Yemeni men glanced at it only intermittently as they quietly loaded a rubber dinghy with explosives. Fahd al-Quoso and Jamal al-Badawi gave last minute instructions to Ali al-Hada, their partner, who climbed into the boat to pilot it. They covered the explosives with tarps.

Starting the engine, al-Hada shouted over the din, "You will tell my brother of my sacrifice?"

Al-Badawi reassured him. "Your family will honor your name. *Al-khaliph* will declare you a hero, and care for your family, and Allah will welcome you into Paradise. Allah be praised." Yet al-Badawi's eyes betrayed him. He looked at al-Hada not with pride or with assurance of eternal rewards, but with a sadness of another young man who would not live to see his sons again. Al-Badawi had no reservations about the necessity of the task. Unlike his less sophisticated partner, al-Quoso, however, Jamal knew everything came at a cost. In this case, the cost would be al-Hada's life.

Fahd al-Quoso, a short, vile bin Laden lieutenant, wanted to leave no doubt as to al-Hada's mission, but his pep talk was less than inspiring. "You will strike a great blow against the great Satan. We have learned our lesson with our failed attempt on the *Sullivans*. This boat is large enough for the explosives. Take yourself to Paradise, and send the Americans to death. They will know after today that even their great warships are not safe from al-Qaeda."

Al-Hada nodded solemnly, but for the first time it dawned on him that he, and not Fahd or Jamal, was piloting this boat to his death. *How convenient*, he noted, even as he threw the transmission into gear. *How convenient that bin Laden himself never seems to lead one of these attacks.* Hada's brief dialogue with himself suddenly collapsed under a mass of ideological slogans and jihadist rhetoric as he, once again, convinced himself that this was "Allah's will." Shunting his questions aside, he obediently powered the small boat across the harbor to the *Cole*. Back at the dock, al-Quoso and al-Badawi follow the small craft with their eyes (it was too obvious to watch it through field glasses).

After a seeming eternity, the vessel pulled alongside the *Cole*, with the only sign that something was coming when al-Hada did not return the *Cole's* hailing. Instead, he stood praying . . . right up until the tremendous explosion next to the *Cole's* hull. Their hearts swelled with pride in their accomplishment, and scarcely a thought passed about al-Hada, or his fatherless sons. Later, al-Quoso and al-Badawi learned that 17 Americans had died in the blast, which left a 40 x 40-foot gash in the side of the vessel. *Allahu Akbar!*

Tora Bora Mountains, Afghanistan, 30 minutes later

Bin Laden's spartan headquarters building sat in an unremarkable valley near the Tora Bora Mountains. Aside from a few bunk houses and supply sheds, the only structures were a couple of training houses and some adjoining firing ranges and explosives pits. Even inside the headquarters, which more resembled a telemarketer's office than terror central, bin Laden only had a few computers, a television or two, two ottomans and a sofa, and a large table littered with maps and postem notes. He did not use phones, unless they were cell phones. Land lines were too easy to track. He easily could have afforded his own radar unit, but to what purpose? The Americans could take it out in seconds with one of their infamous HARM missiles, and it just offered another target.

No, he thought, *the militaries of the world have been relying increasingly on technology. It was time to go "low-tech"---to defeat the western powers, he would not attack them at their strength---their military and economic power. He would attack their weakness. Their liberties. Their tolerance. He would use their very values against them. Allah would not be so foolish as to expose His people to such freedoms, which only lead to corruption and impure lusts. MTV indeed. The Americans will find that their most powerful warships are all but invulnerable to Russian or Chinese ships, but not from hundreds of small crafts that swim around them at every port, which are needed for supplies. Perhaps a missile cannot take out their Pentagon, but there are other, possibly deadlier, methods.*

He sat staring at the satellite map on his computer screen as Malid pored over research bin Laden had requested about the

Pentagon and Wall Street, when one of his many cell phones beeped. Bin Laden knew who was on the other end when he answered.

"Results?" he asked Quoso

Al-Quoso answered with obvious pride. "The Americans cannot move the vessel. It has a huge hole in the side. Many dead."

"Did you videotape your attack?"

"As you ordered. Ali al-Hada died a martyr. What do you want us to tell Sameer about his brother, or say to al-Hada's sons?"

Bin Laden snorted, "Tell them what you want. His death does not concern me. We will make a recruitment video of this blessed event. All the infidels will shudder."

Puzzled, al-Quoso questioned bin Laden. "But Ali is a hero, *Khaliph*. A martyr."

"Yes," bin Laden said without conviction. "Let Allah decide his status. His death does not interest me. Tell Sameer and the boys what you wish. Just get me that video. The Americans will find this attack is just the beginning."

Malid looked at the video. Smoke pouring from the warship's hull. Litters with red crosses on them taking wounded men off the vessel---and body bags. Many of them. That they were enemy combatants somehow did not salve his conscience, especially about Ali. Yet bin Laden cared not that he had sacrificed himself for . . . *for what? Bin Laden? Islam? Certainly not for the Prophet.* Malid went cold when he looked at the reaction on bin Laden's face: a satisfied smile.

Then bin Laden hit a speed dial on his phone and heard his uncle's voice.

"Yes, Sharif?" Khalid Sheikh Mohammad, with papers strewn all over his Karachi apartment, had been working all morning.

"Is your plan on schedule?'"

"It is. They have learned nothing since the Bojinka plot . . . ."

"That failed, I will remind you . . . ."

"Yes, Sharif, it failed, but the next attempt will not use bombs on planes."

"No, it will not. Let us pray it is more effective than your Bojinka plan to blow up several airliners simultaneously."

Bin Laden could not see Khalid Sheikh Mohammad break into a smile. "Oh, I assure you, Sharif. It will astound the world."

Air France Flight 203, en route to Prague, Czechoslovakia, May 30, 2000

Mohamad Atta, a 33-year old Egyptian with close-cropped hair and an expressionless countenance, popped open his seat belt before the flight attendant even finished her instructions for passengers to remain seated. His butt was numb from the flight from Paris, on top of the New York-Paris flight before that. All he wanted to do was stand up . . . and, of course, at the moment that was forbidden. He stared at the petite, middle-aged flight attendant. She scarcely looked big enough to push a drink cart, let alone resist him if he decided to slash her throat. That was for another day. Right now, he sat, expressionless, concealing the utter contempt he had for not only this woman, but for all westerners. She was lucky. This was not her day.

He had no visa, nor did he need one. His last instructions indicated he would need go no further than the duty free section at the Prague Airport. Dressed in slacks and a coat, Atta passed for a European, or, at least, a typical Muslim worker in Europe---one of the millions who now held the low-wage jobs that many Frenchmen and Germans would no longer take. He carried no weapon, although Atta knew he could easily slip what he needed by airport security.

Within moments the aircraft rolled to a stop and Mohamad Atta entered the duty free section at the Prague airport, but, unlike all the other passengers exiting the plane, did not join a line to be processed. He wouldn't be staying that long.

At times, despite his extensive training and near-fanatical preparation, Atta committed fundamental errors of covert operations. In this case, he simply was unaware that Czech secret police watched a feed from the security camera, and took copious notes as another man approached him. Indeed, the other man---not Atta---was the subject of their interest. His name was Ahmed al-Ani, the Deputy Foreign Minister of Iraq, who had entered the country the previous day, and the Czech authorities had tailed him from that moment on. Unlike Atta, al-Ani had virtually no experience in undercover operations, and thus was unaware of his "tail."

Like Atta, the Iraqi wore a nondescript suit and draped a black overcoat across his arm. He carried only a briefcase. Plump and already sweating, the diplomat greeted Atta with a perfunctory bow.

"I bring you greetings from President Saddam Hussein."

Unimpressed, Atta did not return the greeting or the bow. "I hope you brought more than greetings."

The response unsettled al-Ani, a man used to receiving deferential treatment from most with whom he interacted. "You understand it is very dangerous for my nation to be seen talking to representatives of Osama bin Laden."

Atta clenched his teeth and hissed "Your president was not concerned about such contacts when he was given immunity by *al-Sharif*, despite the fact that he is no more committed to Allah than the westerner infidels."

Al-Ani suddenly found himself on the defensive. *Who was this insect anyway?* Merely to encounter a contrary word was unusual in Hussein's circles, where al-Ani had only heard fawning gratitude--- *most of it insincere. Now this . . . this Egyptian is lecturing me? Your scrawny Contractor should meet my Rais-I Wazir or his sons some day*, he thought. *Uday, especially, could instruct him in real terror, person-to-person, not remote, faceless bombings.*

With each moment, al-Ani's contempt for Atta and bin Laden grew. Nevertheless, the diplomat had his instructions, and would not be derailed by Atta's impertinence, lest he himself face the unpredictable rage of Uday Hussein and his pet leopards.

"We already have too many visible contacts," al-Ani noted, regaining his composure. "The training facility at Salman Pak can be seen by the Americans' satellites. Do you think they are unaware of the 737 fuselage where you practice?"

"That is not my concern. Just give me what I need," insisted Atta, keeping his voice low.

As one of Saddam's long-time ministers, al-Ani had at one time finely-honed survival skills. But two decades of artificial security in Baghdad had dulled his sense of danger. Like Atta, whose failure was one of arrogance, al-Ani did not notice the Czech security cameras that quietly whirred, capturing their exchange. He thought he had discreetly slid a small envelope to the Egyptian, although when Czech officials saw the transaction it looked clumsy and amateurish.

"It is as you requested," al-Ani contemptuously stated. "You have no visa. You may not stay. Board the next plane out. I am instructed, however, to ask you one question: is the plan as they say?"

For the first time, Atta's stone expression changed and his mouth curled up into a menacing smile. "What do they say?"

Al-Ani felt a sudden churning sensation in his stomach. "A direct attack on America. Bigger than before. Genuine revenge for their infidel invasion and embarrassment of the Holy Lands."

Atta stared at him, his tight smile frozen in place. *You care nothing for the Holy Lands. You want revenge for your fat president.* Then Atta's smile disappeared, replaced by a coldly evil stare. "Why do you care?"

Atta's reply surprised al-Ani. *Is this man stupid? Does he not know the obvious?* "We have provided much of your funding recently." Al-Ani snapped, "Rais-I Wazir wants to know what his money has gone for. Besides, certainly our country is at risk of retaliation whether you succeed or fail." Like most in Saddam's circle, he never called Saddam "Saddam" and rarely addressed him as "President, but rather called him "Rais-I Wazir"---"Great Leader."

"Fail? Retaliation? Have you not learned the lessons of Mogadishu? *Sharif* has. The Americans are cowards. Bleed them and they run." Atta now waxed philosophic as he stared at the ceiling, as though he were lecturing a group of new recruits.

"But they never left us," al-Ani countered. "They are still in Kuwait---a Muslim country! Their infidel feet still trod the sand of the heretic Saudi Kingdom, mere miles from our border. Your "sharif" may be safe in the mountains of Afghanistan, but the Americans can invade us again whenever they wish. Their aircraft still fly uncontested over our soil!"

Atta shifted his gaze from the ceiling to al-Ani, and the thin smile returned. "Which is precisely why they must be driven out of the Holy Lands forever. Khobar Towers. The embassies. The warship. All of these were a mere preliminary to the great strike that is coming. Surely even your pompous president understands this. You have nothing to fear from the weak and cowardly Americans. Allah is on our side. Tell your president he will be pleased with this operation. Very pleased."

Bin Laden is one man, and one man is difficult to find, even for the Americans. A country is not. Al-Ani did not bother with the Muslim farewell of peace. What was the point? And the sooner he got out of Czechoslovakia, the better. Looking back at Atta, al-Ani gestured, "The next plane . . . ," then tipped his head as if to ask, "understand?" Atta shot back a defiant nod.

One hour later Mohamad Atta handed an Air France ticket to Paris to a boarding agent and within minutes was free of Czechoslovakia. Once airborne---and alone, as there was no one in the first class section next to him---he slid from the little envelope several transaction slips bearing the numbers of his accounts in London and Florida, revealing that Ahmed al-Ani had deposited nearly $1 million on behalf of Saddam Hussein. Atta surveyed the information, shoved it back inside the envelope, and snorted as he closed his eyes. *Do not think this has bought you immunity from jihad. Even as the president of Iraq, you are not safe. Your faith in Allah is a prop. A sham. It will be exposed as such. Sharif will deal with you in the same manner as the heretics in Riyadh and Cairo and the infidels across the ocean. Do you not remember Sadat? In the meantime . . . . thank you for your "contribution." It will serve Allah well.*

Chapter 2

June 2000, Cranbury, New Jersey

"Rod, put that box over there next to Michael Jordan."

Rod Trainer's mother was busy painting a large mural of Michael Jordan, firing a jump shot in front of a frenzied Bull's crowd, on Rod's office wall.

"I want to give her plenty of space," he replied, admiring the partially-completed work of art. "We can't mess up the winning shot." Rod set down the box with his office items on the floor without taking his eyes off Jordan's number 23. Then he noticed something unusual about the front row of fans.

"You put me and Liza and Daniel and Douggie in the picture?" he asked incredulously. Penny Trainer, spackled with paint, merely looked over her shoulder and smiled. A talented artist, Penny had thrown in a few special touches.

"Liza, check this out. Mom put us and the boys in the mural as fans."

"Terrific, honey," she answered unenthusiastically. When Rod chose the paint scheme for his office, he'd asked to have a mural of Jordan rather than a serene landscape or a modernist swirl of color. *Hey, it's his room*, she acknowledged.

And this is mine! Liza Trainer gazed at the state-of-the-art kitchen in their new home. Twin GE ovens for her baking projects, an extra-wide giant Kenmore refrigerator (with ice-maker and cold water dispenser), and, past the cooking area, a spacious dining area with a polished hardwood floor beneath a liberating sunroof. She'd soon have it decorated with wicker and flowers, having already selected the scene from *Southern Living* that she wanted to replicate. *Even though New Jersey's not the South. It'll still work.*

The two boys, Daniel (named for his grandfather, Richard Daniel) and Douggie, played among the boxes. Liza was sure one of them would bump into a stack, and knock them over, but she resisted the temptation to make them leave her sight. There was something peaceful about their play amidst such chaos.

Liza and Rod had begun building their dream house in 2000. It was only 10 minutes from their existing house, but had much more room and a basement for the boys. Rod's position at Pandora Corporation provided them with plenty of money, if it came at a cost of him being constantly gone. Liza had worked part-time at Pandora until Daniel came along in 1997. Douglas, whom they all called Douggie, followed two years later, and combined they forced Liza and Rod to re-evaluate their relationship.

Most of Rod's clients with Pandora were in New Jersey, but increasingly he got accounts that were further away, and as he spent more time on the road, he increasingly ignored Liza and the boys.

She marveled at how far they had come. Their "perfect marriage" had nearly crumbled under Rod's compulsion to sell software and serve clients in faraway states. He was rarely home. Frustrated, in 2000 Liza e-mailed him a list of questions with some rather blunt instructions:

"Fill this out, then we'll talk when you get home," she wrote.

Among the questions were how many nights a week Rod would be home for dinner? How far in advance would he inform her of travel plans? *It was a step in the right direction*, she thought. While their answers came out fairly close, Rod still hadn't come to the realization that he was putting career and work ahead of faith and family.

Finally, after a major client abandoned him, Rod had an awakening. Selling more software wasn't going to bring fulfillment.

"Liza, where's that can of red paint? Mr. Jordan's jersey is too pink." Mom studied the swooping figure of Michael Jordan on the wall with a combination of displeasure and bemusement.

"Mom, I think I put it in the garage, but, to be honest, I don't have a clue right now. We've moved so much stuff in over the last two days."

"Well, His Air-ness needs to dry anyway. At least this coat." Daniel whizzed by. "Watch your hands, Daniel. This is wet paint." *It'll be a miracle if there aren't paw-prints all over this before I'm done.* "How long do you have before Rod goes out on the road again?"

Liza, now fully engaged in unpacking the coffee maker and mixers, had already put the calendar up on the fridge. That little piece of paper with the pretty pictures still regulated their lives, not too different from the days of the factory whistle. "Tuesday. Down to North Carolina again, then back the next day."

"I don't know how you two do it. Richard and I would have split up for sure if he'd been gone that much. The world seemed more stable then, I guess. Course, Richard never made the kind of money at IBM that Rod makes at Pandora." Penny never missed an opportunity to praise her only son.

"Yeah," replied Liza, now absorbed with hooking up the toaster oven, which, naturally, was the wrong color for the kitchen. "It's the old tradeoff. Money for time." Then she abruptly changed the subject. "I don't believe this. I could have sworn I matched the paint chips in this room to the toaster and microwave, but they both look yellow in here instead of ivory. Now I'll have to get new ones."

"If they're new, I'll buy them from you. Our toaster oven is nearly gone, and the microwave will be due soon." Penny breezed through the kitchen to the door leading to the garage in search of Jordan Red.

"Let me try them out in here, and see if my eye doesn't adapt. At least Rod's here long enough to see what the kitchen and his office will look like before he has to leave again."

Woodside, New York, March 2001

"Patty, don't you forget your dy-hickey-hedron-thingey after I put so much work into it." Shannon Callahan examined the oddly-shaped, ten-sided geometry project that sat on her already-crowded kitchen counter. Despite her best efforts, it still looked like crap. *Weren't the colors supposed to line up?* She and Patrick---always "Patty" to her---fought with that thing for two hours last night, and she was glad to be rid of it. *Why is it all <u>his</u> assignments end up with me working on them? I wish these damn teachers would get a clue. Kids don't do these things, parents do.*

Patrick thudded down the stairs, dragging his overloaded backpack behind him. It ricocheted off each step. Thud! Thud! Thud! Then came the ever-present jingle of the dog's collar as Spike waddled down the stairs after him. Spike had one job in life: get Patrick up in the morning. After that, the only thing that broke his sleep was an occasional snack and an afternoon walk when the weather provided.

"You walking to school today?" asked Shannon. "The weather's finally decent." She hoped her slightly overweight Irish son would at some point begin to see the value of exercise. So different from Sean. And his dad.

"Nah. There's no way I can carry this thing and my backpack and not mess this up." Patrick threw some instant flavored coffee in a cup of boiled water and stirred.

"Guess you have a point, but be careful with that. I'm not making it again!" *As if I ever should have made it in the first place,* she didn't have to add.

"Hey, I don't want to work on this thing anymore either. I'll grab the bus."

"Fine. Your dad will pick you up today in front of the school---are you staying to play in stage band? And where's your trombone?"

"Yeah. Tell dad to be there at 4:30. I left my trombone in my band locker because I knew I'd need it today."

"And you knew you wouldn't practice, either, right?"

"Right," Patrick replied, unapologetically. He hated the trombone, and played it only because of the school's music requirement. Patrick already had substantial savings account targeted for a guitar He planned to ditch the horn as soon as possible, but for now, it got him on band trips. He gulped the coffee down, then carefully carried the dydechehedron out the door as the bus pulled up.

"Have a good day," his mother said, trying to be as cheerful as possible.

"Kaaay," Patrick shouted back, unenthusiastically.

Spike stood on his hind legs and managed a few barks until the bus pulled away, then, convinced he had chased it off, again circled Shannon's feet, awaiting a crumb or morsel that might fall from the counter.

Finally, she thought. *Sometimes it seemed to take forever to get the team out of the house.* Sean had left a half-hour earlier for wrestling practice. What a difference. She hated comparing her kids, but Sean got himself up early, worked on his wrestling after practice, and studied any materials the coaches gave him. His homework was done, usually ahead of time. He'd filled out his college applications and scholarship forms---to the extent that he could---late in his sophomore year. *Patty, on the other hand . . . .*

Michael had the early shift at the station on Mondays and Tuesdays, late on Wednesdays and Thursdays. Fridays and Saturday shifts rotated. Right now he probably was fixing a high-calorie breakfast for Engine Company #71's crew right about now. She Windexed the counter where Patrick, as usual, had left his cup and spoon, along with a small puddle of coffee and some donut crumbs. *This may not be the Hamptons, but my house will never be dirty.* She bent over to put away the Windex when she felt the dull ache in her back again flare up. *It hasn't been right since last year. Never do dead lifts. Never do dead lifts. God! NEVER DO DEAD LIFTS.*

The back pain was bearable, and, in fact, occasionally it was a distraction from the fact that she often had no feeling in her hands.

Which was worse? Pain or numbness? Eight years earlier, Shannon went to doctor after doctor, each of whom missed the symptoms of spasticity and tingling, until one bout of numbness started to take over her body. Only then did Michael get her to a hospital where, finally, a neurosurgeon uttered the crushing words, "Multiple Sclerosis." By that time, she was losing sensation from her toes to her torso. Massive infusions of steroids reversed most of the effects, but her hands never fully recovered feeling. She still occasionally dropped glasses and had trouble grabbing slippery things. If she really wanted to feel a texture---like Spike's fur---she rubbed it against her face.

A weekly injection of interferon held the disease at bay, beating it into remission, at least according to the last MRI. When she heard the news that there had been no increase at all in any of the lesions, she was so excited she forgot to ask the neurologist if any of the spots on her brain had actually shrunk, as Michael was sure they had. The irony was not lost on Shannon: of all people to get a disease affecting the muscles, a fitness/exercise instructor was a pretty interesting draw. *And they say God doesn't have a sense of humor*, then, the old Irish guilt resurfaced as she corrected herself. *I know, God, You didn't do this. Gotta blame somebody. Never ask "why me?"* a comedian, of all people, once said. *You only have the right to ask, "why now?"*

Shannon kept it secret from her classes, her boss, and most of her close friends. Pity? Absolutely not. They didn't need to know. *I'm not Annette Funicello or Montel.* Worse, people just treat you different. *It's not contagious*, she wanted to scream, but, of course, human nature fears that any weakness spreads, just as in the animal kingdom. Unfortunately, some things could not be hidden, like the horrendous effects of the interferon that she had to poison herself with every Friday night. While the boys and Michael got pizza and watched a movie or went to a game, Shannon stabbed herself with a six-inch pre-mixed hypo filled with a beta-seron that attacked the MS---and virtually everything else in her body. It gave her the equivalent of the flu. She didn't vomit, but came pretty close. There were the chills, accompanied by a severe headache, and above all, an inability to focus. Every Friday night. Boy's night out, mom's night to puke. *Try explaining that to your kids' pals, or to family friends.* For more than eight years Shannon had hidden the disease from all but her mother and brother, and, of course, Mike and the boys. Mike understood, even though every week she ragged on him as though he didn't. The boys? Well, how could teenagers "get" a disease like this? They resented her for being sick, most of all because it inconvenienced them. Movie versions of little Haley Jo Osments who would lovingly put aside their lives and gladly endure a sick parent never met MS.

So, like clockwork on Sundays she got on her treadmill in the basement to purge the toxins through sweat and endorphins, and to rebuild her body for the week ahead. Normally, she taught several step aerobic classes and two spinning/cycling/weight training classes each week. *More of a schedule than most 20-year-olds,* she proudly noted. And, normally she would go to the gym on Mondays and teach the 9:00 circuit-training class. But in August 2001 she switched her schedule to attend a Bible study at her church, some tape series about the Book of John. So Monday's routine was now: Get to church. Take the goodies she'd made the night before. Clean up. Walk Spike. Start making dinner. Everything on her mental list, everything in order, everything like clockwork. Michael would be hungry when he finally came in at 6:00, assuming, as did all firemen's wives, that there was no emergency call.

Church in itself was a hoot, especially for an ex-Catholic. But Shannon Callahan was not one of the Scots-Irish converts to Presbyterianism or Anglicanism or any of the "nearby" Protestant faiths. She went all the way to other end of the spectrum, to the modern Pentecostal "Word of Faith" movement. She heard a couple of preachers comment that ex-Catholics were the easiest to convert to the "faith" movement, because they had no prior baggage of reading the Bible through a denomination's eyes. Quite the contrary, in her Bible study, her---*admittedly shallow?*---understanding gave her a background that nobody at her Bible study seemed to possess. This, too, would have made her the object of great curiosity if she didn't remain as guarded about her faith as she did her disease. *Nobody needs to know the details of either.* Anyway, her conversion (and a few sessions with a good shrink) helped her to ditch most of the Irish pathologies. Two decades ago she quit drinking, so that little "Irishism" was gone, too.

And, in what was perhaps the most telltale sign she'd abandoned Eire, Shannon loved to cook and bake. She toted a small plate with a slice of poppy seed bread she'd made for the girls at Bible study over to the table, where she sat down and again looked over the lesson for this week. "How did John feel about the disciples? How do you think John's family felt about him being in the disciples?" *Who the hell cares what they 'felt?' Can't this woman just tell me about John? Who was he? Guess that's too much to ask these days. Gotta know how people feeeeeeeell. Maybe that's why people don't read the Bible any more. We don't need a 2000-year-old book to know how people feeeeeeeeellll.* Spike waited patiently for a poppy seed crumb to fall, then began licking the carpet when it did not.

Shannon and Michael had married 18 years ago, and here came Sean right away. That's usually cause for great celebration in Irish families, but again, she and Michael weren't typical. She didn't treat her husband like an adult child, and their relationship did not thrive on avoidance. They actually enjoyed each other's company; they both loved food (Michael had to be part Italian, she thought); and had the boys not come along they still would be traveling. Michael, still a nominal Catholic, some time ago had ditched most of the trappings of his faith. She'd even seen him start to read the Bible from time to time, a trait she encouraged by leaving him scripture verses apropos to his job or to family life. He accompanied her to church many times, with the understanding that they go to St. Andrew's on traditional occasions. While both boys were more Protestant than Catholic, Patrick knew more about the Bible than most Sunday School teachers. Reluctantly, the Callahan grandparents had abandoned the dream of having grandsons grow up to be priests. Shannon and Michael both thought more in terms of business or law for their sons.

Neither better be a firefighter, Shannon had determined. *The Irish need to get out of that profession. No, Sean and Patrick will both go to college, and they better not ever come back to Woodside. They better not make any girl a firefighter's wife.*

As she read the Book of John, she heard the mournful wail of a siren in the distance. Probably police. Could be fire. The linear equation of a fire wife raced through her mind: Every siren is an emergency. Every emergency means danger. Danger walks with death. Someone has to respond to every emergency. *Michael is a "someone," and Michael's in danger.*

June 21, 2001, Hollywood, Florida

Waleed al-Shehri shouted over the techno sound of the "Chemical Brothers" blasting through his CD player. "We're leaving around 9:00. Yes. Cheetah Club, as usual." He continued to unpack his few boxes in his newly-rented apartment at the Bimini Motel & Apartments. The CD player had, of course, been unpacked first.

His older brother Wail al-Sheri, had only gotten in from Boston the night before, where they had stayed at a hotel in Newton. They would again visit that hotel. Meanwhile, he toted a large box from the car into the ground-level living room. "Will Abdul be there as well?" Abdul was Abdulaziz Alomari—if that was indeed his name---the third member of their cell, who had been staying in Lauderdale-by-the-Sea, but who was visiting a friend in Hollywood. Neither Wail nor Waleed knew who the friend was, nor were they encouraged to ask.

"Yes, he will be there," laughed Waleed. "Americans have plenty of whores." Suddenly, he realized what he had said. To Waleed and his compatriots, all strippers were whores, but they had been warned that such comments would call attention to them. While the hotel manager, Joanne Stanley, had been friendly enough, like any other American she could not be trusted. If she had heard this, she would be suspicious, and he swore by Allah not to utter such sentiments again.

Nevertheless, I spoke the truth. Bitches! With their ample bank accounts, Wail and the others had no trouble picking up women. *Even without the money*, he thought, *my brother would be successful at landing these whores.* Wail, the better looking of the two, resembled comedian Ray Romano. On the other hand, Waleed's big chin and high forehead made him less appealing, though not ugly, and he had his thick, bushy hair going for him. Neither man wore a beard---*as per our instructions*---and neither looked particularly menacing. For that matter, neither did Alomari, who might even be considered handsome. In short, they looked---and acted---like all-American boys, if, perhaps, . . . *swarthy?* They laughed easily, and spent freely. They blended in.

All except Atta.

Mohamad Atta was the kind of person who caused the hairs of your neck to stand up. He didn't need to say a word to be creepy. At 33 years old, Atta, was a true believer who was indicted in the 1993 World Trade Center bombing along with Zacarias Moussaoui. He successfully evaded American law enforcement for years. Although four of the five men in Waleed's cell were Saudis, Atta, an Egyptian, was their undisputed leader, and by far had the most training in aircraft. It hadn't come easily. His hostility to authority had caused more than one instructor to refuse to give him flying lessons. Even the trained men in Waleed's cell, some of whom had killed before, feared Mohamad Atta. They dealt with him the way one does an asp.

The CD flipped to "Chrystal Method," and Waleed gyrated to "Busy Child" as he unpacked nondescript clothes. *These 'techno' bands. Chemical Brothers. Prodigy. The westerners know how to make music that causes your body to move.* Every night when they weren't preparing for their mission, Waleed and Wail partied as though they were already in the afterlife. *There is nothing in all Islam like American "techno,"* thought Waleed, ignoring the nagging question of why he enjoyed it so much.

Perhaps they had grown careless with their parties, but his trips through American "security" at airports convinced him that, if anything, they had been overly cautious. After all, they had all been in the United States for a year without raising an eyebrow---not at the airports, not at the flight schools, not even obtaining their drivers' licenses. Atta, who had been in the country the longest, had enrolled in a flight school along with Alomari and learned to fly. No one seemed concerned that, despite practicing in twin-engined Cessnas, the two continually asked questions about the flight characteristics of large Boeings. At no time were they so much as questioned as to their intentions, or their background. All the Americans cared about was cash. *And we have plenty of that*, smiled Waleed.

Each of them managed to get jobs, rent apartments, and, for all intents and purposes, act normal. None gave up Islam, but at first they observed it privately and quietly, taking care to make no comments to Americans, particularly Christians. And, again at first, none carried a *Koran* or *Hadith*. No one had a prayer rug visible, or prayed openly. To the extent possible, they were to shed the appearance of being "Arabs."

But it didn't take long for them to drop their guard. None of them followed some of the suggestions that they had been taught during their training: put a Bible in a prominent place; wear a cross or crucifix; fly and American flag or hang one from your apartment window. There was no need. To most Americans in Florida, they were invisible. *Bin Laden had been wrong about this much: America's vaunted intelligence services did not even know they were in the country. The American obsession with "tolerance" deflects uncomfortable questions. Remember the manual: when challenged about your Middle East status, assume a pained look. Play the victim. The questions will cease.* And they did.

Increasingly, the group had met in public, especially at the Pink Pony strip club where they could watch these brazen American women flaunt their bodies and jiggle their breasts---an experience Waleed did not find all that distasteful. "Acting American" involved drinking, did it not? How could they not partake of alcohol? *To not drink such beverages would itself evoke suspicion. In this case, did not the cause of Islam demand he disobey its very laws? And Americans seemed to appreciate these nearly-naked girls, therefore how better to fit in than by likewise enjoying them? And Atta seemed to enjoy the women more than anyone: together, that night, they spent $300 on lap dances.*

Waleed marveled at the entire situation. *In the belly of the Great Satan. No! In the VAGINA of the beast! We are literally raping the West's women here on American soil, and their corrupt life enables us to do so!*

As the alcohol set in, though, the party grew less cautious. Waleed openly referred to "impending bloodshed" and all of them uttered an increasing number of anti-American sentiments without concern. When they left, Wail even left a copy of the Koran on the table where he had just enjoyed a lap dance. As they readied to leave, the waitress brought their change and said (with little conviction), "Thank you. You boys have a great night now."

"Allahu Akbar!" Waleed responded with contempt.

Parkersburg, West Virginia, US Army Recruiting Station, July 20, 2001

"Jo, do you know where you are going? What did Sgt. Grady say?"

Donna Miles had promised she wouldn't cry when Joanne was sworn in, but the scene was too much. Even burley Gary had fought back a tear or two when he looked at the tiny little blond raising her right hand and swearing to defend the United States against enemies foreign or domestic. They knew what to expect, because Gary, Jr., was inducted just a year earlier, but that didn't diminish the emotion of their little girl joining the U.S. Army, even though she wouldn't leave for basic training for two months.

"They told me I'll be doing basic at Ft. Jackson, South Carolina, so I won't be too far from Gary at Ft. Bragg," Jo chirped as she ambled back to the car with her parents and sister, Beth.

"Well, Gary said that at least they feed you well. You're just a wisp."

Gary Miles, Sr. had seen life through the windshield of a Kenworth diesel, and knew that the Army offered Jo a way out. He was not concerned with her weight nor her teenage demeanor. After all, she was a "mountain girl," as everyone said. She could take care of herself.

"Dee," Gary interjected, "if Jo put on any weight, you'd be pushing that Atkins diet on her. Relax. She'll be fine. Did they give you a list of what to bring?"

"Yeah, and it ain't much. Three pairs of underwear---nothin' silky. One change of clothes for free time, no halter tops . . . ." then, looking down at her chest, she broke out in a giggle. "Like I need to worry. Then it said one pair of good running shoes. Eyeglasses. And a pair of white athletic socks. Guess I got it pretty well covered."

"I'm worried, Jo," said her mother, sliding beside her in the back seat while Beth took shotgun in the front. "With Gary, Jr., well . . . ."

"He's a *boy*. Is that it?" Jo scowled.

"Well, yes, if you want to know the truth, he's a boy. Er, a man. It's not that I don't think you can do whatever you set your mind to, Jo, but this is a big commitment. You can't back out if you don't like it. You can't come home if you break a nail."

"Mom, it ain't like there's a war on or anything," Jo laughed.

Gary, Sr., who already had the engine running and had started backing up, suddenly put his foot on the brake and put the car in park. He turned and peered over the back of the seat. "Jo, we all agree that you made the right choice. We support you. This is probably the only way you're going to be able to go to college. But you listen to me, and never forget this: the army exists for one reason and one reason only, to kill people and break things. And it's fine so long as you are the one doin' the breakin'." He didn't have to say, "But . . . ."

For a moment, Joanne's smile vanished. Gary made his point, then turned and put the car back in reverse, and headed out of the Grand Central Mall parking lot, before he added, "Anyway, ain't nobody ever made a Miles run yet."

The message was not lost on Jo, who looked at her mother. "I know what I'm doin' mom. I'll be careful, and I'll keep up with Gary. Don't you worry. Your little daughter will come home, and bring back enough money for a college education, too. And I'm tougher than you think!

July 24, 2001, Yankee Stadium

Rod Trainer held each boy by the hand as they wound their way past two elderly Chinese men---one, oddly, in a Mets cap---to find their seats along the left-field line.

"You ready to see Derek Jeter hit a home run, Douggie?" Douggie just smiled and nodded enthusiastically, taking in the wonders of Yankee Stadium. Of course, Douggie had no idea who Derek Jeter was.

"I am!" added Daniel, sucking hard on the Coke Rod had bought on the way in. "De-rickk Jeee-terrrrr," he growled. "Derickk Jeeee-terrrr."

Liza, trailing the boys, smiled at the scene of her 220-lb. husband negotiating the obstacle course of the Bronx's finest citizens as he crawled over one fan after another to locate their seats.

"Right here," announced Rod. "J-110, 111, 112, and 113."

A burly, dark-haired man in a blue FDNY cap eyed them with a mixture of concern and amusement. "See ya got your hands full, there," he noted to Rod, pointing at Daniel's Coke, which, now tilted, was seeping out from around the straw, heading for the neck of a heavily pierced teen in front of him.

"Oh, crap. Daniel, watch your Coke!" Rod managed to deflect the drip toward the empty seat to the right of the teenager, who was focused intently on his date, equally pierced. Fortunately the seat where the drip ended up was empty, so no damage, save a sticky butt for whoever got H-112. "Thanks," Rod said, nodding to the man in 114.

"No problem," he said, gesturing to the boys. "Got a couple myself, but they're a little older now."

"And you didn't bring them to the game?"

"Nah, one's on a band trip to Los Angeles and the other has wrestling practice. Besides, neither really likes baseball all that much."

Rod surveyed the man, and concluded that, as the cap indicated, he probably was a fireman. But it was more than the cap. He was a big guy. Tough. Irish. Rod liked him immediately.

"Rod Trainer," he said, sticking out his hand, while holding Daniel's Coke precariously in the other. It continued to dip at a 45-degree angle.

"Michael," he replied, returning Trainer's firm grip. As an afterthought, he added, "Callahan." Both smiled, then a brief silence ensued. Aware of the awkward moment, Michael filled the void. "So, this your first game at Yankee Stadium?"

"Oh, heck no. But it's the first with the boys. We live over in Jersey, and my dad grew up a White Sox fan. But I thought these two should see Yankee Stadium."

"Can never start 'em too early. Wish my boys liked the game, but . . . ." Michael started to drift as he stared at the Yankee bullpen where Mariano Rivera was throwing gently. Well, as gently as Rivera can throw.

Rod noted a certain disappointment in Michael's voice, so he quickly interjected, "Yah, different strokes. My dad hated football, but I love it. To this day I can't get him to a Giants or Jets game. You with the fire department?"

"Engine Company 71," he said, still following the smooth delivery of Rivera. "We're over on the Upper West Side."

"Oh, yeah," Trainer nodded, although in fact, he didn't have a clue where the Upper West Side was. Except for a few landmarks, Rod didn't know the Bronx from Staten Island. He'd probably spent more time in Pandora Corporation's headquarters than in the City. He glanced at Liza, who now had the boys as settled as they could get in the uncomfortable Yankee Stadium seats. She and Rod had agreed before coming to the game that if Daniel and Douggie lasted through the sixth inning, they were doing well, and they were prepared to leave when the kids got restless.

"Must be exciting," Rod said to Michael.

"What?"

"You know, being a fireman and all. Rescuing people. Being a hero."

Michael stared at Rod for a moment, then nodded. "Yah. Being a hero's always great." *Somebody tell that to that rook Danny Shaugnessy who forgot to check the door for heat last week at that tenement fire in Queens. He just turned the knob. Jesus, how often did they go over that in training? Check the door, Danny. Damn it, check the door! You open a hot door, the flame is attracted to the oxygen outside. It blasts out, like napalm. You're covered before you can even scream for help. The force usually knocks the wind out of you, and even if your buddies are right there, you'll be lucky to escape with a few burns. Danny wasn't lucky. His nearest squad member was ten feet away, dragging a hose. Danny should have waited. He won't get another chance. The funeral was last week. Heck, even when we do everything right, we still don't always do the job. The 1911 Triangle Shirtwaist Factory fire was a legend---how the ladders only reached six floors up---but the fire was on the eighth floor. All women and girls worked in that factory, and in panic they started to jump. Oh, the firemen had nets all right. But nets hold one person. When three or four jumped at a time, the nets just ripped. I hope I never see people jump from a burning building. If that happens, I've failed.*

Derek Jeter, Tino Martinez, and Jorge Posada had now moved to the top steps of the Yankees' dugout as the stadium announcer, in his familiar clipped voice, uttered the famous words, "And the Yankees take the field." Cheers erupted and Michael and Rod obligingly stood with the rest of Yankee Stadium to acknowledge the Eastern Division leading Bronx Bombers. Next came the "Star Spangled Banner," followed by another massive Yankee cheer.

"So, how many you do a month?" asked Rod as they reclaimed their seats. Liza shuffled three hot dogs down the row, gesturing to the boys to take one and pass the others down. Douggie had almost devoured his already, while Daniel still clung tightly to his. He focused intently on Bernie Williams in Center Field.

"How many what?"

"Fires. How many you put out a month?"

Too many, Michael thought. *Even routine runs were never routine. A year ago, a six-year vet, Reggie Carlson, from Engine Company 16 responded to a call on a car fire off Sixth Avenue. No biggie. Routine. It was an old Chevy Vega. Small car, just a little smoke. The guys thought they had hosed it down with foam pretty good when a spark must have hit a breach in the gas tank of the Ford Econoline van just a few feet away. The Ford sailed ten feet in the air, and one of the tires shot straight out like a discus. It went straight for Reggie, just like it had a tracking beam, and caught him square in the head. Broke his neck instantly. How do you tell Reggie's wife that her husband was killed by a rogue Goodyear tire?*

"We probably get one or two legitimate calls a month---fires, not someone who smelled smoke or left a gas valve open, but a real fire. It's not all that romantic." *Danny Shaugnessy's body was so blistered they couldn't have an open casket ceremony. The blast had taken the skin right off his face. Literally, the guy was a skull on a body. Looked like something out of a horror movie.* "Most of the time at the station is spent either training or cooking. It's amazing how much food preparation goes on in a fire house. We all take turns, so eventually most of the guys become decent cooks." *On Eddie's nights, we manage to eat the bare minimum, then sneak out to McDonald's or the Indian restaurant down the street.*

Rod nodded, unaware of people like Danny or Reggie. "Whoa," he said, changing the subject. "Look's like Rocket has his stuff today," pointing to Roger Clemens. Clemens had fired three straight fastballs past Nomar Garciaparra for his first strikeout of what would be a 10-whiff day.

Callahan smiled and nodded. Great day for Rocket.

He and Rod would barely exchange another dozen words that sunny day. Rod talked with the boys, joked with Liza, and munched on his hot dog. Liza made sure Douggie didn't get too much mustard on his Yankees baseball shirt---*ugh, too late!*---and enjoyed the sun. She looked at the Chinese men conversing profusely in what she thought was Cantonese, though it had been a decade since her missionary trip to Indonesia even exposed her to a modicum of Asian languages. And then there was nice fireman whom Rod had befriended. They had hit it off well, though both were into the game now. Even the boys were attentive---*whooosh*, the Rocket put down another batter. Liza was a people watcher, so it was fine with her if Rod and the boys were into the game. She'd just look at . . . .

. . . the guy sitting just behind Douggie, to her left. He was an odd sort. Middle-eastern. She had noticed him out of the corner of her eye earlier, but now something seemed strange. He and the other Arab-looking fellow---she didn't know that his name was Saeed Alghamdi---hadn't said a word since the Trainers sat down. Not a "C'mon, Jeter." Not a "You call that a strike?" Not a "You blind, ump?" They had stood during the national anthem, and they stood every time the crowd came to its feet, but something wasn't right, because they never reacted to things on the field, but rather to whatever the crowd did. The crowd stands up for the 7th inning stretch as policeman Daniel Rodriquez, the "Latino voice of patriotism," sang "God Bless America," and they stand. The crowd sits down, they sit. No chatter between them. No high fives. Not even a "Praise Allah." Curious. Maybe they are just getting the hang of America. Maybe not---maybe something less benign.

She began to watch the pair as unobtrusively as she could. They didn't frighten her nearly as much as they interested her from a cultural perspective. She didn't know that the one seated right behind Douggie was named Ahmed al Haznawi, or that he had been trained to blend in, to act "American," even to the point of attending football and baseball games. She didn't know that this was part of his cover. Liza Trainer had no idea that al Haznawi and Alghamdi had recently moved into a motel in New Jersey . . . from Hollywood, Florida.

Off and on, Liza Trainer made mental notes on the two men. In the eighth inning, with one batter out, Bernie Williams hit a high foul that drifted left, hooking right toward Douggie. He had his kid's glove ready, eyes closed. Rod stood by with his own glove, ready to catch it for him. Then, at the last minute, the wind caught the ball and pushed it back one row, just behind the Trainers and Michael Callahan. Michael reached back.

Ahmed al Haznawi uncomfortably realized that the ball was headed straight for him. He had to act normal. What did a normal American do in this situation? He reflexively reached up. His hand and Callahan's both shot toward the ball...

August 1, 2001, Logan International Airport
American Airlines Flight 11 to Los Angeles

Actor James Woods settled down in first class, along with four other men. He had just visited his mother outside of Boston, where he feasted on her specialty corn bread and baked beans. Woods' mom managed on her own (his dad died years earlier), but she was slowing down. He'd already brought up the assisted care facility once, without much response. Woods knew his mom would make the right choice, and probably not procrastinate, so he didn't push it. He'd be back next month to see her again.

Now it was back to work. Having finished his final voice-overs for his last film, "Riding in Cars With Boys," and a new script sat on his first-class tray. It had possibilities. A screenplay adapted from David McClintick's 1982 book, *Indecent Exposure,* about actor Cliff Robertson's battle with studio head David Begelman in the 1970s Hollywood check-forging scandal, the script called for Woods to play Begelman's boss, Alan Hirschfield. Hirschfield who refused to fire Begelman---his golden goose---even after the director's crimes were obvious. Finally, the studio's board overruled Hirschfield, and the matter seeped into the press.

Of course, actors thought all scripts had promise, and Woods always looked for the best in a script. That explained why Woods worked constantly. Good movies, bad movies, starring roles, bit parts, cameos, off-beat---it didn't matter. Like his acquaintance, Michael Caine, Woods took any role if he wasn't already committed. More often than not (though he certainly wouldn't say so) he made a film excellent by his presence. Some actors decided many parts were beneath them after they won an Oscar nomination. Not Woods. He'd appeared in more than 70 movies---the majority coming after his best actor nomination for his role as psychotic killer Gregory Powell in "The Onion Field." While not possessing classic leading-man looks, Woods' long face, cleft chin, and easy smile made him versatile enough to do comedy, drama, and even voice-overs for cartoons. Woods inverted the old Hollywood saw, "there are no small parts, only small actors," making even the smallest role big.

Now he stared at the script based on McClintick's book, which he had read years ago. The book had been a bestseller: it was a compelling story from the early 1970s featuring tragic figures, beginning with actor Cliff Robertson---an Academy Award winner himself---who noticed something fishy with his paychecks. When Robertson investigated, he found that Begelman had been forging his name---and those of many other actors and actresses---on checks to cover his gambling habit. Begelman was a successful studio head who oversaw production of such blockbusters as "Close Encounters of the Third Kind" and "Taxi Driver." Yet he was stealing from his own cast members.

But the story, and the tragedy, only began there. Begelman's boss, Alan Hirschfield, learned of the improprieties, but rather than fire the producer, Hirschfield sought to protect his talented box-office Midas. Finally, the board forced the reluctant Hirschfield to fire Begelman. At that point, Robertson, who should have been lauded for his efforts to root out corruption, was blacklisted for several years. It was worse for Begelman. In the 1990s, broke and alone, he shot himself.

Plenty of material here, thought Woods. Hirschfield, the role Woods was slated to play, had uncovered Begelman's fraud, then rationalized his actions. *Can't lose the cash cow*, thought Woods. *It's only a little fraud. Only forging a few checks. Cliff Robertson can afford it.* Woods had already started to try to think like Hirschfield.

What the hell does Robertson want, anyway? Does he really want me to fire a successful producer over . . . principles??

Woods pored over the script for more than an hour when he noticed something odd. None of the four men who sat in first class with him had moved. They hadn't eaten, or even drank anything. *All four are Arab, or Middle Eastern.* His interest piqued, Woods began to apply his astute observational sense of people---how they move, what they do with their hands; when sitting, with their feet; what they eat, what they drink; what they watch or listen to; when they talk, what they say. The more he studied them, the more unusual their actions seemed.

No pillows. Not one of the men had slept. Woods knew that much. No headphones, no entertainment of any sort. And no work. What kind of person---let alone persons---travels from coast to coast without eating, drinking, or going to the bathroom? They don't have briefcases, so they aren't working on the flight. They don't have walkmans or CD players, so they aren't entertaining themselves. Maybe their diet doesn't allow them to eat airline food, but they didn't bring any food on board, and haven't drank anything.

Now Woods started recall his observations of the men earlier, as they came on board the aircraft. *No bags. Not even a single carry-on. Who goes from one end of America to the other without a damn carry-on bag?*

Suddenly the men seemed to warrant a closer inspection, and Woods made mental notes. He thought it ridiculous that Congressmen and Senators often called actors as witnesses because they played a movie role related to the real-life issue, but there was something to the fact that actors do basic research for parts. He'd only been in only one hijacking movie, a 1980s film called "Raid on Entebbe," but he'd played more than a fair share of psychotics and thugs, giving him some insight into the criminal mind. Suddenly, he recalled his research like he had just read it---*hijackers displayed unusual behavior, had no bags because they didn't need them. And their tense, almost rigid, body language is not normal.* They never spoke to the flight attendant---*more than that, he could tell they didn't respect women. They spoke to each other in low hushed tones.*

Awwww crap. These guys are going to hijack this plane! Just what I need . . . . then Woods realized that he had personalized a potentially deadly situation, and mentally reprimanded himself.

At that moment, the lean actor stood up, feigned a stretch, and as nonchalantly as possible walked to the galley area where a blond, thirty-ish flight attendant changed coffee filters. She had recognized him earlier, and smiled.

"Yes, Mr. Woods." Her name tag read "Yvette."

"Yvette, I don't want to cause an alarm, but I think we may have a problem here."

Her brow furrowed. "What would that be?" Yvette was used to prima donnas complaining about the wine in first class or a business-class person using the front "exclusive" lavatories.

Woods leaned in---and defensively, Yvette leaned back. Quietly, Woods told her "There are four Middle Eastern men in first class. I've been watching them for more than an hour. I'm sure you noticed they didn't eat anything or drink anything."

Suddenly, she seemed relieved that she wouldn't be dealing with a medical emergency and wouldn't have to perform open-heart surgery with a spoon. "Oh, yes," she smiled. "Maybe they aren't hungry," and returned to the coffee pots.

Flustered, Woods replied in measured tones "Yvette, I study people for a living. That's how I learn parts. It is unusual, no, downright weird for four men to board a plane, none of them with any luggage, none of them with any work or entertainment, for a *six hour flight*, then to sit almost at attention for more than an hour. No reading? No sleeping? No bags? I'm telling you, there is something wrong here." He really wanted to say "something sinister," but could tell that Yvette still wasn't all that concerned. Nevertheless, she again looked over his shoulder. She checked under their feet. *He's right--- no bags. People fly first class so they can relax. These guys look like they haven't relaxed since the Bee Gees were hot.* Her mood began to change. Woods could see her reviewing her training manuals in her head, and watched the warning lights click on behind her hazel eyes.

Now, she again looked at Woods, and in a whisper said, "I'm going to ask the first officer to come out." She knocked on the cockpit door. Shortly, the first officer, a tall man appeared. A Texan, no doubt. *Aren't there any pilots under six feet?* Woods wondered. *And don't any pilots come from Wisconsin or Iowa?* Captain Charles Rayburn had reddish hair, closely cropped, looked to be about 50, and had the former military demeanor of so many civilian pilots. After Yvette whispered something in his ear, he moved further into the galley, closing the cockpit door behind him. Woods still stood with his back to the four men in first class.

"Captain," Woods cautiously began, "I'm well aware of the implications of using the word 'hijack' on any airliner, but I'm very concerned about those four fellows over there. Can you look over my shoulder?"

Rayburn tried to unobtrusively glance over Woods' shoulder, then again returned his eyes to the actor. "Yeah," he said with a non-committal reply.

This could go better, Woods thought. "I, ah, . . . I think they're planning to hijack this plane. I haven't seen them move in almost an hour and a half, let alone eat, drink, or piss. They brought on no carry-ons. They have no briefcases or walkmans, nor do they have any business materials, briefcases, or cell phones. Who gets on a six-hour flight with absolutely nothing to do . . . unless your purpose is to hijack the aircraft? And while I've watched them, they seem to be taking mental notes about the plane---the position of some of the personnel, the amount of room, and so on."

Rayburn continued to look disinterested, but he inconspicuously surveyed the four. Apparently he shared Woods' assessment.

"All right, Mr. Woods. Go back to your seat. I'm going to lock the cabin door . . . ." he turned to Yvette, "and you are not to open it or knock unless you call me first. If you knock without a prior intercom call, I'll know you are not doing so of your own volition, and I will not come out. I'll alert the tower of our concern, but unless those men make some clearly illegal or overtly suspicious move, I can't do much more. After all, it is no crime merely to look unusual, and we don't want any lawsuits."

What did you expect? Woods thought. The actor knew that the next move was the airline's. He did not know that later, both the pilot and the flight attendant would file separate reports to the FAA of the suspicions behavior of the four men. Those reports would be buried under stacks of other materials, and not read until September 15, 2001. Meanwhile, for the next five hours, Woods uncomfortably returned to the script, all the while keeping an eagle eye on his four co-passengers in first class.

Several hours later, James Woods deplaned from Flight 11, safe and sound. The men walked off, said nothing, and made no suspicious moves. *God. I'm paranoid. I probably terrified that poor stewardess and created a truckload of paperwork for Rayburn.*

Woods drove back to his home, where, exhausted, stuck his key in the door and walked into the foyer of his house. His girlfriend, Traci, drowsily traipsed down the steps.

"So," she said, kissing him on the cheek, "how was your flight?"

He dropped his bags on the tile where they landed with a loud thud, still reflecting on the four first class passengers. "Well, aside from the terrorists and turbulence, it was fine."

Chapter 3

August 20, 2001, Logan International Airport
American Airlines Flight 11 to Los Angeles

Security cameras caught a sullen Mohamad Atta as he strolled through the security screening. Just prior to walking through the metal detectors, Atta emptied his pockets, putting a box cutter, some change, and a set of keys in the plastic basket that he passed around the detector. The security guard said nothing about the box cutter as she shifted her attention to the next person in line.

Atta fought the impulse to smile. *Their security is worse than Sharif prepared us for.* He thought they might at least confiscate the box cutter, although Atta had a backup plan.

Moments later, Wail al-Sheri walked through the same detector, carrying a pocket knife. He, too, passed through without incident. Then, a few minutes later, Waleed al-Sheri and Abdul Alomari also passed through security, each with a deadly instrument, and each without even so much as a raised eyebrow. Each man had purchased a one-way ticket with cash. Since none checked a piece of luggage, they didn't even have to answer the inane questions from the baggage-check people—"Did you pack your bags yourself? Have your bags been in your possession at all times?" Aside from their images on a security camera, they left no trail.

When they boarded the aircraft, Atta sat in seat 1-C; Wail in seat 3-B; Waleed in 3-C; and Alomari in 7-A. Satam Sugami did not make this dry run, but had he done so, he would have sat in seat 6-C. Three men in first class, two at the very front of coach. The only difference between their practice runs and the real thing next month was that Sugami would wear a belt with fake explosives so as to better control the passengers.

Atta buckled his seat belt, then made mental notes---this was his third trip---of how many flight attendants there were, where they worked, how they responded to different passenger calls. Wail and Waleed did the same, while Alomari recorded movements and locations in business class. As before, during a flight of more than five hours, the men scarcely said a word to each other, and none brought any work or entertainment. They neither ate nor drank, but they got what they wanted.

The following day, they rented a van and drove back to Florida, comparing their observations on the flight.

"There is one flight attendant in first class at all times. She will be easy to overpower," said Atta. Wail nodded in agreement. "Immediately after the aircraft levels out, she moves to the galley to begin a drink service. I can take her there and hold her as Wail gets the second officer out of the cockpit. I will threaten to cut her throat if he resists. He will come out to negotiate, at which point Waleed, standing behind him, will kill him. I'll slit the bitch's throat, then kill the pilot. Wail will immediately take over the co-pilot spot until we get the pilot's body out while Waleed controls the other passengers in first-class."

Alomari picked up the narrative. "Satam and I will stand up when you give the signal. He will reveal his 'explosive' vest, and I will take the nearest flight attendant hostage. This will keep the business/coach class under control until matters are too far along for the passengers to react."

Waleed drove as Atta studied the men in the van. "We will go to paradise that day. There can be no other alternative. Do you understand?"

All grimly nodded without hesitation. Atta wanted to be certain.

"We will all die that day. Am I clear?"

"We will strike a great blow as martyrs to Islam. Our names will be remembered forever!" Waleed expressed the views of the others who again nodded enthusiastically.

"Mohammed, we have settled in our minds these issues long ago. You need not worry about us," added Alomari. "We only need to make sure that we have planned this down to the last detail."

This was the answer Atta wanted. "You all got through with your knives and box cutters?"

Again, all nodded.

"No searches, frisking, or questions by the guards?"

"Yes," Wail observed. Atta's head snapped up. "They actually pulled me aside. But a box cutter is not illegal. They let me pass," he laughed. "I could have brought aboard one of those American Bowie knives, I think."

The ever-dour Atta grumbled, "Very well. This was our last test. Next time, we will destroy the icons of American excess and opulence and strike a blow for Allah that the world will never forget."

Attorney General's Office, Washington, D.C.
September 5, 2001

Attorney General John Ashcroft, along with several FBI and Justice Department officials, stood rigidly silent as Robert Mueller was sworn in as only the sixth Director in the history of the Federal Bureau of Investigation. One man---J. Edgar Hoover---had held that job for half of the Bureau's existence, a fact that hardly minimized the honor, or the responsibility.

Mueller wore a blue suit and dark tie, jokingly referred to as "the uniform" inside the Bureau, but otherwise looked unexceptional. He could pass for any mid-level government bureaucrat. Inside the Bureau, he had compiled a solid, but hardly spectacular, record. Perhaps the most that could be said for Robert Mueller was that he had the good fortune not to be tied to any of the Bureau's disasters, such as Waco, the intel failures associated with the Oklahoma City bombing, or the Richard Jewell case. From that standpoint, he was the ideal stealth candidate---no baggage to challenge in congressional hearings. Of course, that also meant no significant accomplishment. A cipher, to some extent.

And ciphers made presidents nervous.

Mueller completed his oath of office, whereupon Ashcroft stepped forward to shake his hand.

"Bob, I don't envy you," said the Attorney General, gripping Mueller's hand. "It's a big job. More often than not, you'll be unpopular, even when you do the right thing. Especially when you do the right thing."

Ashcroft knew about personal assaults. Defeated in a close Senate election in Missouri, he had been named Attorney General by the new president, George W. Bush. Liberal groups like People for the American Way pulled out all the stops to block his nomination. That, he expected. What bothered Ashcroft most, though, was that many he considered friends---fellow senators, who knew there was not the slightest racist bone in his body---turned on him for political reasons and denounced his nomination. Later, in the cloakrooms, they had the gall to come up to him as though nothing had happened. "It's all politics," shrugged one northeastern senator with a smile, having just moments earlier used hateful and slanderous language to denounce the Attorney General. In the senator's mind, of course, "it's all politics" constituted an apology. Ashcroft smiled, and shook his hand. His Pentecostal background demanded that he forgive, but he couldn't forget. After that hearing, John Ashcroft knew who he could trust and who were the good liars.

Mueller, of course, despite years in the Bureau, had yet to learn the depths of partisan rancor. He seemed oblivious to the opposition he would engender from former friends and allies merely by heading the FBI.

He turned to Ashcroft and said with sincerity, "Mr. Attorney General, restoring the honor and dignity of this office will be at the top of my list."

Ashcroft's smile disappeared, replaced by a somber mood. "Bob, the Bureau has had little to brag about here in the last few years---the Richard Jewell thing. Los Alamos. Robert Hansen. You know what I mean. It won't be easy to restore the luster of what was once considered the finest law-enforcement agency in the world. But the President has confidence in you and so do I. You know what I was always told growing up: when you have a tough job to do, call a Marine!"

"Thanks, John," Mueller replied with a laugh. "And thank the President too."

"I'll see you at the cabinet meeting."

As the Attorney General walked away, Mueller turned to his assistant, Ben Steinberg, who had just handed him the daily briefing report. "Let's hope we don't have a Waco to deal with," Mueller said, comparing the briefing notes in his head to this week's agenda items. "Who knows? Maybe the FBI's role has changed. It seems like all the Justice Department does any more is investigate Microsoft and Martha Stewart."

Steinberg took the report as Mueller initialed it at the bottom. "Yes sir. I have your agenda for the week ready. It's on your desk."

Mueller waved Steinberg off and walked into his new office for his first day as Director. *The days of Dillinger are over. Long live the Matrix.*

Meeting Room, Federal Bureau of Investigation HQ
September 7, 2001, 10:50 AM

Every week, the FBI Director met with the heads of all the Departments. Mueller had patiently sat through several initial briefings on personnel and cyber-crime. *Slackers and hackers,* as Mueller labeled these briefings. Next up was the Director of the Counter-Terrorism Division, Paul Andrade, a man whom Mueller scarcely knew. Of course, he barely knew many of these people, and certainly didn't have a read on any of them.

Andrade, a man of 52 years and extensive experience, took the podium with his notes. He still had all his hair---*too much hair for a man his age? And it is black. Jet black.*---and was remarkably fit, easily the equal of many field agents. Other department heads joked and chatted with those around the table, but not Andrade, whose demeanor squelched any informality. He wasn't stiff, but surely in control.

Like the briefers before him, Andrade picked up the remote to the slide projector---*Does everyone have to do Power Point stuff these days?* Mueller thought---and began to review the terrorist attacks on the United States in the past 10 years.

As the first slide came up, Mueller suddenly sat up a little more in his chair. It was a picture of the World Trade Center with smoke billowing out.

"In 1993," Andrade began, "the World Trade Center was attacked using a car bomb detonated in the garage. This attack was masterminded by a Saudi Arabian named Osama bin Laden, who fought with the *mujahadeen* in Afghanistan against the Soviets. The WTC bombing killed seven, and wounded a couple of dozen people. It showed considerable capabilities to gather important information, including details on the construction of the WTC itself. Fortunately, the bomb did not do any permanent damage to the building, thanks only to poor positioning of the van by the terrorists."

"Since that time, bin Laden set up shop in the Sudan, where he remained until 1996. At that time, Sudan apparently drove him out of the country, and he relocated---'fled' would not exactly be appropriate here---to Afghanistan, where he has essentially been under the protection of the Taliban government. Since he has been in Afghanistan, his terrorist network, called 'al-Qaeda,' or "the Base," has plotted a series of strikes against the United States, our allies, and even Middle Eastern countries who have, in his view, become heretics."

The new slide revealed the long, thin face of Osama bin Laden, photographed with his trusted aide and one-eyed Taliban cleric, Mullah Omar. Bin Laden wore Afghani-type robes, a small Afghan turban, and his face was lengthened further by a salt-and-pepper beard. Omar, shorter and rounder, sported the cleric's turban and wore small round glasses---sort of a Middle Eastern Michael Moore without the smirk.

"In 1996," Andrade continued. "we broke up a plot in the Philippines, also traced back to bin Laden, to blow up several airlines over the Pacific. Two years later, terrorists directly tied to bin Laden bombed the U.S. embassies in Kenya and Tanzania, killing 224 people, including 12 Americans. We arrested and tried a Saudi, a Lebanese, a Tanzanian, and a Jordanian. One had a diary, revealing intricate connections to al-Qaeda."

The slides advanced through scenes of devastation of the two American embassies, smoldering ruins, and bloody, wounded people staggering out. Mueller now leaned forward, his palms on the table. *My God. Had this happened inside the United States, we'd be at war with someone.*

He interrupted Andrade's lecture. "Our policy is still to treat terrorism as a 'law-enforcement' issue? Is that it?" Mueller's question carried a strong whiff of disapproval, which Andrade immediately perceived.

"Yes sir. So far, we have no other mandate."

"All right. Please proceed."

"Last October, a cell associated with al-Qaeda obtained a boat similar to the supply craft that our naval vessels deal with in every foreign port. We know at least three men were involved. They filled the boat with explosives, and one of them sailed it into the side of the *U.S.S. Cole*, killing 17 American sailors. Two Yemenis were indicted, but we do not have them in custody."

"In summary sir, Osama bin Laden has been persistent, deadly, and increasingly bold in his attacks. Al-Qaeda strikes are well-planned and well-coordinated, and not just against us, but anyone they deem a heretic or outlaw nation, including Muslim states like Kuwait and Saudi Arabia. Bin Laden has made no secret of his desire to assassinate the Saudi royal family or any 'moderate' Muslim leader who cozies up too closely with us or any western nation. That said, America remains his number one target."

"And what prompted this hatred of the United States, or do we care?" asked Mueller in a disgusted tone that betrayed his contempt for theories that terrorists were merely products of western oppression.

Andrade replied that some of the intelligence on bin Laden ascribed his violence to the U.S. presence on Islamic "holy ground" in Saudi Arabia during the Gulf War. "There is a view," he stated with little conviction, "that we have somehow provoked him."

Mueller sensed Andrade's skepticism. "But you disagree?"

"Mr. Director, we've had some sources confirm for us that this guy went way over to the dark side long before Desert Storm. He's been gunning for the west for almost 15 years. In my opinion, the Gulf War was an excuse."

With that assessment, several around the table shifted uncomfortably. Mueller, on the other hand was impressed. *Thank God for a man who doesn't mince words. Andrade has some spine.* The Director stood, then started to pace as he talked. "I don't like this one bit. The Bureau can't really do anything but react to thugs like this bin Laden. We don't have the authority to arrest him on foreign soil, especially where there is no treaty of extradition . . . even if we could do it, which is a task far beyond our resources. But I want you to put whatever discretionary resources you have on this guy and his network. And I want a review of all the bomb security at the WTC and at the main government buildings in Washington. If he tried to bomb us once, he's certain to try again.

Chapter 4

September 7, 2001, Woodside, New York

Michael's voice sang out excitedly on the other end of the phone. "Hey, it's me. I got the schedule for the weekend, and I'm on for Friday, off Saturday and Sunday this week." Michael sounded excited, for unbroken weekends were rare in the Callahan household. But for Shannon, the message had an entirely different meaning.

"I guess I can't take my shot Friday night," she replied, fatigue already in her voice. "I can't leave the boys unsupervised, and I'm too sick to get up Saturday. I'll have to take it Saturday night."

"Can't you miss it this week? We almost never get a weekend to go out."

"And who's going to take care of the boys? My mother sure can't."

"Shannon, the boys are teenagers. They are old enough to take care of themselves for an evening," he pleaded.

Michael was right, of course, because the boys were 17 and 15. And Sean was usually not home anyway on Friday nights any more, while Patrick often had to play at school with the pep band. But someone had to go drop him off and pick him up---she wasn't about to let him walk the streets of New York alone, and he still couldn't drive. No, it wasn't that. It was the disruption of her patterns that she disliked. On the other hand, she and Michael *didn't* get out much.

After a long pause, Shannon finally asked, "Do we have the money?" That was always the first sign that she was about to relent.

Michael recognized the pattern. *If she's asking about money, she's already decided we can afford it.* "Yeah. I've worked overtime. We can afford a nice dinner. Patrick will be ok at home for three or four hours."

"Well, let's go to that new B-B-Q place out on Long Island." Shannon never chose what she called "chi-chi-poo" cuisine, which usually consisted of a tiny spoonful of some oddly-sauced meat and a sprig of parsley for $50 a plate. Instead, she searched out restaurants that featured "American style" cooking, and, especially, good desserts. "There is a pie place right near there, too." Then, another pause, "That's *if* I feel good enough."

"Ok. But I have a feeling you'll want to get out of the house."

You're not the one that has to put on makeup when you're in such a fog you can't tell the difference between blood-red and pink. But Michael meant well, and they did not get out much. "I'll try. Let's see how I feel. See you later."

Shannon and Michael usually got right to business on the phone, and never lingered with long "I-love-yous." Even in their dating days, they had not dwelt on syrupy nostrums. In 18 years of marriage, he never called her "baby"---*well, occasionally during sex*---because she found that demeaning, and she had only called him "honey" one time---the only endearment she ever used. That was when they had cut short a vacation with the two of them to Orlando when Michael suddenly developed heart palpitations and irregularity. After returning home, and having the family doctor insist that he go to a hospital---and not drive himself---Michael broke down as he and Shannon walked to the car, sobbing, "I'm sorry. I'm sorry." She took him in her arms and said, "Oh honey, it's ok. It's ok." Michael took his role as protector and provider seriously. In his mind, for the first time in their marriage, he let her down by being sick. "We're a family," she said, comforting him. "You don't have to apologize for being sick. God knows I'm sick enough."

Her words struck home with Michael, and he pulled it together, got to the hospital, and after a battery of tests determined that the only thing wrong with him was an excess of caffeine. He went on decaf the next day.

Other than that time, the Callahans seldom slobbered over each other. That didn't mean they were impersonal or detached in anyway: quite the contrary, Shannon and Michael did everything for the boys---*probably way too much*---and loved each other deeply. But public displays bothered them. They found something suspicious about couples that constantly kissed and cuddled, for within minutes the same lovers would be throwing ashtrays at each other or signing divorce papers. And since both Shannon and Michael had gone the divorce route in previous marriages, neither had any intention of letting the other go in this one.

Another siren? Shannon listened more closely. *Is it me? Am I the only one who hears these?* On Sunday, right before Michael sat down to watch the Giants, the phone rang and a young fireman from Station 70, Michael's sister station, had been killed when a floor gave way. A Hispanic fellow, John Martinez, just two years on the force. Another fire funeral. Another grieving widow---she had two kids also, both under five---and more of those bagpipes. Shannon had never met the kid, and Michael only saw him once during a drill. But those pipes made everyone your relative, and she cried for someone she never met, and for the children he'd never know.

September 9, 2001, Chestnut Hill, Massachusetts

"Here you go, Audrey. This is the place." Mario Lombardi turned to his passenger, a mid-20s white woman sitting in the back seat of the Cadillac limousine, still applying lip gloss while smoking a cigarette. Her courtesy ride came from "Day and Night Encounters," a local escort service ("for the most discriminating of gentlemen," according to its ad). Mario had driven for the service for as long as "Audrey" could remember. Of course, Audrey wasn't her real name. She once told Mario she'd had taken it from the man-eating plant in "Little Shop of Horrors," but, like so much about the prostitution business, that was probably a lie too.

"Thanks, Mario. Thirty minutes. If you don't see me in 45, something's wrong." She brushed back her blonde hair, whose telltale roots showed that part of her wasn't genuine, either. Nor were the size 38s she stuffed in the leopard-skin blouse.

"Fine. I'm right out here if you need me." Mario checked the limo's clock: 1:30 in the afternoon. *What kind of guys get time for sex parties in the middle of the day?* Such afternoon trysts were unusual, even for some of the things Mario had seen. "Oh, wait, what are the names? You know the drill. I have to have names."

Audrey paused getting out of the car to stamp out the cigarette butt. "They're A-rabs," she said in her thick Brooklyn accent. Then, looking at her thin call sheet which she kept tucked in her purse, studied the names. "Ok, I don't know which of these two I have---they're brothers. One is Wail . . . ."

"Wail? Like wailing and moaning?"

"No, it's spelled, er, yah, it's spelled that way. Like wail. You know, like 'I'm gonna wail the tar out of you?' Anyway, his name's Wail Alsheri and the other one is Waleed."

"Wally? Like Wally Cleaver?"

"No, Mario. W-A-L-E-E-D. Arab, ya know?"

"So you got both of 'em or just one?"

It's none of your damn business, she thought, but then realized he was just being protective. "I think I have one. If it's both, it'll cost 'em double," she added, as she slammed the door. "Course, if it's both I might be a little longer. That's why I said give me 45 minutes."

"You got it." Mario pulled the limo over to an empty parking spot about 200 feet from the Park Inn on Route 9. He flipped on the radio to take in the latest on thrift from Clark Howard, the "Consumer Warrior," and re-checked his Baretta tucked underneath his jacket. *Just in case it's too long*, he thought.

He was surprised when, after only a half an hour, Audrey came out.

"They want me back again tonight, at 9:00," she sighed, lighting a Camel.

"Randy little buggers," observed Mario as he started the car.

"You don't know the half of it. They're pigs," she replied, completely oblivious to the religious overtones of her comment. Then, she gazed out the window. Mario, of course, knew better than to ask what the other half was.

September 10, 2001, Newark International Airport

"Rod, I can't believe you're getting on another airplane in less than 24 hours. Isn't your butt sore?" Liza Trainer seemed to drag herself through the lobby to baggage claim, looking for carousel #6, marked "TWA 1455 ROME."

Liza and Rod had just completed a whirlwind trip to Italy, thanks to Pandora Corporation, but Rod had to go to San Francisco the next day.

"Someone's got to pay for that tennis bracelet," Rod said, pointing to Liza's wrist. "That shop in Florence has already sent my VISA card through the roof." Actually, the bracelet was partly a token of peace---a concession for his having tried to bring the laptop computer along. (*"You're not bringing THAT thing, are you?"* Liza had asked in her pained voice. Rod explained that if he didn't keep up with his e-mail, he'd be spending the entire night after they returned having to catch up.) Now, tired as he was, it seemed even a worse decision than before.

"I know. I guess it's worth it," she said, admiring the bracelet. They didn't even know if the diamonds were real, or if the $1,200 was even remotely close to the value of the item, but Liza knew one thing---it looked good on her wrist. "Did you call Mom while I was in the bathroom?"

"Yah. The boys are OK. They will meet us at the usual spot."

The "usual spot" was a rest area along the parkway. "It's raining," she said, looking out the endless glass of Newark International. "We won't be able to chit-chat." *Which is good. I'm beat, and I have all this unpacking to do.*

"Then we'll just have to say hello and goodbye quickly. They'll bring the boys."

Liza remembered not too long ago when they called it the "baby exchange," when Liza and Rod would give his parents the boys as they left for short vacations to the Bahamas or Florida.

"I wish I'd gotten the flight to San Francisco from here today," Rod added, as they boarded the tram to the baggage carousel. "By the time I get home, I'll have to turn right around again."

"No, it's ok. I need you home for a while, if even for a few hours. The boys need you home."

"Well," he winked, hugging her, "you got me." Then, seeing his distinct bag with a red-white-and-blue ribbon on it, pointed, "There's our bags."

The Trainers drove home, stopping to pick up the boys. When they pulled the minivan into the driveway at 5:00, and got inside the house, they were greeted by a note from Liza's mother: "meatloaf and macaroni and cheese in fridge; apple pie in dish." Rod shook his head, saying, "Your mom is really something. To come over here and do our cooking for us so we don't have to go out again, well, that's pretty amazing."

Actually, it's stunning, thought Liza. *The woman's a saint.* But Liza could not remember a time she hadn't though of Mom as a saint, even in the difficult teen years. Liza couldn't remember ever delivering a typical teenager's "you-don-t-love-me" or "you've-ruined-my-life" speeches directed at her mom. Even when Liza went on a missionary trip to Indonesia---Indonesia, for God's sake, *literally, for God's sake*, she laughed---Mom didn't object. Maybe she knew what God had in mind there.

Liza heard Rod playing in the living room with the boys already. *I see Rod didn't wait to give them their presents from us.* Douggie had a wooden train, which he moved along the coffee table. Daniel seemed puzzled by his gift---a miniature statue of Michelangelo's "The David."

After dinner, Rod bathed the boys while Liza cleaned up the kitchen and unpacked. By 9:00, she was drained, but still had one more task. Calling her mom wasn't unpleasant, but as tired as she was, Liza wished she could postpone it. No such luck.

"Hi, mom. Yah, the flight was fine. Oh, the trip was great. We saw Florence and Rome. Hey, thanks so much for the food. It was a godsend. I was really debating whether to even stop at the grocery store on the way home, and just took a chance, and didn't. So you were a lifesaver."

Liza made some more small talk as fatigue swept over her. "Mom, I have to go. I haven't even had a chance to talk to Rod after dinner, and he has to leave tomorrow for San Francisco. No, it's ok, he'll be back by Wednesday. Short trip. You know Pandora, INC. Yah. See ya, Mom. Love you." *Finally, a shower and bed.* Rod was still on the computer, finalizing his schedule for Pandora's meeting tomorrow. *Rod will probably leave early, like he always does. We will talk on Wednesday. Where's he flying out of tomorrow? Forgot to ask.*

PART TWO

THE DAY

Chapter 5

September 11, 2001, Logan International Airport

"Good morning and welcome to American Airlines Flight 11 non-stop service to San Francisco. . . ." As the desk attendant rattled off the boarding procedures, Mohamad Atta glanced at Wail al-Sheri. There was no need for words. All five men had said their prayers earlier, and they had rehearsed this particular flight repeatedly, having made the actual Boston to San Francisco trip three times. They would not fail.

"Now boarding first class passengers . . . ."

Atta, looked at Wail and Waleed, and all three slowly stood, having this time brought carry-on bags for show, although they had the box cutters, knives, and mace in their coat pockets. An elderly man---*a Jew?* moved in front of them, and while inside Atta snarled, outwardly he gestured for the man to go ahead. *It's the least I can do, seeing as though soon you will be ashes.* Another, younger man, an executive, took the seat opposite Atta, as the other conspirators found their places. Atta sat in 9D, an aisle seat. They sat down and stared straight, watching Alomari slid in across the aisle from him in 9G, while al-Suqami walked past them to assume his seat in row 10. *Allah be praised, today we shall strike the Great Satan as never before.*

Al-Suqami carefully concealed his "bomb" beneath his coat as he took seat 10D. He had easily walked through security because he didn't have a bomb at all. But the passengers wouldn't know that.

Astonishingly, almost all the terrorists carried with them a copy of Atta's handwritten instructions: "shave excessive body hair, wear clean clothes and clean shoes, bathe, bring knives, and all papers and passports." Authorities would later find some of these papers---or pieces of them---at the crash sites.

Although the boarding process seemed to go on infinitely, at last the cabin doors were closed and the big Boeing 767 pulled away from its gate and lumbered onto the runway with 11 crew members and 81 passengers on board.

There are only five crew members who count, Atta reminded himself: the two men in the pilot's cabin, the woman in first class, and the woman and man toward the front of the business/coach cabin. The rest are too far away and separated by too many people to be a factor in the outcome. Atta's thumb ran along his box cutter that this day would taste infidel blood, and fondled his small dispenser of mace. We must act immediately after the plane has climbed to altitude. New York is not that far. At that point, al-Suqami would stand up to announce that he had a "bomb," and Waleed and Wail would spray mace, then kill the flight attendant and purser. Atta would move to the cockpit, mace the pilots, and slit their throats. Al-Omari would remain in the back to help al-Suqami.

It was 8:00 a.m..

September 11, 2001, Logan International Airport

"United Airlines Flight 175 to Los Angeles is in its final boarding. If you have tickets for United, Flight 175 to Los Angeles, please board at this time." As the desk attendant lowered the microphone and attached it to its velcro holder, Mohald al-Sheri quickly handed his boarding pass to the woman collecting them. He had been in the bathroom, praying. His cousin, Marwan, was already aboard, along with three other men in his cell. Although any of them could fly the aircraft, if things went according to plan Mohald would direct the great bird into one of the World Trade Center towers in about 45 minutes.

It was 8:14 a.m. . . . .

September 11, 2001, Washington Dulles International Airport

Salem Alhazmi, seated in 5F, and his brother, Nawaf, in 2A, stared straight ahead as the Boeing 757 hurtled down the runway on what everyone thought would be an uneventful trip to Los Angeles.

Once airborne, their task was to handle the First Class flight attendant and the pilots; Khalid Almihdhar, seated in 12-B, and Majed Moqued and Hani Hanjour, would take care of the business-class passengers.

Khalid did not notice the pretty blonde who gazed out the window. Michelle Olin, a prominent author and television news personality on the political shows, reflected on her recent celebrity status. She had just finished a book on the last days of the present administration, and was flying to Los Angeles as part of the book tour. Her husband, Solicitor General of the United States, Cal Olin, had played a key role in arguing the 2000 election before the United States Supreme Court, and Michelle intended to call him once they achieved cruising altitude. As she turned from the window and glanced across the aisle, she saw Khalid and politely smiled. He gazed at her vacantly, as though he were a dead man. *Or she, a dead woman.*

Olin snapped her eyes back to the front. Khalid's look sent a chill down her spine.

It was 8:25 a.m. . . .

September 11, 2001, Logan International Airport

"Jan, we've got a delay," said Rod Trainer into his cell phone. "No, the flight was delayed. Actually, we got out on the tarmac on time, then have sat here for a half hour. Oh, wait, we're moving. Ok, here we go. It looks like we're actually going to get airborne here soon. I'll call you en route."

Rod had called Jerry Toonan, another Pandora employee whom he was scheduled to meet in San Francisco later that day. The delay on the tarmac allowed Rod to get his laptop out and send a few e-mails. Now, with the plane moving, he had to put the laptop away. He had not paid attention to the four Middle-Eastern men who sat in rows one through six. Nor did he know that one of their number was missing.

A fifth hijacker, known only as al-Qahtani, had been denied entry into the United States in August at the Orlando airport and had not found a way into the country. Immigration agents questioned al-Qahtani and became suspicious when he could not give specifics about who he would be staying with or what he was doing. They put him on a plane back to Saudi Arabia. As the officials took al-Qahtani in custody, just a few feet away Mohammed Atta was using a pay phone to call a number in the Middle East.

Ziad Jarrah, Saeed Alghamdi, Ahmed al Haznawi, and Ahmed Alnami, three of whom were "unindicted co-conspirators" in the 1993 World Trade Center bombing and who had gotten into the country despite being on an FBI watch list, were not concerned about the loss of Al-Qahtani. Four of them were plenty to capture this aircraft. Large as it was---another Boeing 757---the men counted only 38 passengers and seven crew. Only four of those, including the two pilots, would be in rows six through one. As with the plans for the other planes, one of their number, Alnami, would stand up and announce he had a bomb, exposing his realistic-looking vest laced with "explosives." Sufficiently distracted by Alnami, the other three men would use mace and the box cutters to subdue the first-class cabin attendant and the forward business-class attendant, threatening or killing both instantly, depending on their response and that of the other passengers. Using one woman as a hostage, Jarrah and Alghamdi would coax the pilot or co-pilot out of the cockpit, kill him, then kill the other American in his seat as Jarrah slipped behind the co-pilot's controls.

No, al-Qahtani would not be needed.

Rod Trainer stashed his cell phone and flipped up his tray table as the huge Boeing lumbered down the runway. *One quick meeting, then back to Jersey. I'll be one tired puppy. Liza was right. I should never have agreed to this meeting.*

It was 8:45 a.m. . . . . .

Flight 11, On Approach to World Trade Center, Tower 1

Mohamed Atta put the whimpering of the wounded flight attendant just outside the cabin from his mind. She was incapacitated, blood flowing from her throat. The purser was dead. Before anyone could figure out what was happening, Waleed and Wail had taken control of the cabin after 20 minutes in flight. Even the pilots, whom bin Laden warned might be difficult because they had military training, were convinced first of all that it was a standard hijacking, then, only later, were they maced and killed. Disabled by the gas and buckled into their seats, they were helpless to react as the box cutters slashed their jugular veins.

All had gone as bin Laden predicted: the passengers were cowed by Al-Suqami's "bomb," and the mace and shock of the attack subdued the others. More important, the terrorists counted on the passengers' ignorance. Since none of the passengers or crew suspected the real intention of Atta and his fellow hijackers, few of them thought it necessary to be heroes. Instead, as bin Laden had predicted, they would "play it by the book"---a typical hijacking where the hostages are released.

What Atta did not know was that just before they killed him, the pilot, Captain John Ogonowski, a Vietnam vet and former fighter jock, triggered a "push-to-talk" button on the aircraft's yoke the moment the hijackers took over. Although Atta demanded he turn off the transponder (which he did at 21 minutes into the flight), Atta did not see Ogonowski push the button every time the terrorists started speaking, It was from Atta's careless boast, "We have more planes. We have other planes" that FAA controllers instantly started to ground all aircraft, and which, as it turned out, may have saved numerous other targets in London, and contributed to the information that soon reached Rod Trainer and the passengers of Flight 93.

Nor did Atta know that back in coach class, flight attendant Amy Sweeny used the GTE Airfone to call the American Airlines flight service manager, Michael Woodward, at Logan.

"Michael," she said clearly but quietly, "This plane has been hijacked. The suspects were in 9D, 9G, and 10D. They had a bomb. I could see the wires."

She turned to Betty Ong, who was behind her in the rear jump seat, and pointed to the receiver, indicating to her to get on the phone to American Airlines.

While Woodward talked to Amy, Ong got on another Airfone and called American Airlines' North Carolina reservations, which patched her through to headquarters in Dallas.

"I don't know, but I think we're getting hijacked," Ong told a supervisor on the other end. "The cockpit isn't answering their phone, and people can't breathe in business class."

Ong spoke coolly, with no panic in her voice. "They've stabbed the purser and the first flight attendant. I think there's mace or something. Wait . . . someone's coming back from business."

A passenger had snuck back from business class when one of the hijackers was distracted with the flight attendant. Ong paused, absorbing the information. "There is a bomb, and no one can breathe . . . some sort of gas, and we can't get into the cockpit."

She looked puzzled. *Did that mean they tried to get into the cockpit and it was locked? Did they overpower the hijackers?* In the rush to get information out, she didn't ask.

A few rows up, Sweeny continued to provide information to Woodward. "Michael, what I'm getting is that the guys in first class stabbed the first attendant and the purser, while one guy in back stood up and showed everyone his bomb. I saw it. One of the other Arabs in business class went into first class. We think they maced the front of the cabin and the pilots."

By then Woodward was patched in with Dallas, as well, so he was getting, if on a delayed basis, Ong's comments too. Having punched up the seat locations, he knew that 9G was Abdulaziz al-Omari, 10B was Satam al-Suqami, and 9D was Mohamed Atta.

"Amy," he said, "can you see where you are?"

"I see water. I see buildings. Oh my God. It's New York. We're flying low. Really low. Oh God . . . ."

Mohamed Atta, in the pilot's seat, could see the gigantic towers looming straight ahead. He had to do little to line up the aircraft as it screamed over the New York City skyline. He would cut a swath through the 94th through the 98th floors, though he wasn't nearly skilled enough to aim the plane precisely. It would be enough.

In these, his final moments of glory, Atta felt incredibly empty. He'd pondered his last words, even rehearsing a few lines, maybe to shout into the microphone to the passengers. Yet now, with the monstrous tower looming before him, and the jet under his control careening toward it, Atta had no great slogans, no final utterances, no prophetic words for his fellow hijackers about to die behind him.

In a voice almost resigned, hardly full of Jihadist fury, he exclaimed "Allahu Akhbar!" The rejoinders from his compatriots echoed behind him, "Allahu Akhbar!" Atta closed his eyes, but saw only black.

It was 8:46:50 a.m. . . . .

World Trade Center, Tower 1, Offices of Cantor Fitzgerald

"Laura," said Sheila Armstrong as she breezed by Samantha Egan's desk, "I've got a stack of papers here for Uncle Ben's signature." Sheila, one of Jeremy Klein's executive secretaries, had come down nine floors from Olympus, as Cantor employees called the 105th floor. She would never call Ben Klein, the boss's brother, "Uncle Ben" to his face, although he wouldn't mind.

Cantor Fitzgerald bond traders had affectionately dubbed him "Uncle Ben" after Jeremy's boys came to the office one day and told everyone about his weekly visits to Jeremy's house to play video games with Jeremy's son, Josh. The easy-going Ben, a 37-year-old kid who loved toys of all sorts, especially the electronic variety, relished the moniker, and within a few months, almost everyone privately called him by that name. Some even circulated a joke computer-generated picture of Ben's face on the old "Uncle Ben's" rice box. Ben only laughed.

It was the kind of casual liberty that no one would ever take with Jeremy, the driven CEO of Cantor Fitzgerald. No, Jeremy wasn't a guy to have a beer with, or go to a hockey game with. He didn't take to friendly ribbing or office jokes. But the man knew securities sales. Everyone at CF respected his acumen, and, indeed, most sought to acquire the morsels of knowledge about leveraging assets and corporate debt that dribbled from his brain in unguarded moments. Ben, on the other hand, did not know the intricacies of the securities game the way Jeremy did, but at pure sales, no one was better.

As different as the brothers were, Jeremy eagerly anticipated the day when Ben would be a full partner, and would co-manage the company with him. Ben's relaxed style belied his talents in selling securities to high-dollar clients better than anyone since the famous Charles E. Merrill virtually created the "middle-class investor" in the 1920s. If Jeremy supplied the analytical ability and organizational brains, Ben was the charm and the personality of the firm.

On Monday, September 10, Ben took Jeremy and his wife to dinner at an Upper West Side Japanese restaurant. They then attended a rare Michael Jackson concert, which made for a late night. Even so, Ben made it to the office early the next morning, as usual.

"Actually, he's at the copier," said Sam, bobbing her head toward the copy room, past the desks of several bond traders. Sam, Ben's gatekeeper, protected him from the myriad of CF employees who just like to shoot the bull with Ben, well aware he loved shooting the bull with them. Unlike Jeremy, no one picked Ben's brain for price/earning potentials or unfunded debt levels of potential clients. Rather, Ben was more likely to fall victim to an inter-office debate about the New York Jets' wisdom of starting Vinnie Testaverde over Chad Pennington. And from such discussions, Sam had to protect Ben at all costs. *God knows, the man could not protect himself from such weighty subjects*, she thought.

Sheila nodded without breaking stride. "Was he in early today?" she asked, looking back.

"Of course. Why?"

Sheila stopped for a moment, then walked back to Sam's desk. "He and Jeremy hit the town last night---even saw Michael Jackson."

"You're kidding! Jeremy's a Michael Jackson fan? Who woulda' thought?"

"I know. He doesn't seem like the 'moonwalking' type, does he? Anyway, he's late. He called a few minutes ago. Decided to take his son to school today. But I'm not surprised Uncle Ben's in already."

"Me either. When I took this job, I thought they were joking when they said he gets here at 7:00 and expects you to already be here," added Sam. "You know, I heard rumors of the old Drexel-Burnham-Lambert group when Michael Milken ran the bond side of things---before he went to prison---and Laura Rothstein told me that their people had to be there at *five in the morning!*"

"Not this lady," snorted Sheila. "Takes me an hour just to look this good." She stepped back and swept her body with her arm in jest. "No way I'm getting up at three in the morning to come in to an office. There's not enough money in New York to get me up at that hour."

"Know what you mean," added Sam. "But the good side is that we're off by four. Ben has us staggered, and probably a third of the people are out of here after three o' clock. I checked all this out with my sister before I took the job."

Sam's sister, the human resources manager at Cantor, who had practically begged her to come to work for the company, finally prevailed. She convinced Sam that it was the chance of a lifetime. Given CF's growth over the past two years, who could argue?

"Anyway," Sam continued, "I suppose they know that they get what they pay for and they pay for what they get."

"Oh, I know. There's not another bond house in New York, except the real elite, insider companies, that pays as well as the Kleins. Gotta give 'em that. They treat their employees right with the stuff that really counts," Sheila smiled, rubbing her thumb and index finger together. "I can manage to crawl in here at 7:30 for that kind of money."

Suddenly, Ben rounded the corner from the copy room.

"There's Ben," observed Sam. "Do you suppose he's learned a few moves?" Then, just loudly enough for Ben to hear, Sam started singing "Gotta be startin' somethin', ya gotta be startin' somethin' . . . ."

Ben blanched as he got close enough to hear the lyrics. "Ok, ok. So I saw Michael Jackson. So what. I admit it: I'm stuck in the '80s."

Both Sam and Sheila looked at each other then, let out a spontaneous "Oooooooh!" Ben started to crack up. "Am I gonna get this all day? Don't you dare pull out a sequined glove. It was a good concert, what can I say?"

Composing herself, Sheila held out the stack of papers. "Jeremy left these last night for your signature. He needs them today." Sheila pointed out the yellow signature tags wedged in the stack of papers. Then, unable to resist, threw in, "Ya know it, ya know it" to which Sam added, "Sham on."

"Ok, you two. Quit." Ben lifted the stack of papers from Sheila's hands. "Did Jeremy put you up to this?"

"Uh, no, actually," noted Sheila. "He's not in yet. He had to drop Josh off at school."

"Well, when he gets in, tell him . . . ." Ben paused for effect, then, in a voice loud enough to be heard by anyone eavesdropping, stated, "I think we can close the Inesco deal today."

Sheila and Sam exchanged surprised looks, and a low-level buzz started to percolate in the office. "Really?" asked Sheila in amazement. The initial public offering for Interstate Energy Service Company had consumed much of the bond department for the past two weeks, and until late yesterday, no one thought Cantor Fitzgerald had much of a chance to offer the IPO. "Did you tell Jeremy this last night?"

"No. It was 99% sure, but I didn't want to say anything until it was certain and I had confirmation . . . ," holding up the copies of faxes of the agreement-in-principle, "which I got this morning."

For CF employees, such a deal had far-reaching consequences. At the end of the year, everyone at the company benefited from pro-rated company-wide bonuses, right down to the janitors. It was a remarkable share-the-wealth program that helped the company maintain one of the lowest employee turnover rates in the industry. And Uncle Ben had come through again, signing a major client---one whom even Jeremy thought unattainable---to a multi-million-dollar deal that would stake every one in CF to a very merry Christmas indeed.

"Ben," said Sam in shock, "that's amazing. Isn't that the biggest single sale we've . . . er, you've . . . ever made?" By now word had spread through the 101st floor, causing other traders gather round.

Beaming, now, Ben nodded enthusiastically. "Now do you see why I wanted to go to a concert last night?"

Sheila picked up the cue. "I guess you could say . . . 'You're BAD, you're BAD, ya know it, ya know it."

"No you don't! Stop it!" he laughed. "I swear, if you people start dancing I'll personally fire the lot of you!" Amidst what had now become a crowd, Ben addressed the troops: "Good job, all of you. We're going to have some heavy work ahead of us, but the payoff is going to be huge. Congratulations to all of you." The small semi-circle broke out in applause, then began to dissipate, each person back to a cubicle.

"Look, Sheila," Ben added quietly, "call me as soon as Jeremy gets in, OK? Don't tell him yourself, no matter how tempting. And try to make sure no one else gets to him with this news. I know it will be hard, but I *really* want to surprise him."

"I understand, Ben. I'll put the 105th floor on lockdown until you get up there."

"By the way, what time did Jeremy say he'd get in?"

"Jeremy's driver, Jimmy called, and said he'd just driven them to Josh's school, so I'd say within a half hour."

Ben looked at his watch. It was 8:46. He walked by the large windows of the 101st floor, when he thought he detected a large bird heading for the building about 10 floors below. *Strange, it's a big sucker.* Fascinated, he walked toward the window for a better look, when suddenly he noticed that everyone had started to gather near the windows. Some were pointing. And someone was . . . *screaming?*

He put his face to the glass, looking down, and felt the building shudder.

That's no bird.

It was 8:47 a.m.

World Trade Center, Tower 1, 94th Floor

Soro ("Ellen") Matsui had only been in the United States for a year. The Bank of Yokohama had transferred her from Yokohama when she got her promotion, after she spent a year in the Singapore branch, where she picked up a distinct British accent. Ellen specialized in corporate finance, especially electronics firms. From her office on the 94th Floor of the World Trade Center, she had a window on the world. Today, she had a meeting a 10:00 in the Chrysler Building, and was running a little late.

One of BoY's American borrowers was struggling after the dotcom bust, having invested heavily in online music. *They should have known better*, Ellen concluded, stuffing the last papers in her briefcase. *Napster didn't solve anything. "Music sharing" isn't going away, and we should have known better too.* Now she had to reduce BoY's exposure.

Ellen glanced out the window just as she snapped her briefcase shut, barely in time to see a monstrous, silvery shape closing in.

By the time it registered on Ellen that the shape was a Boeing 767 hurtling at her at almost 400 miles per hour, it was too late for her---or anyone else on the 94th Floor---to even scream.

Flight 11's forward wing tore into the tower 20 feet from where Ellen stood. Fuel cells in the wings ripped open, spewing out the 10,000 gallons of jet fuel for a few milliseconds until a spark hit the main tanks, blasting the fuselage to shreds and sending an engine nacelle like a projectile through the building like grapeshot. Ellen disintegrated in a fraction of a second. The flaming engine continued on, out the other side, spiraling several hundred feet away, bouncing once on a car, which it crushed, then rolling to a stop against a subway sign. As the rest of the Boeing shredded itself and exploded, its massive 2000-degree fireball burst all windows on the entire floor, propelling bond traders and secretaries out of the building out like human corks shot from champaign bottles. A secondary blast jetted down the elevator shafts, melting 10 of the 104 elevator doors, then, as the flame was sucked upwards in the shafts by air currents, belched like a fiendish skyrocket, blowing out elevator doors for the next 10 floors before dissipating.

More than a thousand red-hot rivets perforated a senior executive, "Fred" Tanaka, and a Fed Ex delivery man, Jaime Morales, like a sieve of bullets. Shards of molten metal penetrated chairs and computer screens, lungs and limbs. One junior trader, hurled from his desk more than 100 yards from the impact point, dangled from the edge of the building for brief seconds until the flames consumed his hands. One floor up, an analyst, blinded by the heat and smoke, literally stumbled out the open 95th story portal. Thankfully, most people near the impact zone were numbed into instant shock by the blast, and few actually felt their horrific wounds during the scant seconds of life that still remained.

Those not instantly killed by the shock, the fireball, or ejected from the building by the force of the explosion had only seconds to realize that they were being cooked alive, barely long enough to scream before the searing heat vaporized their vocal chords. Isoroku Nomo, whose grandmother had been burned badly at Nagasaki, stood just a few hundred feet from the impact, which ripped him in five pieces, firing his disfigured head out of the building like a wobbly cannonball. An executive standing behind him had been slammed through four dividers, then impaled on the melting metal leg of an upside-down table.

Just outside the immediate blast zone, the unfortunate YoB employees were no better off. Smoke overcame anyone within a few minutes not instantly killed in the blast. Lungs were fried by the superheated air of the jet fuel mixture.

The angle of Flight 11 took out parts of the 95th through 98th floors, and sent heat and smoke up through the floor and ventilation of the floors above, while fireballs shot down the elevator shafts as the building shook and convulsed. People immediately above or below the immediate impact point had virtually evaporated. Further up, in Olympus, some had seen the airplane's approach and had started screaming. A few took to the stairwells instantly, unaware that the lava-like concrete quickly hardened into impassible walls. By the time they got to the 94th Floor, the stairwells had turned into smoky incinerators.

Anyone above the impact point was already doomed. They had mere moments to make a decision on how they would die. Even below the impact point, merely stopping to ask a question---"What was that? Did something hit us? Are the elevators working?"--- constituted a delay of mortal proportions, because instantly all 97 elevators (plus the six freight elevators) were shut down by impact and the flame. Not one person made it out above the impact point.

One elevator shaft not hit by the flame contained about 20 people who were trapped for 15 minutes. Finally, the elevator mysteriously started again, opening its doors to the lobby where the bewildered people exited amidst amazed firefighters and piles of debris.

Meanwhile, at the impact point on the 94th Floor, jet fuel spread the flame spread rapidly consuming the whole level, igniting the floors below and above. Within minutes, smoke billowed out of the 99th and 100th Floors: somewhere around Floor 100, a man hung out a window, frantically waving a white coat in distress.

Some desperately went up to the roof, praying that helicopters could rescue them. Under "normal" fire circumstances, perhaps some could have been lifted off by choppers. A New York Police Department helicopter was already on scene, but found that the antenna and the numerous lines and cables on the roof made any kind of rooftop rescue impossible. The winds were too precarious, to even hope to shoot grappling cables into the building.

Brad Hayes, sitting in the NYPD helicopter co-pilot's position, shook his head to the pilot. "We can't get down there. Tell the Department, no air rescue. He watched in horror as figures began to emerge from the windows and fall. Those in the floors above the blast recognized they weren't getting out. Within minutes, they called loved ones, aware that their moments of life were fixed, and short. As desperation mounted, more than 200 people jumped.

"Good God! Did you see that?" Hayes pointed to the jumpers, and the pilot, Ian Kellan, at first squinting, now saw the same thing.

"They're *jumping*?" he said, shaking his head. He maneuvered the chopper so that they now looked straight at the tower, and saw frantic people clawing to get next to the windows---the last source of air. Anything to get away from the flames. Another leaped, falling in a jackknife position. "They're jumping," he noted again, softly into the microphone.

"We can't do anything here." Hayes gestured with his thumb to return to base, and the pilot nodded helplessly. They banked southeast past Battery Park, where Hayes could see the Statue of Liberty to his left. Then he noticed another airplane to his right . . . and low. *Really low! That thing is going to pass right under us!*

"Holy cow!" Hayes shouted as he and his pilot watched the plane fly under them---*a plane flying below a helicopter??*---and both turned to follow it through the lower glass bubble on their chopper. It was heading straight for the World Trade Center, Tower 2.

Hayes didn't wait for the impact before calling in. "NYPD Chopper Six, I repeat, NYPD Chopper Six. We have another aircraft heading for the towers. This is a terrorist attack. I repeat, a second aircraft heading for the towers. We're returning to base. Out."

Chapter 6

World Trade Center, Tower 2

"Holy hell!" David Costello pressed his face to the glass in his office in the south tower. "My God! An explosion or something next door. Jesus!" From his 104th floor office on the north side of Tower 2, he could see the billowing smoke, although he heard nothing. Almost instantly, however, the odor of charred bodies and seared metal began sifting through the tower's ventilation system.

"Get out of here. Clear the building *now*," he shouted. His secretary and two subordinates started packing up. "Leave that stuff," he instructed. "Go. Go now. Evacuate. Don't wait."

"But isn't our building safe? Isn't that an accident?" one of the secretaries asked.

"We aren't going to wait to find out," Costello replied, grabbing her arm. "Let's go. Move."

The three of them briskly walked past rows of offices, where, inside, they could see gaggles of people looking at the carnage across the plaza. One of his associates started for the window, a woman named Linda Maslowski. Costello took her by the arm, too. "Leave the building, *now*. Don't waste time. Don't get anything, not even your purse." She saw the intensity in his eyes, nodded abruptly and followed his party down the stairwell.

They'd climbed down more than 15 floors when Costello said, "Keep going. Everyone keep moving. I'm going to check outside, and join you. *Keep moving*."

He exited the stairwell and went into the 89th floor, where he gazed upward at the gaping hole and fire almost across from him. In the giant gash in the side of the north tower, he saw figures, human figures, some hanging from the side. Then one jumped. Then another. Costello felt an icy stab in the pit of his stomach as he watched. Later, he recalled the clothes they wore, and could see their faces---faces he wouldn't forget for years. Fighting back the wave of nausea that swept over him, Costello bolted away from the window back for the stairs, leaving other on-lookers to gasp and watch, hypnotized.

Back inside the stairwell, Costello joined a stream of evacuees. He didn't see his group, and now was a good two to five minutes behind his party. He moved as fast as the crowd would let him, covering two and three steps at a time when he could. *It's not fast enough*, he thought.

World Trade Center, Marriot Hotel Complex

Columbia University seemed an odd place for Constantine Cataris, a good Greek Orthodox boy. Oh, he more than belonged there academically and intellectually. His studies on the history of banking panics and financial institutions were internationally regarded, and a quick search in the academic databases showed that he was cited nearly as frequently as some Nobel Prize winners, although certainly few in the general public had heard of him. Constantine---or Connie, as everyone at Columbia called him---liked it that way. Anonymity did not bother Connie in the least.

He looked like an academic---often slightly askew, office papers stacked high. He played squash instead of basketball, listened to opera instead of Nellie. So in many ways he fit the part, unless you knew him. Connie's father was Spartan, literally, and married a nice girl from Naxos. Connie, his brother, and his two sisters grew up in D.C., and he was used to big cities, so New York didn't bother him. Despite Columbia's overpowering climate of liberalism, where race, gender, class, defined everything, Connie nevertheless easily stood his ground in debates, thanks to his superior mind, and, besides, a good mix of political views existed within the business school, which was not generally true of the rest of the campus.

Of course, the B-school situation was unique, and Connie knew it. Hell, at almost any American university, the operative phrase was *" Who's zoomin' whom?"* as Aretha Franklin once sang. That's the new academic mantra in America. Who's oppressing whom? It was straight out of Marx and the *Manifesto*. Of course, the faculty and the administrators all knew it. Occasionally the students figured it out, but parents and donors rarely did. They blindly went on funneling money to these sick cows of higher learning, assuming that, after all, *it's the IVY LEAGUE! It's COLUMBIA.* But the truth was, COLUMBIA, like most of its sister institutions, was sick. It was near terminal. Decades of ignoring the key principles that made America great had produced the desired result. History classes no longer dealt with important ideas or key developments, but "themes" designed to show the evils of America and the West. Sociology classes explained why those who chose not to work were "victims," or why those who murder are "misunderstood." Philosophy professors reaffirmed that there was no God, and that man was little better than a "tool-making animal," and yet offered the goofy paradox that animals should have all the "rights" of humans. Political Science insisted that American government was hopelessly corrupted by money and dominated by the "elites."

In his own research on economics and finance, of course, Connie had called into question several of these myths. Government regulation produced financial instability---not the reverse. Private markets worked pretty well, unless they were strangled by bureaucracies. Entrepreneurs, not the state, produced wealth. But each new study he churned out, none of which could be refuted by his peers at academic conferences---seemed increasingly like firing a pea shooter at an elephant. To add insult to injury, he couldn't even make the elephant mad. The academic system hurdled along its fatal path, sucking genuine knowledge and spiritual understanding into a pathetic vortex of nihilism and hate. Every university had a few voices who still spoke of honor, western values, God---but they were overwhelmed by entire departments of "women's studies," "gay studies," or "peace studies."

That's a good one, Connie laughed. *Peace studies. The solution to everything is to let the enemy kill you. Yah, you're at peace all right. You're dead.*

These trends, among other things, had prompted Connie to work on other projects. He was a fellow at the Hudson Institute, as well as board member of a small New York bank---a position he inherited from his father. Amazing how much more real his economic theories became when bank employees and thousands of depositors relied on him to make the sound and moral decisions for his company.

As he did three days a week---an academic's cushy schedule---Connie left before Jan, and his two girls, Nikky and Sophie were up. He'd call Sophie later that day, as he often did. For now, he re-focused on his speech about global financial structures to the National Association of Business Economists in the Marriott Hotel at the World Trade Center complex.

Connie followed his normal habit of taking the train from the Hartsdale Station near Scarsdale to Grand Central Station, and from there he grabbed the subway to the City Hall stop. Coming to the City never bothered Connie. He'd grown up in big cities, worked at Northwestern in Chicago for years, and was not intimidated by the tall buildings and bustling streets, even though any time he left Jan and the girls, he felt a brief, small tinge of foreboding.

Dumb, he reassured himself. *I've never been mugged, never even been yelled at by a NYC cabbie. I work downtown all the time.*

Sophie, the youngest, was born with an eye problem that had been corrected by surgery, but not until she had virtually lived at the hospital for about a year. At times, Connie wondered if she would ever attain full sight. When she did, in gratitude Connie felt he owed God a renewed attention to his family---an inclination that neither Jan, Nikky, or Sophie did anything to dissuade. They had enough money for him to be home several days a week. It was a blessed life indeed.

Actually, it was a life that Connie's phenomenal intellect and skill with both numbers and history had brought them. He could, at the drop of a hat, go to work for a brokerage or a financial consulting firm and made double or triple what he earned at Columbia. But then . . . *then I'd be working for myself, and I wasn't put here to just benefit me. As bad as it gets, the university is my mission field. I'm put here for a reason.*

The Truth was a noble goal, and few found the Truth in the statistical potpourri of antebellum economic data better than Connie. Had he been corrupt, he easily could have twisted any finding to advance a particular political agenda, and, no doubt, with great fanfare from the press. Instead, he let the numbers speak for themselves, with a unrelenting resonance that few Marxists or Keynesians could resist. And today's excursion into finding the Truth, insofar as it involved economics, was making a presentation about the International Monetary Fund at the World Trade Center Marriott on the World Bank.

Tuesday was a beautiful day. Not a cloud in the sky. Connie wanted to walk the four blocks from the City Hall stop to the World Trade Center. He'd visited the WTC many times, usually in a professional capacity, yet oddly enough, he had never really studied the buildings.

There's time. The sun is out. Look at the World Trade Center. Really look at it. Truly amazing.

He'd read the stats: more than half a million square feet of glass, 200,000 tons of steel, 1,200 bathrooms, and every floor covered an acre. When everyone showed up for work, the towers contained 50,000 people. But today, it wasn't the massive size that impressed him as much as the beauty of the towers.

Enjoy the view. It is a perfect sky. Flawless.

As he looked up, Connie remembered that the architecture critic Vince Scully had once derided the "twin towers" as giant boxes, lacking in grace or style. Today, however, as Connie walked the World Trade Center Plaza, he thought they were beautiful. They positively shimmered.

How incredibly majestic they are against such a blue sky. Why have I never noticed this?

After walking the half perimeter in front of the two towers, Connie finally headed into the Marriott, where he located the large ballroom. Dutifully pinning on his name tag, he grabbed the obligatory glass of orange juice so that he would have something in his hands during idle conversation. Other participants were taking advantage of the copious food provided at such shindigs, including bacon, eggs, potatoes, but Connie wasn't hungry. Besides, he hated talking on a full stomach. Even at a fairly non-combative conference like this, critics couldn't wait to slice and dice. He held his own in these exchanges, but even after many years, he developed a knot in his gut.

Better lay off the bacon.

It was 8:46 a.m. . . . .

The president of Morgan Stanley had gathered his notes and placed his water glass to begin his breakfast speech, then Connie would have his turn in the morning session. He recognized a few of these people, knew others from previous meetings and conventions, and knew still others from their name tags, mostly by reputation. Amicably he sipped coffee with an economist from MIT and some banker from London as they pondered the future of the Euro.

Then he heard . . .

a *subway? No, it was an approaching train. No, it's over our heads.* The cavernous ballroom shuddered and industrial-sized coffee pots rocked. The lights went off momentarily, then flickered back on. New Yorkers in the room looked at each other. They well knew the 1993 bombing, and Connie got word that the head of the Israeli central bank was giving a speech that day.

They're bombing us because of an Israeli?

Few people spoke: all knew a bomb had gone off. Within seconds, everyone stood, then moved out of room in an orderly and quiet manner. *This is remarkable. There is no panic, no questioning, no screaming, no running, no hysteria.* Hotel representatives gently directed people to the appropriate exits. Connie prayed, crossing himself. *Holy God, Holy Mighty, Holy Immortal, have mercy on us!* He repeated this to himself, in English and in Greek, all the way to the nearest exit, then onto the plaza. Emerging from the dark hallway, Connie suddenly stumbled into blinding sunlight. He squinted, then instinctively looked to his left, to the first tower.

It's on fire.

Smoke poured out of Tower 1, the North Tower, but it didn't mesmerize Connie as it seemed to do others. Along with perhaps a hundred other people from the ballroom, he kept moving, yard after yard, until finally he stopped to look up at grey-black plume billowing out of the side of the building.

That's no accident. OK, Connie, one foot in front of the other. Keep going. This is serious. We're being attacked. Keep moving. There is a street sign.

Connie realized he was nearly a full block away from the Marriott, somewhere to the south, and then looked down at his feet, where debris covered the ground.

Origins unknown, he wanted to say, but he knew better. *These pieces are from an airplane.* One hundred feet away, a small crowd of people gathered around . . .

. . . an aircraft engine?

Now it was raining, except it wasn't rain.

It's confetti. Confetti?

Connie stretched his hands out, collecting shards of what was 8 ½ x 11 paper that still blew out of the offices. *But there is something else here. What is this other stuff?* Did he want to know? Some of it was the remnants of office furniture, copy machines, telephones. *Flesh? Did I really see that?* He looked at a half of a picture of what was, in another time, a happy couple, and resisted the urge to pick up a handful of this confetti---to touch it.

These are human lives. Or pieces of lives.

To his right stood an economist from the conference, the fellow from London. A voice came from behind the two of them, "A plane hit the building." Another voice---a large black woman---simply sobbing. "Oh my God. Oh my God." Then another woman wept hysterically as she saw a body sailing 80 floors down, seeming to land right next to her, even though it was nearly a block away.. Others looked up, mesmerized by the jumpers. Connie couldn't look. Instead, he could only stare at the eyes of the others, who followed the people as they fell . . . all the way down.

Connie blurted to his English colleague, "It's bin Laden." The Brit stared back blankly. Anger welled up inside Connie: *This guy doesn't even know who bin Laden is. You shouldn't come to the World Trade Center if you don't know who Osama bin Laden is.*

He nearly turned to look at the tower with everyone else when a voice inside him suddenly shouted *"Leave,"* but his legs wouldn't move. He was nailed in place.

Engine Company #71, 8:48 AM

"We got a fire at the WTC. Let's go, let's go. All units." Callahan clapped his hands together hustling the men along. As per his habit, he walked around the firehouse in "pool shoes"---the flexible waterproof slippers that people wear to the beach to keep their feet from frying. He found that they not only worked well when water got inside his boots, but they further insulated his feet within the heavy boots.

The dispatcher's alert had all the members of Engine Company #71 in their gear within a minute and a half, and the truck was rolling by 8:51. Already the members knew things were bad. There had never been a "borough call" before as long as any of them had been with #71. A "borough call" was above a "five alarm" fire--- which is thought to be the highest-level emergency situation. A five-alarm fire meant that 15 engine companies and 10 ladder companies would be dispatched. A company had four officers and up to 25 firefighters, meaning that a five-alarm fire brought out 420 firefighters. Today, that wouldn't be enough.

"Ever fought a fire in the WTC?" asked Brian Brennan, a rookie who'd only been with the force a few months after graduating training. He looked at the other men in the truck, and the answer lay in their eyes. What he saw made his face pale.

"Not a big fire, and never in the top floors," answered Ed Young, a 20-year vet.

"We've *never* fought a big fire in the Twin Towers? I thought the place was bombed in the early '90s."

"It was," replied Young soberly. Young recalled going to the WTC that day. "Arabs tried to take out the WTC with a truck bomb, but all the fires were on the first couple of floors, where we could get to them easily."

And these are on the top floors, Brian thought as he completed Ed's sentence. *No ladder goes that high. Aircraft will be hard pressed to drop slurry because of the winds. Holy Mother of God! They've never fought a fire like this before.*

New York City has 12,000 firefighters. Today, we're gonna need all of 'em.

Other veteran firefighters saw the fear in Brian's eyes, but steeled themselves with a confidence that defied logic, and Brian took reassurance from them. *Ok, they must know what they're doing. They've done this a hundred times before, I'm sure. Yeah, this is tough, but we'll get it. That's what we do. We're firefighters."*

"Movin' out," shouted Callahan. "Roll 'em." Engine #71 pulled out the doors as Young, the last man, leaped on.

Weaving through traffic, Engine #71, followed by ladder #12, arrived at the base of the WTC within minutes. Without pausing to look up, the crew donned their heavy jackets, helmets, and grabbed their oxygen tanks, and marched into the massive, five-story lobby, whose windows lay in shards on the ground outside. As they walked in, three people came running out of a stairwell on fire. One of the firemen had a small extinguisher and put them out, and paramedics quickly took over.

Methodically, Chief O'Bannon, a loudspeaker in one hand, and a radio in the other, made a quick introduction. "This is Henry D'Onofrio, who is in charge of maintenance here. He tells me that all the elevators are out."

D'Onofrio looked exasperated. "Out, hell! I was standing right over there when I heard the explosion, then there was a 'swoosh' and

I instinctively knew that something was coming down the service elevator. I don't know why, but I dove behind the reception desk in time to see this fireball blast the doors out. One door hit a woman square on, and knocked her outside about 30 feet. I think someone got her already. Then, just as fast as it came down, the suction took the fireball right back up, like nothin' happened."

He surveyed the firemen as they stared at him dumbfounded.

"Don't you get it? These elevators ain't 'out,' they're *incinerated*," he concluded.

Oh my God, Brian thought. Everyone there knew their job had become much tougher.

"Boys," said O'Bannon. "You're gonna have to climb."

Young looked at O'Bannon in disbelief. "The fire's on the 94th Floor, Chief. Chief?" Young wasn't a Rhodes scholar, but he could add. *It will take us an hour to get up there by stairs---those people will be dead by then. There won't be an 94th floor left.* Then, almost as an afterthought, he asked, "Was it an airplane?"

O'Bannon nodded grimly. "It's war. We're at war. This was deliberate," and the hard eyes of the firefighters showed they understood. "Come on, we'll set up a mid-level command post on 23. Call in when you get there."

His instructions were interrupted by a sharp crash. Some object hit the outside lobby roof. *Debris?* Another instantly followed, then several more. Human bodies of jumpers were hitting the overhangs and glass skylights that extended out from the base of the Tower.

As the cause of the sounds sank in with the firemen, one probie puked all over the lobby. Brian wanted to, but held it.

Another engine crew, with a pair of French television documentarians, had actually been responding to a suspected gas leak less than a block from the WTC when the cameraman heard the sound and turned his lens to the sky, capturing the only film of the aircraft hitting the building. They relayed the word quickly, and O'Bannon picked it up on his radio. He already calculated the time, the distance, the likely heat of the fire, based on the color of the flame and smoke.

It was a standard question on the lieutenant's test: "What is the expansion factor of a one-hundred-foot steel beam as it reaches the inherent heat level of 1200 degrees Fahrenheit?" Translation: if this fire is 1200 degrees---as it surely looks like it is---the floors don't have very long before the collapse. Unless they can put out the fire quickly, the people above Floor 94 have no hope. Even if the fire is brought under control, it could take days to get them out with ladders and ropes. With the smoke, they won't last more than a couple of hours.

Callahan began to run other numbers through his head. He actually knew a little bit about the WTC. It's designer, Minoru Yamasaki, had based his concept on the bamboo reed made square. A reed, he reasoned, would bend in the wind, not break. Except, unlike a reed, where all the weight-bearing was on the tube, Yamasaki designed the twin towers with 60% of the weight borne in the center of the building, using the core of elevators and stairwells, and 40% placed on the outside walls. This increased the usable space in the towers by about 1/3, but it also meant that anything that compromised the middle of a tower would utterly destroy it, as the outer shells could not sustain the weight.

If that occurs, thought Callahan, *the building will come straight down, imploding in on itself, rather than breaking off. And if that happens, two-hundred thousand tons of steel, more than used in the longest suspension bridge in the United States, will drop straight down.*

Callahan was shaken out of his thoughts by Ed Young, who turned to his crew and calmly instructed, "Saddle up. We have to hoof it. We'll do 10 floors, then rest a minute. We have to have something when we get to the fire."

Firemen instantly slung heavy hoses, axes, and other equipment over their shoulders and started up the stair well. Michael

Callahan, toting a hose, brought up the rear, and shot a glance at Brian Brennan.

"How long does it take to hike 90 floors?" Brian asked, causing most of the activity to halt momentarily as he was met with stares. "Oooooo-kay," he shrugged, and movement continued upwards again. Everyone knew that it took about a minute to climb one flight of stairs with gear, but obviously they were going to slow down after several flights, no matter how many breaks they took. To climb 90 floors would take close to two hours, even under good circumstances.

These people don't have two hours. Not even close.

The party marched off---whether confidently or not, Brian couldn't tell---as D'Onofrio remained behind to assist the Chief.

They had climbed steadily for almost ten minutes. Only about 75 more stories to go before they started encountering fire. Suddenly, WTC 1 shuddered again. *Aftershock?* wondered Brian. Enclosed in the insulated stairwell, they could not see what had happened outside.

It was 9:02 a.m. . . . .

World Trade Center, Tower 1,
Offices of Cantor Fitzgerald

Julius Farrelly, a CF trader, looked outside the windows of the 103rd floor. He was pacing back and forth dialing numbers on his cell phone. *Try Jeremy. What the hell.*

Farrelly punched in Jeremy Klein's number. To his surprise, Klein answered on the first ring.

"Ben?" Jeremy breathed desperately.

"Uh, no, Jeremy, it's Julius Farrelly. I'm a trader on 103." He didn't wait for a response. "I don't know what you've heard or seen, but a plane hit the building and we've got big-time smoke. We can't get down. They're telling us the elevators are all out and the exits are full of smoke and fire. Can you help? Can you send help?"

Tears welled up in Klein's eyes. Jimmy had headed the limo toward the WTC the minute he heard the news, and he was watching the horror on his TV in the car.

"Julius, it doesn't look good. You've got to find a way to get down."

"OK," said Farrelly, glumly. "We'll do what we can. Thanks, Jeremy. I gotta call my wife."

Klein buried his face in his hands, bawling like a baby. The cell rang again, and Jeremy grabbed it.

"Jeremy, this is Marybeth." Marybeth Taylor was his administrative assistant.

"Are you inside?" Jeremy asked.

"No. I was late. I missed the train by a minute. And to think I was complaining about that."

"So you're all right? Where are you?

"I'm outside Tower Plaza. Jeremy, our people . . . the smoke is everywhere up there."

"I know," said Jeremy, staring at the screen. "I'm a few minutes away, but who knows with the traffic. I may have to walk. Do you know anything about Ben?" Then, realizing Marybeth had just started dating a bond trader, he added, " . . . or any other of our people?"

"No. I tried you first. They can get them out can't they, Jeremy? I mean, the fire department is good. They do this stuff all the time." It was a plaintive appeal, and one to which both knew the answer was "no."

"Get to the northwest corner, near West Street, where it's safe. When I get there, I'll try to find you."

Marybeth felt a deep rumbling in her chest as she saw a huge shadow blow by her. A massive 767---another plane---maneuvered to hit the tower dead-on. She clicked off Jeremy without even realizing it as she stared at Flight 175 closing on the tower at 450 miles per hour.

United Airlines Flight 175

Marwan al-Shehhi pulled the 767 into a wide turn. It was a move he had practiced countless times---albeit in smaller aircraft---in Florida. He'd read every manual, and worked in every way possible to simulate the big jet, but even then he wasn't ready for how effortlessly the enormous aircraft handled. And his study had been accelerated because he practiced only two basic control operations--- flying in a straight line from Logan, south into New Jersey, then turning northeast to New York City, lining up the airliner for the WTC South Tower.

Except he wasn't going to get a straight-in shot. He'd slightly mishandled the aircraft and was coming in at an angle, and a little lower than he wanted. No matter. Didn't the Americans have a saying, "Close only counts in horseshoes and hand grenades?" And he was flying a massive hand grenade---a flying bomb filled with jet fuel and shrapnel that would in an instant be the jet's airframe.

Behind him he heard the groaning of the maced first-class passengers. The flight attendants made no noise: both lay outside the cabin with their throats slit. Still further behind, Hamza Alghamdi kept coach class at bay with his "bomb."

Allahu Akhbar! The aircraft crossed the plume of smoke drifting from the north tower, then banked straight in to the side of the south tower. Al-Shehhi had no idea that the dip of the right wing downward brought the plane in at an angle that would affect seven floors directly by the explosion---two more than the first airplane. His only last thoughts were, *Sharif has done it. He has taken down the symbols of American greed.* And just for good measure he goosed the throttle right up to the moment of impact.

It was 9:02. . . .

World Trade Center, North Tower

Only a handful of CF employees on the 102nd Floor, who were now choking under the rising clouds of ash, could see out the windows. What glass hadn't been blown out by the impact of the aircraft now were being smashed out by people with chairs or by hurling computer monitors. Anything for air. They would deal with the heat later.

Sheila Armstrong had crawled over to a zone on the southern side of the tower, where the smoke was less dense. In the process, she pulled herself over several bodies, several charred, but none, that she could tell, still breathing.

She was surprised at how quickly she went from a stunned realization of what had happened to a dull fatalism, completely bypassing panic. Evan Shockley, a mortgage bond trader, had gone down one of the south stairwells and gotten to 95, where he encountered flames so bad that the heat turned the handrails red. He staggered back up and reported to others. Sheila had worked her way around the building, but so far had found no one who had come back with good news about a way past the 94th Floor. Shockley was just another negative report, but no one needed to tell them that the floor was starting to heat up rapidly.

By now, most people had learned that there were no stairwells still functioning. Crouching near a blown out window, Sheila looked down. The smoke wafted away from her spot, but she could feel the heat eight floors up from the impact point. People crowded around open windows, looking out over the lattice-work side more than 100 stories down. A few had cell phones, and were frantically trying to call home. One or two still tried to talk to the fire department.

Sheila knew no help was coming. She couldn't bring herself to jump, but was terrified of burning alive. *Maybe I'll just be overcome by smoke and go to sleep?*

One of the equities bond specialists—Sheila didn't know his name—choked uncontrollably, hacking and grabbing his throat. Julia Kastle, a woman she'd had lunch with once or twice, slumped a few feet away on the floor, sobbing. "Why did they do this to us? Why did they do this to us?"

Sheila wondered if anyone "did" anything, or if a pilot had a heart attack or there was some unfathomable malfunction. *Maybe we're just poor dumb bastards. Maybe there's no one to blame. Maybe it was just an accident. A horrible, stupid accident.*

Then, in a heartbeat, she knew she was wrong.

Outside the window, another airliner blasted past Tower 1, heading straight into Tower 2.

It's no accident.

The plane momentarily disappeared from her sight behind the building, only to emerge out the corner of the other side in a spectacular explosion, almost parallel with her floor. Flame and glass burst out from the side, along with a hail of metal and confetti of disintegrating paper.

Sheila had no where else to crawl. She was alone. The smoke obscured everything in the room. The heat now got nearly unbearable, and soon she would either choke or burn up. Sheila pressed her face to the glass one more time to look at Tower 2, then slumped back against a chair leg. She began to cry, and not just for herself.

It was 9:04 . . .

World Trade Center, Marriot Hotel Complex

It took several seconds for Connie to accept what he was seeing. Smoke roared out of the towering structure above him, and he was now covered in a confetti of paper and dust and . . . *human remains.* Connie finally shook himself.

The small voice again said *"Get out, now!* The London economist standing next to him---*I didn't even get his name, and don't want to embarrass myself by craning to look at his tag---*suggested to Connie, "Maybe we should go to NY Fed."

A government building? thought Connie. *If this is only the first wave of attacks? . . . .* "I don't think that's the safest place to be. This is an attack."

"Attack? How do you know it was an attack?" the man asked. He still didn't move, and Connie wasn't going to debate. He headed for subway, when something caught his eye.

Up there.

God. No. God Almighty. No, please.

It's another plane.

A 767 flew straight over him, then maneuvered a little toward Tower 2. Connie saw it long before he heard it, but he felt it as soon as he saw it. *This is the work of demonic forces. I feel an overwhelming presence of evil. I'm watching pure evil incarnate.*

Then the impact---again, seen before heard. Then more confetti, which soon turned to large particles of dust that Connie figured out was the remnants of ceiling tiles. People, who up until now were transfixed as they stared at the smoke and flame, started to run. Bigger debris might be close behind. As Connie walked more rapidly, he noticed a stream of people walking toward the World Trade Center, oblivious to the destruction ahead, like a school of fish swimming into a net.

To his left, a car, or what remained of it, sat contorted and smoking where something had completely flattened the roof, and yet no large piece of debris was in sight. *Whatever it was, it bounced off the car!* Then an even more astounding thought occurred to him: *I can see for almost a block in every direction, but can't see anything. It has bounced completely out of sight!*

I need to get out of here, now! He moved even more quickly. People stared, vacant-eyed, right past him at the inferno, but Connie had seen enough. Walking deliberately, he reached the City Hall stop, and to his astonishment, the subway not crowded at all---no one was trying to get out. Connie waited as the train pulled in, and borrowing a cell phone, tried to call home. *No answer. Surely there was nothing in Scarsdale. Or is there? What about the nuke reactor on the Hudson. Is this an attack across the nation?*

A 30-ish man in a dark suit---at least, it was dark before the confetti covered him like terrible dandruff, giving him the appearance of the "before" picture in a Head and Shoulders ad campaign---stood in the subway car a few feet away. From that point on Connie would think of him only as "Dandruff Man." Perhaps an executive, Dandruff Man stood there in a suit that yesterday would have cost $1500. Yesterday, this man would have gone berserk if someone had spilled a cigarette ash on that suit. But yesterday was September 10.

"Were you there?" Connie blurted. *That was pretty stupid. Of course he was there. What's the confetti from?*

The man took no offense, but stared vacantly at Connie. "I saw everything. The planes. The . . . I saw . . . I saw people jumping. They hit the pavement . . . ." and he started to weep, ". . . right in front of me. They cracked when they hit, like a whip." Now he was bawling like a baby and Connie understood. "Their . . . they just came to an immediate stop and their bodies . . . flattened out. Some . . ." he paused, and composed himself, then seemed distant, " . . . some just turned into a ball of red. Guts, brains, spread out everywhere." Then, Dandruff Man stopped as abruptly as he started, as though the horrors he had seen shouldn't be shared with a total stranger. Maybe a psychologist, maybe on a couch. Maybe months, or years, later.

Connie stared at Dandruff Man said nothing until they reached Grand Central---Connie's stop, where he turned to say something. *Like what? "Have a nice day?" Good to meet you?"* Instead, the two gazed at each other as Connie gently bobbed his head. Then he blurted out "I can't believe this. We'll never be the same---our city will never be the same."

Then tears welled in Dandruff Man's eyes, and without a word, he grabbed Connie and hugged him.

I've never hugged another New Yorker in my life, thought Connie. He gave his best reassuring smile, then turned to find the 10:00 train for Scarsdale. He stepped on board, and to his left was a woman, pacing, talking on a cell phone.

"It's *what?*" she screamed. "Oh my God! Oh my God."

Connie looked at her, half in horror, half befuddled. She let out a sigh of desperation: "The tower came down. It collapsed completely."

Connie's mouth fell open, and she continued. "My sister says a giant cloud of dust is blowing through the city." Then, she added, as if it weren't obvious, "Anyone inside is dead now."

She snapped her cell phone shut, and within moments the quiet sobbing of the train car was buried under the sounds of the Scarsdale train leaving. Moments later, the New York Transit Authority shut down the subways. Connie literally caught the last train out.

He did not know that behind him hell itself was opening its jaws.

Chapter 7

American Flight 77

Michelle Olin watched the surrealistic scene: the dark-skinned man stood up and announced he had a bomb, while two others grabbed the first-class cabin flight attendant and put a box cutter to her throat. One of them pounded on the cabin door, and, while she couldn't hear the exchange, she got the gist of it: "Send the co-pilot out or we'll slit her throat."

Surrealism turned to horror. No sooner had he come out of the cabin, hands up in a non-threatening gesture, than a third man stabbed him from behind. He plunged forward, right into an elderly couple seated in the first row. The cabin erupted in screams as the man went inside the cockpit, but no one moved because of the "bomber." Olin burrowed deeper into her seat, hoping they wouldn't notice her, and fished for her cell phone. She diverted her eyes long enough to miss seeing the first hijacker slit the flight attendant's throat. The man who went in the cockpit never came out. Suddenly, the plane lurched, then began a swift 180 degree turn, heading back for Washington.

They killed the pilot too. They are flying this plane. This is no normal hijacking.

Stunned, Olin dialed her husband. *They have to know what's going on. Someone has to tell the people on the ground what's happening.*

Cal Olin picked up his cell. "Hello!"

"Cal? Listen to me carefully," Michelle began, speaking quietly and remaining slumped well down in her seat. From her perspective, none of the hijackers could see her. "Some Arab-types have taken over this plane. I think they've killed several of the crew. We have turned around and are heading back toward D.C." She checked her watch, and did some quick calculations. "We've been airborne for about 45 minutes. I don't know what they want, or where they are taking us, but it isn't good. One guy in the back claims to have a bomb. Cal, I think the pilots are both dead. Cal, I love you."

Cal had not interrupted, but now, tears welled up. He gathered himself. "Is there any chance you're wrong?"

"No," Michelle said, rather serenely. "We aren't going to make it. Listen, it looks like they have knives and . . . ." She noticed movement out of the corner of her eye, and quickly snapped shut the phone and sat on it.

"Michelle, I love you, I . . . . Michelle? Michelle?" Then Olin heard the dead tone.

Hani Hanjour, whose job it was to police the back part of first class and the first rows of business class, walked through, brandishing a container of mace and staring at everyone. Olin avoided his eyes, and he pivoted and turned back into business class. The plane made a sharp descent, only it wasn't heading for Dulles.

It was 9:20 . . . .

World Trade Center, Tower 1, 9:22 A.M.

His lungs heaved to suck oxygen out of the thick air, and Brian Brennan's legs screamed with pain with each step, even with two brief rests at Floors 10 and 20. He had climbed to the 30th Floor, and they weren't even half way up. At the 23rd Floor, a captain set up a command post, where he and one fireman remained. The rest of the men started up the stairs. They hadn't gone more than a couple of flights more when, through the haze and dust, he heard Michael Callahan guiding people down, and a stream of shocked, dust-caked figures staggered past them.

Callahan ask one question over and over: "What floor did you come from?"

So far they had yet to find a single person from above the 60th Floor. Not one.

Maybe we don't have as far to go as I thought, Brennan glumly noted. It wasn't reassuring. It meant they might have to fight fires for 35 floors. It had never been done. *It isn't gonna happen now, either. That's too much fire.*

The pace of the unit slowed down markedly. They climbed 10 floors in five minutes, then the second 10 in 10. Now, it was taking close to 12 minutes to do 10 floors. Brian heard rasping and labored breathing, and they weren't even close. In 1993, the evacuation of the building took one hour and 20 minutes. That was people coming down, not walking up, burdened by fire-fighting equipment.

And what do we do when we get there? No one's really talked about that, have they?

If the interior pumps were fried, they'd likely have no water to fight the fire. The best they could do would be to save whom they could and get the hell out. *Maybe we can cut away some of the debris so the burn is controlled straight up. Maybe we can burn the top floors. There is no hope for those people, but if we can save the rest of the building, and the hundreds of others who might not be able to get out for a while . . . .*

What the hell are we doing here? It started to dawn on Brennan that they really didn't have a plan. *No one has ever fought a fire this high before. People on the first few floors---maybe up to four or five---could jump into nets. No net in the world can catch someone falling 90 floors.*

Brennan heard Callahan again. "What floor? Ma'am, what floor?"

As he turned the corner in the well, he saw the woman Callahan was talking to. He couldn't tell if she was black or white, and only concluded that Callahan knew she was a woman because of the dress. She looked like a giant chicken leg, rolled in flour, grey from top to bottom in soot and ash. Irreverent as it sounded, Brennan made up a name for her on the spot---"Ashley"---and "Ashley" looked at Callahan like a soldier who had been in combat.

"There were six of us," she said numbly. "All six of us. We were at Liza's desk looking at pictures of her new granddaughter. It was like the floor just opened up. They just disappeared. Liza was *right next* to me, then gone. Something, this explosion, came through the roof, and there was this fire everywhere, and . . . then this hole. . . . Oh God! She had a new baby! She had a new baby."

"Ma'am," Callahan tried again, "What floor were you on?"

The woman managed to compose herself. "I was on the 54th Floor. We found this stairwell, and just started walking. She was *right next* to me . . . ."

"Ma'am, have you talked to anyone above the 54th floor?" She looked dazed, her eyes frozen on his firefighter's gear. "*Ma'am!*" He repeated, and snapped his fingers in front of her eyes. Her head jerked, then she shook her head and started down the stairs.

Callahan shot a glance at the men in his unit. "I doubt we're gonna find anyone above 90. Let's go. Steve, call O'Bannon. Tell him the 54th is the top-most floor where we have survivors so far."

"I can't reach him, Mike. We haven't had radio contact for about five floors. Nuthin' but static."

"You're kidding," Callahan said incredulously. His men stared at him, now panting from their climb, hoping for any word that they still had a chance to do something when they got to the top. He couldn't think of anything to say. "C'mon, guys. Let's keep climbing."

O'Bannon was at the other end, feverishly trying to call his teams to tell them there was a second strike, on Tower 2, trying to tell them that while they were going up, they should have been going down.

Engine House #71, 9:30 A.M.

"Damn it. The bastards!" Vinnie LaScala screamed at the 8" television screen as he saw the second airliner plunge into the South

Tower. Alone in the office, Vinnie had drawn the duty of calling in all available firemen and watching the fort. Right now he did not know that the luck of the draw had saved his life.

"Sources at the Pentagon tell Fox News that the terrorist group al-Qaeda---the same group that masterminded the 1993 World Trade Center attacks---is apparently behind this attack. Sources say that the airliners were hijacked and . . . ." The ringing phone in the firehouse office interrupted Rita Cosby's report. Vinnie hit "mute" and yanked the receiver up to his ear, then composed himself.

"Engine Company #71 Firefighter LaScala speaking."

"Vinnie? That you? This is Melvin."

"Melvin," gasped Vinnie. "This is war, man, this is war. They took out the other tower. You see that? Get down here."

"What? What are you talking about?" Melvin was one of the two blacks in the engine company, and he was off duty today. "My beeper went off, so I called."

Vinnie was pacing, the cord of the phone dragging the body of the phone all the way to one end, then all the way back to the other as Vinnie walked. Each time he reached the end of his stride, the phone came close to the edge of the desk. All the while, he kept staring at the screen.

"You ain't watchin' this?" he fumed.

"Watchin' what, Vinnie? I'm in the basement working on the plumbing to the sink when my beeper goes off."

"Melvin, look at the television. Hell, stick your head outside and look at the smoke."

Running upstairs, Melvin burst out his front door to look toward Manhattan, seeing two thick plumes of smoke. "No way. What happened? Are *both* towers on fire? No way."

"Melvin, we're at war. Get in here now. This is an all-borough alert. You hear me? Every firefighter in the City needs to get in here.

Everyone is recalled as of now." Vinnie slammed the receiver down and released the mute button.

Cosby continued her report *". . . the FAA has unconfirmed reports of other hijacked airliners. Repeat, we are getting word that the FAA has reports of as many as three other airliners that have possibly been hijacked. We are following that . . . . Just a moment. We have a report of another airliner in the New York area . . . ."*

"Come on! Bring it on!" Vinnie threw a phone book through the office's glass divider. You want some of us? Huh? You messed with the wrong country, you bitches!" He hurled a log book across the room, where it split on a chair, sending papers flying.

Chapter 8

United Airlines Flight 93

At 8:42, Flight 93 took off from Newark and climbed above the New York-New Jersey skyline on this clear, perfect day. As it climbed, smoke started to pour from the World Trade Center in the distance.

"Everything ok?" Captain "Dell" Franz asked ground control.

Newark was unaware of the impact at that moment, for the reply came back, "Everything is fine." Franz and his co-pilot, Kevin Wilkins, continued climbing to altitude, performing routine tasks. But as Flight 93 got over Pennsylvania, and the second plane hit the WTC, a new, cryptic message was sent to all United pilots: "Beware cockpit intrusion."

"Confirmed," radioed back Wilkins. The two pilots exchanged puzzled glances.

"What was that all about?" asked Wilkins.

"Check in with Cleveland. See what they know."

Wilkins set his frequency for Cleveland, and said, "United Flight 93, calling Cleveland Tower."

"Cleveland Tower. Go ahead, 93," came the response. Kevin couldn't tell, but the voice seemed tense. Nevertheless, he tried to be pleasant.

"Good morning, Cleveland," chirped Kevin.

It was 9:26 a.m. . . . .

Cleveland Tower, 9:28 A.M.

"Don, I'm getting some weird stuff on United 93." Luke Forlane had been an air traffic controller for 15 years, and the worst he'd had to deal with was a mechanical mishap on an Airbus flight from Buffalo. Normally, he wasn't a worrier, but today he'd already gulped four aspirin with no relief.

His boss, Don Bandow, did not need any more grief today. Whatever was going on in New York---and the messages were still jumbled, but it appeared a couple of airliners hit the World Trade Center---was peripheral to his immediate problem of a slew of bomb threats that started coming in. He didn't know that Logan International was receiving similar bomb threats at the same time.

"What the hell is going on in the world today," mumbled Don, walking up behind Forlane's screen. "We've gotten five bomb threats already today. Ok, Luke, what kind of weird stuff are you getting?"

"It's . . . It sounds like screaming."

Don picked up the auxiliary headset and tuned to Forlane's frequency. "Raise 'em."

Forlane spoke into his microphone. "United Flight 93, do you copy? What is your status, 93?"

There was no response. Forlane and Bandow exchanged troubled looks. Other controllers began to patch in. Then they heard voices on the channel, but they weren't using protocol.

"Get out of here" they heard. *Get out of here."* It was English, but Luke couldn't tell if that was the pilot's voice or not. What he heard next sent a bolt of fear into his gut. It was the sound of choking---*or gurgling?* Given the proximity to the microphone, Forlane knew it was the pilot. He slowly stood up at his station, his knees weak.

"Holy Mother of God," he mumbled, crossing himself, turning to see the other controllers with equally stunned looks.

It was 9:31 . . . .

World Trade Center, Tower 1, 105th Floor

On the 105th Floor, home to the offices of Cantor Fitzgerald, people frantically tried to call loved ones and leave farewells on message machines. The smoke and heat had grown considerably worse. Already, dozens bodies littered the floors, people who had passed out from smoke. Dozens of others congregated around the gaping holes where windows had been blown out, gasping for fresh air.

Eric Magalene, an equities broker who had only come on the job last week, briefly looked at his fellow employees and said, matter of factly, "I'm not waiting to be burned alive. Good luck to you all." He stepped on the window sill and without a further word dove headlong down to the pavement. Some of the women screamed, mainly because they knew the only choice that remained was the type of death they would encounter in the next few minutes: flame, smoke, or a few seconds of free-falling followed by oblivion. One woman, still crying, quickly followed him, leaping without a word. Many more gasped as the smoke gripped their throats, and crawled steadily away from the floor, which seemed to get hotter by the second. A crowd of 30 employees became 20, then 10. One man, a trader near retirement, had both hands outstretched and prayed, thanking God for a long, prosperous life and asking His mercy on his family.

Twenty-four stories below, a man actually climbed out the window and managed to scale two floors down the side of the World Trade Center. A photographer caught him on film, clinging to the outside of the building like Spider-Man. Minutes later, Spider-Man vanished.

It was 9:40 . . . .

Fitness Pros Gym, Woodside, New York

Finally, Shannon thought, *I get some time to myself.* She loved her workouts and enjoyed listening to tapes while she ran on the treadmill or did the elliptical walker. But she always kept her eyes on the television monitors in front of the treadmills, even when she didn't listen to the sound of the news broadcasts. It was a habit.

Tying her shoe, suddenly Shannon noticed no one else was exercising. They were . . . *standing? Watching TV? What's going on?* Some woman talking head on CNN looked grave. Shannon hated her look, and called her "Elvira" after the old horror-movie hostess, "Elvira, Mistress of the Dark." *Can't they do something with her makeup? She looks terrible.* Shannon quickly learned why. Taking her headphones off, she heard the announcer.

". . . *and it appears a second aircraft has hit the North Tower of the World Trade Center. Both buildings have been hit by airplanes, and it is now appearing that this was no accident. To repeat, an aircraft has hit Tower 2, the North Tower of the World Trade Center, and both buildings are on fire. This appears to be a deliberate attack of some type.*"

Shannon's knees buckled and she would have fallen over if she hadn't grabbed the handle of the treadmill.

Michael must be on his way there. . . . Or worse, is already there.

She staggered backward somewhat, leaving the treadmill running, and sat on the exercise bicycle behind her, when she realized that there wasn't a sound in the gym except for the hum of her treadmill and the ominous reports coming from the broadcast. A wave of nausea swept over her, and she brought her workout towel up to her mouth expecting to puke. It passed momentarily, but her mind now raced.

Where is he? Surely they wouldn't go up into that tower would they? How do you fight a fire that high?

Shannon raced back to her locker, digging out her cell phone. Maybe Maureen Carlson knew something. Her husband was in the Department too. All she heard was a dull, dead sound as hundreds of cells around New York City were overloaded and several crashing. She needed to leave, to get home, but she didn't want to go to the locker room to change. On the other hand, if there was bad news--- *Bad news? Are you kidding? No, what if there is worst news?*---she didn't want to hear it on the gym floor. She raced out of the locker room to her car, and flipped on the radio as she swung the car out of the parking lot and began the ten-minute drive home.

World Trade Center, Tower 1, 35th Floor

Callahan's firemen reached the 35th Floor, where they encountered a large group of people from the 71st Floor. They had left when they first felt the impact, and hadn't looked back. With the firemen going up, and the people coming down, two single-file lines formed. Two men carried a disabled woman, and another helped a man on crutches. The firemen stared into the eyes of these survivors, who methodically descended, step after step. A few minutes later, they would be directed to the elevators through the mall underneath Tower 1, with emergency workers urging them on. From there they went several hundred feet to another broken escalator that led them back up to ground level and Church Street. One man headed south on Broadway, stopping in Trinity Church, which was open, to pray.

Chuck Kehoe, one of Callahan's firefighters, suddenly remembered he had a pager: it flashed the news, planes strike both World Trade Center towers in terrorist attack.

"Hey, Mike," said Kehoe. "Tower Two's been hit too."

Callahan stopped, and looked back at the line of men. "Are you serious? That's what we felt?" *My God, and we're stuck 35 floors up in a giant match that's burning down.*

Suddenly, the can-do confidence with which the firemen started their climb vanished. Many started to think they were now on a suicide mission. Callahan waited for any sign that any of them wanted to turn back. None did. He checked his radio, but could not raise the command center. Without further orders, Callahan turned and started climbing again. It was getting even harder. The heat grew more intense, and men, already struggling under the added weight, slipped on the puddling sweat of the people struggling to get down the stairs.

They had climbed five more flights---*are we at 40 or 41?* Brian had lost count---when they heard the chilling sound of a low rumble. But it wasn't coming from below them—like an earthquake—but from outside. The south tower of the World Trade Center, its support structure melted by the superheated airplane fuel, collapsed and the tower began to fall in on itself. Witnesses outside heard an eerie sucking *swooosh* as the air surged, then the floors start to pancake in a massive cloud of debris, dust, and steel.

Michael Callahan heard it, and stopped dead in his tracks, and closed his eyes.

It was 9:50 a.m., and the South Tower started its deadly implosion.

"Evacuate. Evacuate. Raise anyone you can. Get out of the building," shouted Callahan, struggling to keep his voice under control. *Even going down the stairs, this isn't going to be fast.*

Woodside, New York

Without even pulling the car all the way in the garage, Shannon raced inside the house and flipped on the television. She'd made it home in nine minutes, speeding most of the way. As she picked up her phone to call Maureen, she stared at the image she had seen at the gym---two towers, plumes of smoke curling out or each. *No change,* she thought. Maureen wasn't in. Maybe she'd try . . . *What was that? Something going on in the tower?*

CNN's camera remained focused on the smoking buildings when, suddenly, the South Tower seemed to turn into a giant dust mushroom. Literally, the floors of the tower where the plane had hit just evaporated, yielding a cloud of debris and dust that rolled out along the sides, flattening out as the building imploded. As the upper levels crashed to the ground, about 20 of the top floors tilted at a 45-degree angle and then fell as a single section. Plumes of dust sprayed out from the sides like a grotesque skyrocket, and entire walls could be seen plummeting downwards like fighter planes shot from the skies, trailing smoke and debris.

Shannon dropped the phone and fell backwards against the refrigerator. *Is Michael in that building? Except . . . there's no building now. Oh my God. God help us.*

Flight 93, Over western Ohio, 9:45 A.M.

"Operator? Listen very closely. My name is Rod Trainer. I'm a passenger aboard United Airlines Flight 93 out of Newark International. We have a hijacking situation."

His voice was calm and unwavering. Operator 15 knew that this required a supervisor, and she said "Sir, I'm not going to let you go, but I am going to bring a supervisor on the line." She waved over Liza Anderson, a GTE Airfone Customer Service supervisor. She said solemnly, "Hello, Mr. Trainer. I understand you have a hijacking situation. My name is Liza."

How ironic is that? thought Trainer. *I can't talk to my wife, Liza, but I end up talking to a phone supervisor named Liza.*

Methodical and thorough, Rod, with information supplied by the flight attendant sitting next to him, began relating the numbers to Liza:

"There are 27 passengers in coach, 10 in first class, five flight attendants, and no children aboard. At least three people have hijacked the plane. Two of them had knives, and one has a bomb strapped around his waist with a red belt. Guys with knives are in the cockpit, and have locked themselves in. They told people, including the flight attendants, to sit down."

"They can't see me, because the guy with the bomb closed the curtains to first class, apparently not wanting people to see into the front part of the plane."

Liza asked if there were any casualties.

"I could see two bodies—men—on the floor. They didn't look good. I think they were the pilots. We think they may be heading back to the airport---the plane has definitely turned around."

By now, a small group of men on phones had gathered in the rear of the aircraft, all gathering information. A New Jersean named Kyle Belz, seated not far from Rod Trainer, had called his wife, Cheryl, from somewhere around Cleveland. He asked Cheryl point-blank, "Another passenger who talked to his wife said that passenger planes had crashed into the World Trade Center. Is that true?" She said, "Yes, they are doing that."

He asked if his plane was headed back to New York, and she said there was nothing left of the towers, when yet another passenger, Todd Burton, talking to his wife, was told that the terrorists had hit the Pentagon. He relayed over to Belz, "They seem to be taking planes and hitting landmarks on the east coast."

Bunett said, "I think they are bluffing about the bomb. They wouldn't blow us up if they needed the plane as a weapon."

Already, Rod and Kyle had developed a strategy to try to take back the aircraft as a small group gathered around. Flight attendants were filling coffeepots with boiling water to throw at the terrorists. Rod and Kyle looked around at several strong men who could overwhelm the hijackers—Lou Nelson, a store manager who was a solid 220 lbs., Mack Beckham, a 6' 6" rugby player, and Ralph Galliendo, a California Fish and Game agent. In addition, some of the women aboard had training in karate. Each person seemed to come to the same conclusion simultaneously: *We've got to regain control of this plane, or it will be used as a flying bomb against some target.* It was only their delay on the ground at Newark that provided a window whereby they learned the fate of the other planes.

Kyle looked at Rod. "Is this plane on a suicide mission?"

Sweat broke out on his forehead, and Rod nodded. Mack dropped his head and let out a low whistle. "God," he said. He heard cursing from some of the others.

"We can't let them fly this thing into the White House or the Empire State Building. We have to do something. If they are going to destroy this plane, we better make them do it before we get over a city. One way or the other, we have to get this plane back or we're all dead anyway."

All around he saw eyes that met his with solemn agreement and reluctant nods.

"We have to take this plane back, or die trying." Again, everyone agreed.

Kyle took over. "OK, here's the plan. I'll go first, then Rod, then Mack, and whoever else wants to come. We'll use the serving cart in case he has a gun, sort of as a shield, and steamroll the guy. I'll try to take the guy with the bomb. The worst he can do is set it off."

Now the flight attendants leaned in, anxious to be a part of the resistance.

Kyle addressed them next: "You scald the other guys with the water. Don't worry about us---we'll try to use them as shields. Try to watch out for the knives and box cutters. If we get that far, maybe we can break open the cockpit door and either kill these guys or get them out."

"Who'll fly the plane?" asked Mark.

They looked around. None in the immediate group had flight experience. Rod looked at one of the flight attendants, named Carlie. "You stay back. After we attack, follow behind us and see if any of the passengers can fly a plane. If not, I'll do it. Hey, how hard can it be? These things land on auto pilot," He smiled grimly.

Rod meant to be reassuring, but the notion that they might not have a pilot even if they succeeded caused even Kyle's neck muscle to twitch. No one else had a better idea.

All the time, Rod had kept Liza Anderson informed and on the line, holding the phone where she could hear the discussion.

"We're gonna do something," he told her. "I don't think we're going to get out of this thing, and we're just going to have to step out on faith. We're going to jump the guy with the bomb, and try to get control of the plane back."

Liza sensed the desperation. "Are you sure you want to do that?"

"We have to. We have no choice. Would you recite the Lord's Prayer with me?"

Fighting back tears, Liza said, "Sure."

"Our Father which art in heaven . . . ."

Meanwhile, Kyle explained the plan to everyone. "We all on the same page?" Several nodded. He saw determination and, in some, fatalism, but no one opted out. These Americans were not going down without a fight.

"Ok, once we go, no one stops. We either get this plane back, or we die trying, because if they take it where they want to go, a helluva lot of people are going to die." Again, more somber nods. Tears welled up and cell phones were snapped shut as passengers closed with "We're doing it." "I have to go." "I love you." "Say goodbye to the kids."

"OK," said Rod with finality. "Let's roll."

Rod and Kyle pushed the food cart in front of them straight up the aisle. Only two of them could fit, so Mack climbed over seats and passengers like so many high hurdles. Astoundingly, he kept pace. As they charged up the aisle, they heard other shouts of encouragement from those too old to help. "Kick their asses." "Give 'em hell." "Go get 'em, Americans." "God bless America."

As the little band gained momentum, the flight cart burst through the curtains in business class, where 20 feet ahead of them, Ahmed Alnami stood with his hand on a string attached to a red belt that appeared to have explosives on it. Instead of yanking the lanyard, he turned pale and scrambled back into first class.

"They are coming," he shouted to al Haznawi, who alone stood guard over the First Class cabin.

"What are you talking about?" demanded al Haznawi.

"The passengers you fool. They are coming up the aisle!"

"Ladies and gentlemen," announced Jerrah in his thick accent in broken English, trying to confuse the attackers. "Here it's the captain. Please sit down. Keep remaining sitting. We have a bomb aboard."

Rod and Kyle burst through the First Class curtains as al Haznawi pounded on the cabin door. "Let us in! Let us in! The passengers are attacking!"

Jarrah, at the pilot's controls, rocked the plane sideways. The sudden lurch threw Rod onto the lap of an elderly woman who pushed him back to his feet. Kyle retained his footing and Mack, already crawling over seats, was almost on top of Alnami.

Alnami put out his hands in self defense, then let out a "woof" as the dumb-waiter slammed into his mid-section, knocking him backwards into al Haznawi. Other passengers now stood to throw dishes, debris, any object they could find to attack the terrorists. A laptop slammed into his head, sending blood spurting into his eyes.

Inside the cockpit, Jarrah and Algahmdi looked at each other with horror. Mohammad Atta had not prepared them for a passenger revolt. He had assured them the Americans would behave like timid sheep. Jarrah knew he had to regain control of the situation quickly. "Cut off the oxygen in the back," he ordered. Algahmdi threw the switch, but it would take minutes before the tactic had any effect.

Outside the cockpit, Mark leaped over the last aisle of passenger chairs and landed square on Alnami's chest, pounding him mercilessly in his already-bloody face, inches from al Haznawi, who ignored his fellow hijacker and frantically beat on the door.

"Let me in!" he screamed, but as he turned back, a flight attendant hurled boiling water at his face at the same time Rod slammed a shoulder into his sternum. He let out a piercing howl, just as Algahmdi foolishly opened the door behind him. Still bellowing in pain, al Haznawi fell backwards through the door, with Rod wrapped around him. Both tumbled into the cockpit. A horrified Algahmdi kicked Rod in the face, knocking him back. Stunned, Rod toppled outside the cockpit far enough for Algahmdi to roll up al Haznawi's legs like a futon, balling him up so he could slam the door. Suddenly, Kyle's powerful hands kept the door open, then he wedged his foot in the crack for leverage.

Algahmdi kicked Kyle's foot out of the seam, then, grabbing his box cutter with his free hand, slashed Kyle's knuckles. Kyle roared in pain, momentarily letting go of the door as Algahmdi pushed it shut.

"What of Alnami?" Jarrah asked coolly.

"He's down. They have him already."

"They won't give up," Jarrah coldly noted. He checked his bearings. They were still at least 10 minutes from Washington D.C. and the White House. *Not enough time.* He opened the throttle to full speed.

Outside the door, Kyle, Rod, and others pushed the cart out of the way and looked for anything they could use to break into the cockpit.

"Here," shouted Rod, his head still spinning from the kick to the face. "A fire extinguisher!"

Mack took it and smashed the butt down on the door handle, which flew off.

Hearing the compartment open again, Jarrah swore. The door swung open and several pairs of hands grabbed Haznawi who by now was splayed backwards diagonally against the instruments with his feet toward the door. The passengers dragged him feet first, into the galley, again throwing scalding water on him and kicking him. Alghamdi tried to get out of his seat, but now he was as helpless as the United Airlines pilots whose throats he slashed just minutes earlier. Kyle wedged himself inside, ignoring Alghamdi and instead grabbing the pilot, Jarrah, in a vise grip around his neck, pulling him out of the seat.

He would have succeeded except for the seat belt.

"Give the controls to me," screamed Alghamdi. "Allah Akbar!" But Rod, who squeezed in behind Kyle, punched Alghamdi square in the nose, cracking his cartilage and spraying blood all over the cockpit. Alghamdi let out a high-pitched scream as Rod ripped his hands off the controls.

The 757 rocked wildly as Jarrah struggled to stay conscious against Kyle's powerful grip that continued to tighten around his neck. But the belts kept him in the seat just long enough. He pushed the control stick straight down, plunging the aircraft spiraled into a steep dive, breaking Kyle's hold and sending him reeling backward back with the force of the descent. Rod, too, was pushed backward, but retained his lock on Alghamdi's hands. They had already been flying low, and Jarrah put them into a vertical dive. Even if the passengers had the piloting skills to save the plane, it was too late for a lumbering monster like the big Boeing to recover.

Rod looked through the cockpit window to see Pennsylvania farmland directly beneath them. "Jesus, receive me into your kingdom," he said, loudly enough that he heard an "amen" from someone behind him.

Flight 93 hit the hard ground like a bomb, exploding in a fireball, plowing out a 50'-deep crater in the Shanksville countryside and scorching the tree line. Smoking parts flew in all directions, but the impact of the blast was down, not out. Flight 93 had become a meteor instead of a missile directed at the White House.

Listening in on the open phone, Liza Jefferson heard the sounds of combat, the shouting, the struggle, followed by the sickening sound of dead air. Her body sagged, and she covered her eyes with her hands.

Chapter 9

World Trade Center, Tower 1

When Callahan's men reached the second floor mezzanine where there was a direct exit walkway, it was obstructed by debris. Callahan noticed outside one of the blown-out windows, on the plaza, chairs had been lined up for a concert around the golden globe.

There are people in those chairs. No, not complete people. Then it dawned on Callahan that the concert never took place---that the bodies and body parts he saw there were from the jumpers.

The command post is abandoned. This is bad.

"It looks like World War III down here," said Callahan, coughing through the dust. The men started moving debris, and found they could clear a door. "OK. Through here." He received grim but energetic nods from the other firefighters.

They started across the large walkway that connected the WTC to other buildings, but Callahan held them up as they continued to hear the bodies and falling metal slam on the causeway above. "Wait a minute---we don't know if we can dodge all this. You guys will wait here a minute, I'll check it out." Again, nods.

"I'm coming with you, Mike." It was Brian Brennan.

Callahan paused, then jerked his head. "Come on, then."

They quickly crossed through a passageway filled with dust, their flashlights barely cutting through the din. When they found a set of doors ahead, Callahan half expected them to be locked, but they swung open. Down the hall, Callahan could see other doors, probably leading to one of the other WTC buildings. *Damn, I've lost my bearings. I don't know which building that is.*

He pointed to the doors, and Brennan sprinted over to them, crossing the long hallway in a few seconds. The doors were open, too.

"This looks good," Callahan said. "We can get out here. Oh, and try your radio. See if you can hail anyone."

Brennan checked his radio. More static. "Sorry, Mike, nothin's working."

It seemed like eternity, but finally they saw the doors to the WTC lobby. *But no firefighters! Where were the men I left here?*

"Where'd they go, Mike?"

"I don't know. Maybe they found another way out." Callahan checked his watch: 10:28. Then he heard the low rumbling, followed by the swoosh of air pockets as entire floors collapsed. Only this time it was right above them. He had never heard a sound like that before, like a mountain falling in on top of them.

"We won't make that cause way!" Callahan frantically looked around. "B Stairwell. Move!"

Above them they could hear a familiar pattern. BOOM. . . SWOOSH . . . BOOM. . . SWOOSH as each floor imploded and the air was sucked upward. It sounded like a massive train sweeping by, only it was above him, an earthquake and tornado rolled into one. The whole thing took eight seconds---Callahan was sure it took longer, because he and Brennan made it down one more flight before the entire stairwell seemed to give out under them. All went dark, and while he couldn't see what was happening, he swore he was surfing. Literally, the floor of the stairwell was both collapsing and sliding downward over other debris. Somehow, Callahan didn't lose his balance, but he did lose Brennan, who disappeared in the dark void. *This is the end. A firefighter's end.*

He sailed downward, yet his feet never left concrete. *I'm surfing on a damn slab of concrete underneath a collapsing building!* Finally, his "board" smashed abruptly against something---he couldn't tell what in the dark---and he was covered with pellets of rock, gravel, concrete, and, above all, dust, or, at least, it *felt like* rock, gravel, and dust because he couldn't see anything. The train sound stopped, replaced by occasional pops of frayed electric wires, which provided a moment of light, and the continued rainfall of debris.

Wherever I am, I'm alive, and I'm underneath what was the World Trade Center. How far underneath, he had no clue.

"Brennan? Anyone?" There was no response, and fear gripped Callahan that he'd not only die down here, but die alone.

"ANYONE DOWN HERE?"

West Street, Two Blocks from the North Tower

By 10:25 the North Tower looked like a massive smokestack, its upper floors entirely obscured. At 10:28, it began its implosion as the radio "spike" antennae fell straight through floor after floor. Unlike the South Tower, the North Tower did not tilt at the top, but flattened straight down, its dust and debris spewing out from the middle like a grey volcano. In less than two minutes, the second of the two tallest buildings in New York had vanished.

Vinnie LaScala had put on his firefighter gear while still answering phones. When the first off-duty fireman came in, LaScala said, "The station's yours. I'm going down to the WTC."

"Vinnie, wait. You can't just run out! Vinnie!" But it was too late. He was already hoofing it to the scene of the attack.

That had been more than 20 minutes ago, and once he got to the WTC grounds, he found command vehicles buried under rubble, firemen walking around covered head-to-toe in soot and ash, and saw no faces he recognized.

"Hey, anyone see #71?" he asked a pair of older firefighters who sat taking oxygen from an EMT truck. Both shook their heads. "I heard they were in the North Tower," one of the men said, and Vinnie realized that was the one still burning. No sooner had he started toward the building when he heard the awful noise and turned the other way, taking whoever he could with him. Then he saw the onrushing tidal wave of dust and debris, and for a split second, he was tempted to plant his feet and ride it out, before common sense took over.

Vinnie leaped toward a doorway, which, as it turned out, led to Yao's Supermarket. He fell through, on the floor, as the dust and debris tsunami thundered past. Mr. and Mrs. Yao (or, that's who Vinnie thought they were) held each other tightly behind the counter, unable or unwilling to speak. After a few seconds, when it was clear that dust---and not debris----was all that remained, Vinnie gave them a thumbs up and went back outside. Perplexed, the Yaos returned his thumbs up.

Tora Bora Mountains, Afghanistan

Since fleeing the Sudan in 1996, Osama bin Laden had alternated between one of his training camps near Pol-e Khomn, about halfway between Mazar-e Sharif and Kabul, and his main headquarters on the Afghan-Pakistani border opposite Peshawar. After Bill Clinton had tried to blow him up with cruise missiles in 1998, bin Laden moved frequently, and Clinton's missiles did significant damage to the facilities at Pol-e Khomn. But forewarned by informants in the Pakistani intelligence service---who, in turn, were notified by the White House as protocol for getting flyover clearance for the cruise missiles---bin Laden had evacuated all of his troops. The missiles hit an empty camp.

Bin Laden returned to Pol-e Khomn not long afterward. There was little rebuilding necessary: after all, what is a terrorist training camp but a few firing ranges and some buildings to practice taking hostages? The most difficult thing to move was the ammunition and arms, but even those could be relocated in a matter of hours.

Now, with the moonlight reflecting off the imposing Tora Bora Mountains in the distance, bin Laden sat in a small shack with only Zawahiri and Malid, gently stirring a goat stew. It was late for dinner, but, then, tonight promised to bring great news. Methodically bin Laden served up a portion to his physician and his assistant, along with a traditional Afghan pita-type bread, and then ladled the stew into his own bowl. Both men quietly ate, Zawahiri rocking back and forth, awaiting the vibration of his cell phone.

Malid stared, apparently lost in thought. Bin Laden had kept most of the details of this event from him. He knew little of what was happening tonight---*actually, yesterday, in America*—except that it was big. Many in the camp speculated bin Laden was going to assassinate Clinton, having failed to kill George Bush. Others thought a massive round of truck bombs was planned for America, England, or France.

Whatever it is, Sharif has been extraordinarily cautious. I have never seen an operation run so tightly. Malid knew only that, somehow, Khalid Sheikh Mohammad was right in the middle of it, and that money had come from Iran and Iraq. *Lots of money. But money for what? Truck bombs aren't that expensive.*

Since the cruise missile strike, bin Laden had increased his security even more. He avoided using any land telephone lines, and conducted all his conversations by cell phone. Still unaware that the CIA had found ways to "hack and track" his cell phone numbers--- although without the speed or reliability they needed to respond fast enough to kill him---Zawahiri now awaited a cell call from one of bin Laden's former "sleeper" agents in New Jersey, a man named Moqtar. It was not his real name, nor did bin Laden even know the man's name. He was a recruit from al-Zawahiri, and had been planted years ago for one specific mission. Moqtar was to deliver a first-hand damage assessment.

Bin Laden patiently slurped his stew, checking his watch, calculating the hour in the United States. At long last Zawahiri's cell phone vibrated. He clicked it open, "Wait. Tell Sharif."

The man gulped, aware he was now talking to bin Laden. Then blurted out, "Sharif! It was incredible. Both towers are down--- utterly eliminated. They didn't just burn and leave the lower part of the buildings. Both totally collapsed. I can see the skyline from here. No part of them remains. You have done it, Sharif!"

Bin Laden flashed his eyes at Zawahiri, and gave him a cold affirmative jerk of his head. Zawahiri's face broke out into a broad smile. Malid still looked on, puzzled.

"And Washington? Are the White House and Pentagon also destroyed?" Bin Laden sensed that the plan had not been entirely effective.

Moqtar hesitated. Unlike Saddam, bin Laden did not have a reputation for meting out punishment to those who brought bad news, but there was always a first time. Moqtar cursed the fact that he had to be the one to tell bin Laden that part of the plan had failed. Bin Laden sensed the change in Moqtar's mood.

"What happened to the Washington planes?" he snapped.

"Sharif, the Pentagon plane came in too low. It hit just on the edge of the building. The destruction is massive. Many Americans dead."

"But," bin Laden replied, repressing his fury, "the Pentagon remains?"

Moqtar could feel the anger from thousands of miles away. "Yes, Sharif."

"And the White House?" bin Laden coldly asked, already suspecting the answer.

"We do not know what happened. The aircraft went down somewhere in Pennsylvania, without damaging anything except an empty field. There are rumors that the American government had the plane shot down. Others say the passengers staged a revolt. It is still a magnificent victory, Sharif!"

There is no more to be gained from reprimanding this fool. He is a mere scribe---a reporter. Bin Laden decided to cut him off graciously. "You have your instructions, Moqtar. May Allah bless you. We are not finished with the Great Satan." Although he was unaware that his cell transmissions were intercepted and, on a delayed basis, translated and analyzed, he still exercised great caution when speaking on any phone, and routinely kept the channel open for mere minutes. He flipped off the cell phone and passed it back to Zawahiri.

"Both towers are down, but the Pentagon was only wounded, and the airplane targeting the White House was destroyed before it got to Washington."

"Towers, Sharif?" asked Malid. "What happened?" Bin Laden's face broke into a broad smile as he explained the attack in detail. "Thousands dead," he said, closing his eyes as if to replay it in his mind. "Thousands."

Malid was shaken, but tried not to show it. *Thousands of innocents? For what purpose? What was accomplished other than death?*

Zawahiri interrupted his thoughts. "We must move immediately with the second wave, Sharif," offered Zawahiri. "Activate the attacks on Los Angeles and London and Chicago."

Bin Laden angrily waved his hand. "Do you think I did not already do so? There is something wrong. Use the contacts---get Moqtar to call me back. There is more I need to ask him."

Zawahiri assented, placing a call to a German al-Qaeda member, who relayed the coded instructions to a Londoner, who then relayed them again to Moqtar. After fifteen minutes, bin Laden's normally steel resolve began to fray as he paced outside the small shack. Finally, the cell phone vibrated again, but before the Saudi could speak, Moqtar exclaimed, "They grounded all the planes within 30 minutes. Heathrow is shut down. There is no attack on Parliament. The second wave cannot occur."

"It is not possible," bin Laden snapped. "The Americans could not have moved so quickly."

"Yes, it is true, Sharif. The FAA grounded the planes after the second aircraft hit the New York building. Every pilot was instructed to land immediately within a certain radius. If the plane was close to its destination, it was allowed to complete the trip, but otherwise all planes will be on the ground within the hour. No overseas flights are admitted in without a fighter escort."

Bin Laden stood stunned, breathing heavily, holding the phone at his side. Zawahiri sensed immediately something was wrong. "The Americans reacted faster than you expected?"

"Yes," bin Laden nodded, now starting to pace. Moqtar still hung on the other end of the line from New Jersey, neither aware that CIA analysts were tracking the call and plotting coordinates in Afghanistan while the FBI moved on Moqtar's location. "How could they have responded so quickly? I should never have changed the original plan. We should have taken all 10 planes at once."

"And risk that the CIA or the FBI would have put the pieces together earlier? It's a miracle they were as incompetent as to miss the clues from Ramsi Yousef and the earlier bombings. They have many of our people in custody, but their weak, western values will not allow them to use torture to extract confessions. No, the more ambitious plan would have been marvelous if it had worked, but I fear that even the Americans could not have failed to detect what was about to happen."

Bin Laden reluctantly agreed. "I suppose you are right. But I miscalculated. I thought the American bureaucracy and the financial power of the airlines would force the weak American politicians to keep the airports open. At the very least, I thought the anger of stranded passengers would require the government to permit at least some flights on a reduced level." By now, bin Laden had completely forgotten Moqtar on the cell phone.

"This new president is not as easily intimidated as the previous one," Zawahiri offered.

"Bah! He is no different. You will see. He will send some missiles at our camps. He may even order some aircraft to bomb the mountains. But the Americans will never again risk their mighty ground army in combat, especially in the Middle East. Even against Saddam, they carefully avoided invading Iraq, because they feared the *fayedeen* and the *mujahadeen*. It is a show army, designed to impress the cowardly Europeans and the corrupt Russians. It is no different than the beautiful and impotent Swiss guards around the Pope, or the elaborately-clothed horse guards who supposedly protect the Queen of England. No, the Americans will not use their army, and certainly not in Afghanistan."

"Perhaps, but we did . . . " (and Zawahiri carefully used "we" here) "er, miscalculate the rapidity of the aviation system's response."

Suddenly bin Laden realized Moqtar still waited on the cell phone's open channel. Uttering an Afghan curse, he jerked the phone to his ear. "What is happening with the law enforcement agencies? Have they started a crackdown on Muslims?"

Surprised to again be a part of the conversation, Moqtar had to shake himself alert again. "Um, no Sharif. So far they have done the expected things---tightening border security, airport security. But no one is rounding up Muslims. The statements from the New York mayor and the president---he's only made one brief speech from that school---have been entirely devoted to New York and Washington, not revenge."

Bin Laden passed this information on to Zawahiri and grinned. "The fools! Even now they don't understand us. They will no doubt send the vaunted CIA to try to negotiate with the Taliban for our extradition." At this suggestion, Zawahiri beamed. The Americans were so predictable.

Malid had sat quietly, piecing everything together. It was clear that no matter how devastating the attacks were, they came nowhere near to succeeding as planned. *Does he really understand what he did? He has declared war against the Americans in a way they cannot ignore. Before they thought it was a game, a minor irritant, like a gnat on an elephant. Does he really believe they will do nothing? And is this what a mighty religion has come to? As a child, I heard Imams preach against the sins of the Mahdi, who butchered innocents in Khartoum out of "obedience" to Allah. How is this different?*

Bin Laden again addressed Moqtar in the cell phone. "Contact me at our appointed time with additional information. We have already exposed ourselves too long, though I doubt the Americans are clever enough to track these discussions. At that time I want to know the changes in security, and, most important, the policies that the

American government plans to introduce to 'counter' the threat we now pose." He clicked the cell phone shut, still lamenting losing the long-planned second strike on Parliament, Los Angeles, and the Sears Tower. At one time, before Zawahiri talked him out of it, bin Laden had 10 aircraft in five cities on two continents all striking major civilian targets within minutes of each other. But the rapid reaction by the American FAA had even grounded flights coming out of Europe and England, halting not only the Los Angeles/Chicago strikes, but nullifying the London attack.

"Perhaps you were right, my friend," bin Laden said to Zawahiri. "Perhaps the plan was too ambitious. Instead of ten planes and ten explosions, we have three. Nevertheless, we destroyed the center of their financial empire and struck at their vaunted military command center. They will never forget this day!"

Maybe that is not such a good thing, Sharif, thought Malid.

"Malid," said bin Laden, "as per the decision to add 'insulation,' you will be the go-between for the next operation."

"The next operation, Sharif?" Malid felt sick. If the previous operations were any indicator, more innocents would die.

"Yes, Malid, one that will hurt the Americans like nothing so far."

Allah have mercy, thought Malid.

"For now," bin Laden continued, "we must leave here. Get my driver, and collect your things. We move quickly. Tell no one else we are leaving."

Panic? thought Malid. *Is this the Lion of Afghanistan? The great Sharif?*

"You fear an American attack *here*, Sharif? I thought you said the Americans lacked the will for such a strike." Malid followed him into what served as a bedroom.

"One cannot be too careful," bin Laden said, throwing things in his small bag. "Move, Malid. We will leave in 15 minutes."

So the Americans are not as weak as you let on. This Bush president has you worried, does he?

Chapter 10

Fort Bliss Texas, September 11, 2001, 9:00 A.M. local

September in El Paso always provided a respite from the scorching heat of August, especially for soldiers at the Army's Fort Bliss, where long marches in the Texas desert challenged even the strongest. At the 507th Maintenance Company, supply clerk Pfc. Joanna Miles, had begun September 11 as every other, learning to check her ledger and distribute food, equipment, and personal items.

Since leaving basic training and arriving at Fort Bliss, Miles had traded her M-16 for a clipboard, tracking down missing equipment and supplies, calling depots to complain, and, above all, filing paper after paper.

When the first airliner flew into the World Trade Center, Joanna Miles had been in a warehouse cubicle on the phone, where she seemed to spend endless hours, this time trying yet again to gas masks that had been on order for weeks delivered to the 507th. She no sooner had gone round and round with a quartermaster's adjutant than she had a new problem to deal with---a missing shipment of spare parts for Hummers. Although she took the gas masks seriously, in truth they could wait. *After all, we ain't goin' to war.* And sooner or later, HQ would figure out they had too many, someone would connect the dots, and the little blonde private at Ft. Bliss would get the gas mask orders.

But the missing Hummer parts concerned Jo.

She knew autos enough from her brother to know that Hum-Vees were popular, and yet expensive. Without doubt, a hot black market existed for Hummer parts. And no doubt, more than a few Hummer parts "just happened" to find their way into the civilian auto parts shops while some quartermaster types pocketed some "retirement" money on the side.

It isn't gonna happen on Pfc. Miles's watch.

"Corporal Quinones, 327th Quartermaster," answered the young, bored voice on the other end.

"This is Pfc. Joanna Miles, 507th Mechanical at Fort Bliss. We have a problem here: we are missing 10 transmissions; 30 spare ignition sets; 35 batteries; six spare tire mounts; and over two dozen various orders of nuts, bolts, and minor parts for three different varieties of Hum-Vees. I've reported this before, I've sent in the papers. Enough is enough. Now, do you handle this or do I go to your superior?"

Quinones was stunned that a private, let alone a girl, would use such a tone with him. Irritated, he answered, "Look here, *private*," he snarled, "how about you begin with the transaction request?"

"Fine," she replied, all business. "It's number C-420753-6, dated August 3, 2001. As you'll note, that's six weeks ago, and plenty of time for you to get us our parts."

This is crap, Quinones thought. But rather than argue with her, Quinones decided to let the computer do his talking. He clicked on several windows until requisition order C-420753-6 appeared. Sure enough, the items were just as she read them, and, sure enough, the date was August 3.

"We show those item were shipped on August 22. You should have received them on the 27 or 28." *There. It's solved. Now get off my back.*

"Well, we didn't receive anything. Do you have a signature on the receipt." Miles knew she had not signed them in, nor had anyone with whom she worked.

"Hang on." *Damn pain in the ass girls. Who let them in the Army, anyway?* Quinones had to actually get up and dig through some paper. He pushed his chair back from the desk and went into the next room, where he yanked open a massive file cabinet and tracked the slip number. After several minutes, he returned to the phone. "A Cpl. Paul Armstrong signed off on these on 27 August," he said, the routed receipt slip in his hand.

"There is no Cpl. Paul Armstrong in the 507th," Miles noted. "I'm gonna need a copy of that, because I think we may be heading for a JAG investigation here. We did not get these parts. I hope I'm wrong, but it seems to me we have someone with a little auto repair business on the side."

Damn it. Not JAG. "Uhhh, look. I'll get that off today, and see that my Looey gets a copy of your request for the form."

Well, he's covering his own butt, but at least he's cooperating. "Thank you, corporal."

"Lessee," Jo said softly to herself. "It'll take a week for him to get the paperwork to me, a week for the acknowledgment to get back and for my copy to reach the Captain, so they'll get to investigating this about the time I muster out."

Miles no sooner filed the papers and stamped them than her bunkmate, Pfc. Kelly Jamison, came running in. "Jo," she said breathlessly, "look-at-the-TV." It was all one word. "Someone tried to blow up the World Trade Center."

Jo shrugged, vaguely remembered the 1993 bombing. "So? They tried to do that before. What's the big deal."

"No, you-don'-get-tit." Again, all one word. "Planes. Someone flew *airliners* into the towers."

It still didn't register. *She didn't mean airliners. She meant Piper Cubs. Bad, but, hey, it's not like Oklahoma City. Now, that was a bombing.* Jo put down her clipboard and ran over to the rec hall with Johnson. *She has to be exaggerating. We aren't at war with the Japanese, and they're the only ones to ever have suicide planes.*

Moments later, Miles and Jamison jogged through the door to see a thick khaki crowd huddled around a couple of televisions. Someone had brought in his own private TV and had it plugged into a different channel. *This ain't good. Anything that needs two TVs ain't good at all.*

What in the world? Both towers, burnin' to beat all. She started to ask someone what was going on, only to pick up side conversations about the Pentagon.

"What is this about the Pentagon, Sarge?" she asked a three-striper standing nearby.

He didn't even look at her, but kept his eyes glued to the screen to his left. "Terrorists hijacked a plane and flew it into the Pentagon, too."

"Too? You mean that the planes that hit the World Trade Center were flown by terrorists? How did military aircraft get by our defenses?"

He turned to her with a look that said, *"When did you fall off the pumpkin truck?"* "The terrorists hijacked our own airliners and flew two of them into the WTC and a third into the Pentagon, and word is they have more." Jo's stunned look softened his mood slightly. "It's an all-out terrorist attack on the U.S. If I read this right, we're at war."

At that moment the rumbling started in the second tower, and a gasp went up from the crowd of soldiers. Most were recruits who had put in their time, and there were a few "lifers" and grizzled vets, but they were all stunned. Jo heard quiet curses, *"Jesus Christ!" "Oh, my God." "Those poor people." "This is war!"* She looked at Kris Johnson, who had tears streaming down her cheeks.

"Do you know anyone there?" Jo quietly asked, meaning the WTC. Johnson started to sob, her head bobbing. "My brother was there."

"Your brother was in New York?"

"No, at the Pentagon. He's in the Air Force."

"Oh my God, Kel, have you been able to talk to him?"

"No. I just found out when we came over here that the Pentagon had been hit too."

Jo didn't know what to say. "The Pentagon's a big place." One station changed its coverage from the collapsed building to Washington, D.C., and Jo saw the smoke billowing out of the gaping hole in the side. She put her arm around Kelly's shoulder and walked her outside into the warm Texas air. "It'll be ok, Kel. They'll get our people out of there." But even Jo knew that this was merely the beginning, not the end. *Whoever did this can't be allowed to get away with it.*

She'd heard her family talk about Pearl Harbor---her grandfather used to sit at the dinner table and tell stories of how he was working the coal mines in 1941, and how that December Sunday morning they had dressed for church. They had just finished the service---Baptist preachers could go on and on---when cars started to come by the church, honking their horns, with people yelling that America had been attacked, that the fleet had been sunk in Hawaii by the Japs. Typically, people hadn't gotten accurate information---it was not the "fleet," but it was several battleships and some auxiliaries, with two thousand casualties. *In broad daylight. On a peaceful day. With no warning. A vile, sneaky, barbaric attack. Just like today.*

Tempe, Arizona

What were the chances of this? Our first game of the season is . . . a BYE? Thomas Palmer could already hear the jokes about the inept Cardinals, whose pathetic 3-13 season in 2000 seemed right in line with previous team records from the 1990s. *Yep, already sportswriters had wondered if the Cardinals would lose their opener. Ha ha. Jerks.*

Palmer was mystified how the NFL schedulers, in all their infinite wisdom, could have any NFL team open the season with a bye. Yet there it was: *"September 9. Open Date: Arizona."* So while the rival Dallas Cowboys were stinking up Texas Stadium against the Tampa Bay Bucs, scoring only six points with a rookie quarterback, and while the Eagles lost a nail-biter in overtime against the then-powerful Rams, here were the Arizona Cardinals . . . watching on TV.

Normally, if a team played a Sunday game, players had Monday off, but it varied from team to team. Most teams started work on Tuesday, usually with a breakfast at 7:30 and strength/conditioning work at 9:00. Sometime around 10:30, they would report for a team meeting, then break up into offense and defense, then further divide into linebackers, linemen, and so on.

Yesterday was different, though, because of the bye. On Monday, the Cards had film sessions, except, with no film of themselves to grade, all the time was spent preparing for the Redskins. No football player ever complained about too much preparation time. But in reality, players are creatures of habit, and of superstition. Anything that breaks the habit, and anything that disrupts the numerous superstitious rituals of players, is unwelcome. The bye forced all of the Cards out of their habits, which was to say it barely affected Palmer, who refused to allow himself to become a slave to a routine. He didn't believe in blessed bobble-head dolls or magic rubber bands wrapped around his wrist or lucky jock straps that you didn't wash all season. He hadn't even minded when he got #40 at the Cardinals, abandoning his ASU #42. No, Palmer didn't need any tricks. He did it the old fashioned way. He was better conditioned, stronger, and meaner, and better prepared than his opponents. And he wanted to win more than almost anyone, saving, perhaps, his old ASU teammate who now quarterbacked the Cards, Jake Plummer.

So that meant that Monday he watched film . . . and watched, and watched, until he was sure he knew every pass pattern the Redskins would run the minute they lined up. It didn't hurt that all the good tight ends---a safety's one-on-one cover responsibility---were in the AFC.

At least I don't have to worry about Tony Gonzales or Shannon Sharpe. Heck, even Wesley Walls isn't in my division.

He went to sleep Monday night, satisfied that insofar as it fell to him, the Cards would not lose their opener this week.

With their schedule off, the Cardinals would report for a practice on Tuesday, with a "walk through" at 10:00 and a full-pads practice after lunch. Palmer was determined to follow his normal routine as much as possible. He woke up at 6:00 and then showered, even if he was just going to get sweaty all over again. After that, he would flip on Fox News for background noise, eat, dress, and then head for the Cards' southwestern-style Tempe workout facility off Elliot Road.

The commute could not be taken for granted any more. Even with the new freeways, Phoenix traffic had outpaced the highway's carrying power, and congestion was common. Normally, Palmer left his apartment in the South Mountain foothills near Awatukee and jumped in his Dodge Ram truck about 7:00. Even if there was a traffic jam, he knew enough side roads to get to the training facility.

Today, the crew at Fox was discussing something about President Bush's stem-cell research speech, the details of which bored Palmer. He tuned it out as he slurped a cup of the darkest blend of coffee he could find, when he heard something odd on the television that caused him to turn the sound up.

" . . . it appears an airplane has hit the World Trade Center North Tower, that would be Tower 1. Flame and smoke are now coming out of the tower. The extent of the damage is not known . . . ."

Huh. Wouldn't surprise me. Sky Harbor is right next to the center core of Phoenix. I'm amazed no jet has ever flown into the Bank One building.

Putting away his coffee cup, Palmer went in the bathroom to brush his teeth. He grabbed his gym bag, which contained only a few personal items that he took to practice. He usually wore the same clothes home that he wore to practice. Unlike some of the stylin' brothers, he saw no need to dress for practice or home games. Snapping off the light, he grabbed his keys and aimed the remote at the television when he saw that now both towers were burning.

What the hell?

He flipped up the sound on Fox News.

" . . . both towers have been struck in what officials are now saying is a terrorist attack using airliners. . . ."

Airliners? Airliners flew into the buildings? They used airliners as missiles?

" . . . and a report that another airliner has hit the Pentagon. This is now confirmed: a third airliner has plunged into the Pentagon. There is smoke coming out of the Pentagon, and it is confirmed that another airliner has struck the Pentagon. At this point, we do not have any word from the FAA as to how many other airliners may still be up there that have been hijacked."

Still drawn to the images, Palmer fished his cell phone out of his pocket and hit the auto-dial to his parents' house. His mother answered immediately.

"Hi mom. Listen . . . '

"Thomas? This is horrible."

"Yeah, I'm just now turning on the TV, but looks pretty bad."

"They say it's Middle Eastern hijackers---the same group that tried to blow up the World Trade Center ten years ago."

I think that was in 1993, but no matter. This is serious. "Is David over there?"

"No, he's at his place." David had an apartment in Chandler.

"OK. I'll call him. I'm coming over there. I'm sure the Cards will cancel practice today."

I bet a lot of "normal" life in America gets canceled today.

Before calling David, Pat hit the auto-dial for Heather, his fiancée. She was sobbing when she picked up. "Oh my God, Tom. What did these people do?"

"Heather, it's all right. I'm going to come over. I needed to make sure you're ok, and now I've got to call David. I'll be over in a little while."

"Tom, my cousin lives in New York. Right in Manhattan."

Soberly, Tom replied, "Look, Heather, before this is over, I have a feeling we're all going to know someone in those towers or who was there today. See you soon." He ended the call, then punched in David's number aggressively, anger starting to build within him. *Who do these people think they are? A bunch of hijackings are one thing, inconveniencing people and all, but blowing stuff up is different.* David's phone rang several times, and Tom almost gave up before finally David's agitated voice answered, "Yeah?"

"Dave, this is crazy. Who are these assholes?"

"Man, there's a fourth plane---did you hear? A fourth plane went down in Pennsylvania somewhere, and now they are thinking that the passengers found out what was in the works and stormed the cabin."

Rage started to build in Tom, although he had learned from years of football to control it. "They aren't gonna get away with this. I don't know much about this guy Bush, but he strikes me as someone who isn't going to put up with this, not for one minute."

"Are you on your way over here? You won't believe it. Tom, the World Trade Center just collapsed! I don't mean, parts fell off, or it fell over---it went straight down in a gigantic cloud of dust! The whole tower. The other one's still on fire."

"On my way. Be there in five, bro. You know, we gotta do something."

"I know. I'm with you, I think Bush will do something."

"No, Dave. *We* gotta do something. We can't sit this one out."

David paused on the other end, then, his voice grim, answered, "Yah. I know. This demands blood. See you in a minute."

Chapter 11

Ground Zero

"Brennan? Hey! Anyone?" Callahan sat in pitch black, taking an inventory of any equipment he still had with him. He had his fire department radio, but had avoided using up the batteries. It hadn't worked when the building was up, so it was unlikely it would work now. That meant that Maydays or other distress calls had to be kept to a minimum---only made if he thought rescuers were close. His flashlight was gone. The oxygen tank still was on his back, but he lost his helmet somewhere. It was dusty, but he could breathe, so there was no need for oxygen at that moment. Carefully he felt his "surfboard" below him---the concrete block that had sailed him to safety. It was now split in half, and he was sitting on the larger section.

Callahan felt nothing underneath the concrete, so he reasoned he might be on some sort of ledge. Searching with his hand, he found a small rock or piece of cement, which he threw just a couple of feet in front of him. It made a sound after a short fall, leading Callahan to think he was a few feet up from some solid floor . . . *but how solid?*

Ok, so I can go down if I need to . . . if it doesn't collapse more. He threw a few more pebbles in a fan pattern to make sure he had hit a floor, and not just another piece of debris. It sounded like he was indeed only a short distance from a floor. Carefully Callahan inched his body over the ledge of the "surfboard" and, uttering a prayer, let go and dropped. Thankfully, his feet touched down only perhaps two feet below. Then he noticed something . . . the darkness was lifting a little. He looked up and saw that what that once had been black now was grey smoke with shards of light peeking through.

There's a hole up there! It's been there all along, only I couldn't see it through all the dust and smoke. Sure enough, there was an exit to this place. In the dim, but improving light, Callahan suddenly heard moaning, and he as he moved towards it, he heard another voice.

"Hang on, chief. We'll get to you." It was Brennan, but who was he talking to?

"Brennan!" Callahan shouted.

"Mike, that you!? Thank God you're Ok."

"Who else is down here with you, Brian?"

"I've heard from Kehoe and Rogers---they appear to be about 100 feet from me, but for now we're all staying put, as we hear things shifting. Then there's the Chief."

"Which Chief?"

"Chief Prouty. About 50 feet from me there is a big gash. He's at the bottom there, somewhere, and his legs are buried." Then, more quietly, Brennan added, "Mike, he ain't gonna make it. He needs help, big time, and we can't get to him."

Suddenly it dawned on Brennan that it was getting lighter. "Hey, I can see you Mike!"

Callahan had half-crawled, half-duck-walked over to Brennan's location. He smiled and the two men exchanged an emotional handshake.

"There's a way out of this, kid. I could see a shaft up above from where I was about 100 paces back."

Quickly he called out to the other men. Both Kehoe and Rogers hailed him back.

"Does anyone have a radio? Mine hasn't worked."

"We've been trying, Mike, but no luck. None of the frequencies seem to be operating."

"OK, listen. There is a shaft of light about 100 feet back from where I came. It appears to be a way out, but we have to climb. We'll have to come back for the Chief."

Joe Rogers had dropped down to where Prouty was. The elderly man was in pain, but his lower body was increasingly going numb. "Mike, Chief can't move."

"I know, Joe. We'll have to get someone back down to him."

Chief Prouty suddenly lurched upward as far as he could--- now able to see the outline of Rogers' face---and grabbed Rogers by the arm. "Tell my wife and kids I love them. You tell them, you hear me?" Then he fell backward, dead.

"Mike, Chief just died."

It was a sad moment, but no more so than the whole day. Callahan realized that this was no time for sentimental ceremonies. "Look, you guys, you need to carefully come over here to me and Brian. We're gonna climb out that hole."

Then Callahan heard several short, staccato beeps . . . *of a cell phone?*

Joe Rogers called his wife on a cell phone. "It's me! Yah, we're ok. I can't talk, but we found a way out." Then there was a pause. "Of the World Trade Center." Another pause. "Huh? Oh my God. Look we gotta go. We'll be out soon."

"Joe, tell me you didn't have a cell phone this whole time," Callahan's rage started to build. "We've been here in the pit of hell and you had a *damn cell phone!?*"

Rogers, who had been crawling while talking, stopped like a deer hit by a semi. "God, Mike, oh God. I'm sorry. I don't know what I was thinking. I never thought the phone would work down here. I'm sorry. . . I'm . . . ."

The man is losing it. Back off, Callahan. No point beating him up now. We've all been through hell. Leadership is knowing when to chew someone out and when to let it go.

"Forget it, Joe. Let's just get out of here. And don't use up your cell batteries. We may need them."

"Dontcha want to call for help?" asked Brennan.

"And tell them we are where?" replied Callahan. Brennan thought for a minute, then nodded.

The four could now see each other's faces in the dingy tomb. They took a moment to congratulate each other on their incredible luck. Then Callahan broke the mood. "Ok, boys, like I said earlier today, let's climb."

Woodside, New York

Shannon had phoned everyone she could think of---the station, other stations, wives of other firemen. No one had any information, and most were even more panicked than she was, if that seemed possible. Information coming from the FDNY was patchy, and utterly incomplete. The brass didn't know which units were inside the buildings, who was assigned where, or even who had reported back. A few wives started to get calls on cell phones.

By now word had spread throughout New York. Schools were shutting down, frantic families tried to contact each other. Sean got a ride with a friend, and would be home any minute. Patrick was going to walk with several other kids from the neighborhood. Normally, there was no way Shannon would let Patty walk, but she couldn't leave the phone, and everyone was in as desperate straits as she, so there were no free rides.

They knew something horrible had happened to the Twin Towers. They probably didn't know their dad was underneath one when it collapsed.

Shannon finally got through to the engine house. A firefighter named Terry Shills answered.

"This is Shannon Callahan---my husband, Michael, is a firefighter in 71. Can you tell me anything about him? About his unit?"

Shills was a replacement from another borough. He had no idea who even worked at 71, let alone who had reported in. "All I can tell you," he said, "is that guys are trickling in, and the first thing they do when they get in here is call their families. So you might want to stay by the phone, but other than that, we don't know much more than you do. Almost all the units, except for a skeleton reserve to fight any other fires that might come up, are down at Ground Zero."

Ground Zero? My God, is that what they are calling that now? It's that bad?

As controlled as she could manage, Shannon thanked Shills and punched in Maureen Carlson's number again. This time there was an answer.

"Chuck?" said the frantic voice on the other end. It was Maureen, and Chuck was her husband.

"No, Maureen, it's Shannon. Have you heard anything?"

"Oh, Shannon, oh my God, oh Shannon," she sobbed. "Both towers came down. Chuck had to have been in there."

"Maureen, you don't know that. In fact, if they went to Tower 1 first, on the first impact, there's a good chance they might have evacuated when Tower 2 came down---and we didn't have any firefighters in Tower 2 yet." *Do you believe that yourself, Shannon?*

It was enough to calm Maureen down, but not much. "Calls are coming in from guys who got out. They are saying that hundreds of firefighters were killed when the building collapsed."

"Look," said Shannon. "I just talked to a firefighter holding down the fort at #71. He said it's total chaos and confusion, but that guys are straggling in." *I called her hoping for some reassurance, but I'm having to console her!* "We just don't know where the boys are right now. They'll start reporting in."

"Chuck was talking the other day about the Big One. I tried to tell him he was dwelling on the negative. Maybe he knew something I didn't."

"Maureen, they *all* talk about the Big One. How else could they do their jobs. Look, I need to clear the line in case Michael or the boys are trying to get through. But as soon as you know *anything---anything, you understand?*---you call me. Ok?"

"Sure, Shannon. And you do the same. Hey, thanks. I'm usually not a blubberer. But I have a real bad feeling about today."

Shannon hung up, staring at the TV, whose cameras were focused on the cloud of smoke rising from mid-town Manhattan. *How can you not have a bad feeling about today after this?*

Cranbury, New Jersey

Laundry, laundry, laundry. It seemed like it never ended, especially after a trip. Liza Trainer had awoken after Rod left, had a Spartan breakfast, then attacked the laundry baskets that vomited out their soiled refuse. She'd done three loads already, in between making the boys their Fruit Loops, changing Douggie's diapers, and getting him and David dressed.

Then came the lists. Liza was a list-a-holic. She made lists for everything---groceries, chores, appointments, phone calls. *A day without a list is a day without organization.*

She put on *Sesame Street* for the boys while she took a shower, then got ready for a grocery store run. Since no one had shopped since she and Rod went to Rome, the cupboard was bare indeed.

"Come on, guys. Let's go get some goodies."

"Can I have a car?" David said. One way Liza had found to enlist the boys' cooperation in grocery shopping is to let David have a "Matchbox" car when they came to the display toward the middle of the store. Of course, the last third of the store wasn't nearly as easy to cover, given that he wanted to open the car right away, and Douggie wanted to stick the little Porsche in his mouth.

"We'll see how you behave. If you help mommy, I think we can swing a car." She had them nearly outside the door when the phone rang. Normally, she'd have let it ring, but there was something today that told her to answer it.

"Hold on guys. Wait right there." Both stood at the door while Liza grabbed the receiver off the phone on the kitchen counter, half expecting it to be Rod. Instead, it was her friend, Ellen.

"Liza, I know Rod is traveling today. Do you know what flight he's on?"

What an odd question for a friend to ask. "No, I didn't check. He's going to Oakland, I think, and . . . ."

Elaine cut her off. "Turn on your TV. Don't you know what's happening?"

Puzzled, Liza slipped on the television. "What channel?" she said, impatiently.

"Liza, it doesn't matter. All of them."

All of them. Oh God. Then the two burning towers came into focus. "Is that the World Trade Center?"

"Yes. Liza," she paused, "someone flew *airplanes* into the buildings. Do you know Rod's flight number?"

Then it hit her. *Was Rod on one of those?* She listened, Ellen in one ear, the new reporters in the other, then picked up that two other airliners were missing. *What flight was Rod on? I didn't pay attention. What airline was he even on? It wasn't Oakland. It was San Francisco. He was headed to San Francisco. But he usually flies Continental Airlines, and they said the missing airliners were United and American.*

"Rod usually takes Continental out west, I think. He's a pretty seasoned traveler, Elaine. Look, I'm going to phone Continental right now. I'll get back to you."

Liza dialed Continental and reached a customer service rep, who, for his own security reasons, couldn't tell her if Rod was a passenger or not. But the 7:00 from Newark departed with no problems, and the later flight was grounded. *Was Rod on the first, or still waiting with the second? And if with the second, why didn't he call on his cell phone?*

Only then did Liza start doing the math. Rod left too late to get on the first flight. But there was a United flight that he took from time to time. *Oh God.* She fought the terror that started to build. *"We are not given the spirit of fear, but of love, and of power and a sound mind."* Breathing deeply to calm down, Liza attempted to get United Airlines Customer Service on the line . . . just like hundreds of other people concerned about their friends or loved ones. It was no use. She hit computer recording after computer recording. Finally hanging up in frustration, she called Ellen again. Her husband Daryl answered.

"Daryl, I'm worried about Rod. I can't get through to United. Can you do me a favor and find out what flight Rod was on?"

"No problem. By the way, Elaine is on her way over." *Why? This sounded worse all the time.*

Ellen rang the doorbell just a few minutes later. Liza had just watched the reports of the attack on the Pentagon and saw the first WTC come down.

"I got here as quickly as I could," she gulped, bustling through the Trainer doorway. No sooner had Elaine closed the door behind her than CNN had another announcement.

"We are now getting a report of a fourth airliner, one of those out of contact, and it appears to have crashed in Pennsylvania. This was a United flight . . . ."

Liza's knees buckled and a wave of nausea swept over her.

"It is believed this United flight---flight 93---was en route to Chicago . . . ."

Liza's head jerked up. *Rod was going to San Francisco*, she thought, and began to stop shaking.

Her reprieve only lasted seconds.

"We have a correction, the United flight 93 was on its way to San Francisco . . . ."

"Oooooaaaaaaa," Liza moaned as the tears came. She collapsed to her hands and knees, gasping "No, no." Ellen kneeled beside her, "Liza. We don't know anything yet."

Tears streaming down her face, Liza said, "No, Ellen. I know. That was Rod's plane. I know." Then, instead of weeping uncontrollably---despite the hole in her heart the size of a basketball---Liza felt an incredible peace sweep over her. She looked at Ellen and asked, "Can you watch the boys? I need to be alone." *My God. I need to think. What will I do without Rod? Oh, Lord. I need You.*

Her knees weak, Liza struggled upstairs to her bedroom, where she alternatively cried and thought about her life---her family---without Rod. Yet she knew it was not a mourning of hopelessness. Her husband was now safe, in the arms of the Master. And the peace flowed over her like a gentle stream all over again.

Chapter 12

Ground Zero

Despite improving light---the dust seemed to be settling, perhaps---Michael Callahan still struggled to see exactly where he was going. Step by step he climbed, with Brennan a few feet behind, then Kehoe and Rogers. They wanted to stay spaced out enough that if Callahan loosed a wall of debris, all of them wouldn't be buried. On the other hand, they had to stay close enough that if one got in trouble, the others could reach him.

Even though they had been missing for a couple of hours now, Callahan had no way of knowing that directly above them multiple buildings were still on fire---FDNY had decided to let #7 World Trade Center burn, as there was no saving it. He could still hear intermittent pops and crackles, accompanied by low rumbles and shudders. Besides #7, other buildings sagged with compromised structures that could collapse at any minute, but, of course, that was above ground. Nor did Callahan know that FDNY had more than 300 missing firefighters---entire companies---and that no one had a reliable accounting of who was missing and who was safe.

Firemen trickled into stations all over Manhattan, some too shell-shocked to provide basic personal information. In those cases, the guys at the station obtained what they could from the markings on the fireman's helmet, coat, or, if necessary, wallet. Most were lucid, if stunned. They had seen, up close, what the world saw in Technicolor, and despite the danger and chaos, what most of them witnessed first hand failed to capture the awesome destruction observed by the rest of the world. Some had barely escaped from the pits and carnage that Michael and his group of firefighters now battled.

Callahan thought it took an hour to climb 50 feet to the hole where the light poured through, only by the time he got there, it was again covered with smoke and haze from a half-dozen fires. Placing his boot on a piece of sheet rock and grabbing a protruding steel rod, Callahan pulled himself through the opening, out, above ground.

What he saw nearly knocked him back into the hole. *This is a scene from Terminator! Everything's on fire. Is this what the bombing raids in World War II looked like?*

For several minutes he just scanned the scene, now oblivious to Brennan struggling up through the hole behind him. Brennan didn't even make it all the way out before he was staggered by the apocalyptic vision.

"Holy God. It's a war zone. We must be at war. I don't even see our guys."

Brennan's voice snapped Michael out of his momentary lethargy and depression. He grabbed Brennan's arm and hoisted him out.

"Everything's on fire, Mike," Brennan observed. *To say the least, it's still dangerous here!*

"Come on. Let's get the other guys out and clear out of this place before something else collapses."

Kehoe had already popped his head out, uttering a string of profanities, followed by Rogers.

"Ok. We need to get out of here." Pointing to a burning hulk, Callahan said, "That appears to be WTC #7 there, so we ought to be able to get to Broad Street this way . . . ." And, as he turned to head back past what was Tower 1 just a few hours ago, Callahan again stopped. All that remained of the giant tower was a huge pile of rubble, a single lattice-work side of the building, now leaning at an angle, and, oddly, two steel beams standing in the middle . . . in the form of a . . . *cross?* Michael shook his head. "This way. Let's move."

They high-stepped and climbed over cement and steel, all jagged edges and broken blocks. Kehoe grazed a razor-sharp sheet, and it sliced his leg open.

"Jesus," he screamed. "Damn it." He spread his pants, and concluded that while he was bleeding like a stuck pig, the wound was not too deep. "Keep going, guys. I'm ok. Let's just get out of here." Callahan nodded and again led the way.

They had moved only a few more steps when the building to their left simply exploded. A gas main had blown, hurling debris and fire all over them. A 30-foot geyser shot out like a flamethrower, knocking Kehoe on his back and setting Rogers on fire. Brian raced to put out Rogers, when a second explosion hurled cement, brick, and steel on them. A four-foot slab landed square on Kehoe's ankle and he screamed in agony, as a second chunk crushed his skull in mid-scream. Rogers had caught the full force of the second fireball and had collapsed in a burning hulk.

"No!" yelled Brennan, rushing for Rogers. "Hang on Joe!" Callahan cried, "No Brian! The ground is giving way." Callahan felt the blast loosen the rubble beneath their feet, opening a small chasm that quickly threatened to engulf the men. Brennan sank through the shifting ground, saving himself by grabbing a steel girder. Callahan slid below him. It was as if a dump truck had loosed its contents right out from under them. Callahan found a small hunk of concrete, and ducked to avoid the avalanche of dirt and metal. "Hold on, Brian. I can push you out."

Feeling Callahan's hands at his butt, Brian used the extra leverage to pull himself out of the hole. He crawled to his knees and leaned back over the hole, then reached back down. "Come on, Mike. Grab my hand." Extending his arm toward Callahan, Brian heard another blast from the building behind him. He went flying sideways as another wave of debris fell on Callahan.

"Brian!" Callahan's yelled, but the voice got further away.

"Mike. My God, Mike. Mike!" Brennan leaned as far into the hole as he could when he felt the tremor of the giant rubble pile shifting yet again. "God, no, MIKE!" Then more steel and dirt caved in. Right where Mike Callahan had been.

Woodlawn, New York

Both boys walked around the house quietly, as if a sudden noise might trigger the wrong type of phone call. Shannon had used her cell to stay in contact with the Fire Department and with other wives, but right now, too many of them were awaiting some word of their loved ones. She knew only too well that anyone other than a FDNY official telling them their husbands or sons were ok was unwelcome, even if it was the voice of a friend in a similar situation. Shannon didn't want to be the one to intrude on their private hell, making it worse by adding her own.

It had been six hours since the buildings collapsed. Brian Brennan had been found by searchers sometime around 1:00. He didn't know where Michael was. The last thing he saw was a small mountain of debris shifting and swallowing Michael up. As far as he knew, Michael was buried under 100 feet of what remained of the World Trade Center.

Shannon cried, good and hard, when Captain Chuck English of the FDNY called her. He let her talk to Brennan---*thank God that kid is ok, because Michael really liked him*---and while her heart told her to hold out hope, already she was preparing herself that Michael would never come home again. She hadn't told the boys everything. Instead, she told them their dad was still missing, but that the rescuers had a pretty good idea where he was, and that he would come home. It was probably a lie, but Shannon figured since no one knew for sure, it was better to tell them a lie than to give them all the details. *There is hope*, she reminded herself. *Until you have a body, there is hope.*

But common sense asserted itself again and again. There is only so long a man can live if buried below ground without oxygen. No one knew specifically where to look for Michael. By the time Brian took the first search and rescue team back---after being delayed for hours by the needs of hundreds of other missing firemen---he couldn't even point to the exact spot where he had last seen Michael Callahan.

So she waited, determined not to blubber and bawl. But quietly she had actually looked at some of Michael's insurance policies and bank accounts. She was practical enough to know that the boys had to be fed and schooled, and that bill collectors didn't grieve for long.

Then the phone rang.

"Hello?"

"Shannon, Chuck English here. I'm gonna give it to you straight. We couldn't find any holes or openings anywhere in the area where Brian said Michael vanished. Without a clear lead, I can't get Department authorization to use any special resources to search for him. He'll be a part of the site-wide rescue effort."

Which means that if he was alive, you've just let him die. "I understand," Shannon said, choking back more tears. "How long before you get to that zone?"

"At the rate we're going, it will be several days before we get the entire site covered. In the mean time, we have dogs going all over the site. If they so much as pick up a single scent, we'll stop what we're doing and dig at that spot."

"Thank you, Captain. Please keep me informed."

"I will, Mrs. Callahan. You be brave. It ain't over 'till it's over. You know we won't quit."

"I know." Shannon hung up the phone, knowing that very soon the nature of the WTC site cleanup would demand that they do exactly that, quit. A piece of property that valuable, in the middle of Manhattan, couldn't sit empty for years while people dug around for fingernails and bone matter of loved ones. Gruesome, but that was a fact. *Michael is likely in the grave he'll remain forever. Right now.* She buried her head in her hands and sobbed, trying not to let the boys hear her.

Tora Bora Mountains, Afghanistan

"We have CNN, Sharif!" Al-Azni adjusted the small television, which now via satellite picked up CNN. Al-Anzi had spent the last 45 minutes driving bin Laden in a dirty SUV through mountain trails, a few miles from the camp, to a small secret cabin that the world's most famous terrorist kept for emergencies. He had never seen bin Laden's retreat before---a small, two-room shack powered by a generator with its own outside well. He had spent the next fifteen minutes setting up the satellite receiver and bringing in bin Laden's gear from the SUV.

Bin Laden, Malid, and Zawahiri gathered around, sipping their tea and peering at the images of rubble at Ground Zero. Both nodded approvingly, but Zawahiri's eyes grew solemn and rested on bin Laden. Malid kept silent as Zawahiri spoke.

"They will come after you this time. It may be half-hearted, but they will make some gesture."

"It is no matter," offered bin Laden. "No nation had successfully invaded Afghanistan. Should the Americans try, they will fail like the Russians and the British. More likely, they will launch their missiles and perhaps fly some bombers over, but they will not topple the Taliban. Our friends in Kabul will string them along, being sufficiently apologetic. They will, no doubt, distance themselves publicly from us...no matter...it will only be temporary, if at all."

So why, thought Malid, *do you have a plan to assassinate of the leader of the Northern Alliance? Are you concerned that the Americans may prove more determined than you let on?*

"Sharif," Zawahiri responded, "the Americans moved rapidly. They not only grounded all aircraft immediately, but so did the British. Our entire second wave attacks in Chicago, London, and Los Angeles are nullified. I spoke to Khalid Sheikh Mohammad earlier, and we agree that the ambitious plan for hitting ten targets will have to be scrapped. None of the planned follow-up attacks can occur. The cell charged with taking out Big Ben found itself grounded at Heathrow!"

Typically for a bin Laden operation, few people knew all the components of a plan. Zawahiri, most likely, had the grand scheme in his head, but Malid only learned some of the details of the plot in pieces, and when he did, its grand scope astonished him. Zawahiri plotted for the hijacking of a dozen airliners in two countries, striking 12 prominent targets nearly simultaneously. He was not surprised, however, at the speed of the American reaction.

"Do you trust the Taliban to protect you?" Zawahiri asked. "They are brigands and thieves! They will give you up to avoid a confrontation with the United States."

"Be patient," bin Laden snapped. "The Taliban are brothers in Islam, far better than the heretics in Riyadh or Damascus. They are more clearly practicing the Koran than anyone right now. They will not be intimidated by the Americans."

Malid was stunned. He knew the Taliban were the most extreme variant of the most extreme form of Islam. No mullahs or clerics approved of their teaching. They submitted to no outside clerical examination of their doctrines. Quite the contrary, they had been nearly universally condemned by the most respected religious men in Islam. *Now bin Laden elevates them to the status of holy men?*

Bin Laden continued. "The Taliban know that the Americans are famous for words and threats, not action. They will not risk the deaths of thousands of soldiers to come after us."

And, Sharif, thought Malid, *that is why we just relocated from our main camp to this isolated hut? Because you think the Americans will not respond?*

Oblivious to the skeptical looks from Malid and Zawahiri, bin Laden continued with his lecture. "Have you so soon forgotten Mogadishu? No, these Americans will rush about frantically for a few days, then gradually return to their lax security."

Zawahiri set his tea cup down. He avoided Malid's eyes, but both of them shared the same thought: the Great Satan would not forget so easily.

Malid had another thought---likely one that Zawahiri did not share. *Perhaps Osama bin Laden is not the brilliant leader I once thought.*

September 12, Parkview Hospital

Eight in beds. Twelve waiting. Twenty treated. Five sent home who probably should have been kept. Regina Waterford scanned the list of patients in Parkview's emergency room. *Thank God it's easing.* For more than 24 hours, Waterford and other ER doctors had worked on a never-ending stream of victims from the WTC sites. Most came in with breathing disorders from the smoke and dust. Many with burns. Several with shattered bones from falling debris, injuries received in the line of duty while rescuing others. *We never saw the worst. We won't. What's left of them will need DNA testing to identify. And those who jumped . . . .*

Yesterday had been Regina Waterford's day off. Like most Americans, she had been going about her life, surfing the net for some of the latest medical technologies, keeping her TV on low in the background, when she heard the reports had stared in horror at the catastrophe. Like most Americans, she knew instantly her life had changed, but for now, the only thing that mattered was getting to Parkview, where she would be needed.. When she got there, every doctor and nurse who could be reached was already treating patients. Her first was a Puerto Rican woman with severe burns. She'd apparently not been in the WTC towers, but was close to building #7 when flash explosion got her. Waterford cleaned and dressed her as best as she knew, but her expertise---such as it was---was in pediatrics, not burns. No matter. Specialists would be swarming in soon anyway. At least Waterford could put the poor woman out of her pain for a while.

Next up, a guy in a t-shirt, torn pants and some sort of slippers. She read the admitting nurse's notes, but they were (*as usual*) stupefyingly incomplete. She drew back the privacy curtain only slightly so she could look at the guy. He lay on the bed, head turned to the side, apparently asleep, shoes still on. *Are those pool shoes?* Looked like a contusion of his head, and the arm looked to be in bad shape. *Definitely dirty. Course, we've had hundreds of people in here coated in dust. Local hospitals have treated thousands of glass wounds, burns, and debris-related injuries.* Regina pulled the curtain closed and briskly walked to the admitting nurse.

"That John Doe you admitted in bed #6---can you tell me any more about him?"

Joy Lelane was the admitting nurse, scanned through her notes. They'd had hundreds of patients since the events on September 11, and she couldn't remember the patient. "Not really. He was picked up several blocks away by a policeman, who brought him in. The cop already took off. This guy was apparently in this shape when they got him. He obviously can't talk right now, and the cop didn't say much."

"You know anything else? Any ID?"

"No, Regina, that's it. Any idea who he is?"

"Not yet. Maybe someone who worked in the WTC and got out. When he wakes up he can help us." Waterford turned and went back to cubicle #6, where she found her patient stirring.

Checking his pulse, she saw his eyes flicker. "How you feeling?"

He saw only a dim shape at first, then, gradually, the details of Waterford's pale blue medical jumper crystallized. "Ummmmmm. Owwww." He grabbed his head with his right hand, then, when he tried to move his left arm, he moaned. Waterford had seen the wound when she cursorily examined him the first time, but he wasn't bleeding badly and there were no signs of internal hemorrhaging, so she had waited to stitch it up until, possibly, she got some information out of the guy.

"You're ok, but you took a pretty nasty whack on the head and you need to keep that arm immobilized. We need some X-rays. Could be broken. Nothing serious, though, but we need to check you out, and I'm to have to stitch up that head wound."

"Where am I," he asked, before bursting into a spasm of coughing. He looked around, seeing only the ER curtains on all sides.

Lotsa smoke inhalation, like everyone else. "You're at Parkview Hospital. I'm Regina Waterford, and we should have you on your feet in no time, if we can find you some better clothes."

"What happened to my clothes?" he asked, looking at the torn shirt.

"You don't know??"

He closed his eyes and grabbed the bridge of his nose. "I recall taking off a coat. I was hot."

Waterford envisioned a suit an tie. "Who are you?"

Squinting, he slowly shook his head. "I don't know. I don't know my name. Don't you know?"

Waterford frowned and shook her head. "Can you remember anything that might help us figure out who you are?"

His eyes closed, saw something: *Yankee Stadium.* "Yankee Stadium. That's the last thing I remember."

She tilted her head slightly. "Are you a ballplayer or a fan?"

"I don't know. But there's something about Yankee Stadium."

"You don't remember anything about what's happened in the last 24 hours?"

"No, what's happened?" His eyes showed he was completely sincere. There were flashes of darkness, light, and what looked like smoke, but he couldn't tell.

"Are you a New Yorker?" *This is getting weird. Eight years in ER and I've never encountered a genuine amnesiac.*

"I don't know. We're in New York now, right?"

Oh boy.

"Hang on here just a minute. I'm going to stitch your head up. But I need you to talk to our staff psychologist. Unfortunately, they're just a little booked, so it's gonna be a while. In the mean time, we probably ought to get you into one of these gowns. We need to look at your x-rays, which ought to be up any minute."

He took the gown, but didn't put it on. "How long have I been here?"

"You were admitted 45 minutes ago. It's where you were before that has me concerned."

"So, what's wrong with me?"

"Well, obviously you have some head damage, and that probably accounts for your memory loss. We don't think it's permanent, but I'm no specialist, and, well, it's gonna be days before you see one. You might start getting things back any time, but, like I say, it's not my field. Your arm is badly bruised, but apparently not broken---although I'm going to check the X-rays to confirm. Otherwise, you're in pretty good shape." She studied him, looking between his vitals on the chart and the man in the bed, then put down the chart. The patient in the next cubicle moaned in pain.

"What do you remember about Yankee Stadium?"

The man close his eyes. *It's a ball. Someone hit a long fly or foul ball---can't tell---and I'm reaching for it, and there's a guy behind me and he's reaching for it too.*

"Sorry, not much. I was at a game there, but I can't remember anything except reaching for a fly ball."

"Were you there with anyone?"

"Hmmm. Not exactly 'with' him, but a guy behind me was also going for the ball."

"So no one else was with you?"

He closed his eyes again. There were shapes to his right, but he couldn't make them out. They were small---*kids?*

"Can't tell."

"Ok, well, we'll work on it. Meanwhile, a little rest won't hurt you." Waterford picked up her clipboard, pulled the curtain as the moaning next door increased, and punched the extension for the staff psychologist, then checked the head and arm x-rays folder at the pick-up bin. She ordered an MRI of his head, and instructed a nurse come in with the splint, but, seeing no break, knew that a full cast would not be necessary. Of course, all this was as time permitted. No telling when they would get back to him, especially since cubicle #5's moans had graduated into screams.

Ground Zero, September 12th

Coolio was a powerful animal, a German Shepherd with a black muzzle and sad eyes. He was also among the finest trained firefighters in the FDNY, except that he didn't fight fires: Coolio found buried survivors.

Like dozens of search and rescue dogs, many brought in from around the country, Coolio received a ride to the WTC site early on September 12. Anyone still buried would have to be found within 48 hours, or there would be almost no hope. Before it was over, the search and rescue teams would employ more than 100 dogs, with Coolio one of the first on the scene. He was trained to search for human scent buried underground. After four hours of unsuccessful work, without so much as a "hit" on a scent, Coolio was becoming depressed.

Kevin Elam, Coolio's handler, knew that a depressed dog would not work efficiently, and had himself been trained to give the dog intermittent successes by "burying" a firefighter that the dog could "find." Members of the search and rescue task force volunteered to take turns being "found" by the dogs so they would not give up. A volunteer from a Wisconsin fire department, named Rick, had laid down next to some girders and other members quickly piled dust and debris on him. Then Elam guided Coolio to the general area, where he quickly picked up the scent and scratched at the ground around Rick's leg until he had exposed a good part of Rick's foot.

"Good boy, Coolio," said Elam, continuing the charade. "You found him! Way to go." He popped a dog treat out of his jacket and Coolio wolfed it down. He had to repeat the charade again that afternoon. There simply weren't any survivors.

At 4:30, Elam led Coolio to one of the supply stations for a water break. He could work all day without food or water, but the dog couldn't. Nevertheless, Elam grabbed a bottle of water for himself, pouring part of it over his dust and smoke-covered face.

The dog's getting depressed. We need to arrange another "victim" to be "found."

Elam and Coolio worked for another three hours, with no success, when he saw Captain Michaels gesturing to him.

"Elam!" Despite the fatigue, Elam stood up and slowly walked toward Michaels, ordering Coolio to follow him.

"Listen," said Michaels, "we know you aren't having much luck out there. The training people suggested that perhaps we ought to try another approach with a couple of the dogs. I want you to go home. Get some rest, and get back here at 6:30 tomorrow morning with Coolio. We're gonna give the dogs something more specific to work with. We have a bunch of clothing items from missing brothers."

"Cap, they ain't bloodhounds," said Elam.

"I know that, but the trainers said this might work. It can't be any less successful than what we've been doing."

He's damn sure right there. "Ok. I'll be back tomorrow."

"Just make sure the dog is rested. They're worried that the dogs are breathing too much soot---that it might be ruining their smellers, ya know?"

"We'll be back." And with that, Elam headed back to one of the FDNY transports that took him to the station, where he was able to get a ride from the cops back to his apartment.

Chapter 13

Woodside, New York

Shannon spent much of the evening praying. After she and the boys pushed a little food around on their plates, they cleaned up and the two boys went to their rooms. Neither had much to say. They knew their dad was missing, and that "missing" meant, in all likelihood, buried beneath hundreds of tons of steel and glass. Shannon knew plenty of Bible verses for such an occasion, but they seemed hollow now when she, herself, was doubting them. *Is it true God held Michael in his hand? If so, where is he? Why didn't You protect him, Lord? "All things work out for those who love the Lord?" Prove it. How did this day "work out" for Michael?*

Almost immediately she began to repent of her bitterness. It wasn't God's fault that the buildings collapsed, or that evil men stole airplanes to destroy them in the first place. *"The thief comes not but to steal, kill, and destroy," Jesus said. Well, these men surely were of the devil, because they stole planes, they killed people, and they destroyed those towers.*

"Oh, Michael . . . ." she sobbed. "The boys. You won't see them graduate, grow up. . . ."

She'd already been through the arguments with God. *It's not fair. You're not faithful. Why didn't you protect him? Why him? Why ME?* And despite praying, her heart ached and her head throbbed, and she just couldn't understand.

Except . . . *Only believe*, Jesus said.

"Fine," she said quietly. "What do you want me to believe?"

You know, came the reply.

But he's missing. Lord, if he was in that building . . .

Only believe.

"Only believe," she repeated out loud, and for the first time since the phone call her heart felt a little lighter.

Ground Zero, September 13th

How do they want us to do this?" Elam had Coolio's leash in one hand and a large black coffee in the other. He hadn't slept much last night, and doubted that Coolio got much rest either.

"We're gonna give the dog a piece of a fireman's clothing---something brought from the station. Give the dog an hour. If he doesn't have a hit in an hour, come back, and give him a new piece of clothing."

What does that make the odds? Even if we had 100 dogs here, and half of them get hits, that's only 50 guys before nightfall. But what the hell. We gotta try something.

"Fine. Give me a piece of clothing."

The captain handed him a box with shirts, socks, and other items from missing firefighters. Elam pulled out a jacket from the top, where someone had written a name with a black marker---"Callahan." Elam gave Coolio the scent. "There you go, boy," he whispered in Coolio's ear. Answer the Callahan family's prayers." He let Coolio off leash, and the dog, enthusiasm renewed, took off, nose to the ground, starting in small circles, then making concentric, ever-widening circles. Coolio broadened his circles for perhaps a half an hour when he started to head away from Ground Zero, zig-zagging as he went, keeping the scent right in the middle of his path.

He's going away from the WTC. What the hell?

"Coolio, what are you doing?" Elam almost ran to keep up with the dog, who snaked between debris piles and onto Broad Street, where he darted between emergency workers and police. "Coolio, the site's back that way!" But Elam knew better than to correct a search and rescue dog, or to use a sharp tone, especially when the animal wasn't deliberately disobeying. "Man, you're gonna get me in trouble. Now I've gotta explain this to the Cap."

Crap, I knew this wouldn't work. They're trying to make these German Shepherds into bloodhounds. We're wastin' time when he could be looking for guys who still might have a chance.

Within minutes, Coolio had Elam down an alley, close to a dumpster, where he began to sniff at a . . . *jacket? A fireman's jacket.* Then the Shepherd turned right out of the alley, away from Ground Zero, and zig-zagged down the street, stopping every few hundred feet to make small circles that started to get bigger until he headed toward Parkview Hospital at a run. Elam jogged to keep up with the animal.

Woodside, New York

After several rings, Shannon picked up the telephone. "Yes?"

"Shannon, this is Chief Knox."

Another chief. How many has she spoken to in 24 hours?

"I'm contacting all the families of, er, firefighters who are still missing."

"Yes, Chief?"

"Ah, we just want you to know that we're doing everything we can. The search teams are working round the clock with thousands of volunteers and . . . ."

"And you haven't found anybody, isn't that right?" Shannon knew the answer.

"Well, we found one woman this morning . . . ."

"But not a single firefighter."

"No, no firemen. But I want you to know that if you need anything, we have an organization set up to help with shopping, getting financial information, whatever you need. If you want someone to come to the house, we can arrange that."

"Thank you, Chief. I don't need any help right now."

When she hung up, she noticed Patrick and Sean standing in the door. Their heads fell. Every phone call now became a source of hope. Funny, in wars, a telegram or phone call or visit was always a bad sign. That's because you assumed your loved one was alive until told otherwise. But now…

"Sean, Patty, hang in there. There are thousands of people still working there. It's too early." *Do you believe that crap, Shannon?*

Patrick put his hand on Sean's shoulder, and covered his eyes. He'd been crying, off and on, all day. *Don't you let those boys down, Lord! You owe them a father.*

Only believe, came the little voice inside. *Do you know who I said that to?* The question was as audible as a doorbell. *Do you know Who I said that to?* It came again.

Shannon thought, *Who did He say that to?* Then she remembered: it was the father of a little girl who was already dead. Jesus said to the father, "Only believe" when she was already dead . . . before He brought her back to life!

Only believe. It came again.

"Fine," she mumbled, none to convincingly. "I'll believe the man who died is brought back to life." *What choice do I have at this point?*

Parkview Hospital

"I'm sorry, sir, you can't bring that dog in here!" The woman at the emergency room registration desk flew out of her chair, aiming to block the door, but Kevin Elam allowed Coolio to lead, ignoring the fact they were heading into a medical facility.

"You know where you're going, boy? We ain't exactly supposed to be here, ya know!"

Coolio dragged him straight to a curtained area, then, without waiting for his master to pull the curtain back, ducked under it and barked. By now the whole emergency room staff descended on Elam.

"Hey, buddy, get that damn animal out of here!" shouted an intern, grabbing the leash above Kevin's hands. "What do you think you're doing?" A nurse punched a number on her desk phone. "Get security to ER, right away." Then, turning to Elam, tried reason, "Sir, sir you *have* to get that animal out of here. No, no, no, no . . . ."

But by now, Coolio had virtually dragged Elam and the internist wrestling with him into the curtained cubicle, where he saw a middle-aged man with a splint and a head dressing.

"Who are you? What's with the dog?" asked the patient, as he raised himself up on his elbows. Coolio approvingly sniffed the smiling man from head to toe, as Elam struggled with the intern.

"Hang on!" he shot to the intern, then, turning to the man on the bed said, "Michael Callahan?"

"Who?" asked the man, as three pairs of hands from security guards pulled Elam out of the cubicle, Coolio grudgingly dragged behind him at the end of the leash.

"Coolio says you're Michael Callahan," the man yelled as he disappeared behind the ER doors.

"Who's Michael Callahan?" Then he paused for a moment: "Who's Coolio?"

Woodside, New York

"Not the phone again," moaned Shannon. "I can't take FDNY telling me they are 'doing everything they can.' That and two dollars will get me a Starbucks."

The phone would not relent.

"Sean, will you please answer that?"

Shannon heard only murmurs in the next room as Sean spoke to an unidentified person. Then, he appeared in the doorway with a puzzled expression on his face.

"Mom, it's somebody at Parkview Hospital. I think you better talk to them."

New York Depository Trust

It had taken Connie all day to get home from the World Trade Center on September 11, even with the train to Scarsdale. Traffic was bad, but often he remained in a fog. He took out his car keys and put them back in his pocket twice before reaching the car, then wondered where the keys were. He took a wrong turn in his own neighborhood, driving three blocks out of his path before shaking his head and turning around. When Jan finally saw him---a ghostly figure---neither said a word for endless minutes. They both knew how close he'd come to not standing in front of her.

Over the next two days, Connie's emotions went from relief and shock to outrage. He thirsted for revenge, and even, for a moment, toyed with enlisting in the armed forces. He realized he was too old and, by military standards, probably too soft, despite regular games of squash. But then he knew numbers and finance, and had worked with the president's Council of Economic Advisors. He put in a call to Louis Guzzo, his friend on the Council.

"Lou, Connie here . . . . Yeah, I'm ok. It was close. No, I really don't want to talk about it right now. Suffice it to say I saw things no one should ever see. Look, I want to help. I don't know what I can do, but I know I can do something. There has to be someone who can use my talent."

Lou thought a moment, then replied, "In fact, you're right. You are way too valuable to sit on the sidelines, and we've got a helluva mess at the Depository Trust. The President and the Treasury Secretary both want the stock exchanges back up and running as soon as possible, both to prevent further erosion of the panic they know will occur when the markets reopen, and to send a signal to our enemies that they haven't won. For that to happen, we need the banks to be able to clear checks and other accounts. You might be useful down there."

"At the Depository Trust? Sure. What do you need?"

"The explosions destroyed many of the phone systems, dozens of brokerage houses were either obliterated or had significant operations damaged when the towers collapsed, and the communications between banks are all screwed up. You've worked a lot in operational risk---your name came up in discussions the other day, actually. Specifically, hell, I don't know what would be involved. But if you can get down there today, I'm sure they could find something for you to do. I'm leaving in 20 minutes."

"Done. I'll be there as soon as I can," then suddenly realized he didn't have a clue as to whether he could even get into the City or make it to the Depository Trust. Still, Connie was relieved to be in the fight.

After exiting the train, it took Connie more than an hour to get to the Depository Trust, and even then he only got into the now-tightly guarded building by accident when another economist he knew showed up at the same time with an FBI agent. Inside, Connie donned the visitor ID and phoned the internal number Lou had given him. It was the office of the president.

"Alan Graebner's office. This is Nicole Ervin. I'm the executive vice president. How can I help you?"

Her voice was pleasant enough, but Connie could sense that the last thing she wanted to do was to "help" anyone.

"Hi, I'm Constantine Cataris. Lou Guzzo, I believe, gave you a call, and . . . ."

"Oh, Professor Catarkis!" Her tone changed instantly. "Lou said you were a whiz at banking and operational risk issues."

Connie blushed. "Uh, that's 'Cat-ar-is, no "k," and I wouldn't go that far. Anyway, he said maybe I could be of assistance to you, and I want to do whatever I can, both for you and for our country."

"Absolutely, Mr. Cataris---sorry, Professor Cataris. Very well, if you'll come up to my office---the guards will let you through---we have a thorny problem here that you are uniquely equipped to handle."

"I'll be right up."

Moments later, Connie was admitted to the president's office by two uniformed guards. He was greeted by a short, dark-haired slim (nearly anorexic) woman in a dark suit, and it was obvious she hadn't slept since the attack. Beneath her glasses, dark rings made her look like a raccoon.

"Hi," he said, extending his hand, "I'm Connie Cataris."

"Hello, I'm Nicole Ervin." Despite her fatigue, she bubbled with energy. "Thanks for volunteering to help. We have a huge problem."

Only one? Connie thought. *Maybe five thousand dead. The towers down. American markets are set to tank in what some insiders think could be a crash of 1929-type proportions. I'd say you have freaking Armageddon.*

"As you know, there is great concern in the White House and Treasury Department about turmoil in the financial markets when we reopen." She grimly looked at him. "Frankly, we expect a dive---a big dive. We want to prevent a total collapse."

"Not a lot you can do if people start selling their stocks," he offered. "It's a free market, after all."

"You're right about that. What we want to do, though, is ensure that there are no non-market factors that accelerate or exacerbate the downward trading that we know will occur. Right now, our major concern is that the problems with the phone lines and communications will exaggerate fears of people that 'something is wrong,' and that this, in turn, will lead to a panic, and we especially want to guarantee that the banking system is safe."

"I'm with you so far."

"I'm sure you're aware that the Wall Street Depository Trust Corporation handles---er, handled---all the market clearing for the exchanges?"

"Yes. I've never been here before, but I know how it operates, what it's job is."

"We need someone down there right now who can start contacting all the bankers, basically making sure that all the transactions can be executed when the NYSE is back up and running. As I understand it, you've done a lot of consulting with these banks on operational risks and that many of them have already put in place some of your recommendations, which is why we especially wanted you. You already know what they are doing."

Connie thought for a moment. "Why me? Every one of these banks has their own specialists."

"Because right now we need someone that isn't tied to any one particular bank. Also, down the line, we want people who know the big picture, who can explain the structure to people they are talking to, and who can lay out the consequences of failure. In short, it's a perfect job for a teacher!"

She's good, Connie thought. "Fine. Tell me where to go, what passes I need, and who to work with, and I'll start immediately."

Shown to a desk with the last computer readouts from the Depository Trust and a stack of data from New York Stock Exchange, Connie set down to work. His was a unique talent. Able to scan columns of financial or banking data and, in a heartbeat, circle the unusual or highlight an outlier, Connie plowed through the numbers. Seven hours later, he realized he was hungry, and he thought briefly about trying to find something to eat before grabbing another stack of papers. It was another six hours before he went home.

Parkview Hospital

While the hospital attendants labored to calm down Elam and Coolio, finally extracting from Kevin what the situation was, Regina Waterford finally answered her pager. When she reached the admitting desk, she found Coolio patiently sitting next to Elam, who was drinking another coffee.

"I know you've told others," she said, "but tell me what you're doing here with the dog."

Elam studied Regina, then launched into the events of the past 36 hours with the missing fire crew. "I contacted the animal rescue unit, and they will be here any second to take Coolio back. He's still needed back at Ground Zero."

For a moment, the gravity of what had happened weighed on both of them, when, outside, an SUV marked "FDNY Canine Unit" rolled up.

" 'Bout time. I put the call in 30 minutes ago." Elam knew the driver had done a remarkable job getting there in such a short time, but he had to let off steam somehow.

"Yeah, yeah," Dan Hieland snorted, waving off Elam. Hieland had been pressed into emergency taxi service, as there were only a few drivers trained to handle the dogs. "Come on Coolio, man. Let's go for a ride." He took Coolio's leash and led him out to the SUV, then headed back to Ground Zero. The dog energetically bounded into the SUV.

Waterford watched the dog depart, then looked at Elam skeptically. "So you think your rescue-dog-turned-bloodhound found a missing fireman? That would be a first."

Elam was convinced. "This guy's FDNY." She waved him along, and they walked back through the emergency doors.

"Well, can't hurt to check. All he told me was that he remembered something at Yankee Stadium, but he wasn't wearing any fire gear. Come on, our mystery man has been moved over to 4-A," she said, swinging back the curtain to reveal an empty bed.

Ground Zero, Fire Department Command Center

"He *what*?? Why didn't you just use the dog again? You what? Terrific," Chief Knox shouted sarcastically. He covered the mouthpiece and rolled his eyes at Captain Burt Allen. *They already sent the dog back here*, he mouthed, and it was Allen's turn to roll his eyes.

"Well, can you track the guy down?"

Kevin Elam, on the other end of the phone, was agitated enough. "With what, Chief? Do you want me to try to pick up the scent?"

"How did he get out? I mean, wasn't he hooked up to tubes and crap?"

"One IV, but he took it out. Look, what do you want me to do?"

"Ok, ok, hang on. How sure are you this guy is FDNY and not some homeless guy?"

"Chief, I found the jacket. How does a fireman's jacket get six blocks away from the World Trade Center?"

"How the hell should I know? We had a damn airplane engine land four blocks away. It's possible. I mean, if he took off his jacket in the hole, just after Brennan saw him, ... Ah, hell. It is unbelievable I guess. So what do you want to do? It's already too late to use a new dog, and I bet even Coolio couldn't find that scent now."

"Well, why doesn't he just go home? I mean, he knows who he is for Christ's sake!"

"Uh, that's the thing, Chief."

Knox's shoulders dropped and his eyes squinted up as Allen gave him a funny look. "That's *what* thing? The guy *does* know who he is, doesn't he?"

"Umm, not exactly. The hospital staff said that he has amnesia. He could come out of it any time, or not."

The Chief exploded. "So we actually may have *a survivor* but you LOST HIM and he doesn't know he's a fireman?? Hooo—ly Christ." By then, the gaggle of captains and other chiefs next to Knox had stopped their own work and were eavesdropping on the entire conversation, most of them shaking their heads in disbelief.

"Ok, you come back here. You ain't a detective, and you're sure not a dog. In the meantime, I'll talk to the police, and have them search the area . . . that is, if they can spare some men, seeing as though *WE HAVE A LITTLE BITTY PROBLEM HERE!*"

Knox was yelling so loud that Elam thought the cell phone would melt. He clicked it off and turned to Waterford. "Wherever this guy went, I won't be looking for him."

"You're just going to...to *leave* him?" she asked incredulously.

"Look, doc. I can't do anything on my own. I've got orders, and I don't have the dog. I'm sure his memory will come back soon, and he'll get ahold of us." He spun around to leave, then, regretted his tone. "I'm sorry, doc. But I gotta get back."

Chapter 14

The Streets of New York

The pit of hell. That phrase kept coming up as his struggled to see any light at all. Yet, there was light, a sliver at first, then, as he followed it, a stream, then a river, then a cascade. Sunshine, though dimmed by smoke and haze.

Then he felt himself flying. It was a pleasant sensation, as he recalled. Flying. Imagine that. Then he hit the earth, then pain.

He didn't know how long he lay there, but he instinctively crawled away from the smoke. And crawled, and crawled. After a while, he was on his feet, staggering. It's an alley? It was so hot, he took of his coat---it was a big coat---and some boots. Was he a cowboy? The throbbing in his head nearly blinded him, and his ears rang. He got up and staggered another few hundred feet before collapsing again.

How long had he lay there? Who knows. Was it seconds? Someone helped him up. Was it a policeman? He could hardly see, by then, the pain in his head was so great. Then there was the doctor, and the man with the dog.

The whole thing made him nervous. He felt a little better, and nothing was seriously wrong. Something told him to leave. And . . . what's with the dog? Am I a criminal? What if the authorities catch me? Something isn't right---besides being beaten up and smelled by a police dog. Something terrible had happened. Did I do it? Am I responsible for some horrible thing? He decided to leave as soon as the hospital people got the dog out. Sitting up, he disconnected himself from the monitors and pulled the IV out, and grabbed his pants. I still don't have shoes, he noticed. As best as his damaged body would let him, he hustled to the front, where he saw a crowd of people in a heated debate with the man and his dog.

Then an image came to him. Yankee Stadium. Two hands reaching for a fly ball. I need to go to Yankee Stadium. But I'm not getting far without shoes.

There was no money, because he had no wallet in his pants. No keys. At the very least, he needed shoes to get to Yankee Stadium-- wait, Yankee Stadium is in New York, so am I in New York already? I think so. Outside the hospital, he slipped around a corner and leaned against an alley wall and looked down at himself. Definitely shoes. I need shoes. And maybe get rid of this ragged t-shirt. If I'm wanted for something, maybe I should look different. What did I do at Yankee Stadium?

People milled by him, many staring. He ignored them and looked at street signs, though the names didn't register. Are these New York streets? He looked in vain for a couple of names that he knew were in New York---Park Avenue, Madison Avenue, Fifth Avenue, Harlem, but saw none. It was still dim, and he could see large areas closed off by police barricades. The more he walked, the more he became aware of his bare feet. With no money, there was only one way to get shoes, and he wasn't too proud to try.

"Excuse me, can you help me? I've lost my shoes." A young man---a banker type, judging from the suit---stopped and looked him over.

"Man, you look like you've been through the ringer. Were you there? Have you been wandering all this time? Did you just get out of there?"

There? There where? Out? Of jail?

"Uh, yah," he replied, still puzzled. "I was there, and it wasn't fun, but I'm out now and can't remember much. The . . . ah, hospital just released me."

The man's eyes softened, and he reached inside his jacket for his wallet, pulling out $200. "Here. You need this. Get some shoes, some clothes, and a meal, although I don't know what's going to be open around here with all that's happened. They don't even want people on the streets."

What's happened? "Thanks. I'll definitely get some shoes. Thanks."

The man nodded and patted him on the shoulder. "I think there is something open down on Broad Street that might have what you need." He pointed over his shoulder.

Broad Street? That sounds familiar. "Ok. Then I'll go that way. Say, which way is Yankee Stadium?"

Stopping in mid-stride, the man surveyed his raggedy companion, and laughed. "Are you planning to go to a ball game like that? You know, they've canceled the games for a few days."

Looking at his torn shirt, he had to laugh too. "I don't know what I need to do at Yankee Stadium, but I know I need to go there."

"Well, it's that direction," the man said, pointing northwest, "and your department store is right there," pointing down the street to Macy's. "Good luck, pal."

The man slowly extended his hand and the stranger, who had already started off, stopped, reached out and said, "Really. God bless you."

"Thanks. Ah . . . Thank you very much." He crossed the street and headed for Macy's.

Even the homeless are affected by this attack, thought Connie Cataris as headed back to his temporary office of the Depository Trust and the stacks of stock sales documents that awaited him.

Woodlawn, New York

Shannon had been in a positive frenzy since the most recent call by yet another chief. Michael's jacket had turned up near Parkview Hospital, and they thought he might be there. She got both boys ready, and telephoned Maureen.

"We're heading down to Parkview right now."

"Shannon, has anyone confirmed that this man is Michael?"

"Well, they have his jacket," she said into the cell phone, wedged between her shoulder and mouth as she put on her tennis shoes. "Who else would it be?"

"Shannon, anyone can put on a jacket. Hey, it's probably him, but, you know, you might keep something in reserve until you know for sure."

"You're probably right, but, you know what? I *know* it's him. Gotta go. Call you from the hospital."

She and the boys had only been in the car for a couple of minutes when her cell went off again, and, of course it was another chief---Knox again. At least she knew this one.

"Mrs. Callahan, we have some difficult news."

Oh, God. No! Not after getting my hopes up! Shannon swerved the car over to the side, afraid she might vomit if Knox said what she expected him to say.

"What is it, Chief?"

"Ah, it seems that we *had* a man we think was Michael . . . ."

"Had?" Panic gripped her voice.

"Damn it, this is tough. The man we thought was Michael was in the ER when the rescue dog found him---that's when we called you a few minutes ago---but somehow, in the confusion, the guy walked out of the ER."

"He *walked out*?? How can he just 'walk out' of the ER? Wasn't he hooked up to things?"

"Yes, apparently he unplugged himself from his monitors, IV s, and so forth, and got out without anyone seeing him. Now, he doesn't have shoes, and his shirt and pants are all ripped, so he shouldn't be too hard to locate. But he also apparently had amnesia, so he may not know where he is or where he's going."

Shannon felt like laughing and crying at the same time. *He still may be alive . . . if it's him! But is it him? And if it is him, what if he is so lost, so confused, that he leaves New York? God how am I to deal with this?*

By this time, the boys were bombarding her with questions. "Where's dad?" "What's happening?" "Why did you stop?" She waved them off and asked the Chief, "What do you want us to do now?"

"I think it's best if you stay home---there's a chance he may start to regain his memory and get home, and we need someone there if that happens."

"Fine. Thanks, Chief . . . I guess." Shannon snapped the phone shut, and now had the odious task of explaining this bizarre situation to her boys---that their dad *what? Is alive? Dead? Missing? Missing again?*

Yankee Stadium

The grounds were locked up when he got there---the Major League Baseball Association had re-scheduled the New York teams to play away games for a while. Even looking through the iron gates, he kept seeing bright flashes, followed by total darkness. It wasn't a blackout, but it wasn't real. *What am I seeing?*

He moved around the perimeter of the House that Ruth Built, unable to shake the sight of a foul ball coming toward reaching hands. *His hands?*

Then, for the first time, he could see people around him. Someone to his right. A man and his family.

"Rod Trainer" someone said. Was it him? He was shaking someone's hand. Was it Rod's? Or Michael's? When did that happen? Before? He kept walking.

What was it about that ball and those hands? They weren't all his hands. *There is someone behind me.*

He could see a dark shape catching the ball . . . no, wait, the ball popped out of his hands . . . and *into mine?* Now he could see it: the man's black eyes. "Tough luck." He heard himself say, "Tough luck" and smile at the man. . . *who didn't smile back. Is he pissed?* Grabbing his forehead, he leaned against a section of the fence. *What am I missing? Who are these people?*

Tough luck. Rod Trainer. Tough luck. Yankees rule. Huh?

He had said that to the man, "Tough luck." *Who said that to the man? Him? Rod? Michael? Was he Rod?* "Yankees rule!" Someone said, "Yankees rule!" sort of as a "can-we-agree-on-that" kind of comment. Now he knew what disturbed him about this man.

"Only for ten more days," he said. *Huh? What the hell did that mean?* The arrogance in his eyes. Sheer hatred. Why was he even at a baseball game?

Trainer. He caught the ball . . . *or did I catch the ball? Or am I Trainer? Lessee. Am I him?*

The images stopped. No amount of concentration could get them back. He started walking along the fence line, still oblivious to people around him, lost in his memories . . . *or lack of them.*

"Hey, you. You gotta problem?" A burley black security guard bore down on him.

"No problem, except . . . I need to tell someone."

"Well," the guard answered, "there's a phone over there," and jerked his head over his left shoulder. *Anything to get rid of this guy.*

"Thanks . . . ah, . . ."

The guard stopped and cocked his head. "Don't tell me. You don't have a quarter." Without waiting for an answer, he dug in his pocket and pulled out some change. "Here, this oughta take care of your call."

"Thank you. It's just that I'm . . . ," *no, he probably already thinks you're a homeless bum. Are you?*

He didn't know why, but somehow he recalled "berries." *Blueberry? Cranbury. That was it. He . . . or Rod . . . lived in Cranbury, New York. No! Cranbury, New Jersey. Is that where I live?*

Directory assistance came on the line. "Ah, Cranbury, New Jersey. Rod Trainer." As he waited he debated what to say. "Hello, am I Rod Trainer?" "Hello, is Rod Trainer there?"

After three rings a female voice answered. It was a soft, pained voice. "Trainer residence," said Liza Trainer.

"Ah, hello . . . ." *crap, this is harder than I thought.* "I'm calling . . . for Rod Trainer?" He phrased it as a question.

There was silence at the other end for what seemed an eternity. He started to speak again when she said, "My husband is dead."

"Then I'm not your husband?" he blurted out. *God, how stupid that sounded!*

"Who is this?" Liza asked angrily. She'd had her share of nuts in addition to the friends, relatives, insurance agents, and pastors who called, and had not unlisted the phone number precisely for that reason. She had almost started to hang up when the voice yelled "We've met. I need *help!*"

"Who are you? Where have we met?" she continued, impatiently.

"I don't know the answer to the first question. I've been in an accident, and I can't remember. All I know is that sometime we--- you, Rod Trainer, and I---were at Yankee Stadium. I can see that part clearly . . . but, not much else I'm afraid."

Liza knew which game he referred to. They'd only gone to one in the last year. She doubted he was the strange-looking Arab that sat behind them---the one who nearly caught the foul ball. It must be . . . *the fireman!*

"I remember you, now. You're a fireman." She searched for the name, because she had only heard it tangentially. "Mark. No! Michael something. You're a New York fireman."

A fireman. So where are my clothes? My coat, hat, boots . . . . That's who the guy was in the hospital.

"Yes, I think you're right. Michael. That is my name. Michael. . . Callon, no! Michael Callahan. But I can't remember a thing before the cop took me out of that alley."

Liza sat down by the phone. "What alley? Were you at the World Trade Center?"

World Trade Center. Yes. I was there. Somewhere. "It's all so murky. Dark. I mean, literally, all I see when I think of it is darkness."

"Well," Liza replied, "that's probably because it was destroyed. Were you inside?"

"What do you mean, 'destroyed?' You mean one of the buildings that was on fire?" He still saw only black when he tried to focus on the shape of the buildings.

Tears formed in Liza's eyes. "No," she said softly. *God, how hard is this to tell someone else?* "Two days ago Arab terrorists hijacked some airplanes and flew two jetliners into the two World Trade Center buildings. Both buildings collapsed, completely. Nothing remains. They're still counting the bodies, but thousands have died, thousands more are missing . . . . Many firefighters." She heard a groan from the other end of the phone. *He doesn't need to know the rest.*

Then he asked, "Is Rod your husband . . . er, I'm sorry." *Stupid, stupid, stupid. She said he's dead.* "Rod---your husband---did he die in the WTC?"

Guess he does need to know the rest. She took a big breath, even though she had repeated the story for a dozen people over the past 48 hours. "There were two other hijacked planes. One flew into the Pentagon and killed over 100 people. Rod---yes, he was my husband---was on a fourth plane that was hijacked, and the government thinks the terrorists were going to fly it into the White House or the Capitol. But the passengers, including Rod, attacked the terrorists and managed to either get control of the plane or force them down." Then she knew that was too sterile, and she knew he's just ask another question, so before he could say anything, she added softly, "The plane crashed in Pennsylvania. All aboard died."

Michael was silent for a moment. "So your husband was a hero?"

Choking back tears, Liza answered, "Yes. But if you're a firefighter, you're a hero too. Now, don't you have someone worried about you?"

Woodlawn, New York

"Patty, can you answer that? Patty?" *Damn it, the kid hears nothing over those CDs!* Shannon dropped the laundry basked, not wanting to miss a possible update from the chief. A chief. Any chief, at this point.

Yanking up the receiver, she said "Chief?"

"Not yet, but some day soon I hope," came Michael's familiar voice.

Shannon sank to her knees, as the tears streamed down her cheeks as she sobbed, "Oh, my God. Oh, my God. Thank you, God. Oh, my God, Michael. Patty! Sean! Your dad is alive! Oh, God, Michael's alive."

PART THREE

INFINITE JUSTICE

Chapter 15

Washington, D.C., September 14ᵗʰ, 2001

Television cameras followed the President as he crossed the apse of the National Cathedral alone, looking neither left nor right, climbing the few stairs to the pulpit where he would deliver a speech that would heal the nation. Dignitaries filled the crowd, including Bush's father, former President George H. W. Bush, and his wife, Barbara, seated next to the President's wife, Laura. Alongside them was the former President Bill Clinton, his wife Hillary and daughter Chelsea, as well as most of the cabinet, and hundreds of family members whose relatives died at the Pentagon.

President George W. Bush knew he was under growing pressure to unite the nation and give it a moment to grieve. But he could not ignore the boiling national mood for revenge, either. His flat speech Wednesday night had proven unsatisfying, either as a call to arms or as a healing salve. He knew he must do better today.

Even though hundreds crammed into the Cathedral, the angle of the cameras made it appear that Bush was alone amidst high walls and stained glass. From the camera's eye, he carried the weight of the world and the responsibility of a generation.

This was the same man who admitted to having a drinking problem in younger years, and whose happy-go-lucky life style led him to mediocre grades in college and a failed oil venture. This was the same man who mangled syntax, and whose speaking missteps already had become known in the press as "Bush-isms." This was the man who had rescued the Texas Rangers as a baseball franchise but who joked that his most memorable move was trading star slugger Sammy Sosa to the Chicago Cubs.

Just a few months earlier, Bush had won the election by the narrowest of margins---one of the two closest elections in American history. A mere 530 votes gave him the state of Florida, and thereby, the election, by a single electoral vote.

It was then that the incumbent vice president, Al Gore, made a critical strategic error. First, he demanded a statewide recount, which took time. Then, convinced he could "cherry pick" selected heavily Democratic districts and mine "new" votes through a process known as "contesting" the returns, where individual canvassing boards reviewed every single ballot, Gore entered the "contest" phase. This rested on the dubious and unreliable premise that votes already counted would somehow yield a different result if re-counted, and, more important, it cost time. America's Founders set a Constitutional clock in motion with the November election, and presidential electors had to be certified by December. Gore had eaten up a large part of the clock already.

Then, during the tedious process of examining hundreds of thousands of ballots, even the local canvassing boards (mostly Democrats who favored Gore) threw up their hands in frustration, realizing they didn't have time to properly review every vote. Meanwhile, Bush did not idly sit by: his legal team challenged the constitutionality of only counting some Florida ballots and not others under the "equal protection" clause of the Constitution. In the end, the United States Supreme Court agreed, 7-2, that "cherry-picking" was illegal and that the only proper recount would be a statewide recount . . . but by that time, the clock had run out on Gore.

Having received a final concession, President-elect Bush was sworn in. Throughout it all, he quietly and confidently waited at his ranch, never losing faith. It was that faith thing that had so many people so concerned. Bush was the first president to name Jesus Christ as the Lord of his life on national TV. Not some oblique reference to being "born again," or a generic tip of the hat to "God." No, even as a candidate, he went whole hog and uttered the "J-word." God has a way of honoring those who honor Him and His word doesn't return void. David learned that while on the run from Saul's armies; the Messiah said so Himself, many times.

So Bush put his faith into practice. He actually loved those who hated him, entertaining political enemies at the White House, celebrating the achievements of some of his nastiest critics. The man learned the truth of the scripture that said by praying for your enemies, you heap burning coals upon their heads. The more they reviled him, the more he smiled, and, in turn, the more they writhed in anguish.

But the bitter and close contest had left the government as divided as the country. Although the new president managed to get a tax cut and a rump version of "educational reform" passed through the Senate, most of his agenda stalled. On September 10, the most controversial policy issue in the administration was Bush's decision to allow limited stem-cell research on embryonic stem cells. Then, on September 11, he visited an elementary school in Florida, touting his education policies.

There, while Bush sat reading to third graders, Chief of Staff Andy Card whispered something in his ear about a plane hitting one of the World Trade Center towers. *What a lousy pilot,* Bush thought. Like millions of Americans who heard the news, he assumed it was a Piper Cub with a drunk pilot. Then he learned of the second explosion. Bush hastily finished the lesson with the school children, and excused himself.

For several hours, the President was whisked from location to location based on intelligence that revealed that the terrorists actually knew the call sign of Air Force One---a call sign that was changed daily! In short, the Secret Service was convinced that Air Force One itself was also a target, prompting them to keep the Commander in Chief away from Washington for most of the day. Bush's abrupt and at times oddly-worded statement at the elementary school (he called the terrorists the "folks who did this" rather than despicable cowardly murderers) was followed by an equally unsatisfying address from an air base.

Finally, he's had enough. Bush overrode the Secret Service and insisted on a return to D.C., whereupon he made a better speech to the nation---yet one still with a disturbing lack of emotion. Bush later revealed that it was not the time for an "Armageddon"-type speech of retaliation, but even his supporters began to wonder if he was up to the job in this horrible moment. Perhaps the critics were right: he was a lightweight, a man whose lack of intellect or international depth prevented him from seizing the moment.

Perhaps.

Or perhaps Bush, who was more given to genuine (as opposed to *faux*) emotion, worried that he would show weakness on the national stage, giving our enemies hope and solace. As a result, he appeared stilted and robotic.

It soon became clear that the new President was not given to empty threats. He had no intention of going on national television within 24 hours of the attack and issuing vague warnings about potential actions he "might" take. No, he kept his cards close to his vest, and if it cost him a little in terms of connecting with the American public in the initial hours of the trial, it would stand him in good stead later when friend and foe alike would learn that he meant what he said, and said what he meant.

It also became clear, both throughout the Florida post-election battle, and during his first months in office, that he was a deeply religious man who walked the walk of faith. He frequently inserted scripture in his speeches, and not for window dressing. The fact that Bush took his faith seriously outraged and frightened the Left in America more than any single policy that Bush advocated. Just by living, the man exposed the hypocrisy and moral decay of the Left, and for that he could not be forgiven.

But now, in this giant cathedral, even the icons of the Left had to sit silently, lest they alienate the entire American public, the large majority of whom were out for revenge on the devils whose actions now brought these hundreds of mourners together before the unproven President. In the moments before Bush spoke, he sat quietly and prayerfully with his wife. If his faith ever faltered, it was pretty clear hers did not. Following an unbearably emotional series of songs, it seemed impossible for Bush to deliver a speech without blubbering, unless he was on drugs.

The cameras tracked him to the pulpit where he solemnly began.

"We are here in the middle hour of our grief. On Tuesday, our country was attacked with deliberate and excessive cruelty. We have seen the images of fire and ashes and bent steel."

"Now come the names, the list of casualties . . . . They are the names of men and women who began their day at a desk or in an airport, busy with life. They are the names of people who faced death and in their last moments called home to say, "be brave," and "I love you." They are the names of passengers who defied their murderers and prevented the murder of others on the ground. They are the names of men and women who wore the uniform of the United States and died at their posts."

"Our responsibility to history is already clear: to answer these attacks and rid the world of evil. War has been waged against us by stealth and deceit and murder. This conflict was begun on the timing and terms of others; it will end in a way and at an hour of our choosing."

"Grief and tragedy and hatred are only for a time. Goodness, remembrance and love have no end, and the Lord of life holds all who die and all who mourn. . . . As we've been assured, neither death nor life nor angels nor principalities, nor powers nor things present nor things to come nor height nor depth can separate us from God's love. May He bless the souls of the departed. May he comfort our own. And may He always guide our country. God bless America."

Still dry-eyed, Bush slowly closed his notes and walked back across the empty ground that separated him from Laura and parents. Weeping swept over the audience, and tears swelled in the eyes of television viewers and radio listeners. The President had served notice that God's hand had been on him through the razor-thin election, and that His grace now rested on him fully as the nation girded for war. His quiet confidence and spectacularly perfect speech let America's enemies know they had gravely miscalculated. Now the same man who had practiced his faith through a tight election and nerve-wracking post-election contest, hoisted the weight of the world and put it on his modest shoulders as though it were another unpleasant duty.

In the brief time it took Bush to get back to his seat, one could almost hear God whispering in his ear, "You can do this George. I am with you always. And you can do this well, because I go before you. And don't worry about the weight: I've got it." And in his eyes, you saw Bush respond, "I know, Lord. I know. Thank You."

Upon sitting down, Bush's dad reached over and grabbed his son by the arm. It was an unusual moment for the reserved father, and in a single movement his gesture said to the younger Bush, "I wish I could do this for you, son, but I can't. You have to do this on your own." The President squeezed back and his eyes said it all: "I don't have to do it alone, dad. I've got help."

Chapter 16

Situation Briefing Room, The Pentagon
September 15th, 2001

"And you're confident this is the plan you want me to present to the President on Monday?" Secretary of Defense Donald Rumsfeld, who could talk to you like a benign grandfather one minute and rip you open with a cutting criticism the next, grilled his Joint Chiefs of Staff. "You fellahs know me---I'm all for a more unconventional approach---but you'll really catch it from the press and some of your three-stars over this radical of a plan." He laid down the proposed course of action against the Taliban and al-Qaeda that he had reviewed with the Chiefs all morning, and took off his glasses.

"You've got the armchair generals, the people like Barry McCaffrey who get on all the networks, telling the world that this can't work, that we don't have enough boots on the ground. You know that don't you?" Rumsfeld—or "Rummy," as many affectionately knew him---surveyed the men around the table, each of whom had enough medals and ribbons to cover a wall. To a man, each nodded solemnly. The Chairman of the JCS, General Richard Myers, waited for anyone else, and when he saw no volunteers, spoke.

"Mr. Secretary, we can't wait. We can't do a D-Day-type build up that will take six months, nor do we dare just drop some bombs and call it a day." Nods around the table inspired him to keep going. "We've asked Gen. Tommy Franks of CENTCOM to draw us up a plan." Myers pointed to the video monitor from Tampa, Florida, where Franks, the head of Central Command, or CENTCOM, in charge of the Middle East, sat.

"Thank you, Gen. Myers. Mr. Secretary, my team has put together a plan. We think we can get the boots on the ground pretty quickly, but we need to hit these bastards and hit 'em hard. And hit 'em *now*! We can insert Special Ops, Delta, CIA, heck, even probably some airborne or Ranger/Seal units in immediately. We've already got the liaisons set up between the CIA and the Northern Alliance."

At the head of the table, Rummy broke into his trademark grin. Puzzled, Myers paused.

"I'm sorry, General," Rumsfeld said, "and you're on a roll. It's just that the name 'Northern Alliance' always makes me think of Luke Skywalker fighting the evil empire."

Franks saw the humor as well, and smiled. "Well, Mr. Secretary, it is interesting because our guys, *right now*" he said, jabbing the table with his finger for emphasis "are in the mountains riding around with these Afghan forces on horseback while carrying their cell phones and laptops and using GPS to prepare smart bombs to hit the Taliban. And I saw the *Star Wars* movies, and you're right, some of our guys do look like Luke on his Tuan Tuan or Han Solo hanging out with the Ewoks." Then he grew deadly serious. "Except Osama's evil empire will never know what hit it!"

Rumsfeld was pleased. "Very well, General, continue to make your point, and pardon my interruption."

"Yes sir. In a nutshell, Mr. Secretary, this is a new kind of war. We're going in low tech at the beginning, allowing the Northern Alliance---who hate the Taliban and bin Laden---to take some of the northern cities with our support while we get ready for a full-scale push in a couple of months. For now, we can put probably 20,000 forces on the ground in various capacities. We aren't talking heavy artillery, and certainly not Abrams tanks. But we don't think that's necessary right now. We don't want to repeat the mistakes of the Soviets, marching 140,000 men all over those hills. Instead, we have a plan here to fight a new kind of war. Surgical. Precise. Deadly. We won't ever shy away from putting in the troops we need, but our plan calls for a maximum of about 10,000 infantry. Their job is to serve as the 'herders'---to funnel the Taliban and al-Qaeda to targets where we will then annihilate them. Once we're on top of the bad guys, we can call in precision guided weapons and that's our equalizer."

Rummy liked it. He had fought for exactly such a reconfiguration of the military for years, battling the Old Guard/Cold War generals who still thought in terms of massive tank and helicopter formations. The Gulf War had, unfortunately, only strengthened them in their commitment to preserve the status quo.

"Gen. Franks," Rumsfeld said into the monitor, "that is the type of war we have been reconfiguring for. Now, what do you need from me? From the President?"

"Mr. Secretary, the most important thing we are going to need is access. We need bases or over flight rights from Turkmenistan, Pakistan, and Tajikistan. Right now, we already have a secret deal in place with the Uzbekis to a base we call 'K-2' in the south. But we're also going to need all sorts of logistics support help from our current Middle Eastern allies---Qatar, Kuwait, Bahrain, United Arab Emirates, and, of course, Saudi Arabia."

Rummy winced. "The Saudis won't come cheap, General. Politically, I mean. Whatever they do will have to remain quiet."

Franks nodded. "I know, Mr. Secretary. I've been in that region many times and I've met personally, as you know, with most of the leaders of these countries. I understand their, shall we say, special circumstances. But you asked what I needed, and I'm telling you."

"Noted, General. I'm sure the President will get Gen. Powell on these problems right away. Good job, General Franks. Is there anything else?"

For a moment, Franks hesitated.

"Speak freely, General. I'm sure the President wants any insight you have."

"Very well, Mr. Secretary," Franks replied. "Although we have been absorbed with planning for this Afghanistan operation, if I read the President right, he is treating this war on terror like a broader problem---not confining it to a single country."

Puzzled, Rumsfeld put down his pencil. "Go on, General."

"Mr. Secretary, Iraq comes up in almost every plan we do. It affects our flyover---they shoot at our planes constantly---we are daily looking at threat reports about chemical and biological weapons. In short, Mr. Secretary, the United States is going to have to deal with this threat, too."

Rumsfeld stared straight ahead for several seconds. "General, I think the President knows that. Right now, however, our immediate task is to clean out al-Qaeda. When and if the President wants a broader plan, we'll certainly ask you for one."

"Yes sir," Franks replied.

Within an hour, Rummy was on the phone to Bush. "This is no holds barred, right Mr. President? Whatever it takes to go into those mountains and get bin Laden? Yes, sir. Whatever it takes. We have a good man on this---Gen. Franks. You'll have the plan on your desk tomorrow."

Ft. Lewis, Washington, U.S. Army Rangers
2nd Battalion, October 2001

Sgt. Shane "Mick" Roland stood, hands on hips, as a squad of Rangers jogged past him, singing one of the cadences---something about a "Model A Ford and a Tank Full of Gas . . . ." that he'd forgotten. He watched them disappear around the barracks, headed out for Tacoma's thick forest, which, this time of year, would be chilly, but otherwise not too bad of a run.

"Wish you were back at Fort Benning drilling the rooks?" asked Sgt. Jaime Hernandez, or "Chico" as he was known. "Admit it. You want to be teaching young pukes what it means to be a Ranger."

Mick smiled. He indeed missed his days as a drill instructor, but active duty was better. He'd missed the Gulf War and Mogadishu, having only been assigned as an instructor in 1992. Since then, none of his graduates had seen any real combat. Nor had he. In 1999, he had a chance to join a regular active-duty Ranger unit, and jumped at the chance, becoming a part of 2nd Battalion, Alpha Company, along with Chico. Mick had 2nd Platoon, Chico had 3rd.

"Chico, the last thing I want to do is go back to wiping butts and holding hands. I'm trained for combat. I missed Mog. I ain't missing this one."

"You think we're gonna get the call? Clinton just fired off some 'Hawks.'"

Mick stopped dead in his tracks and froze Chico with his icy gaze. "Bush ain't Clinton. We're goin' to war, and we're gonna kick ass."

Chico broke into a broad grin, and slapped Mick's hand. "That's what I'm talkin' about, bro."

But Mick was on a roll. "I got no special insight, but I'm tellin' you what any general knows: we're gonna have to go into Afghanistan, and that means mountains, and mountains mean Rangers, *comprende*?"

"You got that right, *jefe*. If the brass knows what they're doing, we can kick those rag-heads all the way to China."

"Yeah, but already you got CNN, NBC, all those liberal asswipes on TV saying we can't do it, that . . ." Mick assumed a smarmy, gay lisp, "no army has ever conquered Afghanistan. The British failed, the Soviets failed, blah, blah, freakin' blah!"

"The Limeys and the Russkies ain't Americans and they ain't Rangers," Chico said, spitting on the ground. "Didn't we hear this crap before?"

"You mean in the Gulf War? Yeah, absolutely."

"Yeah, they were sayin' that we'd lose 80,000 men invading Kuwait. What a stinkin' pile of manure. We kicked the snot out of the Iraqis and lost fewer than 150 men---and the most casualties occurred in that Scud missile hitting that barracks and in a "friendly fire" shooting by a U.S. helicopter. The 'mighty Iraqi army' killed a grand total of about 80 troops. I don't think you'll find a general in history that wouldn't call that spectacular."

"Unless you're one of the 80. But hey, I know what you're saying. My dad was in Vietnam at the end of his career, and we've talked quite a bit about how much the services have changed. They ain't nuthin' like they were 30 years ago. I think you can say we learned our lessons in Vietnam."

"Yah, Mick, except every once in a while, like in Mog, the generals get amnesia."

"Chico, that wasn't the brass. Hey, I'm no fan of brass, but that was Clinton callin' the shots there. If they gave the Rangers and Delta the gunships and tanks they'd requested, we'd *still* be stackin' the bodies of those Sammie warlords."

"I suppose you're right. At any rate, I don't think we're gonna have a lot of restraints put on us this time. People are *pissed*."

"Let's just hope they stay that way. As long as the public stays behind us, we can take out every rag-head terrorist between Mecca and Malaya, along with anyone who wants to help 'em. Hey, I gotta run 2nd platoon. I'll catch you later, Chic."

"Stay solid, *esse*." The two bumped fists and took off.

Mick got back to the barracks, ready to lead his platoon on a 3-mile run when Lt. Carl Chilton intercepted him.

"Sergeant, pass the word. All troops are to report at 1600 hours in full battle gear."

Mick looked inside at 2nd platoon. *War, huh?* Some of the men he was looking at would not come back . . . *but, if that's the way it has to be, who better to lead the way than 2nd platoon? And if we're going to war, one more good run can only help.*

"All right, ladies, saddle up. Three miles today, and we're gonna beat our previous time by at least ten seconds." Groans went up all around.

"Then, you are to shower and report to drill field in battle gear by 1600 hours, sacks packed, socks stocked, and fear gear! Gentlemen, I think the balloon is going up, and when the balloon goes up . . ."

". . . *Rangers Lead the Way*" came the shout from 2nd platoon. Mick turned and waited outside. Inside, Rangers exchanged solemn looks. There were no hoots of joy, or macho bravado, but rather flinty determination, as the methodically readied their gear.

Suddenly a private ran by. "The President is about to make an announcement." Mick turned to 2nd platoon. "Run canceled. Get out that TV." In a flurry of activity, the Rangers spun the television around as Ari Fleischer, the White House press secretary, said "The President will address the nation at 12:50."

A few moments later, Bush appeared, sitting behind a desk in the Treaty Room. "Good afternoon. On my orders, the United States military has begun strikes against al-Qaeda terrorist training camps and military installations of the Taliban regime in Afghanistan." The Rangers looked at each other. Bush went on to elaborate the distinction between the Afghan people, who were virtual slaves of their oppressive government and the Taliban regime that supported bin Laden and al-Qaeda. It may not have been clear to many Americans listening to that speech that Bush had ordered a completely different response than had Clinton. He carefully avoided giving specifics, but rather promised only justice for the "barbaric criminals who profane a great religion by committing murder in its name. . . .We did not ask for this mission, but we will fulfill it. The name of today's military operation is 'Enduring Freedom.'"

Bush had already made one concession to the politically correct police by changing the name from "Infinite Justice," which carried anti-Muslim overtones. But he signaled this was a total commitment by activating the National Guard and calling up the Reserves, something never effectively done in the Vietnam War. "The battle is now joined on many fronts," he continued. "We will not waver; we will not tire; we will not falter; and we will not fail. Peace and freedom will prevail."

The troopers stared at the set for several moments after Bush finished. If it had meant to be a rousing, rah-rah speech, it wasn't. But every one of them knew that *this time* the United States took this seriously, and that *this* president intended to defeat the enemy, not just slap his hand. Mick broke the silence: "Let's roll, 2nd platoon!" "HOO-AAAH" came the response.

Mazar e-Sharif, Afghanistan, October 2001

Agents in the Company called him "Camel," for his Arabic name, Kham-el Hamzi. A Saudi by birth, he was an American citizen. Camel was also one of the best Pashtun speakers that the CIA could put in the field, and was better-than-average with Arabic and Farsi. For two weeks he had been inside Afghanistan, having driven in overland from Ternez, Uzbekistan, where it met a representative of the so-called "Northern Alliance," a group of tribes in the northern part of Afghanistan that steadfastly resisted the Taliban. Although the Taliban controlled Mazar e-Sharif, their soldiers could not venture far from town, or their headless bodies would be discovered next to the heads on a stake.

Although he knew better from the previous trips, Camel half-expected a Bedouin-type tribesman instead of the rough mountain fighters he usually met. Instead, at Ternez, he was surprised when an 18-year-old in a Nike t-shirt and jeans drove up in a chewed up Range Rover. "Mohammed al-Droge," he said hopping out of the jeep and shaking Camel's hand. Camel nodded, and introduced himself as Abdul Nozri. He seldom used his real name, even in the States, and certainly not in the field.

"Your trip was pleasant," asked Mohammed, flashing a knowing smile (minus a tooth) that the trip was anything but pleasant.

"It is always a challenge, and a pleasure, to enter your country," Camel diplomatically replied, then immediately began to pump the young driver for information. "How close are your forces to Mazar e-Sharif?"

"We operate right up to the city's edge, and the Taliban forces don't dare leave the city at night," Mohammad answered proudly, gesturing him to climb in the Range Rover.

"Sounds like General Masood is in control of the battlefield," Camel smiled.

The young man nodded enthusiastically. "Yes, Masood is a great leader. He has united all the northern tribes---what you Americans call, the 'Northern Alliance,' to evict the evil Taliban. They are not true Muslims. They are heretics, and evil. Worse, they have brought in the Arabs."

Afghans hated Osama's crowd, thought Camel. *Afghans derisively referred to all foreign fighters brought in by al-Qaeda as "Arabs."*

He studied his young driver as the Rover hit 60 miles per hour. For Afghanistan, this was a pretty good highway---two lanes with intermittent potholes. But they were small potholes, and Camel could carry on a conversation if he yelled. Since his objective was to gather information, he made every effort to keep Mohammad talking.

"What are your forces? Are you badly outnumbered?" Based on the CIA's own reports, the Northern Alliance had about 15,000 men, but they were seasonal, and General Ahmed Masood could only count on half that number in any given battle with the Taliban. Still, he wanted to get Mohammad's reaction, partly to see how truthful (or informed) he was, and partly to keep the discussion going.

Mohammad turned and smiled. "General Masood will explain all things strategic to you. It is not my place. But know this: the Taliban cannot defeat us in the north."

Crap! The kid ain't dumb. But something troubled him: *"can't defeat us in the north?" Does that mean the Northern Alliance can't beat them in the south?* The central part of Afghanistan, which was flanked by Kabul on the Pakistani border and Herat on the Iranian side, was where all intel put Osama's main bases.

So the rat can scurry over to his friendly enclaves in Pakistan when he needs to. Camel knew that Bush already had put pressure on Pakistan's "President" and military strongman, Pervez Musharraf, to seal the border, but everyone knew that even if Musharraf made a determined effort to do so, it would take virtually the entire Pakistani army to clean out the area around Peshawar in the northern part of the Sulaiman Mountain Range. Musharraf was making all the right noises, but how effective he would be . . . *well, I'm not holdin' my breath,* thought Camel.

The kid said little else until they reached a series of dirt roads that seemed to turn into and alternating landscape of desert and small mountains, until they pulled into a large camp, bristling with pickups, horses, and above all, guns. Every man not only carried a weapon--- usually the Russian-made AK-47, but at least one bandolier slung across his body.

Mohammed escorted Camel to a tent, which, from the outside looked spartan. Inside, Camel found it cozy, with the earth floor covered by rugs, pillows, and mats. A makeshift fireplace in the middle of the room was necessary for the cold Afghan nights, and small desks and chairs were arranged so as to focus on the several maps pinned to the far tent wall. It was low tech, but effective.

A moment later a short man with a beard, wearing a flak jacket and a short, Afghan headdress entered the room. "I am General Masood," he announced, bowing, then extending his hand. Camel bowed, shook hands, and said, "I am honored. My name is Abdul." Masood looked at him skeptically, as if to say, *"We both know this game,"* and paused. Finally he said, "As you wish, Abdul."

"I assume you are from the CIA, and I assume that you will not be the first American agent to come to Afghanistan."

"Actually, I am a Saudi. Otherwise, you are correct, general, but unfortunately, large numbers of our men will not arrive for weeks."

"And in the meantime, you want us to fight the Taliban for you, is that correct?"

The general obviously knows the score. Camel considered his options, following the CIA playbook of desirability, but, sizing up Masood, decided this was the time for truth . . . or, at least, a measure of it.

"Here's the situation, general. Americans are pissed, big time. Do you understand that phrase?" Masood smiled and nodded enthusiastically. "This time, we're not going to fire some cruise missiles at Osama. We're going in and kick ass. You're familiar with that phrase?

Another knowing smile from Masood.

"Yes, you're absolutely right. We need help until our people get here---but they *will get here.* In the meantime, I'm prepared to offer you an unprecedented level of intelligence support, air power, up-to-date weapons, and anything else we can provide---except American troops---until those forces get here. One way or another, the Taliban will be gone. We aren't going to play "pick the leader" for you Afghans---and I know, you probably don't have a lot of reason to trust us on this, but that's a fact. Our only goal here is to make sure that *whoever* is in charge of Afghanistan does not support terrorists and is not a throwback to the 8th century in terms of their religion. Democracy, parliament, spin-the-bottle, we don't give a crap, as long as you are 100% terrorist-un-friendly. Am I clear?"

During Camel's exposition, several of Masood's lieutenants had joined them in the tent. Camel, suddenly noticing them, surveyed their looks. They were smiling.

He added, "and we plan to assist our friends here with unprecedented amounts of money. Still with me?"

They were all grinning like they had been handed the keys to a condo in Venice Beach.

Masood crossed his arms, studied the agent in front of him, then looked at the map. "We hate the Taliban, and not just because they are political rivals. They are bad for our people. They have set back progress---what very little of it there was in Afghanistan---30 years. But to take in these Arabs as friends and to link our tribes to these attacks . . . . It is completely condemned by the Koran. We fought the Taliban without you. We will fight them with you. We welcome your help, but you do not mind if we, shall we say, question your promise to leave after toppling the Taliban and capturing Osama bin Laden. If you do, well enough. If you overstay your welcome ...

He looked at Camel with a lifted eyebrow, and Camel responded with an understanding nod.

"Regardless, if we---and you---are successful, there will be some work to do in rebuilding the nation back to where it was before the Taliban . . ." he added, "and before you leave."

Camel agreed. "Yes, my government is fully aware of its responsibilities. Masood, the government now is different from the last one, and I know these may seem like empty words to you. But this president realizes that we cannot give "place to the devil," I believe the Bible says. We cannot allow conditions to be such that terrorism seems a good employment choice. So Afghanistan is key, not only to getting rid of al-Qaeda, but in establishing a country that won't *tolerate* groups like al-Qaeda."

Masood surveyed his lieutenants, few made any motion, but he knew their mood. They all agreed. "Well enough. Each day brings its own trouble. For now, the concern must be with the Taliban forces in Mazar e-Sharif. To this point, we have been unable to dislodge them. They have too much artillery and too many armored vehicles. What can you do about that?'

"Plenty. One of my assignments is to be a liaison between you and six more men who will be here tomorrow."

"*Six men*! You propose to aid us with six men?"

"General, these are only the most advance guard. They are Delta Force soldiers who are experts in laser targeting. Whatever they target, or "paint" with their lasers, will be destroyed by American aircraft and missiles that you will never see. They will quickly eliminate---or at least, greatly reduce---your problem in Mazar e-Sharif with artillery and armor."

Masood was a shrewd combat leader, but he had only seen vague references to such weapons from the Gulf War. He held up his hand, palm first, to Camel, instructing him to silence while he conversed quietly with several of his officers. They gestured enthusiastically.

"My officers tell me you can do this with a great degree of success."

"We can. If the United States removes the enemy's armor and artillery, can your forces take the city?"

Wondering if he had just made a deal with the devil, Masood confidently replied, "We can."

"Good. Then by tomorrow, my team will arrive by helicopter, and we can commence offensive operations at your command."

The Americans, thought Masood, *will certainly bring a new form of 'enlightenment' to the Taliban!*

"General," yelled the Ram. "The CNN news crew is here to interview you."

Masood liked the Ram---his name was Ahmed Phalevi, but he was as clever a scout as anyone had ever seen. He could get into the most impassible mountain valleys, hence, "the Ram." He had been a loyal member of the Alliance for close to two years, and Masood trusted him with his life.

Two men walked behind Phalevi, one with a video camera on his shoulder, the other with a microphone extended and a cord reaching back to the first. Masood dutifully walked over to meet them. He had been contacted several weeks ago about an interview. Anything that helps bring down the Taliban.

"Blessings be upon you. Where would you like to talk?" Masood asked gesturing to the mountains behind him. When he turned back, he saw that the cameraman had extracted a gun from the camera. He had no time to reach for his own pistol. Six shots hit him square in the chest before his soldiers gunned down the "CNN" crew.

He would not know that his assassins had been sent directly on the orders of Osama bin Laden.

New York City

For months now, Connie Cataris had buried himself in work. There had been a couple of funerals to attend, but he hadn't known the people particularly well. He never spoke of his experience that day, and never even told Jan about the falling bodies. More than once he pondered the randomness of the event. *Some people were there by accident. Some were saved because they were late. Some things are out of our control. Some things are in God's control, and I'm not Him.*

It was too much to dwell on. Instead, he pored over bank data and the stock transaction reports. He had helped the Depository Trust reopen without incident, connecting back up all the accounts that it was possible to repair, and while it certainly wasn't perfect---the markets dropped hundreds of points in the weeks after 9/11--- America's economy had survived. Many industries would never recover, Connie knew. Insurance, airlines, some tourism would be permanently scarred by the terror attacks. The airlines were already barely solvent, and the insurance companies had needed a special congressional bailout to protect them from 9/11-related claims.

Nevertheless, the U.S. economy crept back, and Connie took some small pleasure in knowing he had helped stabilize the system. But sometime around November, as he hoped to wrap up his work, Connie noticed---almost by accident---some disturbing transfers and stock sales. It appeared that an overseas group, *l'Joliette du Mer*, had an inordinate amount of activity in the week before 9/11, particularly in airlines and insurance stocks. He hadn't caught it in the immediate aftermath of the terror strikes as Connie had been focused on the bank systems, but when the markets stabilized, the irregularities stood out even more.

On his own, Connie started to crunch the data seven ways from Sunday. No matter how he sliced it, it appeared that someone from a French company, *l'Joliette du Mer* had inside information that the attacks were coming. Now, he had taken this as far as he could. Connie picked up the phone to call the Council of Economic Advisors.

"Lou? Connie. Oh, yeah, the banks were pretty sturdy. I was surprised how many of them adopted my operational recs that I made some five years ago. But in the process of doing that work, and cross referencing it with the Stock Exchange data, something kept jumping out at me."

He could hear the seriousness in Lou's voice on the other end. Lou knew Connie was given to understatement, if anything. For Cataris to suggest that there was something amiss meant that he had overwhelming evidence. "Connie," he replied, "this is out of my jurisdiction. You need to be running this by the FBI, a guy named Paul Andrade. I think you'll find him a good listener."

Within moments, Connie punched in the number Lou gave him at the FBI.

"Office of Counter Terrorism," came the female voice on the other end.

"Uh, hello. My name is Constantine Cataris, and I'm calling for Mr. Andrade. I was told to contact him if I found anything in my analysis."

"Mr. Andrade is in a meeting. Where are you calling from?"

"I'm working with the New York Depository Trust. Lou Guzzo at the Council of Economic Advisors said I should . . . ."

"Oh, just a minute. I have a list here of people that Mr. Andrade said to put through immediately if they called, and you're on it! Please hold."

Connie smiled, then frowned. *I'm on a list. That's either very good news, or very bad news.*

Shortly, Connie heard a voice on the other end. "Professor Cataris, thank you for calling. Lou said you had something that might be of interest to us?"

"Uh, yes, Mr. Andrade. Well, as you know, I've been working on stabilizing the banking system and stock market. This has required me to cross-reference variables . . . ah, excuse me. Economists' habit of drifting into 'academese.'"

Andrade laughed at the other end. "It's quite all right. However you have to explain it to me."

"Very well," Connie continued. "In a nutshell, I think I have evidence of stock tampering and maybe insider trading prior to 9/11."

"Are we talking New York brokerage houses?"

"No, sir. We're talking foreign influences."

"Care to be specific, Professor?"

"Not over the phone, sir. I think we need to get together. I need to show this to your analysts. If this is what I think it is, 9/11 just took on a whole new slant."

"From what Lou said, I agree. Can you be available tomorrow? I'll fly up with my key people. I'm going to bring a couple of CIA fellows along, too, Agents Harrison and Jackson. As you know, the President has insisted that we cooperate better on anti-terrorism, and he's damn well right on that."

CIA. My God, what am I into. Connie paused for a second or two before remembering Andrade had asked him a question. "I can meet you then. Uh, that will be fine. Do you want to come to Columbia University?"

"No, I think we're going to need something more secure. I'll arrange for us to have the conference room of the Federal Reserve Bank. 10:00, OK?"

"Fine. I'll see you then." *CIA. For God's sake, I'm an economics professor, not a spook.* Connie hung up the phone, then stared at the stack of data in front of him. He hoped he was wrong about what he found. For the first time in his life, he hoped he wasn't as smart as he knew he was. *Connie, you are up to your neck.*

Chapter 17

Skies over Ternez, Uzbekistan

Chico obsessively cleaned his fingernails with his K-bar knife while Mick stared straight ahead, working his gum intensely. Interesting, thought Chico, that the K-bar---a cross between a Bowie knife and serrated line-cutter---was not developed by the Army or even the Marines but the Navy. *Damn pollywogs. Even a blind chipmunk finds an acorn now and then.*

Mick, sitting across from him, remained totally in the "zone." It was his ritual before a mission. He wouldn't talk to anyone until they disembarked, whether by parachute or, as they would later, march off a ramp. Sitting in silence, his mind replayed the mission over and over, even if it was only something trivial like setting up a camp, which they would do later, and prepare for ground transport to Afghanistan, which they would do within 36 hours. Their briefing was full of "TBDs"---to be determined, as events on the ground unfolded. So far, they knew they were to set up a camp, pick up ground transport to a Northern Alliance base outside Mazar e-Sharif, and integrate with the Northern Alliance forces under Ahmed Masood. They had all heard about him. He apparently was the only one with the connections to pull the NA tribes together, if you can ever "pull Afghans together" to do anything.

A voice came over the intercom: "Descent. Five minutes to land."

The Rangers put away walkmans and Chico sheathed the K-bar. Mick finally snapped out of the zone and gave Chico an encouraging nod. "You ready, *esse?*"

Chico replied with the Ranger acknowledgment, "Hoo-aah."

Within minutes, the 130 bounced onto the primitive airstrip—"landed" would be too generous—and the Rangers poured off the rear ramp. They assembled near a small building. Colonel S. C. "Scamp"

Meadows did not look pleased after meeting with the Afghan interpreter.

"All right, Rangers. Our job just got tougher." Grim looks were exchanged among the soldiers. "The NA commander, Gen. Masood, was assassinated while we were en route by a couple of Osama bin Laden's henchmen posing as a CNN news crew. Right now, as you might imagine, there is a little bit of turmoil in the NA to see who their new leader is, and, if you know anything about Afghan politics, this could get a little dicey. That doesn't change our mission: link up and work with *whoever* comes out of this as top dog. Meanwhile, don't do anything to appear to take sides among the NA tribes."

"Hoo-aaah" came the mass response.

"Now fall out. Lieutenants have the info on where we pitch camp. Dismissed."

Meadows turned to his interpreter and asked, "Now, who the hell is in charge?" All he got in return was a shrug.

Tora Bora Mountains, Afghanistan

"Excellent. So much for General Masood." Bin Laden smiled broadly as he listened through his cell phone. Then his smile suddenly faded. "They have?"

He flashed a concerned look at Malid and Zawahiri, then masked it. "Keep observing and report regularly."

"Problem, Sharif?" asked Malid.

"Not at all. Masood is dead. There apparently are some American Rangers at Ternez, but it is a small contingent. There is nothing to worry about." He smiled the benign smile that Malid knew all too often concealed a black heart. Bin Laden tried to exude confidence but Malid could read him well.

The Americans have not behaved as you predicted, Sharif. They reacted faster in closing their air space, and this new cowboy president is apparently not intimidated by Afghanistan's geography.

"I shall instruct Mullah Omar to issue a new fatwa against all Americans, man, woman, child. That should give them pause."

"Sharif," protested Malid, "the Koran forbids attacks on innocents" *which didn't stop you from killing thousands in the towers.* "The Pentagon and the towers were legitimate targets of American militarism and economic imperialism. But random killing of women and children? Even Muslims?"

Actually, when Malid learned of the 9/11 attacks, it had sickened him, but it did not surprise him. He knew from the *Hadith* that the Prophet had ordered a horrific punishment on a group of thieves whom his followers caught: their hands and feet were cut off, their eyes put out, and they were left in the desert to die. But they were thieves and brigands. There was nothing in the holy books that justified destruction of innocents, especially without giving them the opportunity to convert to Islam. Still, he knew better than to utter such concerns aloud to bin Laden. Now, a new fatwa against every American? Malid knew Mullah Omar—the infamous "one-eyed cleric"—was a pliant bin Laden tool. He would do whatever Sharif ordered.

How many would die then?

New York Federal Reserve Bank Conference Room

Even when he was fully "put together," Connie had that disheveled college professor look. Today, his red tie was slightly askew at the knot, and the label side of the tie sticking out from behind. He hadn't even noticed that the socks didn't match. Toting his large bookbag, as the documents in question were too numerous and thick to fit in his standard briefcase, Connie was almost a caricature.

Upon entering the conference room, he saw three men in black or grey suits, dull ties, and ominous bulges under their armpits. Off to the side was a teenager. *Odd.*

One man with jet-black hair stood out, however, and Connie somehow knew that was Paul Andrade.

"Mr. Andrade?" Connie extended his hand.

"Professor Cataris. Thank you for coming. This is Agent Roger Coates of the FBI and Agents Cliff Harrison and Lonnie Jackson of the Central Intelligence Agency." Andrade nodded to the three men standing next to him. Each shook hands, but said little. No one even mentioned the teenager standing near the window. *Odd indeed.*

"Can we get right to it?" asked Andrade.

"Absolutely," replied Connie, pulling out reams of data and several charts. "After 9/11 I called the Council of Economic Advisors and offered to help in any way I could . . ."

Andrade broke in already. "You come pretty highly recommended from them, I should say. Seems that you've been offered a job or two in the administration?"

Damn, they do their homework. "Yes, that's right, but I couldn't spend any more time away from my family. Anyway, they put me on reconstructing financial information and checking firewalls and operational systems---nothing spectacular, and every bank has its own guys. I was just there sort of adding an 'eyes in the skies' to all their work. But it did require me to cross-reference banking data with some of the New York Stock Exchange numbers." He paused, then noticed all the agents were still with him, and they were nodding. *At least they are acting like they understand.* So he continued.

"In the process of reconstructing this data, something started to jump out at me. There were several odd trades prior to 9/11. Some might just be flukes---you know, someone selling off American Airlines big because he's cashing in his portfolio. So I tracked most of these, and there was nothing to them. But one continued to bother me: *l'Joliette du Mer.* It's a French company with a history of doing business in the Middle East, especially Saudi Arabia and the Sudan."

Jackson and Harrison exchanged looks, but said nothing.

"I've got some friends at Columbia who are specialists in the Middle East, so without telling them what I was doing, I ran some of this stuff by them, doing a little digging on this company. In the first place, it has nowhere near the liquid capital to pull off transactions like these . . . ."

"Transactions like what?" interrupted Andrade. "You still haven't exactly told us what you found."

Grabbing his head, Connie said, "Damn it, you're right. I kind of skipped to the middle. Ok, I found this . . . ." and he spread out one of his large computer printouts, with columns of numbers, and every so often, one circled in red felt marker.

"Professor, please. We're good, but this is way over our heads. What does this stuff *mean?*"

"Of course. I'm sorry. Ivory tower stuff, you know. Look, these are printouts of transactions in airline stocks---but not all airline stocks. It occurred to me that, say, if I was a bad guy and had an event planned that would change the value of stocks, whatever I did would involve specifically those companies I targeted." He saw some comprehension, but the lights hadn't gone on yet.

"In other words," Connie continued, "assuming my theory is right, bin Laden speculated on American Airlines and United Airlines, as well as CessCO Insurance Company, the main insurer for the World Trade Center. You see these trades that I've highlighted. Every one is either AA, UA, or CCO. Notice that in the 24 hours before 9/11, someone began dumping stock. It has all the earmarks of massive profit taking . . . with insider knowledge."

"I'm a CIA agent, Professor," interjected Cliff Harrison. "I don't get to 'play the market' much. You want to explain how this worked?"

"Yes, of course. Again, sorry. We academics get in our own bubble . . . . Anyway, you are well familiar with a practice called 'buying long,' even if you don't know the term. Basically, you borrow money from a brokerage house, buy stock, hope the stock goes up before your contract is due, then sell just before you have to repay the money."

He saw they all nodded in understanding. "Well, imagine that you borrowed *stock shares* from brokerage houses, then sold immediately while the price was high, but you have to repay the shares in a matter of weeks or months---whenever the contract is due."

"So you benefit if the price falls a lot, say, just before you have to repay the stock, then you buy back in at a much lower price, keeping the profit," added Jackson.

Connie smiled. *This won't be as tough as I thought.* "Exactly. The key is that price has to fall in order to make money. Or, he could have been involved in futures options trading, where you are essentially placing bets on the future prices of stocks. I don't know which it was, only that something is very odd here."

Andrade studied the red circles. "And you think this is bin Laden? Didn't you say it was a French company, *l'Joliette du Mer*? It's not a brokerage exchange. And besides, wouldn't you need more than one to pull this off without all sorts of alarm bells going off?"

"Right." Connie appeared a little flustered. "This is just where we were when I started. This company doesn't have the assets to pull off anything like this. It's just a front for someone with money, but every exchange I traced back from the NYSE related to this ended up in one place."

"*L'Joliette du Mer?* Ok, assuming it seems like something bin Laden might want to do, we're skeptical that he ever had as much money as we thought. What makes you think it's him?"

"Again, I've talked to some of my friends here, all low-key. But it seems that bin Laden and *l'Joliette du Mer* worked together quite a bit in the Sudan. Not so much since he left Sudan, however."

"Sounds kind of flimsy, professor. I mean, you've got apparent evidence here of stock tampering or insider trading, and if you say it's this French company, I can buy that, but linking it to bin

Laden seems tenuous." Andrade saw Harrison and Jackson both agreed with his assessment.

"You got Martha Stewart on less," Connie quipped, but the agents didn't laugh. *Damn! The Feds didn't like that joke.* Connie recovered as quickly as he could. "Anyway, I thought it was a stretch too, until I discovered this," Connie added, pulling out yet another sheet. "It turns out that *l'Joliette du Mer* was one of the main operators in the United Nations 'Oil for Food' program with Iraq. Obviously, this is speculation, but . . ." Connie pulled out one of his charts showing several boxes linked together " . . . I think it worked like this: bin Laden gave the orders, Iraq supplied the money via Oil-for-Food, *l'Joliette du Mer* actually placed the transactions, then made the payouts to bin Laden."

Jackson and Harrison both developed deep furrows in their brows, and shot each other knowing looks. "Ok," said Harrison, "say you're right, why wouldn't Saddam directly fund bin Laden? Why go through these fronts?"

"I could think of plenty of reasons. First, the French and German governments are likely up to their noses in 'Oil-for-Food.' While they can excuse that as "merely doing business," they would not willingly be accessories to attacks on America."

"He's right, there," snorted Jackson. "They heard that line about 'with us or with the terrorists.'"

"Second," Connie continued, "Saddam knows that any direct link to 9/11 will mean an instant invasion of his country, and we wouldn't stop short of Baghdad this time."

Andrade studied the charts, drawn to the red circles that represented millions of dollars' worth of Americans' investments and savings literally going up in smoke. "Professor, what do you think it would take to prove this---to make these links unimpeachable? After all, this is likely to go to the top of the United Nations. I mean, I'm no policy maker, but conceivably it could be the end of the UN, or, at the very least, get it kicked out of this country. It certainly would implicate France and the French government, or, at the very least, reveal them as corrupt or incompetent."

Connie thought about that for a moment. "What would it take?" he shrugged. "Most likely you'd have to get someone inside *l'Joliette du Mer* and find out where those deposits came from, or you'd have to get inside either Saddam's operation or bin Laden's operation---and I'm sure you've already tried the latter."

"That's exactly what I was thinking, Professor Cataris." Andrade paused, then looked at him.

Connie laughed. "You're going to just insert someone into bin Laden's operation? Hey, while you're at it, why don't you make it a college professor."

Andrade, Harrison, and Jackson exchanged looks but didn't speak.

Connie felt his throat tighten. *I don't think I'm gonna like what comes next.* "I'm sure you have trained agents who can . . . ."

"I'll be blunt, Professor: we are in a war. Time is essential. And I'm authorized to tell you something that you don't already know. The CIA operated an office in the World Trade Center. On Tuesday, September 11, we were running a joint training briefing with several FBI agents---a group that collectively included our best personnel in both agencies when it came to dealing with financial crime and national security threats."

Now it was Connie's turn to be slow to grasp the implications. "I don't under . . . ."

"Professor, we lost them all. It was a RICO-type simulation using economic and financial specialists. Thirty-six of our best economists, financial analysts, and specially trained agents in this type of operation. In short, professor, you advanced to the top of our list of experts in a period of a few minutes."

Holy God. Merciful God . . . .

"Moreover, for all we know, Saddam Hussein is at this moment developing chemical or biological weapons and is getting ready to sell them to bin Laden's kooks. And it's going to take us months to get our remaining people up to speed on this material. Let me be clear: no one---*no one*---understands this stuff at this level like you do, or has the experience you do with this particular facet of the threat. But the most important thing is, we need access to this company . . . er . . ."

"*L'Joliette du Mer?*" Connie volunteered.

"Exactly. And the best cover is no cover."

"I don't follow, Agent Andrade." In fact, Connie did follow, and he was getting a queasy feeling.

"You have no connection with intelligence agencies, ever. You're clean as a whistle. As an economist, it would be simple to concoct a cover for you to do what, well, what you *do*---financial research. We could come up with something that would give you an excuse to look at some of the records of *l'Joliette du Mer*. They won't be very enthusiastic, but we can get Chirac to put some pressure on without using the 'Oil-for-Food' information as a threat. They're anxious to do us small favors to show us they really are still our "allies." What if we could get the company to at least let you in?"

"Well, that would be peachy, but while I'd know what I'm looking at with data, I'm no computer genius. What you need is someone to hack their system once I gain access. I can't break into their computers. Can't you do that from here?"

"Our experience is that there are plenty of back-doors once you are on-site, but accessing these from the outside is nearly impossible. That's why having you in there---even if you are 'working' on something totally unrelated---is key. And that's where your graduate student comes in"

"I don't have a graduate student . . . ." Connie said when Andrade pointed to the teenager still standing by the window.

"Professor Cataris, meet Jake Cleland."

He slowly walked over and reluctantly extended his hand, offering a limp handshake. The kid had a brown plaid flannel shirt over a red t-shirt with the word "Prodigy" stitched on it. His pants bagged down to his butt-crack, the legs dragging on the floor, and he wore a green wool cap pulled over his ears with some skull logo that Connie didn't recognize. Connie had seen a few students at Columbia dressed like this, but even his most slovenly male Ivy Leaguers looked pristine compared to the Grunge King standing in front of him.

"'Sup, doc?" the kid said.

Connie couldn't help but laugh, and shrugged as he turned to Andrade. "He's an FBI agent?" Connie blurted incredulously.

Jake rolled his eyes and scowled. "Course I'm not you dipwad."

"I . . . I don't get it," Connie stammered.

Andrade motioned to Jake to sit, then explained, "Jake was one of the Bureau's most challenging cases."

"Cases?" The kid shot Connie a smart-aleck grin. "You mean he's a criminal?" asked Connie.

"Not any more. As part of his plea deal, he agreed to work with us on anything we chose for the next two years. Then he's out, no record, no jail time."

Connie studied the kid. Maybe he wasn't as young as he first looked. Maybe he was old enough to pass for a graduate student. *Connie, what the hell are you thinking?* "So," he said to Jake, chuckling, "what did you do, shut down the lights in Waukesha for an evening?"

Jake snorted and shot him a condescending look, but Andrade answered for him. "I'm sure you're aware of the *Wyrm* virus?"

Connie slowly turned back toward the kid, who leaned against a chair with his arms crossed and a smug look. "You shut down my computer for a month and cost me $800!" A smile came across Jake's face as he gave a "what of it?" shrug.

I gotta admit, I'm intrigued. Ok, Connie, you aren't going to agree to anything, but play along. "Fine, say me and my 'assistant' get inside *l'Joliette du Mer*, and say the kid is as good as you claim. I've still got to read and analyze the stuff. They aren't exactly going to let me sit in front of a computer screen once the see what I'm working on."

"Exactly," Andrade answered, "which is why Jake's going to transfer the data to a terminal we will set up for you at your hotel. You can analyze it there, and we'll have an industrial scale laser printer brought in so you can print anything and everything as fast as you want."

Damn it! This guy has an answer for everything.

"Look, this is a great plan, and I'm sure you'll pull it off, but I'm an economics professor, not a spy---spook? Is that the term now? I have a wife and kids." Connie started to fold up his charts into his book bag. "And he . . . " pointing at Jake "is a criminal at best and a menace at worst!"

Andrade walked over and put his hand on Connie's shoulder. "Professor," he said, looking straight in Connie's eyes, "you were *there* on 9/11. We know you were at Building 3. You could have been buried in the rubble if you hadn't left when you did. We checked up on you: we know you even talked to your brother about signing up in the armed forces."

My God, these guys know everything.

Andrade continued, "We can't make you do this. But if you want to get to the bottom of who did this, who helped bin Laden, and keep this from happening again, we need your help. The United States needs you."

"Uncle Sam wants you." Connie was sure those were going to be the next words out of his mouth. But, on the other hand, his nation had never specifically *asked* him for anything. Oh, it took his tax

money, and more than a few rights. But never in his life had representatives of the U.S. government come to him and said, "Help. We can't do it without you." A certain amount of guilt settled on Connie. *I've never done anything for my country except pay my taxes. I didn't serve in the army. God, what will Jan say?*

Soberly, Connie said, "Agent Andrade, you've got me for one month. If we can't make the case in a month, you'll have to find someone else. And no matter what happens, I get to contact my wife once a day. Those are my non-negotiable terms."

Andrade smiled and shook Connie's hand. "Excellent, professor. Now, say hello to your new graduate assistant," sweeping his arm back to Jake.

Jake stuck up his forefinger and thumb to his forehead. *Loser!*

Mazar e-Sharif, Afghanistan

Within two weeks of the Rangers' arrival, Camel, still known to Afghans as his code name of "Abdul," had made contacts with Col. Meadows. Only Meadows knew he was an agent. He discreetly briefed the Colonel about Northern Alliance customs, troop sizes, and enemy positions. For the most part, he remained just another *mujahadeen* in the movement.

Meadows had followed Camel's advice to stay out of the inter-tribal arguments over who would replace Masood. Finally, General Tek al-Aziz, a Pashtun, emerged as the consensus. He lacked the charisma of Masood, but perhaps was an even better battlefield tactician. With the Rangers' support, the Northern Alliance opened an offensive against the Taliban in Mazar e-Sharif.

For more than a week it stalled. American journalists immediately sounded the claxons of doom, and the inevitable comparisons to Vietnam, plus the predictable word "quagmire," sprang up in editorials and columns across the United States. Camel knew better.

Strongholds held by the Taliban were rotten on the inside--- false shells waiting to be cracked so that the natural yearning of the human spirit would burst free. The Taliban had no support inside Mazar e-Sharif, or almost any other town, for that matter. But they did have the troops and the artillery to give the Northern Alliance a battle. Still, Meadows had mounted some of his Rangers on horses as advance spotters, and they rode out with the Alliance forces, calling down American air support on Taliban positions. "The first cavalry charge of the 21st century," Gen. Franks had called it. Mazar e-Sharif fell unexpectedly quickly as the Taliban scooted south. Now Kabul was open.

Camel had to use caution in dreaming up different excuses to be away from his unit. Once his "sister" was ill, and he had to "return to his home town" briefly to help. Another time, he volunteered to go on a reconnaissance patrol---which took him exactly where he wanted to be anyway. Col. Meadows helped him when possible, requesting an interpreter for some of his forward recon units. Of course, Camel never made it to the units, but conducted his own intel gathering activities.

What he learned was valuable: the Taliban and al-Qaeda had concentrated in Kabul, a little over 200 miles south of Mazar e-Sharif as the crow flies, but, of course, that crow better be able to fly over mountains. From what he gathered, they planned to adopt the "Mogadishu" strategy of forcing the Americans to send ground troops into the city and then inflict heavy casualties, whereupon the American public would demand a withdrawal. Camel knew such thinking was utterly naive, but nevertheless Meadows and Gen. Franks would have to be prepared.

Meanwhile, U.S. forces (and some units of Canadians and British troops) had poured into Afghanistan, moving steadily through the mountainous roads toward the capital. Camel estimated some 5,000 men were there now, plus the Northern Alliance, opposed by perhaps 30,000 Taliban and al-Qaeda fighters. *Is Osama bin Laden among them?* Camel's sources told him he was.

We shall know soon enough. The assault on Kabul will begin within two weeks.

Paris

God, this place was made for midgets.

Connie dropped his bags in the doorway of a so-called "suite" at Le International, supposedly a five-star hotel. He couldn't imagine what the five stars were for. The room was a dump, even by Holiday Inn standards. Connie was an experienced traveler, having spent time in 25 foreign countries, including an extensive stint in Russia and Venezuela where he worked with the governments on currency reform. Yet he never got over how the European concept of "luxury" wouldn't even compare to a Best Western back home. And the food! Ugh! The French drowned everything in sauces because the meat was a cross between shoe leather and volleyball netting.

You'd think they'd get a bed big enough for a normal human. European beds still were tailored for the sub-six-foot frames of Continental men. *You're not at a day spa, Connie. Let's go to work.*

He hadn't seen agents Jackson and Harrison since he got off the plane, by design. According to the plan they were watching him and Jake at all times. That's, "according to the plan." But the fact that he had not seen them left him more than a little uneasy.

After calling Jan and talking to the kids for a few minutes, Connie checked his watch. Show time. He and Jake had a 2:00 appointment with at l'Joliette du Mer with some guy named Arel Chalons, who would provide them access to the records for his "financial research" project. Connie looked at his palms. They were already sweating. He had double-dosed with the Right Guard today, but it wasn't working. His gut felt like he had swallowed a dozen whole walnuts, and he munched handfuls of antacid tablets for the first time in his life.

Connie walked one door down and knocked on Jake's door.

"Yeah, yeah," he heard inside, over music. Where did this kid get speakers? Jake swung open the door, jerked his head for Connie to come in, and resumed tucking a MP3 player into his pocket and draping the headphones around his neck. He walked over and shut off some Euro MTV program on the television, blasting at deafening levels. He faced Connie and spread his hands wide in the Alfred E. Newman, "What, me worry?" stance.

"You ready?" asked Connie. Cause I'm damn sure not.

"Yeah," Jake sighed, "that's what we're here for."

"You aren't nervous?"

"Of what? Some Frenchies finding out I'm crashing their system? Hell, no. That's solid. What are they gonna do, deport me?"

You'd like that just fine, wouldn't you? "Fine, but let's not screw this up. This is high stakes stuff here."

"Yeah, yeah. Chill. The J-man has it under control. You just keep 'em off my ass so we can get out of the land of cheese-eatin' surrender monkeys."

Connie stared at him. I may like this kid after all.

Twenty minutes later they checked in at the front desk of l'Joliette du Mer when an attractive 25-year-old brunette in high heels---really high heels, Connie thought---walked up and extended her hand.

"Professor Cat . . . Cat---err-es is it?" She pronounced the "are" as "err." She can pronounce it any way she wants, Connie thought, before shaking himself. Straighten up, boy. You're married.

"Er, that's Cat-ar-is. Yes. Hello." God, am I drooling? She is really hot. "And you are?"

"I'm Ariel Chalons, executive assistant to the president, Mr. Lanier."

Touché. Ar-eee-el, not Arel.

Connie gestured to Jake, who still wore his headphones. "This is my student assistant, Jake" then, noticing the headphones, slapped him in the chest. Jake glared at him, but took the headphones off and turned off his MP3 player and offered his traditional limp handshake.

"Yes," she added, unimpressed with the kid, and scarcely more so with Connie. "Well, come with me. We got your request and have an office set up for you. You want to look at the financial data from before World War II, is that correct? Something about the impact of reparations on the French economy?"

"Yes, Ms. Chalons, that's correct. We think that we can show a direct economic link between the French response to the Smoot-Hawley Tariff and the decisions not to re-arm in the face of Nazi threats, especially if you correlate . . . ."

"Fascinating, professor," she cut him off, "and I'm sure you'll find what you need here. If you need anything else, Ms. Lecompte is just down the hall."

Works every time. The old academic overload trick. She won't be asking any further questions about his work.

"If I can be of further assistance to you, let me know." She gestured to a small room with a pair of computer workstations and reams of binders from the 1930s. "Now if you will excuse me," she added, hoping the two Americans needed as little assistance as possible.

She strode out, with every step accentuated by her phenomenal legs on top of those high, high heels. Bad boy, Connie. Bad, bad boy.

Jake watched Connie's reaction, then rolled his eyes before slumping in the chair and popping up the first screen.

Chapter 18

Tora Bora Mountains, Afghanistan

"We need to leave *now*, Sharif! The American forces smashed through the Taliban in Kabul like tissue paper and are on their way *here*." Malid already had started to pack laptops and gather papers, but it seemed bin Laden and Zawahiri were in denial. *Had he thought himself protected by this silly cave?* thought Malid.

"It is not possible!" bin Laden shouted---itself unusual as the man rarely raised his voice.

Zawahiri had a cell phone glued to his ear. "They are telling me that all of the Taliban and al-Qaeda fighters have fled Kabul! The Northern Alliance is sweeping in from the north, and American Special Forces are to our southwest." He clicked the cell phone off as bin Laden stood in the center of the room with a stupefied look on his face. "Sharif, perhaps we should indeed go. We should move east, to Pakistan."

"The Americans actually sent *troops* . . . " he murmured. Then he grabbed Zawahiri by the shoulders. "We must unleash Allah's Wind. Now!"

Zawahiri vehemently shook his head. "No! It is not ready. We have not established our cell long enough in America. And in Cairo, they only last week got their radioactive materials from Iraq! We don't even know if they have assembled the arming devices."

Malid listened intently to the exchange. *Radioactive material? Iraq? I thought Sharif hated Saddam . . . and yet, Hazzam, our most dangerous chemical and biological specialist was in Iraq for months.* Malid had heard stories of terrorists returning from Iraqi training camps, especially Salman Pak, where a Boeing 737 fuselage had provided hours of practice for hijackers. *What radioactive material?*

Bin Laden uttered a curse---Malid had never heard him curse before. "We have no choice. Order "Allah's Wind" to commence now! It will divert the Americans' attention from us, and it will remind them of their enemy!"

Zawahiri was as ruthless and cold-blooded as they came, but his objections had nothing to do with the death toll of "Allah's Wind"---only its likelihood of success. "Sharif, Allah's Wind is a more complicated operation than the attacks on the towers by several orders of magnitude. It is not just getting two different weapons in place, but it is the precise timing required by the winds. If we are to have our desired effect, we must strike when the weather patterns ensure broadest exposure."

Bin Laden was not persuaded. Jabbing his finger at a map of America, he said "The Great Satan is big enough that no matter which way the winds turn, we will achieve success. My only concern is *here*," he said, flipping the Atlas to a map of the Middle East. "If we act now, can we assure destruction of the Jews and irradiation of Israel?"

What in the name of the Prophet have you two planned? That would start a full-scale war, and we know that the Israelis have their own nuclear weapons. Malid seldom participated in such high-level discussions, but the two terrorists had completely forgotten about him, but he overheard enough. *You would kill hundreds of thousands, perhaps millions, in America? And irradiate the very atmosphere over Muslim countries? Will this not even irradiate Mecca if the winds shift in ways other than you expect?* His thought process was interrupted by Zawahiri's reply.

"It is difficult to say," Zawahiri said measuredly. "The Chicago device has it's own 'distribution source' if you will: the Sears Tower is high enough to essentially make it airborne, which will ensure that the effect is spread over several U.S. states by the winds. But Cairo is another matter. The tallest buildings are all minarets, and there we are not using VX, but a dirty bomb. And, I would prefer a larger device in Cairo. But it will be sufficient to eliminate Israel. The more time we have to increase the 'dosage,' if you will, the greater the destruction."

Bin Laden let out another curse. "How long would you need?" He grew increasingly agitated.

"If you want to abandon some of our safeguards, I could possibly push the schedule by a few months."

"Do so," bin Laden instructed. "In the meantime, Malid is right. We must evacuate."

They hurriedly threw their remaining items into the SUVs. Malid jumped in the driver's seat as bin Laden and Zawahiri climbed in the back of the first vehicle, gunning the engine and spraying rocks all over Mohammad and Karel in the second SUV when a huge explosion threw his truck into a spin and he hit the brakes.

Behind them, the second SUV was nothing more than a cinder.

"There!" shouted Zawahiri, pointing to the sky. Squinting, bin Laden could see a small aircraft, slowly circling.

"That's no American fighter plane! How did that attack us?" bin Laden asked in wonder.

Suddenly, the Predator drone turned toward the SUV.

"OUT!" screamed Malid, and they burst from the vehicle, rolling along the ground and down a gully to their left just as the Predator unleashed another Hellfire missile. The SUV disappeared in a ball of flame.

"By the Prophet! How did they locate us so quickly?" Zawahiri muttered.

"Horses! There are horses just a few kilometers away in the village of al-Kutar," Malid said.

"But we dare not move while that death machine is up there." Bin Laden jerked his head at the Predator, still making lazy circles in the sky.

"No, we must wait until dark and hope that it does not have infra-red imaging, or runs out of fuel. And in the mean time, hope that the Americans do not 'carpet-bomb' these mountains." Malid now was convinced bin Laden had underestimated his foe. *Has he also overestimated his call from Allah? Is he indeed under holy commands, or is he a deranged killer?*

I have no reservations about killing soldiers, Sharif. I can even excuse the attack on the Pentagon and the World Trade Center as a necessary strike on enemy "headquarters." But you are more interested in murdering innocents. And by whose authority? And would you irradiate the Holy City in your bloodlust, even if by accident? Are the Jews so lacking in human characteristics that you can exterminate them? You are not the leader I once thought, Sharif--if you are a leader at all.

Less than 10 "clicks" away, Sergeants Roland and Hernandez, with a handful of Rangers and their scout, Camel, secured a perimeter around a CIA field agent named Johnny Spann while he peered into a computer screen while he used a toggle switch to maneuver a Predator drone over the Tora Bora Mountains. He had fired two missiles at figures trying to flee in SUVs, and while he had destroyed both, he was not confident that he had killed the inhabitants, one of whom looked suspiciously like Osama bin Laden.

"That's it, boys," he announced. "Outta gas. By the time we can get another on station, it will be night, and these boys will be gone. I'm pretty sure that's our guy, though."

Chico and Mick exchanged skeptical glances. They'd heard Agency types before, and they were always "sure" that their intel was right.

"Ok," said Mick, "head 'em back." Chico made a circle in the air with his hand, as the Rangers headed back down the rocky trails to their personnel carriers some five kilometers away. They'd patrolled this area for almost a day, and this was the first contact with the enemy they had. But they were already extended way past their area of operations, and were needed closer to Kabul.

"Don't worry," Spann said confidently. He had already contacted CENTCOM with his information. If a surgical strike didn't take out the target, there was always the less subtle approach. "You won't want to be around here later anyway. Trust me." Chico and Mick exchanged puzzled glances, then, with Camel leading the column and Spann in tow, headed back to their rides.

Paris

Connie watched Sky News as it covered the final collapse of the terror regime in Kabul. He grunted with grim satisfaction. It would not make up for 9/11, but it was something. Connie returned to his stack of readouts. For three weeks, he had daily checked in to *l'Joliette du Mer*, "researching" material related to the Great Depression, while in fact he was a front for Jake to perform his export magic. And, for three weeks, he had searched for the reassuring presence of Agents Jackson and Harrison, but they were nowhere to be seen . . . *as they had told me.*

Jake, as usual, feigned activity over Connie's numbers when anyone was around, but he carefully punched his way through code after code of security. Most of the time, his comments to Connie consisted of monosyllabic requests for food, and "uh" or "yeah." Then, a week ago, he cracked his knuckles and said, proudly, "Dude, check it out," flipping the screen around to Connie.

Cibola! The Seven Cities of Gold! The kid did it. On the monitor were columns of numbers that could only be the Oil-for-Food account, and it took Connie only minutes to spot key deposits in amounts that correlated to the short-selling he had spotted in New York; followed by similar large purchases of stocks that had tanked at bargain-basement prices.

"Good job," he said, grabbing the kid on the shoulder. Jake uttered some inaudible grunt. "Send it to the laptop. We'll print tonight."

Jake's fingers flew across the keyboard and the data began flying out at the speed of light.

"You interested in this?" he asked with the enthusiasm of a narcoleptic slug. He pointed to deposits in the summer of 2001 to another account.

"Could be. Don't know what to make of it."

"What if I could backfill—maybe find out the password user or account holder?"

Connie cocked his head. "You can do that?"

Jake rolled his eyes, then lifted his hands, as if to ask, *"You doubt me?"*

"Of course. Let's see where this leads. The data's already back at the hotel, right?"

Jake nodded, but his fingers did not slow down. "Damn it, dude!"

"What?" exclaimed Connie. "What did I do?"

"Oh, not you man. The security. They're on to us. When I crossed this last password screen I tripped a wire."

Connie didn't want to know, but he had to ask. "A wire?"

"It's a security device that lets a snooper know you are snooping. We've been made." He pushed away from the screen and quickly packed up what few personal items he had. "We probably oughta skate."

Connie, following his lead, said, "You mean someone is going to be coming after us?"

"Sooner rather than later, dude. Let's blow." He brushed out into the hall, then pointed to a fire exit. "There's our ride."

Now Connie's heart was racing. "Do the CIA agents know about this? They know everything, right? They would pick up on this, right?"

"No chance, man. This wire was buried really deep. Their guys never would have found it. 90% of the hackers would never have even seen it," and he turned to smile at Connie, "which is why I'm the best."

They flew down the three flights of stairs and popped through the fire exit, setting off alarms.

Without even seeing the figures following them, Connie could feel that they were close. Out of nowhere, a short, but powerful man shot out of the shadows, lunging---but just missing Jake. He didn't miss Connie, slamming into him like a linebacker taking down a running back. Connie hit the hard Paris street, his briefcase spinning away. Jake stopped and looked in horror as a second taller man stepped out from behind him, grabbing him around the waist and lifting him like a sack of potatoes. "Dude! What the hell? Chill!" he screamed, as the tall man toted him to where the shorter assailant had Connie pinned to the ground.

A car pulled up and Jake was hurled into the car, as Shorty kicked Connie in the ribs. He let out a groan as the air left his body, while Tall jumped into the back seat of the car with Jake.

Shorty turned to get in when his head exploded in a froth of blood and brains. Tall yanked the door shut, and Connie, laying sideways and still unable to breathe, faintly heard Jake screaming, "Connie. Come on, man, help! Get up. Get me out of here!" Then the door slammed as the car rocketed off.

"Jaaaakkkeee," Connie rasped, but even screaming the kid's name hurt his chest. Then he saw a pair of black shoes in front of him, but he still couldn't breathe. He followed the shoes up to Lonnie Jackson's face. "Gotta let us know when you're buggin' out. Come on. Car's waitin'. We need to leave. This stuff is frowned on in France"

They could hear French police horns---you couldn't really call them sirens---approaching. Connie was heaved into a Renault, with Jackson and Harrison in the front. The car sped off. Connie felt breath returning to him, but only slowly.

"Who was that?" he gasped. "And what about the kid?"

"No telling for sure, but it could be French, al-Qaeda, hell, could even be UN people who are pissed at you for uncovering their little scheme."

"You mean you don't *know* who it was?"

"We're spies, not psychics. We'll find out. One thing's for sure. We need to find him fast. He acts tough, but the kid won't last five minutes under questioning from pros, and he'll tell them everything they need to know, plus stuff he didn't even know he knew."

Connie coughed, still gasping for air. "How do you plan to find him?"

Harrison smiled. "C'mon, prof. You don't think we'd really let you guys out of the house without trackers, do you?"

"You planted tracking devices on us?"

"Of course. How else could we afford to hang back so far? And our little bugs say that Jake is right in that building over there," pointing to the Iraqi embassy.

"Oh my God," Connie exclaimed softly. "Can this get any worse? That's the Iraqi embassy, isn't it?" They both nodded.

Then he remembered the data. "Wait, what about the data? We haven't picked that up yet. What if they got to our room?"

"Relax. We picked the stuff up the minute you sent it," Harrison assured him.

"You were in our room?"

"Gotta earn our checks somehow. That's why we were so late taking care of your two playmates. It took us a minute to get there. Now, we gotta get Jake out before he tells 'em everything except where Jimmy Hoffa is buried."

"I'm not going to like this part, am I?" asked Connie, the lump forming in his stomach again.

Harrison put in a call on a cell phone. Within two minutes, a beautiful Arabic-looking female showed up. She was a good 5' 8" with long black hair and dark eyes, and devastatingly beautiful. Harrison introduced her as Fatima, though Connie guessed that wasn't her real name. She and the two agents spoke in hushed tones for a few seconds, whereupon Fatima hurried off to the embassy, disappearing inside.

Jackson pulled out a tracker that had her signal, and he started the car, pulling it around to the side of the building where there was an exit. He kept the car running. The agents could tell, both by Jake's tracker and Fatima's, that the two were close. How she got to Jake, Connie didn't know and didn't ask, but within minutes, Fatima and Jake burst out of the door and sprinted toward the car. Harrison had a sniper rifle ready at his window, but it wasn't necessary. A couple of guards gave chase, too far behind for Harrison to bother. Fatima shoved Jake inside, then piled on top of him, yelling "Go, go!"---the only words Connie recalled hearing her speak. The underpowered Renault screeched off.

Jake and Fatima had both sprawled across Connie's lap, with the girl on top of Jake. Connie noticed Jake was bleeding and bruised and, well, looked like hell.

"Seems they liked you about as much as I do," Connie quipped, and Jake sneered at him through his matted hair.

"Yah, well, the Frenchies didn't get nuthin', so don't freak, man."

"Actually," Connie smiled, "I figured you'd be too stubborn and anti-social to tell them anything. My money was on you."

Jake looked at him for a moment, then bobbed his head.

But Harrison suddenly jerked the car over to the curb. "Frenchies? You mean, "those *Iraqis* didn't get anything from you." He arched his eyebrow up, but Jake shook his head.

"Maybe I'm just a high-school dropout, but I know a Frenchy from an Arab, and that was a French guy who nabbed me and French guys who were questioning me inside the building. You know," he assumed the persona of the French knight in "Monte Python and the Holy Grail": 'Why do you think I have theeessss out-raaaaageous accent?'"

Connie laughed at that one, but Harrison didn't. "Not Iraqis?"

"Dude! Are you deaf? I told you. French. Like Napoleon, *qui? Voulez-vous la couchez avec moi?* French!"

Jackson looked at Harrison and said nothing, but Harrison let out a low whistle as he slipped the Renault back into drive.

Within minutes, they were at a safe location---what appeared to be a shipping warehouse with crates and mealie bags. And Connie's computer was there, already booted up, waiting for him. The printer and reams of paper stood ready.

"Wow. That's efficient. All right, let's see what they're hiding." He scrolled up the files in question, and hit "Print." Hewlett-Packard's most advanced laser printer spat out the paper as fast as Connie could pull it off. Using his red felt pen, he instantly started circling numbers, transactions, and accounts as Harrison, Jackson, and Fatima looked over his shoulder.

"Good, good," he mumbled. "Hey, Jake. Come here."

Jake was still wiping blood off his face, and as he came closer, Connie could see his lower lip was ballooned up like a blimp, and his left eye was almost closed by contact with a fist . . . *or something worse.* "I've got some account numbers here. Do you think you can somehow run these backwards?"

"You mean trace them? Yah, I might be able to at least find the server, and if I do that, and if we could actually go *to* the location of the server, I could hack it."

Harrison and Jackson had dug out some French version of Cokes for everyone, and were finishing their second can each. "So you want us to get you into the server location? That wasn't in the mission description, but . . ." Jackson looked at his partner, "seems to me that's what we have to do." Harrison crumpled his can and nodded. "OK, go for it."

Jake hammered at the keyboard for an hour while Connie continued to circle numbers. Fatima slumped on a pile of mealie bags and, everyone noticed, was asleep in minutes. Jackson and Harrison took turns patrolling the outside of the warehouse and checking the inside for bugs. After almost two hours, Jake announced, "Rue Du Plain. That's where the server is located." He spun around in his chair.

They awoke Fatima and all piled in the car, with Jake nearly on Connie's lap.

"If we're gonna be a team," Connie observed, "maybe you guys should get a little bigger car?"

"Relax, Prof. This shouldn't take too long. If all goes well, this is our last stop," Jackson read the map while Harrison drove to 18 Rue Du Plain.

"Oh, no," Connie moaned. "This can't be right."

"It's right," confirmed Jake.

It was the offices of the United Nations International Education and Social Services Organization.

Washington, D.C.

Had the speech required softer, more feminine phrases, undoubtedly Bush would have pleaded with Karen Hughes, to make a run up to D.C. and help out, but she had left earlier this year. That left the speech in the hands of the untested Norman Nickles.

Bush had a nickname for everyone he liked---and even a few he disliked---and it was inevitable that Norman became "Buffalo," but this time, when the secretary told "Buffalo" come to the President's personal study, Norman Nickles sensed that the mood would not be light.

"Come on in, Norman."

This is bad. The President never calls me 'Norman.'

"Been working on the State of the Union?" asked Bush, gesturing to the sofa while he himself took the large easy chair.

"Yes, sir. I'd say we're pretty close," Nickles answered uncomfortably.

"Hit terrorism pretty hard?"

Where's he going with this? "Yes, sir. Of course."

"Well, we're gonna make some changes."

You haven't even seen it yet, sir. "I don't understand."

"After discussions with my National Security team, we need to specifically identify the threats out there. It was fine after 9/11 to say that we would go after nations who harbored or supported terrorists. But I've decided that we need to stop playing games with some of these countries and let them know we're on to them."

"Sir?" Nickles still wasn't getting the whole picture.

"Norm, I want you to cite specifically the threats posed by Iran, Iraq, and North Korea. Condi will brief you on some of the wording---I know we have to be careful here---but I'm putting these nations on notice as of this speech, particularly Iraq. That may be where we have to start, but as I see it---and as my team sees it---all these rogue states are in it together. Whether or not they are actively trading information or personnel is irrelevant. Their support for terrorism and potential for supplying terrorists is beyond question. And I'm not going to let that fester. I want a speech that paints a clear picture of how they are linked, and just as clearly avoids making accusations we can't back up."

"You mean like involvement in 9/11?"

"That's exactly right. We may have information, leads, and all sorts of hunches that Iraq, Iran, or both of them were involved, but right now we can't prove it. So don't get carried away. I know this is no easy task, especially since we've included North Korea."

"I assume, sir, that's so that this doesn't appear to be a 'get-the-Muslims' speech?"

"Not entirely. The fact is, the previous administration screwed up North Korea badly, trading vital food for promises not to push forward with their nuclear programs." (Bush always pronounced it "nuk-lar") "It hasn't worked. That pot-bellied nutcase Kim Jung-Il has rationed out the food just enough to keep his population from a general revolt, and has developed nukes anyway. Had 9/11 not happened, it is likely we'd be up to our knees in trouble with North Korea. So I want 'em on the list. Maybe we can't deal with them now, but Kim will get the message that we're watchin' him."

"I understand sir. Is 24 hours ok?"

"That'll be fine, Buffalo. Just remember: I'm talkin' to the moms and dads out there who are doing to have to send sons and daughters to clean up these messes. They're gonna need clear reasons for doing so. And, as I said, Condi can give you all the details we can safely release."

"24 it is, sir."

As Nickles walked back to his office, he thought of how someone would have handled a declaration of war against German and Italy in World War II after Japan, a tenuous ally at best, had attacked the United States. *Hitler made such a speech unnecessary*, he recalled. *But what if he hadn't? What if FDR had needed to justify the war in Europe as an integral part of the response to Pearl Harbor? What would he have called it? That's easy. They were the Axis. They were evil. "Axis of Evil."*

Tempe, Arizona, Home of Pat and Ann Palmer

Dear Mom and Dad,

Basic is easy, but don't tell anyone around here I said that! After NFL training camps, the Army's runs and obstacle courses are nothing. Even David thinks they're cake, and we know what a wuss he is. We're careful not to show off, though, 'cause that just brings you more trouble. So we act like everyone else---you know, grunting and sweating, "boy is this hard," kind of stuff.

Judging from the news clippings you sent, a lot of people were surprised that I left the Cards to join the Army. I'm surprised they are surprised. I was reading before I left a book about World War II. Did you know that almost every movie star of your generation---I watched a lot of them on TV for years---fought in World War II? James Arness of "Gunsmoke," Telly Savalas of "Kojak," and even Eddie Albert of "Green Acres all served. Desi Arnaz couldn't get in the U.S. Navy because he wasn't a citizen, but they drafted him into the Army! Some of those guys were real heroes. Walter Matthau, the crusty old coach on the "Bad News Bears" won six Silver Stars in the Army Air Force. Lee Marvin was one of only five men out of 247 who survived an assault in the Pacific. Jimmy Stewart flew B-17s over Germany along, as did Coach Tom Landry of the Cowboys. I could go on and on.

I'm ashamed of my generation. Who from Hollywood has enlisted? Who joined up from the world of music? How many of our cultural icons put on a uniform? I think you know the answer. And you know what? Many of them could have done so without even facing combat. This is a land war---they could have joined the Navy, done recruiting ads, whatever. Well, they have to live with themselves. David and I talked it over, and we couldn't do anything but enlist. We've both put in for Ranger school after basic, and, between you and me, I think we will both get it. Those people, well, one of the things I picked up at ASU was Shakespeare's "Henry V," and believe me, there will come a time in the future when people will sit around fireplaces and dinner tables in America and talk about this time, and "men will call themselves cursed" that they did not do their duty when America needed them.

End of rant. You guys take it easy, and make Dad take you to Matta's for one of those chile enchiladas now and then.

Dave is doing fine. 'Course, as you know, we can't serve in the same regiment because of the "Sullivans" case. But I'll see him now and then. He says 'hi.'

Love, Tom

Camp Virginia, Kuwait

Boot camp was supposed to be the tough part, but as soon as the 507th Maintenance Company arrived in Kuwait, they found out that the real training had only started. Every night, Joanna Miles and her fellow soldiers rolled out of their cots wiggled into protective clothing, donning their masks amidst screams of "Gas! Gas!" Then they ran for the bunkers while they awaited the scream of an Iraqi SCUD missile.

After five or six of these, the drills got routine, but no one got used to the lack of sleep. And lack of sleep made for mistakes—always a problem for a maintenance unit. Just yesterday a sleep-deprived Corporal, Kit Erickson, smashed his hand in a truck jack.

It was ironic. Jo and the other 82 soldiers of the 507th were at Camp Virginia to provide mechanical support for a Patriot missile battery, which existed to protect the 507th and other units from Iraqi SCUDs. *"You scratch my back and I'll scratch yours,"* Dad always *said, and this is as good an example as any.* Jo managed to get through the long days and the sleepless nights by staying busy during the days and exhausting herself to the point that as soon as a raid was over she would topple back into her bunk. *Guess it's a good thing we have these,* she concluded. *Sooner or later we'll get the real thing, and I 'spose we should be ready.*

The rest of the 3rd Infantry Division had been arriving over the past month, and it was almost at full strength. Jo didn't know anything official, but she could add two and two: *When the Third ID is in place, we won't be just standin' around.* And from that perspective, even an advance into Iraq would be preferable to these unbroken days and endless nights.

Chapter 19

Tora Bora Mountains, Afghanistan

The smell was beyond overpowering. *Whatever they're cooking,* Camel thought, *it's a new one on me. And I thought I was used to every smell in Afghanistan.* Nevertheless, he ducked his head as he entered the little hut on the outskirts of Wal-e-Teb, a small village that did not show up on most maps. Three men and a boy inside all displayed toothless smiles and bowed to him, and he returned their greeting.

I have to be nuts. Alone in an unknown location, with no one knowing where I am, and no way to contact anyone. I'll probably end up buried in an ant hill.

They gestured to him to sit, and he chose a rug, where he crossed his legs and steeled himself to eat whatever it was that made that God-awful stink. Then he noticed a shadowy figure in the back of the hut—*and he didn't seem so friendly.* Camel all too quickly found out what the smell was, as it arrived in a bowl. He could make out rice or beans inside, and some sort of gristle or fat, but did not want to know what else was in the odoriferous container.

The boy had set up his visit. Camel had noticed him hanging around for weeks, as if deliberately. Last Tuesday, the kid began talking to him, but with a purpose. He wanted to arrange a meeting . . . but with who? The boy wouldn't say, except to repeat that it was extremely important. Every survival instinct told Camel not to go, but every spy instinct told him he could not afford not to go. This was what espionage was all about. The most he could tell his superiors was cryptic—that a meeting would take place, that it might be important, and that as soon as he knew more, he'd be in touch. *What if this is all about getting some village chieftan getting a year's supply of Baby Ruths or some toilet paper?* Well, he had taken bigger risks in the past. There was no reason to even bring a weapon. *If it comes to that, a pistol won't do me much good, and it will only serve to antagonize if there is no threat.*

As they sat, the conversation was almost surreal, mostly about the food, the countryside, and the Taliban. His hosts had little love for the Taliban or al-Qaeda, or so they said. Camel still half-expected a sharp blade to be drawn across his throat at any moment, and, as best he could without attracting attention, kept his hosts in sight at all times.

Finally, he announced in Pashtun, "Your hospitality is most welcome. I must, however, return to my work. Was there a specific reason you wanted to see me?"

They looked at each other, then turned to the dark figure in the back. After what seemed to be an eternity, he spoke. In English.

"You are here because I asked to meet with you." He moved into the light, but his face was covered.

"And you are?" Camel asked, expecting a lie.

"Call me Mohammad," came the reply, which was a lie.

"Of course," Camel smiled. *Fine. We both know the game.*

"I will, as you Americans say, get to the point."

Americans? He knows more than he lets on. "Why would you think I'm an American?"

"Please. We do not have the time for these games. We are both in danger meeting here."

I coulda told you that. "From whom?"

"I think you know. Now, to business. I can provide you with extremely valuable information."

"Why in the world would you think that I would be interested in it or have the power to do anything with it. I'm a simple interpreter for the foreign invaders." *He isn't buying this, is he?*

"Cease this nonsense! We do not have time. I have told you that we are at great risk just meeting here, and if you wish to play games, I will be forced to find someone else to deal with. If that is the case, it may be too late. And let me be clear: you do *not* want to carry the moral burden for what you might have prevented."

What the hell? This guy is some egomaniac . . . but there is just the outside possibility that he knows something. "Fine. Say I am in a position to do something with what you tell me. What are we talking about?"

The man suddenly seemed to struggle inside---it was obvious even to Camel. Then, after a long pause, he slowly and deliberately told Camel about a plan that dwarfed 9/11. Camel was sick, and it wasn't just the smell of the stew anymore.

Paris

"Tell me you don't want me to try to fake my way into the United Nations social services offices." Both agents returned Connie's plea with stony stares. *OK, Connie, try something else.* "And he . . ." pointing to Jake, with his puffed and bruised face "kind of attracts attention."

"Actually," as agent Jackson leaned over the seat, "you're the only one who can do it now." They managed to crawl back out of the Renault---Fatima first, then Jake, and finally Connie. "We know these accounts lead from 9/11 to Iraq to here. We can't stop: we need to find out exactly how they are connected, and, Prof, you're the only one who can read these numbers. Even the UN would make me and Harrison as agents, although Fatima might be able to accompany you as an assistant."

Connie rolled his eyes. "Another grad student? She's awfully pretty for a typical college student." *Please tell me I didn't just say that.* Connie started to blush, so he continued. "Besides, without Jake, I can't hack into any computers, and they are going to be on the lookout for him."

Harrison busily worked a cell phone, while Fatima just studied the UN office building. Harrison clicked it shut and said, "well, looks like we're gonna have a war. The President's ordered forces to Kuwait, and apparently they have been staging there for some time."

Connie hadn't even paid attention to the news over the last month, but now recalled the President's speech before the UN and that the Security Council had given Saddam an "ultimatum," authorizing the use of force to make him comply. But that was months ago. When the President went back to the UN to get the members to commit troops with another resolution, France was one of three nations that blocked the action. *I should have known then they were hiding something.*

"What do you think we're gonna find in those records, Professor?" asked Jackson. Fatima and Harrison gathered round. Even Jake looked at Connie for his answer.

"We don't have proof of anything . . . ." Connie began.

"I didn't ask you for proof," Jackson responded impatiently. "I said what do you think?"

"I think we're gonna find the UN and France up to their eyeballs with Iraq, and, if the trail from 9/11 leads where I think, we'll find a connection between Saddam and Osama, even if it's only money. But I wouldn't advertise that just yet. Like I say, we can't prove anything except some coincidental deposits and withdrawals from some of the main players."

"Let me ask you straight up," replied Jackson. "Based on what you've seen---where this money trail leads---do you think Saddam was involved in 9/11?"

Connie let out a big sigh. "Maybe not directly, maybe not as part of the planning, but I think the money trail shows that he at the very least helped finance it. Do you think the President knows this?"

Harrison smiled. "That ol' Texas boy is underestimated all the time. They think he's dumb? Hell, he had higher test scores at Harvard and in the military than some of the 'geniuses' who are always knockin' him---no offense, Prof, 'cause we here think you're a genius." Connie started to blush again as Jake rolled his eyes. "Him too," Harrison pointed to the kid. Jake shrugged and gave a *"whatever"* look.

"On the other hand, as far as I know---and remember, the CIA keeps things pretty compartmentalized---you're the only one to have figured this out yet."

"It would be important for the President to have this information, one way or the other," Connie mulled.

"No crap, Professor," Jackson replied. "I don't think we can wait. We need to get inside there, and, unfortunately, we're gonna need to get Jake in there with you."

Connie started to protest when Jake interjected, "They got skateboards in France?"

"Huh?" offered Harrison.

"I said, they got skateboards in France? Get me a skateboard. That will explain my face, easy. No one will even question me."

Kid's pretty sharp, thought Connie.

"Lonnie, why don't you and Fatima split up and try and find the kid here a skateboard? Take the car if you need to. Meanwhile, Prof, you and me and Jake need to come up with a cover story quick, before word gets over to security here from *l'Joliette du Mer*."

It took just 30 minutes for Jackson and Fatima to find a sporting goods store and buy a skateboard. Naturally, it was the wrong color for Jake, but he promptly pulled a couple of skull-and-bones stickers out of his backpack and customized it. "Solid," he stated. "Let's rock."

Cairo

All he knew was that he would receive a package at a future date, and that in the meantime, he needed to make sure that he could get a 3' by 2' suitcase up the steps to the al-Hafa Minaret near downtown Cairo. Jaleel had entered the mosque during noon prayers, kneeling off to the side closest to the minaret. When others left, he ducked into the hallway leading up the prayer tower.

On his way up, Jaleel heard footsteps coming down. It was the *meuzzin* (or crier) who called the faithful to prayer. Jaleel ducked inside a narrow hallway while the *meuzzin* passed, then Jaleel deliberately ascended to the top of the minaret. *Yes, a suitcase will indeed be easy to get to the top.*

He did not know what would be in the suitcase, nor what his instructions were. It did not matter. He knew only that in a week, he was to told to expect another call with his orders. And it almost certainly would cost him his life, which did not particularly bother him. He would follow his orders regardless.

Chicago

Randy Elton, replete with his Sosa jersey and Bulls cap, pushed the button for the observation floor of the Sears Tower, riding up 110 floors with a half-dozen other visitors, including a Japanese couple and, interestingly, an Arab. Elton smiled at the irony. At the top, he followed a routine that he had practiced a half-dozen times already, walking around, pretending to look at the Windy City from 1,457 feet. The Tower was the tallest building in the United States, and eclipsed only by the Petronas Towers in Kuala Lampur, Malaysia.

Of course, Randy Elton was not there for the view, but rather to make mental notes of the location of security cameras, to assess the thickness of the glass, and to judge the reaction time of the building's security. It was easy to do the latter. A woman had a "hysterical reaction" to the height and became unruly, prompting security guards to arrive in less than one minute.

And, of course, the woman had been a member of Randy's cell.

And, of course, his name was not Randy Elton but Randal el-Tahlon.

This tower would make a perfect distribution point. *Sharif was right. This will work.*

Paris

Dominique de Valiere, the dashing, high-profile foreign minister of France, swept his hair back with his right hand and, in the same motion, whisked the cigarette from his mouth, exhaling a cloud of American tobacco smoke. *Marleboro. Humph. The Americans certainly know how to make cigarettes.* He looked at the cigarette in his hand. *Perhaps they are useful for some things after all.*

Valiere hated the United States, and he wasn't sure exactly why. His parents had been teenagers when George S. Patton's Third Army liberated their village. *They* still loved the Yankees. But ever since the golden age of Charles DeGaulle, Valiere saw America as a master, and France a dog on its leash. DeGaulle had broken that leash, but he had not freed France from the need to wait for scraps outside the American door.

No matter. Whether I like them or hate them is irrelevant. They cannot meddle in the internal policies of a sovereign nation like France in this manner.

The messages had come through channels, all guaranteeing President Jacques Chirac full desirability should something go wrong. Now, the trail ended with de Valiere. *Well, not exactly. The trail never ends short of death, and not even then, in some cases.* He waited in a darkened study of *l'Joliette du Mer*, a room he had visited many times. Indeed, it was a room Chirac built with French tax dollars, so that French "academics" would have a comfortable place to pursue their endeavors. *Of course, it's no more than a recreation room for French officials engaging in UN "business."* He sat on a fine sofa of Corinthian leather, stubbing the last of his Marleboro into the ashtray, where it joined three others. *Were it anyone else, I would not be kept waiting.* But this meeting was too essential to miss.

Finally the door opened and a tall figure in a full-length, black leather trench coat stood before him. The man wore a 1950s-era felt hat---which seemed completely out of place with the leather---and his long, straight red hair came down well past his shoulders.

"Citizen Genet," Valiere noted quietly. "Fashionably late, I see."

Genet disliked word games that wasted time. His life was action. Action and death.

"What do you have for me?" The voice came out hoarse, as though Genet---and not Valiere---smoked cartons of cigarettes.

Valiere, seeing Genet would not sit, himself stood. "It seems we have someone very interested in this company. Worse, it seems they may already have extracted some crucial information." He handed Genet pictures of Jake, Connie, Harrison, Jackson, and Fatima. "The last three are CIA agents. The first two are likely as well, though we've not seen them before and they come up on none of our databases."

"You want me to kill CIA agents?" Genet asked incredulously. "It could be done, but I would become a marked man and it would start a stealth war."

"Not the last three---only the first two. Nor, I repeat, do we know that they are agents. Indeed, there are indications they are not, and that the may be amateurs at all this, only very good at their specific tasks. Besides," Valiere continued darkly, now placing his finger in Genet's face, "you are already a marked man. Have you forgotten your sins? As for a war, stealth or otherwise, leave that to the appointed representatives of France, such as myself. What you, my dear Genet, need to concentrate on is stopping these interlopers." He laid out five photos. "Whatever they know, whatever they have, they must not get it to the United States. Our computer security programs indicate that they had attempted to send a rather large file, but we pulled the plug before it got out. We do not think they transmitted it. But there is a good chance that whatever they learned, these two . . ." his finger traveled from the picture of Connie to Jake "know the details. If they get back to the United States, and if they reconstruct something, it would be a disaster for me, for the President, and for France."

Genet smirked. *I wager it would. And what makes you think I care about the President of France, and still less about France herself. She is a sick, cankerous whore. Your transparent front company was easy to penetrate---apparently by a child---and your connections to the Muslim pigs indicates that you yourself care nothing for France. You have let the Mohammedans overrun us in the last decades. They assault our females at malls, they overwhelm our welfare systems in the cities, and they burden our unemployment rolls. And it was politicians like you, Valiere, who not only permitted but you encouraged it. You changed the laws to welcome them, first by the thousands, then by the tens of thousands, until France is in danger of being eaten from the inside. We are drowning in a Muslim tide, and it is, to a great extent, your fault. You are fortunate, Mr. Foreign Minister, that I work only for money, and that I have even less affection for Americans than I do my own countrymen. But a job is a job.*

"And how much of a head start do they have?" Genet asked.

"Perhaps 6-8 hours. We lost them earlier today when they checked out of their hotel."

"You understand that the standard agreements are in place," noted Genet. "No prosecutions, all French taxes and obligations to me and my family forgiven. And, of course, my non-negotiable fee, in dollars, in our pre-arranged account."

Valiere gave a bored nod. "Yes, same as always." He lit another cigarette, looking down at the lighter to make sure he got the tip. When he lifted his eyes, Genet was gone.

Chicago

Won't be long now. Nossir. My big score. Won't be long now. Carl Gilliam looked at the old Dodge Dart as the Jamaicans drove off. They'd come to an agreement---his biggest acquisition in years. Six kilos of uncut coke. Street value in the hundreds of thousands of dollars---maybe over a million if he turned it right. 'Course, he worked virtually alone (no profits to split, that way) and, more important, no one to snitch.

Been long time workin' on this one. Long time. It's ready. Oh, yessir, it's ready. Then Carl Gilliam ain't gonna be Carl any more. Nossir. It be "Cashbox"after that. "Cashbox," that what they goin' call me.

Gilliam knew the streets. He'd run numbers as an eight-year-old, fronted grass and various pills by age 12, and graduated to harder drugs by age 15, when he bought his first gun. A stint in Alton Correctional for Boys only taught him better tricks of the trade. Out at 17, he started his own crack and coke business. He'd had to pay some dues for that. Once the Jamaicans nearly broke his legs, and he managed to get away only when a Chicago police cruiser came by. He'd killed three men, and managed to avoid even being brought in for a line up. It hadn't been easy, but here he was.

Not long now. Took some doing, but he and the Jamaicans worked out an "arrangement." He'd become their best wholesaler, but he knew that wouldn't last long. *Nossir. They be wantin' to cut out old Cashbox as soon as they can work it. Yessir. Old Cashbox got one more big deal left, then I'm outta here. Jamaicans think they be scammin' old Cashbox, but I be scammin' them. Not long now.*

Paris

For an organization with the name "United Nations International Education and Social Services Organization," it had done very little to advance either international education or social services. Indeed---while Connie was no expert---he could not think of one program that contributed to improved education or social services in developing countries. His research in banking had required him to look at lending patterns and at the World Bank, so he knew a little about the UN, and what he knew, he didn't like.

He knew they had stood by during the genocide in Rwanda without so much as lifting a finger. He knew that although some UN relief was sent to Somalia, neither France, nor Germany, nor Russia had sent troops to help the U.S. kick out the rival warlords. When several American soldiers were killed during a raid in Mogadishu, the Clinton administration withdrew rather than destroying the killers. The UN did nothing about the warlords. In Slovenia, in Bosnia, and in countless other counties where oppression and atrocities were occurring, the UN refused to act. It never passed a single resolution condemning the tyrannical governments of Cuba or Red China; it never condemned the Palestinian Liberation Organization's terror activities. Quite the contrary, Connie knew, the UN invited PLO Chairman Yassir Arafat to address the assembly . . . with his pistols at his side! Connie knew the UN delegates cheered when Ugandan murderer Idi Amin called for the "extinction" of Israel.

No, Connie had no love for the United Nations. And now he had to pretend to love it enough to get inside with his "student assistant," who clacked along behind him as his skateboard rolled over the cobblestones with great difficulty.

Thanks to Agents Harrison and Jackson, a phone call back to the states led to a high-level U.S. official calling UNIESSO and presenting the top official there with a request---to permit an American professor specializing in "poverty issues," who was visiting France and unexpectedly decided to do some research there, to be given access to the public archives. Reluctantly, the UN official agreed, but only after he was reminded that the U.S. congress still had not voted on this year's annual budget contribution for the UN. *Besides*, thought Connie, *these types love professors, because they can count on academics to regurgitate their party line.*

Approaching the main desk, Connie announced, "I'm Prof. Cataris from the United States. I was told you would be expecting me."

A middle-aged French woman peered down her glasses, uttered a "huumph," and gave him the guest register to sign. Connie signed, giving the pen to Jake, who drew a picture of a butterfly smoking a joint. She surveyed the "signatures," gave a disgusted "huuumph," and waved them through, pointing to elevator number 1. "Floor five," she called, turning back to reading *Le Monde*.

Connie almost said "thank you," but decided against it. She didn't deserve thanks. He had not noticed that Jake had taken his gum out and stuck it under the ledge of her desk as he walked by.

When the elevator door opened, an Italian man offered a sterile welcome, then with as much condescension as he could muster, showed Connie to his work space and pointed to the archives. There was a terminal in the archive room, and he gestured to Jake. "Come on. Let's make this quick."

Quickly searching for *l'Joliette du Mer*, Connie found the files he needed. Many, of course, were encrypted.

"Your turn," he said, sliding aside to allow Jake to sit down. Connie, meanwhile, tried to look busy by examining boxes of meaningless UN files.

"Export?" asked Jake.

Connie nodded. Jake hit the "send" key. *The kid had broken the encryption in less than five minutes??*

"They may have the same wire on these files that nabbed us at our last little party," Jake added. "I don't see one, but that doesn't mean there isn't some sort of automatic trigger whenever someone looks at these."

By that time, the fact that security guards, or worse, dangerous thugs, might be on their way no longer bothered Connie. *Comes with the territory.* "Can I look at some of these files while you are sending?"

"No prob. Whaddya want to see?"

"Open up something in 2001, say, Spring."

Jake minimized the "send" window and opened *l'Joliette du Mer*, January 2001. Connie scanned a couple of files, but there was minimal activity.

"Hmm. Nothing much here. Try February." Jake produced the February data. Again, no transactions. They repeated the process, but

261

Connie kept a wary eye out for UN employees who might be snooping on them. Still nothing. And again, still nothing.

"Ok, we'll try a couple more and if we don't see anything, we'll just finish exporting and get out. How long?"

Jake maximized the "send" window. "Another five minutes, minimum. These UN dudes have really old crap for equipment. I mean, some of it is probably older than you," he added, looking at Connie. It wasn't a joke.

Connie sighed as Jake maximized the "May 2001" window.

He almost didn't notice it, it was so obvious. Then he looked again. There it was: a deposit of nearly $1 million from the United Nations into the accounts of *l'Joliette du Mer*. But from which account? *Who made the damn deposit?*

Sweat broke out on Connie's forehead and hands. Until now, it was something of a game. In his heart, Connie could not believe he would find what he was now looking at, or, more accurately, he prayed he would not find this. *Connie, my boy, you are now playing international espionage at the top levels with, as we say, "geopolitical implications."*

"Uh," he stammered, tapping Jake on the shoulder, "account number up here. What can you do with it? Can you somehow do a search within the UN data base and find out what account this goes to?"

Jake sensed Connie's sudden discomfort. "Cool. What is it, some prostitute?"

"Uh, Jake, it's a little bit bigger than that." Connie had that queasy feeling in his stomach again and popped two more Tums. No matter what they found now, it was going to involve the UN in the 9/11 attacks, if only as a delivery boy or a holding tank for someone's dirty money.

As always, Jake's fingers flew across the keyboard, defeating one safeguard after another, cracking no fewer than five security codes in a matter of minutes. Connie stared at him in befuddled wonder. "Anyone ever tell you that you really are talented? I mean *really* talented?"

Jake looked up. "Hey, it's what I do." Jake flipped the screen toward Connie so he could read the file.

United Nations Oil for Food Program.

He now felt dizzy. *Mohammad Atta funded the 9/11 attacks with money that came from Iraq and was laundered through the United Nations' Oil for Food Program. The UN has blood on its hands, and Iraq is directly tied to that September day.* Now a wave of fear swept over him like nothing he'd felt before.

"How much time to send, Jake? C'mon, c'mon, send."

Jake maximized the window. *96% complete.* "It's goin'."

Suddenly they heard movement down the hallway, and looked at each other. "We're going to have to leave, *now!*" Jake didn't have to be told twice. In a single motion, Connie swept up his briefcase and started to push Jake out the door. Down the hall, he could see several UN security men coming at them. *They aren't here to help with our research, either.* They were yelling at Connie and Jake in French, but it all sounded to Connie like "You're a dead man."

Yet Jake, stopped, then said, "hold on!" Before Connie could stop him, the kid bolted back in the computer room, where he minimized the "send" window again, then he hurled his skateboard down and shouted at Connie, "Go! Go! I can catch up."

I believe you can, kid. Connie ran down an archival stack toward the red "Exit" sign. It had instructions in French and English not to open the door, because it would trip an alarm. *C'est la Vie!* Connie burst through, and he heard the clack-clacking of Jake's skateboard behind him, and, further back, the angry screams of the security men.

"Come on! This way," Connie waved at Jake, bursting through the door, and Jake pulled a perfect hair turn on his skate board at the top of the stairwell as Connie bounded down the steps three and four at a time.

The men were right on top of Jake, and he could feel hands nearly grabbing his flannel shirt before he performed a kick flip, landing his board on the top railing. He sailed down the rail, sparks flying from the metal wheel brackets. At the stairwell corner, he jumped off, his board shooting into the wall. Jake snatched it in mid-air, and jumped down four stairs at a time, right behind Connie.

"Come on, dude. You geriatric types are slow." Jake passed Connie on the right.

Only one more flight . . . Connie looked back, but the security men were gaining.

Jake blasted through the exit door at the ground level on a smooth concrete sidewalk. He hurled the board down and mounted it again, pushing off with his right foot. "Split up, man. They can't catch me. I'll lure them away."

Connie fought the inclination to be a hero. *You're going to allow a teenager to be a decoy?* But common sense prevailed. "Ok, go. I'm sure the agents will find us." Connie dived behind a shock of trees to his left, as Jake propelled himself down the sidewalk, hopped a park bench, then did a 180 to taunt the security guards. It worked. They all followed him, and in minutes, Connie jumped from behind the trees and headed in the opposite direction. He turned to look in Jake's direction when a car screeched to a stop, the front bumper coming to a halt inches from his knees.

"Get in!" Harrison shouted. He, Jackson, and Fatima, still scrunched in the little Renault.

"Do you guys know you look silly in this car?" Connie asked, scrambling to the door. "I mean, two huge, ugly men and a beautiful woman jammed into what looks like a toy car?"

Fatima said, "Thank you for the compliment, professor."

"We are not 'huge.' We are normal-sized Americans. The French are just small," observed Harrison. "Where's the kid?"

"He went the other direction, on his skateboard. Don't worry, there's no way they could catch him."

Jackson turned on the "Jake tracker," following the beeps down street after street. When they turned near the Arc d'Triumph, there were no security guards in sight---but Jake was practicing jumping his skateboard onto a large fountain nearby, much to the disgust of the Parisians. Harrison pulled up next to the fountain.

"Having fun?" Connie asked.

"Told you they couldn't keep up with me." He flipped the board with his foot, catching it in mid-air. He climbed in the car, squeezing Fatima and her ample breasts even closer to Connie. He didn't seem to mind. Jake wedged the board on top over her lap.

"Was the file transfer complete?" Connie asked.

"Dunno, man. I minimized the window so that they wouldn't see it, but it was only at 96% when I left. If they checked the tool bar when they came in, I doubt that it finished sending"

Jackson leaned over the seat. "What did you find?"

Connie cleared his throat. "It's big. We're gonna need the documentation, but I saw one file from May 2001 that had a check for $1 million deposited in *l'Joliette du Mer*." Still catching his breath, he paused.

Jackson impatiently asked, "And?

"Jake cracked the account numbers. The money came through the UN's Oil for Food Program."

"God," said Harrison. Jackson took off his sunglasses and squeezed the bridge of his nose.

"You got it," replied Connie, slumping back in the seat. "Iraq."

"Professor," said Jackson, turning the car abruptly, "we need to get you home, now."

"Thank God. I'm ready to see my wife and kids." Fatima smiled at him. "No offense, miss, er, ma'am." he added.

"And you'll see them first thing . . . after we take you to the President."

Connie's broad grin disappeared.

Fatima winked at him.

Chapter 20

Cairo

A man dressed in a suit, uttering only the code word, *shalom*, stood at Jaleel's door.

Clever. A Jewish greeting for a Jewish disaster.

"Where is the package?" Jaleel insisted.

"That is why I am here in person," the shadowy visitor replied. " There has been a delay. In case you have not noticed, the Americans and British are active in Kuwait, not to mention Afghanistan. Our delivery has been delayed. I can no longer pick it up in Baghdad. Instead, I must acquire it in Syria, whereupon I will bring it to you."

"And when am I to expect this?"

"Soon. Possibly within a month. No more than six."

"That is a fairly large window. What if I am run over by a mad cab driver between now and then?"

Although Jaleel could scarcely see his face, his sneer was clearly visible: "Then Allah will find another vessel." Then he was gone.

Paris

From here it was routine. Agents Harrison and Jackson would escort Connie and Jake to the Air France terminal, board the plane with them, drop Jake off at . . . well, wherever the odd young man "hung out"---and take Connie to meet the President.

Then he was free. Then he would be another economics professor, having done is part for king and country.

The phone in the room rang, and Connie picked it up expecting to hear Harrison or Jackson's voice.

"Professor Cataris?" It was a man's voice with a French accent.

Connie hesitated. Does anyone know I'm here? *They must. My cover was an economics professor.* He relaxed some. "Yes?"

"Thank God I caught you before you left. I've been trying to find you for a week. My name is Jacques Lestrand---Prof. Jacques Lestrand, of the Economics Department at the Sorbonne."

Connie had heard the name. Thinking for just a moment, he did what all academics do: he ran through the man's publication history. "Yes, I know your work. Inflation during the French Revolution and Napoleonic period, right?"

"You flatter me. It was just a couple of papers."

"No," Connie said, anxious to clear the line for the call from his handlers. "It was good work. As I recall you supported Eugene Black's theory that the inflation came from changes in domestic crop production, and not the excesses of the Revolution."

"Again," he humbly replied, "you flatter me beyond words. Professor Cataris, I realize you are on a tight schedule, but I wanted to just show you my most recent data on French banking during the Great Depression. It's far closer to your own work than my earlier price data."

"I'm sorry, but I really am scheduled to leave within the hour. I don't see how . . . ."

"I've been trying to find you for days, ever since a friend I have at *l'Joliette du Mer* told me you had arrived. I took the liberty to come to your hotel, and I brought the data with me. Please, professor, if you could but give me a few minutes. I . . . I'm embarrassed, but I'm really stuck. Some of this just doesn't make sense, and if anyone could sort it out, you could. I have a feeling you could do it rather quickly. It has to be something I'm just not seeing."

Some men are vulnerable to money; others to sex; still others to the lure of power. Connie's greatest weakness was the unanswered question, the unexplained data, the hidden solution. Something struck him as odd about the reference to *l'Joliette du Mer*, but he brushed it off. "OK, look, I can't leave the room, but if you want to bring it up, fine. Realize, though, I may have to go at any minute."

"Oh, that would be *magnifique*! I promise, this will not take long. I have faith that you can pinpoint the problem in no time."

"Fine, fine. My room number is 317."

"I shall be right up."

Within moments, there was a knock at the door. Connie squinted through the peephole to see a tall man with a briefcase and stack of computer readouts in his arms. He had long red hair. *Typical French weirdo academics. I bet he doesn't bathe, either*, Connie thought, opening the door.

He had scarcely gotten the safety latch off than the door burst inward on him and the man pressed a rag against his mouth. Connie could not scream. He could not even remain conscious as he hit the floor, his head cracking on the wood.

Twenty minutes later, after several unanswered rings on the phone in room 317, Harrison, Jackson, Fatima, and Jake hustled into the room. Computer readouts were scattered everywhere. Connie's laptop and briefcase were gone.

And so was Connie.

Tora Bora Mountains, Afghanistan

Ever since he had met with the secretive figure in Wal-e-Teb, Camel had waited to see some evidence that his warning had been heeded. He passed his information up the channels, where it disappeared in the Langley labyrinth. *Maybe so far, so good.* So far, the horrible attacks described to him by the mystery man had not come to pass.

Camel could handle routine terrorists and bloodthirsty tribesmen. But the images he carried of what could be unleashed still troubled him.

At the same time, he wondered if he had been set up---if now, he wasn't being used to somehow convey information to the enemy, even though he had checked for bugs or tracers on many occasions.

Meanwhile, American bombers had devastated the hills, visible to him in the distance, where all information had placed bin Laden. Camel had not heard anything further from the mysterious figure since their meeting a month ago.

Perhaps the Agency foiled the plot. Perhaps they broke up the cell.

Perhaps.

And perhaps my information ended up in a folder with an overworked analyst. Perhaps the information was given to someone who dismissed it as impossible. Perhaps the Agency acted on the intelligence, but bin Laden slipped into the landscape yet again. Perhaps he is laying low. Perhaps the plan is merely on hold, and perhaps all those images I have battled for a month will become reality after all.

Paris

The first thought Connie had when he woke up was that he was not tied up. After he recalled what had happened, with Big Red giving him the funny gas, Connie forced himself to close his eyes and feign sleep, if only so he could take stock of the situation. *How long have I been out? Where am I? How long will they let me live?*

He had a splitting headache---a side effect of the ether or whatever Red had used to immobilize him. Letting out a low groan, he decided he could not fake unconsciousness forever. He pushed himself into a sitting position on the sofa, four feet from a man in a suit sitting in a chair and, behind him, Red. And, further back, in the shadows, another silent figure he could not make out.

Genet stood motionless as Dominique de Valiere spoke. "Ah, Professor . . . Cat--err---is, is it?" He pronounced the "are" wrong..

Rubbing his forehead, Connie answered, "Cat-ar-is. And thanks for the headache and the kidnapping. Common in your country? No wonder we hate France."

"Please, Professor, no games. We know what you have been doing and you know what you have been doing. I have only one question for you: what have you learned? And, before you answer, I'm sure you realize that given the nature of your investigations---the importance of your subject matter and how it affects France---we will not hesitate to use less polite strategies to obtain our answer. Now, if you please . . . ."

Shortly after he agreed to go to France, Connie had made up his mind that if he ever fell into "enemy" hands, he would spill the beans, totally and completely. He knew enough about spy stuff from novels and non-fiction to know that strong, hardened professionals could not hold out against torture, and therefore he wasn't even going to try. They might kill him anyway, but that was likely going to happen one way or another unless his CIA watchers managed to track him. He didn't even know where the tracker was---*probably in my coat, and I'm sure they got found it by now. Heck, they're probably even using it to throw off the agents.*

"What do I know?" he began, philosophically. "I know, or think I can prove, that *l'Joliette du Mer* is a front organization that laundered money; that the money was given to the 9/11 hijackers; and that money came from the United Nations Oil-for-Food program, which means I know that directly or indirectly both Iraq and France were up to their eyeballs in the deaths of 3,000 Americans. Does that pretty much answer your question, Mr. Valiere?"

The Frenchman was somewhat shocked to see that Connie knew him. "I was not aware, Professor, that you knew who I was."

"Your preening in front of the cameras at every UN speech is hard to miss." Connie's eyes flashed as he baited the minister. "You make it easy to hate France."

Valiere gave an amused sniff. "Preening? Yes, of course you would focus on that. Always 'show-biz' with you Americans. Back to your research: were you able to transmit the codes to the United States?"

Hmm. I hurt him with that one. At that moment, for some reason, Connie decided to lie.

"Yes, the transmission went through. They used me to make sense of the data---only because I knew immediately what I was looking at---but any competent economic analyst could sort this out in 24 hours. So I'm afraid I'm more good to you dead than alive." *God, that was a dumb thing to say. Did Red smile?*

Valiere studied him, dragging out his favorite Marleboros. "You underestimate your talent, Professor. I have done come checking up on you," wagging his finger as if to scold. "Our French economists are quite impressed. More than a few think you are a genius."

Connie rolled his eyes. "It won't take a genius to follow your trail of blood. When this gets out---and it will get out---you and your country will pay more than you dreamed." *Why the HELL am I talking like Clint Eastwood here?*

"Of course, so you say. And so you claim to have found evidence tying the government of France to either the Oil-for-Food payoffs or *l'Joliette du Mer*?"

"Let's see: we have a French company laundering the money and your country's fingerprints were all over the Oil-for-Food kickbacks. And I'm going to go way out on a limb here and bet that when we look at the actual individuals getting UN dirty money, *Monsiers* Valiere and *Chirac* will have received a few francs. Or, should I say, Euros?"

The figure in the shadows shifted uncomfortably, but said nothing. Valiere snorted and waved his hand as if the information he had just heard was nothing more than a roster cut on a soccer team. "Your Union Carbide killed thousands in Bhopal, India. Did that mean your country was aware of its actions? Or condoned them? My nation had no knowledge of what *l'Joliette du Mer* did with its funding."

"If that were true, you would not be here talking to me," Connie said, glumly realizing his likely fate. He glanced at Red, only to see Genet's mouth break into a slight smile. "I'm not good at torture---I'll admit that up front---so I've saved us all time and told you everything. Heck, I'll even tell you the names of everyone I worked with, what our cell phone numbers were, and so on. I'm a loyal American, but I'm not so stupid as to think that you won't get it out of me anyway. So let's just get this over with and have Quasimodo here kill me."

The Frenchman studied him for what seemed an eternity. *Probably trying to decide the least messy way to kill me and dispose of my body without an international incident. "International incident?" France and the UN involved in 9/11 and the kidnapping of an economics professor would be an "international incident?"*

Then it dawned on Connie that even after he told them everything, they would still likely torture him to confirm the information. Still, the Frenchman knew that Connie only had half the story---Jake had the other half.

"Very well," Valiere stated. "Give me your contact number for your agent friends. We'll see if the boy's information matches your own. If so . . . well, there is little we can do, and little difference your death would make."

"No, you don't need to bring in the kid. I told you everything," Connie protested.

"Everything except whether, in fact, the security was breached and the transmission made. And if it has not, well, he is the only other person of interest to us."

Connie began to panic, now having drug the kid into it. He could handle his own death, but didn't want to be responsible for Red getting his hands on Jake. His mind leaped from alternative to alternative. *Suicide. It's the only answer. But how?* Then he saw the window. There were no iron bars on it. "God forgive me," he said.

In a flash, before Genet or Valiere could react, Connie bolted directly to his left---crashing through a glass window. He had assumed he was in some hotel or apartment building but had no idea how high up he was. *God, let it be high, and let me die quick!*

Connie saw the green tarp---no, an awning!---coming at him fast. His body tore through it and thumped onto a pile of luggage, and Connie let out a grunt. Looking up, he could see he had only been on the third floor, and the awning had helped break his fall. *Terrific. Now Red will be after me.* Momentarily surveying himself for broken bones, he found he could move, and swung off the luggage pile in front of an angry bellhop, scurrying to his right as fast as he could go.

Three stories above him, Valiere looked out the window and let out a curse as Genet and the third, dark figure hovered behind him. "He's told us the truth," the Genet said.

"Perhaps," came the reply. "But he already knows too much. This must never reach the public. Do you understand?"

"Of course." The French minister then pointed to Genet. "Bring him back." As the big redhead started out the door, Valiere added, "And bring me the boy!" Genet nodded and disappeared.

Now two blocks away, Connie ran aimlessly, his body aching and his head pounding from the fall and the ether. He knew Paris only superficially, and had no idea where he was. If he could get to a high point, he could locate the Eiffel Tower and, from there, figure out his location. Meanwhile, he searched for landmarks. *No sense running until I know where I'm running to.*

He made a left and found himself in a dead end, and alley. *Damn!* Turning back onto the street, he barely had time to see the Volvo aiming straight at him. Its brakes screeched as Connie dove out of the way, landing on cobblestone that made every joint hurt even more. Laying on his side, he could see Red's boots in front of him. Connie flopped on his back as Genet leveled a silenced pistol at him. "Not here," he growled. "The alley. Move."

Connie gathered himself to lunge at the big man---*that should force him to shoot me and end all this*---when Red suddenly dropped the gun and went into an epileptic-type convulsion. *What the heck?* Then Connie saw the prongs of the Taser sticking out of Red's back, and, six feet away, Lonnie Jackson attached to the other end.

"Come on, Professor," shouted Harrison, scooping up Connie and shoving him in the miniature Renault, already filled with Fatima and Jake.

"How did you . . . ? Oh, right. The tracker." Suddenly Connie got angry. "Where were you guys?? I jumped out a *window!*"

Jackson had leaped behind the steering wheel after shoving Connie across Fatima and Jake's laps. He started the car and smiled. "It was only three stories."

Connie was incredulous. "You *knew where I was all the time*? What if they'd just shot me?"

"We didn't think they'd do that," stated Harrison, matter of factly. "They needed to know what you knew, and we needed you to tell them. We were pretty sure you wouldn't play hero---but the window thing was impressive."

Rolling onto his back, Connie was gazing up at Fatima's dark eyes. Again, she winked and smiled. "Americans," she said. Always the heroes!" raising her eyebrows a hair. Jake, disgusted, just shook his head.

"Wait," sputtered Connie. "You *let me* get taken?"

"Not exactly," answered Jackson. "See, they were gonna make a play for you or Jake one way or another---they still want to talk to Jake, am I right?---so it wasn't a matter of *if* they got you, only *when* and under what circumstances."

"So you had me under surveillance all the time?" Connie's head was spinning. "You used me as bait?"

"Not exactly 'bait.' Prof, no one can protect you 24/7. Haven't you watched enough cop movies to see what happens to people in protective custody? If someone wants you bad enough, and is willing to pay the price, there's no place to hide. But now that they know that we know, and that we know who is behind all this . . . well, you should be safe now."

"So why didn't you kill him?" sputtered Connie. "He'll only come back, like one of those guys in the horror movies."

"Too messy," offered Jackson. "Too public. This is foreign soil, and we still may need him."

Huh? "How do we need a psycho killer?"

Harrison, taking over, held up his hand. "Look, this guy---by the way, the name of the hired killer with the red hair is 'Genet,' although his real name is Jean Olfin, Anyway, we at the Company call him 'Citizen Genet'---this guy probably won't come after you again. What's the point? They know we have you now, and they know you'll be in the U.S. soon. But we do have to get you and Jake out of here now."

"Well, I didn't tell them everything," Connie noted quietly.

Jackson pulled the Renault over to the curb so hard it nearly threw Jake out the door.

"What do you mean? Don't tell me you were a hero after all."

"I lied. I told them we had already transmitted all the information."

Jackson and Harrison exchanged satisfied looks. "So they think, or at least, suspect, that the U.S. now has all the info that you and Jake have yet to reconstruct?"

"That's about it. Oh, and one other thing. You mentioned Red, er, Genet, the killer?"

"Yeah."

"His boss is the French Foreign Minister Dominique de Valiere," Connie announced smugly.

"So? We knew that," Harrison snorted.

"You did?" Connie's life as a spy was hardly paying dividends. First, his heroic leap was unnecessary, then his treasured information proved common knowledge. "Well, just damn! I suppose you know who the other guy in the room was, too." Connie struggled to sit up, but he was too firmly wedged against the softness of Fatima and the jagged edges of Jake.

"Other guy?" Jackson replied. He and Harrison now seemed concerned. "What other guy?"

"There was another guy in the room. Behind Red, er, Genet. He didn't say a word, but I got the feeling he was even more important than Valiere. Maybe even his boss."

Harrison and Jackson exchanged concerned looks and shuffled uncomfortably.

Uh oh! Clearly something the pros did not know! Jackson put the car in gear and headed out of Paris. "All right," he said, "we're getting you back to the United States right now."

"Thank Holy Christ," muttered Connie, still laying across the laps of Fatima and Jake, and wiggled to get up.

"What's the matter?" asked Fatima, smiling. "Aren't you comfortable?"

"No offense, ma'am," responded an embarrassed Connie. "You were, uh, quite comfortable."

"Dude, you are so stupid," interjected Jake, "I would have stayed there and shut up," looking with fascination at Fatima's breasts. Now it was Connie's turn to roll his eyes.

Location Unknown

Dear Mom and Dad,

We've left Afghanistan, but I'm not at liberty to tell you where we are heading. David is still back there with his unit, but I can't tell you specifically where they are, either. No one seems sure if we got bin Laden or not. A lot of scuttlebutt, but nothing solid. If he was in those mountains, he's part of the landscape now. But no one is sure yet if he was there. Anyway, lots for us to do, mostly on patrols with local warlord tribesmen. They have proven tough fighters and, so far, trusted allies.

The Taliban fell apart even faster than we thought. So far, no civil war. This fellow Kharzai seems to have the backing of most of the people---to the extent that any Afghan leader does---and if he can't turn the country into a reasonable democracy, then no one can.

It has been a real experience. I'm just now reading papers from a few months ago saying that we would be in a "quagmire" here. What a joke. It's the enemy in the quagmire. We're killing them in record numbers whenever they show their heads.

Anyway, more later when I can tell you about what I'm doing.

Love you guys,

Tom

Al-Nasiriyah, Iraq

American tanks rattled through the night, blasting anything that shot at them. On their flanks, Humvees and armored vehicles provided a mobile screen, destroying any resistance that the tanks missed. It was a remarkable advance. After two days, the armored column was already beyond some of the southern "hot spots" in Iraq.

It happened virtually overnight: one day, Jo and her unit were in Camp Virginia, Kuwait, then the next day, they were on the move to Baghdad. The Marines and Third Infantry Division had surged north, knocking out initial resistance at al-Nasiriyah. But, as Jo soon learned, the key word was "initial." A massive convoy followed immediately on the heels of the combat units, bringing needed fuel, ammunition, and medical supplies behind the front-line units.

As the 507th headed north, it had stayed on the heels of other units in the convoy. But after two days, sandstorms slowed the 507th down to 15 miles per hour. Before long, Capt. Wesley Carl, the 507th's commanding officer, could no longer see the lights of the vehicle in front of him. Then a truck went into the sand, requiring the column to stop while a wrecker tried to pull the truck out. Carl got word from battalion: his slower unit would have to keep up as best it could, but the rest of the convoy would press ahead. Some 32 soldiers in 18 vehicles struggled to catch up along Iraq's Highway 8, known as "Route Blue."

It took an hour to get back on the main highway. Iraqis occasionally stood by the roadside. None cheered, but nobody threw rocks.

Maybe this won't be so bad, Jo thought. Night descended on the convoy as it crawled up "Route Blue." Marines waved them on ahead. Except, a kilometer away . . . the road suddenly split.

Captain Carl saw lights up ahead, and thought they had to be the lights of the convoy. He followed the lights . . . right into the center of al-Nasiriyah. An Iraqi guard even waved them right into town where he realized his mistake. Carl tried to have the column make a giant U-turn in town, when a truck ran out of gas. Jo and other troopers piled out to form a perimeter while another soldier poured gas into the truck.

My gosh, our CO is lost! He has us in the middle of a town! Jo whipped out her M-16, but it was jammed, even though she had cleaned it daily. *The sand and grit here are unrelenting.* A sergeant quickly checked it, but couldn't fix it, and threw it back to her.

Then came the gunshots. Jo heard several, before the order, "Mount up!" rang out. She jumped in the truck as gears ground and engines roared, but now the Iraqis were all around them, bullets whizzing, trucks bogging in soft mud and sand. The troopers dismounted again, but this time were riddled with incoming Iraqi fire. Two men and a woman went down around Jo instantly. Jo staggered backwards, finding herself next to Humvee, one of the few vehicles in their group still running.

"Get in get in! Everyone. Pile in!" Someone was barking orders.

A sergeant she didn't know was taking over, but there was little he could do. Troops dropped like flies under a hail of bullets from every window, rooftop, and house. The Humvee bolted forward, with Jo crammed in the middle of the back seat between two other soldiers. Her friend, Kelly, was driving, but no sooner had the Humvee built up some speed than an Iraqi truck rolled directly in front of them. There was no time to stop. Jo's Humvee hit the truck dead center and slammed the passengers into the seats in front of them or the glass.

Jo saw the front dash of the Humvee flying at her---or her flying at it. *Bye, mom and dad. I love you.*

Kandahar, Afghanistan

Still. Perfectly still. Bugs of unknown types, like none he'd ever seen before, crawled in and out of Chico's ear. *Do not move.* A hot Afghan sun beat down on him, but the wind was cool, even biting. His body covered by his mountain ghillie---the full-poncho camouflage net that included plastic jute that resembled grass and leaves. *Do not move. Your muscles do not ache. You do not feel pain. You are relaxed.* Chico practiced every calming mental exercise he could think of, breathing slowly but silently.

Earlier a decidedly deadly-looking snake slithered by, but even then Chico remained motionless. A high-value target was possibly coming down the path on the opposite hillside sometime today. *A very high value target.*

Chico was not a sniper by training. He had practiced some, and was a marksman, but so were most of the Rangers. Of all the guys in the unit, though, Chico was the best shot, so he got the assignment. Mick remained about five clicks back, escorted by the mysterious interpreter known only as Camel. Earlier this week, Camel had received a message from a boy in a village in Tora Bora several miles north of here that a person of great interest to us wandered through these hills regularly, almost as a ritual. Indeed, Chico did not know that people in the United States had see these very footpaths on their TV screens on many occasions . . .

. . . as the camera followed Osama bin Laden and Aman al-Zawahiri on network news footage.

Today. Today, I take you out, Mr. Terrorist. Today you go to whatever Islam calls hell. And I'll bet you dollars to dinars you won't be getting any virgins when you arrive.

Then, at a distance of perhaps 1,200 meters, Chico saw movement. Two figures slowly walked up the path, which ran no more than 500 meters in front of him.

It's him. I've got the bastard, right in my sights! As Chico calmly and silently slid the safety off his brand new .308 caliber Patriot Arms "Genesis" sniper rifle, his scope trained on bin Laden's head, he detected three other men, following a good distance behind. *His bodyguards. Well, they won't do you any good today.* Regardless of what he told himself, Chico had only practice-fired the new weapon a few dozen times, and still was not fully comfortable with it.

800 meters. Keep walkin'.

700. That's right, you asshole. Come to papa. Let me put a nice .30 cal round in your head, right above your piehole.

600. Chico fought the natural rising adrenalin. *Keep calm. Breathe. Slow, deep breaths. Exhale as you squeeze.* A professional sniper might not have needed all this self-coaching, but Chico fought to remember all his training.

There. 500 meters. Take the shot. He gently squeezed the trigger...

...just as bin Laden's foot slipped sideways off a rock, pitching him slightly to the right.

Chico's shot ripped a hole in bin Laden's left shoulder, and he heard him howl in pain. Fear gripped Zawahiri's eyes, and the bodyguards ran forward, but not before Chico had another round chambered. *Damn it! The other guy is protecting him.* Zawahiri shielded bin Laden with his body, but Chico tried a "two-fer," loosing another round through Zawahiri's back. The physician-terrorist let out a low grunt as blood splattered, and he went down . . .

but that son of a bitch bin Laden is still up! He was staggering to his right like a drunk, and Chico chambered a third round when a shot landed just a foot away from him. Chico drew bin Laden into his sights yet again when a searing pain shot through his arm. One of bin Laden's guards had hit Chico's shooting arm, but rather than advancing, they provided covering fire . . . *for that rat-bastard to escape.* One dragged Zawahiri while the another effectively shielded bin Laden, and the third al-Qaeda fighters peppered Chico's position with shots. His shooting hand wasn't working well, and he figured he would not get another clear shot at bin Laden anyway, so grudgingly Chico fell back.

Damn it! Your time will come. I ain't done with you! Chico dashed over the ridge, where, in the distance, he could see the dust trail of Mick and Camel's Humvee heading toward him. He took one last look at the party scurrying back up the mountain pass.

You can run, but you can't hide.

Chapter 21

Narbonne, France

It was a small airfield, but it had a helipad, no doubt for the big spenders who frequented the French beaches. Lonnie and Cliff had finally traded the Volvo---itself a welcome upgrade from the tiny Renault---for an even larger Mercedes van, much to the relief of their back-seat passengers.

"OK, Professor," Cliff announced as the Mercedes lurched to a stop near a black helicopter. *Appropriate,* Connie thought. "You and Jake are outta here. We're going to put you on a helo for the *U.S.S. Abraham Lincoln*, and from there, well, you'll probably end up at one of our air bases in the region, then they'll have you on a flight back home."

Jackson came close with a pair of tweezers. "I need you to open your shirt, please."

Connie looked puzzled, but undid his buttons. "What are you gonna do, take a sample of armpit hair?" he joked.

Jackson found what he was looking for---a small thread leading to a tiny transmitter---and he yanked.

"Ow! What the heck?" Connie looked down and a droplet of blood formed above his nipple. Fatima followed behind Jackson and stuck a "Spot" Bandaid on it.

"Now your turn, Pearl Jam," Jackson said, gesturing at Jake. Pulling his shirt up, Jake said, "God are you guys ancient. Pearl Jam went out with Sega."

"Yeah, that's us," Jackson said. "Old geezers. For what it's worth, I loved Sega, especially Mortal Kombat with Scorpion's finishing move. Ok, there you go, guys. Clean as a whistle."

Connie still looked at his Spot Bandaid. "When did you put those in?" *No wonder they never worried about us being searched for the transmitters.*

"Remember when we put you in a twilight sleep for all those tests and injections you needed to come over here? We slipped it in then." Jackson held up the two little transmitters with his tweezers and grinned.

"No wonder they didn't find it," Connie said, shaking his head. He swept his arm toward Norbonne. "So I take it we can't just hop the next Air France flight out."

Harrison chuckled, "No, I don't think whoever is involved here is going to let you just fly out of the country. We've got to be a little bit sneaky, don't you think?"

"Well, they 'let us' get this far, I'd say. So they can't be that dangerous, or that good!"

Jackson and Harrison scowled, then Fatima took over. "Professor," she purred, "perhaps you don't appreciate how talented your guardians are, or how difficult it was for them to get you here without incident."

"'*Without incident*??' You call being threatened by Eric the Red and having to jump out of a third-story window 'without incident?' I call that a *helluva* incident. I thought I was committing suicide back there for the good old US of A. It's not my idea of fun." For his part, Jake looked thoroughly disgusted. *Maybe he's taking my side in this one*, thought Connie.

The agents merely folded their arms, bored by his diatribe. "Look," Harrison interrupted, "You're safe now. We got what we need. You're a damn hero. You've done a good thing, Professor. Now can we just get you back home?"

Fatima squeezed Connie's arm. "You've been through a lot," she added, looking a Jake. "You both have. No operation is without a hitch. But you're ok. All right?"

Jake, ever the voluble one, merely gave his "whatever" shrug. Connie, calmed by Fatima's touch, still could not believe how close he had come to death---but then, he had to admit it had been exciting. *Damn exciting.* And, he and Jake had done something for their country. *Damn patriotic*, he reflected, proudly.

"Fine. Let's go," he replied curtly, heading for the helicopter, which was now starting to turn its big rotors.

"Not us, Connie. Just you and Jake. We still have work to do."

"What? You aren't coming with us? Who'll protect us? I mean, I thought you guys were assigned to us the whole way."

"You're in good hands with the Navy boys. Someone will meet you at each stop, and escort you home." He extended his hand. Jackson came over and did the same. Befuddled, Connie shook it, reached over and shook Cliff's hand, as the big agent punched him in the shoulder. "Great job, Prof. Didn't know ya had it in ya!" Connie smiled, embarrassed.

Then agents slapped Jake on the back. "You're a tough kid. You've got a job with us anytime you want it." Jake paused, then, for one of the first times since Connie knew him, the kid smiled. "Cool. Maybe. Could be fun workin' with you old dudes." He turned toward the helicopter, when he snapped his finger and said, "Hey, my board, man!" Cliff and Lonnie exchanged puzzled glances, then remembered that they had thrown his skateboard in the trunk. Cliff quickly opened the trunk and handed it to him. Jake held it in front of him: "Solid. Don't leave home without it."

Connie started to follow him to the helo when Fatima said, "*Merci, mon* Professor. Your wife is a lucky woman." Then she kissed him square on the mouth. Jake's smile grew even bigger. "That's what I'm talkin' about!" he shouted over the thwap-thwap of the rotors. Connie blushed and climbed aboard.

Within minutes, his adventure would be over, and he'd be airborne for the United States . . . and Jan and the kids. He looked at Jake, who gave him a thumbs up. "Straight!" was all he said.

Connie thought it meant, "Way to go," but wasn't sure.

Tora Bora Mountains, Afghanistan

Osama bin Laden stumbled back into his cave, bleeding profusely from the round that a hidden sniper had put through his left arm. The elbow was broken---likely shattered---and Zawahiri was wounded in the upper right back, but apparently the round did not puncture the lung. Malid had taken over directing the al-Qaeda fighters.

"Sharif, we must move you to Pakistan. There is a place near Peshawar where I can obtain what I need to save your arm---and Zawahiri---but we must go now." He had prepared the SUV for an escape. It would not be long before the American Predators re-acquired them. He could see the pain, and the anger, in bin Laden's eyes.

Grabbing Zawahiri's shirt with his good hand, bin Laden asked, "How long until 'Allah's Wind' is ready?"

Fighting against the pain and lightheaded from blood loss, Zawahiri responded, "I have not talked to our contacts in a week. The American invasion of Iraq has made communications difficult."

"Put it in motion as soon as possible. Do you understand me? As *soon as possible*."

"Sharif, I shall attend to it as soon as we get to safety and get our wounds tended." Malid motioned two of the al-Qaeda members, who came over with a litter. "Move him, now!"

As they lifted bin Laden, he rose up yet again, and looked at Zawahiri: "As soon as possible!" Zawahiri nodded, and bin Laden slumped unconscious. The physician himself flopped on a blanket, and soon both were carried to the SUV.

The trip to Peshawar would take several hours, allowing for time to hide from the ever-present American Predators. Zawahiri and bin Laden were both passed out in the back, with two al-Qaeda guards seated around them. Malid hit the accelerator and the car lurched down the mountain roads toward Pakistan.

Coast of France

As the sleek SH-60 Seahawk lifted off from Norbonne, its twin engines pushing it up to over 120 knots, Connie could see Cliff, Lonnie, and Fatima turning and getting in their Mercedes. *I miss the Renault.* He felt a sting of regret, like a musician or dancer whose Broadway run had just ended---but not too much regret. Already he calculated the hours until he could see Jan and his girls.

It was noisy inside the chopper. Once Connie and Jake were inside, the only crew---the pilot and co-pilot---took their positions in the pilot's cabin. Connie and Jake were alone in the large, empty compartment. For once, Jake did not have his MP-3 player attached to his ear.

"Will you be glad to get back?" Connie asked, making small talk as much as anything.

"Not really," Jake replied in a near-yell. "This was kinda fun, ya know? Like, we actually did something."

"This isn't the first time you 'did something,'" Connie offered, referring to the Wyrm virus the kid had unleashed.

"Yah. So? Maybe it's the first time I did something good. Let it be said "they gave the last full measure of devotion."

It took Connie a second. "The Gettysburg Address? You're a patriot now?"

Jake's eyes grew cold. "Man, you don't know nuthin' about me."

Damn, I blew it. "Look, I apologize." Connie was still in a near yell. "Really. I'm sorry. I just didn't think . . . ."

"What, that I could read?" Jake replied sarcastically.

"Of course not, I meant I didn't think that you would have time for history with all your great talent in computing---I mean, that had to take you a lot of work to figure out all this stuff. When did you find time for Lincoln?"

Jake softened a little. "Actually, the two go together. As I would hack systems, and practice entrances, breaking codes, back doors, I'd start with public, obvious stuff. You know, public libraries. Then I'd get on-line and see if I could change the text of public documents . . . ."

" . . . like the Gettysburg Address?"

"Or the Declaration of Independence." Jake smiled. "Gotta read those things closely and check 'em against the paper copies. You never know when someone has inserted a stray word---like a 'not'--- in something."

"That's what I tell my students all the time, but I didn't really take it too seriously. You've tampered with online documents?"

"Once in a while. Just to prove I could do it. You'd be surprised what the UN Charter really says."

Or not, Connie thought. "You're talking about minor sites, right?"

Jake grinned. "Ever hear of the Avalon Project?"

Avalon. Avalon. "Oh, yeah. They put historical documents, like the Declaration of the Rights of Man or Washington's Farewell Address on line. That's out of Yale. Don't tell me: you hacked that site?"

"Check out the original wording of the Declaration of the Rights of Man and Citizen next time and compare it to their version."

Holy cow. Good argument for requiring students to get real paper documents---as in books---and not just copy stuff from the web. Connie instantly reviewed in his mind how many citations he'd seen in the last five or six years coming strictly from the web. *How many of these have been polluted?*

"Ok," Connie shouted, "so you learned some history. Economics? Political science?"

"You want me to explain Say's Law to you? You want the theory of "critical realignment elections?""

I'd be satisfied if half my students even knew about Say's Law. And they're majors. "I'm impressed," Connie offered. "I bet your parents are proud."

"Mom's so zonked she wouldn't know if I invented the cure for cancer. She freaked when Dad died. Started on the happy pills. She hasn't known what I've done for years." His eyes grew distant, and sad.

Connie felt sorry for the kid. "How long have you been doing illegal stuff?"

"I don't always see it as illegal. Try to think of it as 'exploring as-yet undefined areas of intellectual property law.'"

"Hmmm. You may have a point. No one could say for sure where the courts would go with Napster before they ruled as they did."

"Well, the question is whether the intellectual property of the artist is violated by 'sharing' or not. If I make a videotape of a movie, and 'share' it with 30 of my friends, is that a 'private' use? How about if I trade with them for a movie they taped? Same thing with music downloads: I can listen to it. Am I breaking the law if I hand my headset over to my kid brother or girlfriend?"

This kid is no dummy, and no idiot savant. "Ever think about going to college? I work at Columbia. We could use a student with your talent."

"And listen to profs that are already ten years behind me explain to me what BASIC code is? No thanks."

He has a point.

Suddenly Connie could see agitated movement in the cockpit. He couldn't hear, but he duck-walked up to the open pilot's compartment.

"We've got a problem, Ray," said the co-pilot, pointing out the window. "We're being diverted. I've already radioed for assistance, but if we don't set down they say they'll put us down."

Connie looked out the window to see two unmarked helicopters closing in. They had missiles.

The radio crackled, "American Sea Hawk. You will land immediately at the following coordinates, or we will destroy you."

"What the . . .?" but the pilot's question was cut off by the shriek of a radar lock-on. "Oh my God! They have us locked. Oh crap."

"Ray, get her down. *Set her down NOW!* Don't play with these guys. We ain't armed." The pilot banked the Sea Hawk to the designated coordinates.

Jake had unbuckled and looked out the window. "Guess we're not goin' home yet. Dang. That means I'm gonna miss another episode of 'Pimp My Ride.'"

Connie stared at him in disbelief, before pressing his face back to the glass.

An-Nasiriyah, Iraq

Light, above. Spinning light. Outside, popping like you make with the plastic bubbles they use in packing crates. I used to love to pop those bubbles.

Jo's eyes fluttered open, but she couldn't keep them open long because the light was so bright and the room kept moving. She felt sick. Gradually, the motion stopped. People kept moving in front of her---I'm not moving, they are. Doctors, nurses. Even through the drugs she felt a stabbing pain in her back and legs. They were working on her. Torturing me? No, saving me . . . but it hurts. My back. My legs. It all hurts.

She didn't know she lay in an Iraqi military hospital near An-Nasiriyah, and that she was in a row alongside Iraqi soldiers who had been wounded in battle with the Americans. She tried to turn her head to see who, or what, was on either side, but a blinding pain shot through her, all the way down her back.

How long have I been here? How long have I been unconscious? She had no answers, and the doctors and nurses, none of whom spoke English, did not seem inclined to tell her anyway.

Then, after days---weeks?---in the military hospital, a group of medical personnel moved her to a stretcher, then to another hospital. She did not know that she had just been placed in Nasariyah's Saddam Hussein General Hospital. But she did notice that now, at least, a few of the doctors and nurses spoke English, and that she had her own room. Finally, she managed to sit part way up, where she could see that three of her limbs were bandaged, and outside the door stood a guard (later, she learned, an Iraqi intelligence agent). That night, an older Iraqi nurse came in and sat next to Jo. She began to sing . . . a lullabye, in Arabic.

Jo mercifully drifted back to sleep.

A few hours later, she awoke to a group of orderlies who came in and wheeled her down the hall to an operating room. Not good, she thought.

One of the doctors spoke English to her. "We have inserted a steel rod in your leg, but it is not working. We must amputate your leg."

"NOOOOO!" Jo cried, and started to flail as best she could with her damaged arms. Each movement sent shock waves of excruciating pain down her back.

"We must do this---you are too badly damaged."

"Leave it. The Americans will come," she moaned. "My army . . . my country. They will come for me. They won't leave me. They can fix it. Just leave the leg."

Pity rose up in the doctor's eyes. Reluctantly he nodded to the others, and Jo was wheeled back down the hall to her room.

Then came the procession of nurses, blood transfusions, doctors, more pain. And, interspersed between her own cries, those of the wounded brought in from the field. The staff brought food, but Jo didn't eat. They'll poison you! Drugs worked on her mind.

Jo closed her eyes, and saw the mountains of West Virginia, then her brother Gary. Then mom and dad. Then nothing.

South of France

The Sea Hawk banked back toward the French coast, but Connie couldn't tell where they were. After about 20 minutes, the helo landed on a pad, and military guards swung open the door. They didn't look friendly. Connie and Jake crawled out, then put their hands up. Both pilots were spirited away in another direction.

"Hey, where are you taking them?" Connie knew he wouldn't get an honest answer, and likely wouldn't get an answer at all. It was the latter. Several French paratroopers (*not military police,* Connie thought---*odd*) escorted him and Jake in silence to a hangar. *Surely the U.S. government will be all over this. Is the Abraham Lincoln out there? Would they send planes? Probably not to France. France is an ally . . . or so they keep saying.* Then Connie thought of the trackers. Harrison and Jackson can still find us . . . *except they removed the trackers before we left. God. We are on our own.*

Jake looked at Connie and shook his head. "This isn't cool, dude. I don't think they want tips on how to play 'Everquest.'"

"I have a feeling that whatever tips you know, they are gonna know real soon," Connie observed, as that gnawing in his stomach returned. *And I was that close to getting home.*

A short, uniformed man approached with his adjutants. He looked to be standard military, maybe 50. Out of shape. Snotty. Connie called him Beau Geste, and the officer did not introduce himself.

Maybe some bluster? "I'm an American citizen and I demand to speak to the American consulate," Connie began. "This is an outrage."

Beau Geste was not impressed. "You make no demands on us, *monsieur*. You are a criminal, as is your accomplice, and France will deal with you as she does all criminals." He paced in front of them. There was no need for handcuffs or restraints: everyone knew the professor and his "student" had no where to escape to.

"Nevertheless," the officer continued, "my orders are to turn you over to the Office of the French Foreign Ministry."

"Let me guess. That would be Mr. de Valiere's office, correct?"

Beau Geste disregarded the question. "You will be back in Paris in a matter of hours. Both of you!" and he gestured to the paratroopers at a black Mercedes limo and Connie took the hint. He and Jake climbed in.

Outside An-Nasiriyah, Iraq

Mohammed Odeh al Rehaief, a local attorney, had awaited the Americans' coming for ten years. A Shiite opponent of Saddam Hussein, he had felt betrayed when the local Shiites---encouraged by the Americans to rise up in revolt---had received no support at all from the United States. The American president had privately told them through channels that they would have help, but once the shooting started, everything changed.

Rehaief's own family had participated in the uprising, and he had two nephews captured by Saddam's *Fedayeen* militia. He never saw them again, though the family received word that one was fed to Uday's pet tigers in Baghdad, and the other thrown off a building.

Rehaief did not know who he hated more, Saddam for his brutality or the Americans for their betrayal.

Still, one must make choices. Two devils, one choice.

It was a dark night the first time Rehaief avoided the *Fedayeen* patrols to reach American pickets. After he told them the information he brought, they escorted him to an officer, who interrogated him at length, but, he noted, certainly without torture. Convinced Rehaief's information was reliable, he asked Mohammed Rehaief to return the next night with confirmation about a blond American female being held in Saddam General Hospital in An-Nasiriyah. And, on the assumption that Rehaief would confirm she was still there, the officer, Maj. General Victor Renuart, set the wheels in motion to rescue a wounded POW.

When several Rangers, including Thomas Palmer, showed up at Renuart's briefing eight hours later, they found themselves alongside SEALs, Marines, and some Air Force special operations personnel. "As you were," Renuart said. Palmer and the other soldiers sat.

Renuart pulled back a map of the city, locating Saddam General as he began. "Eight hours ago a local Iraqi attorney---one of the anti-Saddam Shiite groups---came to me with information about a missing U.S. soldier being treated in this hospital. Her name is Pfc. Joanna Miles."

Palmer exchanged looks with others. He'd heard rumors of the fate of the 507th and the myth of this little blond prisoner had already become well known.

"We're going to go get her in twelve hours, pending confirmation of her location today. It will be a night operation, flown by Air Force personnel. The Marines, SEALS, and Rangers will set up a perimeter around the hospital, and one squad will sweep the hospital, find Pfc. Miles, and extract her to the waiting helicopter. This is a snatch and grab. We want no gunfire if possible. You will be in the middle of An-Nasiriyah, heavily outnumbered. If you have to fight, well, it won't be pretty, and we won't get our POW out. Any questions?"

"Ten-shun." Palmer snapped to attention with the rest as Renuart left the command tent. Someone let out a loud whistle.

Paris

During the long drive back to Paris, Connie slept, and dreamed of Jan and his girls at their last Christmas. "Deck the Halls" from Mannheim Steamroller played in the background, and the smell of a fat turkey filled the air. Sophie loved horses, and on one of his academic trips to Arizona, Connie had found a talented artist who painted ceramic horses with incredible scenes. One was stars and moons; another was the Arizona state flag; another was Native American designs. That Christmas, Connie thought Sophie was old enough to handle one of these pieces of art, and he bought her a "rainbow" horse. She loved it, and it became her greatest treasure. One day, Jan, while vacuuming, accidentally hit the desk and caused the horse to fall, breaking its leg. Both Connie and Jan thought Sophie would be heartbroken, but after gluing the leg, she made a little cloth splint, and named the figure "Broken Rainbow."

Then Connie was awakened by a hard shove from one of the French "escorts." He looked out the window to see an airport. It was not DeGaulle International, but a military airport of some type.

"I thought we were going to the Foreign Ministry." Connie knew he would not like the answer.

"Plans have changed," said the paratrooper. Gesturing to the Airbus that sat on the runway a few hundred feet away, the guard said, "Get in."

Jake was already walking in front of him, and in moments they ascended the stairs and heard the compartment door shut behind them. There were no guards. *Where can we go from 30,000 feet?* They both sat, and buckled up. Within minutes, the aircraft was climbing, and the moment it leveled off, the curtains to the forward compartments were pulled back, revealing de Valiere and Genet, or Red, or whoever he was.

"And here I thought you wanted us to see the wonders of Paris," Connie quipped.

Valiere was not amused. "Actually, Professor, you are going home." Then he clicked a remote control and the windows sealed. Red and de Valiere both stepped back into the forward cabin, and a compartment door slammed shut.

Chapter 22

An-Nasiriyah, Iraq

It was dark enough. Darker than usual, because American forces had finally cut the power to the city. Only the emergency lights of a few facilities still had a dull glimmer. One of those dull glimmers belonged to Saddam General.

Thomas Palmer was the third man off the big chopper as it bounced onto the desert floor. Each man moved silently to his assigned position, and thanks to the night goggles, they could see there was no resistance, even though earlier reports said the militia was using the hospital as a regional headquarters. They couldn't take chances: they broke in the doors and used flash grenades on the stunned doctors, nurses, and patients, screaming, "Get down!" as they ran through the halls.

"Who speaks English here?" demanded Lieutenant "Ham" Allen.

A terrified doctor raised his hand and Allen said, "We want to find an American soldier, a female named Joanna Miles."

The doctor nodded and waved for the soldiers to follow him, up a flight of dark stairs. Palmer felt his heart beating hard, half-expecting an ambush. Instead, they came to a hallway with several patients in bed---many behind curtains. *Perfect for an ambush*, thought Palmer.

"Joanna Miles? Private Joanna Miles," shouted Allen.

He ripped back a curtain and saw a frail, blonde figure in the bed. Taking off his helmet, he said, "Joanna Miles, we're United States soldiers and we're here to take you home."

Miles proudly said, "I'm a soldier, too!"

Palmer immediately grabbed one of the cot legs as three other commandos took other ends of the cot. With his free hand, he ripped his Ranger patch off his shoulder and pressed it into her hand. "Hang on to that. As long as you have that, you'll know that we have not forgotten you!" She gripped the patch and held it to her heart.

In moments, they were back in the darkened hallway, and Jo found herself carried downward at a 45-degree angle; then, after that, she remembered crossing a brief patch of desert, then, the waiting helicopter. Palmer looked at her as he set her down. "You're on your way, Private."

They secured Miles's cot, then Palmer started to pull back to his seat as the chopper lifted off. Joe grabbed his hand. "Please don't leave me," she said in a voice barely audible above the rotors. Palmer reached back, stowed his weapon, and sat cross-legged next to Jo's cot, holding her hand the whole way back to base.

New York City

When the Airbus compartment finally opened up, Valiere found both Connie and Jake sound asleep. He motioned to Genet to get them up, and after a few groggy moments, they were all in a darkened limo headed . . . where? Connie thought recognized the neighborhood.

East River, near 42nd Street. United Nations Plaza.

The Mercedes had French diplomatic plates, and passed immediately by security into the garage. Genet escorted Connie and Jake into a waiting elevator, followed by Valiere. Connie didn't notice how many floors they went up, but knew it was more than three, and this time a jump out the window would indeed do the trick if he wanted to end it all. He also knew that even though this was New York City, the UN Charter established an "international zone" for the diplomats who worked here. The UN had its own fire department, postal service, and, of course, police force, and was, for all intents and purposes, an independent country inside New York City.

You may be home, Connie, but you're not in America yet.

As the elevator doors opened, Genet herded Connie and Jake down a hallway, then into a conference room, closing the door behind them. He and Valiere just stood quietly.

"So much trouble from a boy and a college teacher." *I know that voice,* thought Connie. *That accent---it isn't French---it's . . . African!*

"All right, professor. No more secrets." Idi Kofar, the president of the United Nations, walked out. "We know you have traced the money for the Oil-for-Food program to the 9/11 hijackers. Now, what we need to know is, have you seen my name on any documents yet?"

Come to think of it, he had seen something odd. Connie didn't have time to study the exported data before Jake sent it, but that name had appeared . . . Kofar.

He lied. "As a matter of fact, Mr. Kofar, I have not. But your organization appears to be up to its neck in corruption and, given your presence here, apparently terrorism." Connie spoke with as much self-righteousness as he could muster, knowing his and Jake's likely fate.

"You were mistaken, professor. How much money did you find going through *l'Joliette du Mer*? Millions, no? And how much do you think---and you can't prove it, but say you could---how much do you think went into the hands of the 9/11 hijackers."

"At least a million," Connie answered. *Where's he going with this.*

Kofar waved his hand. "It was pocket change out of the Oil-for-Food program. Poor accounting. We didn't know that it had been transferred to Mohammad Atta. We have already fired the person at *l'Joliette du Mer* who was responsible."

"How civic of you. 'Only a million' to a terrorist might as well be billions. It didn't take much for you to finance their undercover activities here for months. That's blood on your hands, Mr. Kofar."

"Nonsense. We were sloppy with an employee; he has been dismissed; and the matter is over. But it cannot become a public relations disaster for a great organization," Kofar lectured. "You understand that, don't you professor?"

"Great organizations don't fund terrorists. By the way, where did the other billions go?" For the first time, Connie actually thought of other slush funds run by the UN. *What an idiot you've been Connie. Who has been getting billions from these clowns for years? The Palestinian Liberation Organization.*

"I get it. Man, was I stupid," Connie continued. "You kept us focused on the Iraq/bin Laden connection---and there is one---but this whole thing was much bigger than just Iraq funding bin Laden. It was all terrorism. You've been using this money to fund Arafat and the PLO for years. Saddam's little payoffs to the families of suicide bombers was nothing: you were supporting PLO terrorism for more than a decade. How could I have been so blind? This what I was trained for in academics---not to miss the forest for the trees. Bin Laden isn't the first terrorist you've funded, only the most spectacular."

Kofar's eyes flashed. "One man's terrorist is another man's freedom fighter. The Zionists have has wielded influence far beyond Israel's size and territory for years, directing the foreign policies of western nations. Someone had to, shall we say, level the playing field. Was the resistance to Jewish occupation of Arab lands 'terrorism'?"

Connie actually wondered if he could cover the physical distance between them and strangle the man before someone shot him. "Bombing innocent people, including school children, can't be called anything but terrorism . . . and pure evil. And you and your 'great organization' are as responsible as the crazed killers who strapped bombs to their bodies. You not only should be ashamed, you should be shot." Connie disgustedly looked at the floor, but Jake's eyes burned into Kofar and Valiere.

Kofar sighed audibly. "We brought you here to reason with you. One way or another, you are not going to be allowed to bring down the crowning achievement of mankind."

"The *UN*? Oh, yeah, that's a real 'crowning achievement.' It ranks right up there with the Ford Pinto and the McRib sandwich." Connie took a step toward Kofar, but Red shifted to interpose himself between them, and the professor halted. "You're going down---you and this whole corrupt bunch of goons. You're all going down. Maybe I . . ." then, looking at Jake, added, "maybe *we* can't take you down," to which Jake nodded affirmatively, "but the info we've sent out will sink this place into the swamp it deserves."

"Please, professor. Do you think you can do that? Can the boy?"

I ain't no boy, you asswipe, thought Jake, but he kept silent.

"You will do nothing," Kofar lectured. "Nor will your guardians. We know your handlers no longer can track you, but even if they could, this is not New York jurisdiction, or even American property, strictly speaking. You might as well be in Paris . . ." or, he smiled, "Nairobi."

He paused, convinced he was wasting his time with Connie. "How about you, my young friend. How are your principles? Do you have a price for cooperation and silence?"

Jake slowly looked up. "What do you have in mind?" Connie shot a look at him aghast, but Jake stared straight at Kofar.

"Well, well. The child has more wisdom than the teacher. Yes, we could arrange something, ah, appropriate for you."

"Give me a number. How much?" Jake countered coldly.

Kofar thought for a moment. "Let's say for $2 million you would develop amnesia, never speak to anyone about this again, and never again work with or for the United States government." He raised an eyebrow?

Jake paused, then countered, "Way too cheap. How about this: I play sphinx in return for you giving yourself up to the FBI, personally paying back $10 million to each of the 9/11 families; plus the UN pays restitution to Israel in the amount of $100 billion, and passes a resolution that terminates this sleazy organization, and we blow this big manure bag up next week and salt the earth the way the Romans did with Carthage. How about that deal?"

Kofar for a moment was stunned. Then Jake crossed his arms smugly, only to have Genet knock him to the floor with shot to the jaw. "Guess your trained Orc here thinks that's kinda high."

Inwardly, Connie beamed, not at Jake getting hit, but at the look on Kofar's face.

Kofar seethed, but only spoke quietly in Genet's ear, "We are finished with these two. Nothing must be done off UN property---we are the law here. We investigate ourselves. Understand?" Genet nodded. "Make sure you dispose of the bodies," Kofar concluded, turning away as the redhead quickly grabbed Connie and Jake, each in a hand, dragging them toward the hallway and the elevator, heading for the basement.

"They're going to have to open a whole new wing of hell for you," Connie shouted. It was the best he could do under the circumstances, but Kofar merely waved his hand as if brushing off a fly.

Western Pakistan

If the Pakistani government of Pervez Musharraf knew about this village, it pretended otherwise. It was close enough to Peshawar that Malid could find a capable doctor---who could keep his mouth shut---but remote enough not to cause undue questions about who the mysterious visitors were.

Osama bin Laden's wound was not as bad as first feared, although he would lose much of the mobility in his arm. Zawahiri, on the other hand, had bled profusely, but was not stable. They had found a small house, if you could call it that, donated by a local al-Qaeda supporter, and the doctor had done what he could, then left. Both bin Laden and Zawahiri were conscious, if in some pain.

"Ayman, we must launch Allah's Wind. The Americans are getting too close, and there is no telling how long Musharraf's forces can be held in check, even by the fear of the local tribal militias."

Zawahiri agreed. "I will activate the operation immediately, regardless of the level of lethality." He brought out his cell phone and began making calls. If the men had not been constantly on the run from American Predators and snipers, they would have read in the papers that some months ago it was leaked that the Americans were tracking some of the cell phone transmissions. First, Zawahiri contacted a European al-Qaeda member who then placed a call of his own. Zawahiri did not know the men who would actually deliver the weapons, nor did he care who they were.

Zawahiri had only two specific instructions to his contacts. First, deliver the weapon in the next week. Second, in each case, make sure it was done on a day in which the wind was blowing east. If possible, and if the winds were right, strike on Tuesday.

Kandahar, Afghanistan

Enough time had passed that Camel had almost forgotten the mysterious figure in the tent months ago. None of the horrors that he learned of that night had occurred. While he did not think bin Laden was dead---at least, the rumors and recurrent video tapes seemed to suggest he was alive---Camel concluded that the military and spy agencies had foiled the terror plot based on the information Camel passed up the chain that he had received in that dark tent.

Until now.

Camel's cell phone rang, and that was very bad news, because only a handful of people had the number.

"It's Mick. We've got something. A kid came to us. Don't know how the hell he found us. Anyway, he wanted you. We pretended not to know you, but it's pretty clear he knew you. He said it was about a meeting you had a few months ago with a stranger. Like everyone you meet isn't strange! Anyway, I just wanted to pass that on. He said to meet him at the same place, tomorrow night. And he said come alone."

The operation is still on! They haven't stopped it. Camel's mind raced through the implications . . . and the casualties.

"Thanks, Mick, although I don't think this is good news. I take it you're in the area? Never mind. I'm not supposed to know. How bad do you think Chico got him?"

"Not bad enough, I'm afraid. And that may be what your meeting is about, if you catch my drift."

"I catch it all too well," he responded glumly. "Tell the kid I'll be there." He clicked the phone shut.

Chicago

So this is what a WMD looks like.

Randy Elton examined the "package" he'd received from his contact. It was a small suitcase, complete with easy-to-roll wheels. Inside, and not yet armed, were twenty standard-size, corked test-tube bottles; one small blob of SEMTEX with a detonator and a tiny timer set for 20 seconds.

And a hammer.

Elton was amused and at the same time horrified at the "strategy" for delivery. He was to take the elevator to the top floor of the Sears Tower, slap the SEMTEX on one of the windows---it didn't matter which---and release the timer. Then he was to take a deep breath and smash all 20 vials with the hammer. It was as low-tech an operation as could be imagined. Exactly as the 9/11 plan had been: who was ready for box cutters and suicide planes?

Just as he would be running out of air, the explosive would blast a good-sized hole in the windows of the Sears Tower at the same time that 20 vials of VX gas released their contents into the air and spread across Chicago, Lake Michigan, northern Indiana and then on to Cleveland and into Pennsylvania. Depending on how fast the wind was blowing, whether or not there was rain anywhere, VX might get as far as Philadelphia, or stop somewhere near Pittsburgh.

Of course, Randal el-Tahlon would be quite dead by then. He would begin dying the minute he breathed the VX. Sears Tower security would be utterly impotent.

And between 100,000 and five million Americans would be dead.

Randy Elton did not appreciate how difficult it had been for al-Qaeda to obtain the VX, an oily substance that is heavier than air and thus exposes those on the ground. It had been used in the 1995 Tokyo terror attack, where a dozen were killed and 5,000 affected, but it was dangerous to make and transport. He had not bothered to ask, nor would anyone have told him, how al-Qaeda got the VX into his possession.

Nor had anyone mentioned to him that the only thing that would destroy the VX mixture was heat, even a normal fire.

Randy Elton/Randal el-Tahlon did not know many things.

He had no way of knowing that this was only half of "Allah's Wind," or that half-way around the world, in Cairo, a man named Jaleel would be setting the detonator to a suitcase nuclear device---a specially designed, small "dirty bomb" that featured . . . sand. The bomb was packed in simple Egyptian desert sand, detonated in the city's tallest Minaret, and, Allah willing, an ample wind would carry it east, and if lucky, northeast to Jerusalem. Swept along by the wind, the sand would cover buildings, vehicles, and, of course, people.

Jaleel was a simple man. He had taken the word of his contact, who spoke on behalf of Osama bin Laden and Ayman al-Zawahiri, that the bomb's effects would never penetrate to the interior of Saudi Arabia, and certainly never reach Medina or Mecca. Some Muslims would die in Jordan and Syria, perhaps, but those were acceptable casualties of war.

New York City

The elevator steadily traveled downward, with Red hovering behind Connie and Jake. He knew neither was up to resistance, and that was what allowed him to escort them alone. Valiere had implored him to take along backup, but to Genet, the fewer hands, the better. Less mess, less cover-up. No mistakes.

"I think this is our last ride, kid," Connie said in resignation. "No CIA to the rescue this time."

"Yeah, well, the UN, the French, and anyone else in this can kiss my ass. I'm not into the patriotism thing. If I'd been old enough, I wouldn't have voted last election. Probably won't vote in the next one unless they run Spongebob Squarepants or that Tweeden babe from 'Best Damn Sports Show.' But these guys are sick. They're worse than street criminals. They've got everything and it isn't enough."

Then he looked at Connie. "You know why I hack, man?"

Connie shook his head.

"So I can take out greedy toadwaddies like that Valiere guy." Jake looked over his shoulder, but Genet was stoic. "And this Kofar--- I've seen him on TV. All peace and love incorporated. All "for the children." Jake adopted an African accent: "'A-mer-i-ca, you must do more for the people of Af-reee-ca with AIDs. You must give more food.' Well, you know what? That's crap. He doesn't care about the poor in Asia or the kids in Africa with AIDs. I bet he has six houses, every one with a swimming pool. *That's* why I hack. It ain't always right. I don't always get the right target. But I get something. At least I'm doing something. If I miss five times, but hit once, at least justice was done once." Jake couldn't see it, but Red's mouth curled into a slight grin with his impersonation of Kofar.

Connie, nodded, but he could barely follow Jake's tortured logic. Still, somehow he related to the kid.

As the elevator slowed to a halt, Genet shoved the two into a darkened parking garage that was apparently sealed off or under construction. He gave them one last push into the light and removed a silencer from his jacket, affixing it to his Walther. Connie instinctively started backing up, knowing that he could not put enough space between himself and bullets.

"You're the only one who's honest in this whole thing," Connie said to Genet, who finished screwing on the silencer. "At least you admit you're doing this for nothing more than money. You're a whore . . . but an honest one."

Red laughed as he brought the pistol up. "And I know you, professor. You and the boy are pawns. I am a mere employee."

"No, you have a choice. . . as do I," and Connie impulsively leaped behind the concrete column as Red loosed his first silenced shot, followed by a quiet curse. The kid had immediately bolted in the other direction, scurrying for a column of his own, and momentarily Genet was undecided as to which target he wanted, belatedly loosing a shot at Jake, which went wide.

"You're on the wrong side of this war," Connie yelled, standing up and sprinting for the next column in line, anything to get away from Red. "Money can't be everything. What will it buy you if you have no country to spend it in."

If Genet heard the words, he did not let on. Instead, he swung around the first column, only to see Connie's heels disappear behind the next some 50 feet away. Red ran for the next column. As Connie peeked around, Genet fired again, blasting out the glass in the fire hose behind Connie. Protected by the angle of the column, Connie scrambled again toward an abandoned Honda SUV and dove under it as Genet came out from behind the column.

"Enough!" he roared. "Come out now and I'll make it quick and painless for you. Otherwise, I put a bullet in that car's fuel tank and you die an excruciating, slow death by fire."

He's got a point. I'm no James Bond here. Connie's hands appeared from underneath the SUV, then he crawled out and stood in front of it, hands in the air.

"Wise choice, professor," and Genet sighted the weapon right on his forehead. Neither man heard the strange squeaking sound of a faucet being turned...

...when a powerful blast of water knocked Genet off his feet. Jake stood thirty paces to his left, where the fire hose was. He trained the hose on Genet, sweeping him across the garage like an ant under a garden hose. Genet managed to level the gun and squeeze off a shot before his head cracked against a concrete column and he let out a moan.

Connie had bounded behind the car, but when he saw Genet literally being washed away, he noticed the open window in the SUV. Crawling into the car, he located the jack in the rear area and ripped out the jack arm, then jumped back out to see a stunned Genet trying to get to his feet. Fifty feet away, the hose still roared, but now it was snapping around wildly, like a giant snake. *No one's holding it! Where's Jake?* Connie ran full speed at Genet, who had staggered upright, only to have Connie's shoulder smash into his midsection, and Red's knees sagged again. As he went down, Connie whipped the iron jack handle across Genet's forearm, producing a crack that let Connie knew he'd broken a bone. The gun went skipping across the garage floor. Genet let out a howl, but Connie wasn't about to show mercy, bringing the tire iron straight across Red's left knee. Another wail. Spotting the gun, Connie took two steps and dove---quite deftly, he thought---skidding up to the gun and grabbing it by the handle. He sat up and trained it on Genet, whose smashed knee and broken arm immobilized him.

Then he started to laugh. "Do you really think they will let you off the grounds? The zone has as many UN police as most small American towns."

He's right. I'm still trapped.

From behind Connie came a familiar voice. "A diplomatic pass will get you out of here."

It was agent Jackson. A car appeared at the ground level opening to the garage, as Harrison got out and removed the pylons.

"I thought you were in Europe? How the heck did you know we were here?" Connie let his gun slide from his hands as Jackson kept his own gun trained on a shocked Genet.

"Remember when we took the tracker out, professor?"

"How could I forget?" Connie replied sarcastically.

"We left one in."

"Huh? What do you mean you left one in?"

Jackson kicked the gun further away from Genet while Harrison positioned the big Ford nearby. "We took one tracker out. But we left one in each of you," Jackson grinned. "We've been following you since Paris, although, unfortunately, a few steps behind." Harrison got out and helped Genet get up on his good leg.

"Where's the kid?" Harrison shouted.

Jake! I forgot about him . . . again. "He hit this creep with the fire hose . . . ." and they looked to see the fire hose still flailing about. "He was right over there."

They ran behind the column, where he saw Jake's limp body laying in a puddle. Jackson took the wheel of the fire hose and shut it off, then ran to Jake.

"He's ok, right?" Connie said, knowing he wasn't. Jackson checked for a pulse, but knew there was no use.

"No, man. He's dead."

"Noooo! Noo!" Connie stared up at the agent, then looked back down at Jake and cradled him, starting to sob. "He saved me. He hit Genet with the water. Genet must have gotten off a shot." Connie looked up at Jackson, his eyes brimming with tears. "This kid saved my life."

Jackson scooped up the lifeless body. "Come on, prof. This isn't the time to mourn." He bobbed his head toward the car. "We're not home, yet. This place can have security all over us at any minute. If Kofar and his henchmen figure out what's happening . . . ."

Connie agreed, and Jackson yelled to Harrison, "Pop the trunk, Cliff. We gotta do this." He started to put Jake's body in when Connie screamed, "No! You aren't putting the kid in a trunk. I'll take hold him."

Cliff nodded, and Lonnie slammed the trunk. "OK, but keep your eye on Red, there," gesturing at Genet, who sat slumped in the back seat against the car door, his arm disfigured. Connie glared at him, white-hot with hate, but the assassin simply turned away. They slid Jake in between the two of them, then Connie climbed in, letting Jake's head rest on his shoulder. Jackson got into the front, and turned, keeping his gun hidden but pointed right at the seat. "If you move," he instructed Genet, "eight inches of seat isn't gonna save you." Genet said nothing and turned away again.

"Why don't you just shoot him now?" asked Connie in disbelief.

"Relax, prof," Jackson answered. "Nothin' I'd like better, but orders are orders. Someone thinks we need this guy for something."

Odd. They said that before, thought Connie. *What the hell?*

The Ford lurched out of the garage, and although Connie expected the guards to stop them, Harrison merely waved the phoney diplomatic credentials he had acquired, and was waved through.

Connie looked down at the top of Jake's head, but then the only thing he seemed able to think of was his own girls at home, and that they would someday be Jake's age.

Chapter 23

Chicago

Jes' 24, Cashbox. 24 hours from now you be rich, and out of Chi-town. No mo' Jam-ai-cans for you. Nossir. Nossir.

As he always did, Carl Gilliam cruised by his transaction spot the day before, scouting the territory for problems. It was clear. He looked for stake out spots and took note of the cars parked on the streets---what makes, models, and then, eight hours later, he'd check them again. Tomorrow, he was going to change his routine. No more selling the product himself. He didn't have that kind of time. Something told Gilliam that the Jamaicans were very close to terminating their business relationship, and that meant "terminate" in the most literal sense of the word. So Cashbox Gilliam found an old crony that was plugged into another gang, and this one time, he was going to sell his load, all at once, and take the money and run.

That right. You gonna run, Cashbox. Go to Vegas. Ain't no Jam-ai-cans in Vegas. Start all over, with lotsa cheddar. That right. Lotsa cheddar. Won' be hard. V-town is tight. Be perfect for Cashbox.

One last survey of the neighborhood convinced Gilliam that it would be a safe exchange.

Yessir, Cashbox. You goin' take the money and run. Jes 24.

Somewhere on the Afghan-Pakistan Border

"You wanted the meeting. Here I am," announced Camel.

"Yes, here you are." The dark figure remained in the rear of the small mountain hut.

"Nothing has come from your last information, so you don't have the highest reliability."

"Fool! The plan was postponed. Don't think you have stopped anything. It will happen very soon---within two weeks."

"So you say. Why should I believe you this time?" Camel shuffled to get a better look at the man, but still could not make out any features.

"Did not my information on the location of bin Laden prove accurate?"

Camel had to admit that it did.

"We do not have the luxury of you clearing information through channels again. You must move, quickly. Bin Laden is hurt, as is Zawahiri. I may be able to stop the operation---I have some of the codes---but I must have their cell phones, which bin Laden and Zawahiri keep on their persons at all times. The AQ members will only answer those particular phone numbers."

"Ok, say my local teams decide you're legit. Say we decide to go get these guys. Where are they?" Camel figured a Mogadishu-type snatch and grab without the fireworks. What he heard next discouraged and depressed him.

"Pakistan."

Camel gulped, then continued. "OK, so say, somehow, we get inside Pakistan and can get to this safe house---why isn't bin Laden in a city?"

"Too many eyes. Too many ears." Then, as if just now realizing what he said, the man added, "including my own, which I think he does not know about. I'm counting on it."

"Why would you give him up? What's in it for you? I mean, you could be leading us into a trap."

The man let out a long sigh. "Are you a Muslim?" he asked.

Camel could lie, but for some reason decided not to. "No. I was born into a Muslim family, but as a teenager I became a convert to Christianity."

The information seemed to surprise the stranger. "So! You are among the most cursed of men."

Camel didn't respond, and the man paused for a moment. Finally, he continued, "Well, at least you have a knowledge of Islam. Fine. Why do I betray Sharif? Because he no longer has any conception of what Islam is. I do not know if he ever did. At one time I thought he was a great imam, a spiritual descendant of Mohammed himself, blessings be upon him. But he knows nothing of the teachings of the Koran. He has desecrated all that Islam stands for."

He clearly was on a roll, now speaking more to himself than Camel. "Jihad? Yes. Holy war? Does the Koran not command it? But slaughter of innocents who have had no opportunity to accept Islam? Violating the most holy sites of the faith? No! That is not the work of a believer, but a heretic."

The man looked at Camel with dark eyes. "If you are a Christian, you will know I hand over Judas, not Jesus of Nazareth. I am saving Islam from an obscene maniac who would destroy it to achieve his own ends."

"And what are those ends?" Camel interrupted, snapping the man out of his philosophical rant.

He paused and considered the question as though he had never thought about it before. "Nothing less than the complete reformation of Islam itself . . . in his own image."

Camel had to admit the man's story passed the smell test. He seemed sincere, the details were consistent, and he had given Camel good information in the past.

"All right. Let's just say---and I'm not promising anything--- that we can get some people in there in the next 48 hours. What exactly do you need us to do? And what will you do?"

"You must provide a sufficiently serious distraction---an attack---that I can get the phones off bin Laden and Zawahiri. Then I can then call the contacts directly, give them the code phrases which I possess. Do what you will with bin Laden and Zawahiri, as long as we get the phones intact. I will find a way to escape and never return, and, for my assistance, you will guarantee that the United States will not target me or my family in any way."

"Only if you do not join up with another terrorist group like Hamas. If you continue a life of terrorism, you're fair game. Otherwise, I think I can safely say on behalf of the U.S. government that you'll be free to engage in politics, publishing, or whatever without fear . . . from us, that is. Of course, you're pal bin Laden will have you in the crosshairs."

"Which is why," Malid said, "Osama bin Laden must not leave this encounter alive."

Washington, D.C.

"Please, show them in." Pacing the Oval Office, the President of the United States, normally warm and friendly, would not be amiable today. His jaw was set, and he would brook no excuses.

Moments later, Idi Kofar and Dominique de Valiere entered the room, and only Condoleza Rice, the newly appointed Secretary of State, and a pair of translators, remained. Bush did not offer his hand. Instead, he circled behind his desk and sat, leaving de Valiere and Kofar standing. Rice, in a dark blue suit, stood to the side.

"This won't take long," he began. "Here's how this meeting works. I talk, you listen. There is no discussion and no debate." He looked at Rice, who pulled out two identical stacks of papers and photos.

"You two disgust me," the President continued, and Rice could not help but stifle a small smile at the President's "un-diplomatic" speech. "Thanks to the efforts of a fine economist---one you both tried to assassinate, I might add---we not only have information that both France and the United Nations benefited from the Oil for Food program, but that you both personally became multi-millionaires off the exchanges."

Kofar, who did not need a translator, started to speak when fire flashed in Bush's eyes and he held up a single finger. Kofar abruptly stopped as Rice shoved one of the stacks of papers into Kofar's hand. Valiere's translator spoke quietly in his ear.

"There is no 'explanation,' there is no elaboration. We've got you dead to rights. Prof. Cataris tracked the money from *l'Joliette du Mer* right into both of your accounts. But," Bush paused, "as you know, that's the least of your sins."

Valiere's knees went weak and he slumped into a nearby chair, his translator now kneeling on the floor speaking in his ear. But Kofar remained standing, defiant.

"We have further information," as again Rice shoved a stack of papers into Kofar's hands, but Valiere was shaking now, so she merely dropped it on his lap, "that the Oil for Food money went directly to the Hamas suicide bombers' families after passing through Saddam Hussein's hands. We even have located two families who have corroborated this through their testimony."

Uttering something in French, Valiere looked ashen. Bush did not bother to ask the translator what he said. He continued to burn holes in Kofar with his glare.

"But as bad as all that is, it still really did not involve the United States until your friend, Mohammad Atta, started drawing money from those accounts, deposited there by none other than the Iraqi foreign minister. And that funding supported Atta and his terrorist cutthroats while they lived here in the United States and while they scouted our airline system, right up to the very moment they flew the planes into the World Trade Center. That, *Mister General Secretary* and *Mister Foreign Minister*," the President stood up and jammed the last two stacks of papers into their hands, "is on you. *You*, now, are in the same category as the terrorists in my book."

He signaled Rice, who pressed a beeper.

Kofar, with all the condescension he could muster, shouted, "Who do you think you are? The nations of the world will not tolerate this! Your paperwork is a tissue of fraud. You can never prove that we received a penny from *l'Joliette du Mer*, let alone allowed terrorists to have it. We are finished here, and you can rest assured this will be a major international incident . . . perhaps one that will bring down your cowboy government."

Valiere took heart at Kofar's speech, and rose as the doors opened behind them. In marched six Marine guards in combat fatigues, not the traditional dress blues, assuming the *en garde* position. Their Lieutenant drew his service revolver and announced to Kofar and de Valiere, "You are hereby detained by the United States government as enemy combatants and are to be removed to a terrorist detainment facility." The Marines looked as though they would relish an opportunity to fire.

Kofar's head swiveled back to the Bush in astonishment, and opened his mouth to speak, but before he could do so, the President walked in front of him, just inches from his face and, his a voice barely above a whisper but full of anger, stated, "There will be no international incident. There will be no support from France, or Russia, or Germany, or any nation that anyone would take seriously. In fact, in confinement, you are going to be making some phone calls to France, Germany, Russia, and a few other countries. You not only are going to apologize to them for misusing UN funds---and here I will have you say 'without their knowledge'---but you are going to explain to them how their own involvement in the abuse of these funds can be corrected by a new direction they are going to take."

Kofar looked puzzled, but the President added, "I'll explain more in due course. Meanwhile, these documents are beyond interpretation. And just as a little insurance, we have more than just documents." He nodded at Rice, who walked to the door.

"Sergeant," she said, and two more Marines entered with a third man . . . a tall redhead who limped in with his leg and arm in casts.

"I believe you both know this man, who has agreed to go public, not only with what he personally heard you say, but what he has on tape."

Kofar's eyes lit up in horror. Valiere slumped back into the chair and covered his eyes.

Genet used his good hand to pull a small tape recorder out. "I knew I was being used---what assassin isn't? But I never trusted a man who would hand our country over to the Mohammedans, who let us be overrun with Arabs to the point that our streets are not safe. Even an assassin has a limit as to what he will bear." Genet hit the play button to reveal the conversation between himself and Valiere. "There are many others. You, too, are prominently featured, Mr. General Secretary."

Kofar staggered back, now leaning against the chair. He turned and hissed, "What do you want?"

The President sat down again, and the Secretary stood behind him. "As I said, this is non-negotiable. Here is what is going to happen . . . ." As Idi Kofar listened, he, too, decided he needed to sit down.

Western Pakistan, Near the Tora Bora Mountains

Mick looked around at his units. Besides Chico and Camel, he had twelve Rangers. He would have liked to have had the CIA guy, Spann, along, but heard that he was killed in the prison uprising not long after the fall of the Taliban.

He wasn't the first, and won't be the last.

Colonel Meadows put Lieutenant Carson Schwelling in charge of the operation---it was decided to go small in hopes of keeping everything quiet---but Camel was really calling the shots. He had the info, and he knew where they were going. Mick and Chico had their own squad of six, plus six men from Delta company not long in from Iraq. One of the guys was a hotshot NFL star who had given up the glory and bright lights to become a Ranger, Thomas Palmer. Mick didn't know him, and the two had barely had a chance to speak since he was assigned to this operation, but the fact that HQ trusted him for this said a lot. That, and the fact that he gave up a fortune in the NFL to play on his battlefield.

They'd driven Humvees to a remote spot 10 clicks from the shacks where bin Laden and Zawahiri were, at least, according to Camel's source. They would know the guy by an Arafat-like black-and-white *kaffiya*, but God knows what would happen if three or four of the guys were wearing that. They had orders not to kill him, especially since he alone knew the codes to call off the operations.

And what operations were those? No one told them, only that they were absolutely critical, and the fact that more than a dozen Americans were inside Pakistan without official authorization and without any verifiable links to the White House made Mick just a little uncomfortable.

His orders were only to move the 10 kilometers by night, achieve total surprise, kill whatever bodyguards or al-Qaeda types resisted, and kill or capture Osama bin Laden and his doctor, al-Zawahiri.

"Believe it or not, that ain't the big prize," he told his men in the briefing 12 hours earlier. "The number one objective of this mission is to allow 'Arafat' (which was the code name they'd adopted for Malid, even though no one knew his name) to abort a couple of terror strikes." No one had told them whether one, or more, of those strikes would be in the United States, but most concluded there could be no other reason for such urgency. And the fact that bin Laden was viewed as a tangential target unsettled them.

Whatever it is, it's big---so big that bin Laden is the booby prize in this op.

According to "Arafat," Camel said, there would be two al-Qaeda guards at designated spots. But bin Laden wanted to avoid having too many guards, lest they draw attention from the Predators. Once the guards were eliminated, the teams were to attack the two buildings simultaneously. They would not know which one bin Laden and Zawahiri were in, nor where "Arafat" would be---but the three would be together. If they did their job, "Arafat" would be able to abort the mission, though he could not do anything to reveal the location or names of the terrorists without giving away the fact that they had been compromised, whereupon the terrorists would likely do their thing as quickly as possible.

If that happens, Mick concluded, *there's gonna be a lot of dead people.*

Chico would be in charge of Bravo squad, taking the far cabin. Mick would have Delta squad with the near cabin. Camel would be with Chico, Palmer's men with him. He didn't feel altogether comfortable without his own guys, but these were veteran Rangers. If they'd had more time, Delta Force would have drawn this assignment, but their window of opportunity was too narrow, and the D-boys couldn't get there in time.

Now, two quick *twap twaps* of silencers took out the AQ guards, leaving the huts standing exposed in the moonlight. *That's another thing I don't like: we have a moon to deal with, and the less light the better.* But again, Mick couldn't pick his times and dates. Slowly, stealthily, more than a dozen men surrounded the two cabins. If all went well, within minutes Osama bin Laden would be dead.

Chicago

It was a good day to die. Randal el-Tahlon had prayed, and throughout the morning taken care of his personal affairs, checking his will and bank accounts. His wife and son knew nothing about what he was doing. They did not even know he was a member of a local al-Qaeda cell, nor, according to protocol, should they. *It would be Allah's irony*, he thought, many times, *that my own wife would be a member of a different cell!*

He had kept the weapon at a U-store it he had rented months ago, awaiting his orders. Once, he recalled, the manager had casually asked him what was in the suitcase.

"A saxophone," Randal replied. It satisfied the manager, who drove off in his golf cart. But there were a number of questions Randal el-Tahlon had never asked.

Does this gas degrade over time? No one bothered to tell him. Dying for Allah did not trouble him, a meaningless death did. *Can anything destroy the gas?* He just assumed that it was not rendered impotent by water, and hadn't even considered the thought of rain in Chicago. *Heat?* He did not know that high temperatures virtually destroyed its lethality. With more time, Randal el-Tahlon might have learned these things, but, then again, it would not have mattered.

At 9:30 he reached the storage facility, and carried his little suitcase downtown. Randy Elton had taken care of everything.

Almost everything: he'd forgotten his cell phone at home.

He drove downtown to the loop and parked in a garage off LaSalle that he had scouted weeks before, then walked west down Adams to South Wacker Drive. In moments he would be dead . . . along with thousands, if not millions of American infidels.

Western Pakistan

Malid had expected the Americans to strike at night, and he had his identifying *keffiya* close to the mat where he lay. *Would anyone notice him putting it on when the Americans attacked?*

Osama bin Laden slept just a few feet from him, and, a few feet away from him, Zawahiri snored. They slumbered thinking that their al-Qaeda guards protected them---even more so, that their supposedly secret location provided security. *Again, overconfidence, Sharif.*

For what he was about to do, Malid had no regrets. He may have worked with infidels---perhaps even demons---but he had grown to see bin Laden as the biggest demon of all. Did not the West have its own false prophets? He had read, years ago, about a San Francisco preacher to lured his followers into a South American jungle and poisoned the lot of them. *Sharif is doing no less, indeed, he is visiting destruction on Islam on a greater scale than the Christian crusaders could have dreamed.*

Malid was still pondering his betrayal of bin Laden when Khalil got up from his mat, rubbed his eyes, and trudged outside to urinate.

What in Allah's name is this idiot doing?

Khalil, eyes half closed, pushed open the cabin door and walked into the moonlight, locating a nearby bush. He pulled his robe up, and as he looked down, saw a human hand . . . *a human . . . arm!* Drowsiness faded as adrenaline surged through his body and he let out a scream. "Sharif! Sha . . . ." Then a silenced round punctured his windpipe. He gurgled and plunged forward, his robe still pulled up, but he had given a warning, and the light-sleeping bin Laden burst out of bed.

American Rangers surrounded the buildings as fire erupted around both huts. One Ranger corporal, near to a small window at the furthest building, was shot through the head at close range. Bin Laden gestured to Zawahiri, who ran to the middle of the room and rolled back a carpet, revealing a trap door.

Rangers now scrambled alongside the huts, but did not want to use grenades as they might kill their "inside man," whom none of them had seen yet. As al-Qaeda fighters grabbed their weapons and started a stream of fire at the soldiers closing in, Malid grabbed his *keffiya* as he feigned looking out the window and quickly switched out bin Laden's cell phone. *One down!*

He searched for Zawahiri, when he saw the trap door. Zawahiri was now pushing bin Laden toward the escape route. *A tunnel! How many ways can this reprehensible creature escape?* Beside Malid, an al-Qaeda rifleman exploded as five rounds tore through him. Only two others in the room, firing out. *But Zawahiri is getting away, and with him, the phone.*

Outside, Mick's squad hugged the wall, then smashed through the door. Malid stood in front of them with the phone in his hand. He had become distracted by the trap door and forgot to put on his *kaffiya*. Mick gunned him down where he stood, *keffiyah* still in his hand. Right behind Mick, Thomas Palmer leaped through the door,

321

just as the trap door slammed shut. The last fighters in the room collapsed in a hail of bullets, as Mick surveyed the room.

"Bravo, come in," said Mick into his headset radio.

"Delta here, Mick." Chico's voice was on the other end. "Clear here."

"Clear here, except the rats went down a sewer."

"You and Camel got our informant there?"

"No, Mick. He's not here. Nobody's wearing a headdress. He should have been in this cabin with bin Laden."

"Damn it!" Mick screamed into the microphone so loud that it nearly burst Chico's eardrum. He turned and looked at the man behind him---the one with the phone in one hand and the *keffiya* in the other. "I don't believe this. We just killed the one guy with the codes. Now we can make a call, but won't have the right passwords for the guy to listen to us."

"Sarge," Palmer pointing to the tunnel. "We've gotta go get bin Laden. He's down there. Lemme go, Sarge."

Mick knew Palmer was right, but the first man in would probably be sacrificed. Someone would surely be waiting for them. "You sure you want this, Palmer?"

The Ranger stared back with unflinching eyes.

"Ok, go. Go!"

Palmer set his rifle aside, drew his pistol, and leaped through the trap door down into the tunnel. At the bottom, he had to get on his hands and knees---bin Laden and Zawahiri were crawling. *Well, Thomas Palmer can crawl faster.*

Meanwhile, above, Chico, Camel, and the rest of the troops had joined Mick in the first hut. "Did we screw up big time?" asked Chico. Camel and Mick could only look at each other, knowing they had.

"Our only chance now," Mick stated in a flat tone, "is to catch bin Laden alive. What do you think are the odds of that?"

No one had to say the obvious answer. "Ok, I'm followin'. Chico, send two more, in thirty second increments, after me. Pistols and knives only." Chico shouted "Hoo-aah," and Mick himself dropped in. "Remember," Chico added, "since our guy's dead, we need bin Laden alive."

Chicago

It was his pride and joy. The big, black SUV with the XM radio, a television in the back, and the heavily tinted windows made Carl Gilliam feel invincible. He had recently gotten the special "spinner" rims that kept turning even when the wheels stopped, providing a terrific optical illusion. And today, it was all gassed up and ready to drive to Vegas after one last deal.

He looked over his shoulder to the tarp that covered the six kilos of coke that he would unload today and he---and his money--- would be out of Chicago forever.

It be payday. Yessir Cashbox, it be payday.

Eight hours ago he'd checked the rendezvous one more time, and satisfied himself that it was clear. Now, just two blocks away, near Wacker and Franklin, he'd become a rich man.

That was when he saw the police lights in his rear view mirror. He loosed a string of profanities.

Nonononono. They can't be comin' for you. No, hell no! Not today. This is payday. Not today.

It didn't matter why they wanted to stop him---as it turned out, he had a broken taillight---only that he didn't dare give them an opportunity to search the SUV. Right then, Cashbox Gilliam decided to run, and he hit the gas.

Chapter 24

Cairo

Jaleel did his best to check the weather the previous night, and it appeared the wind was definitely blowing to the northeast. Early this morning he would climb the minaret and detonate his suitcase bomb. By nightfall, much of Cairo and the southern parts of Israel would be sprinkled with radioactive particles. By tomorrow morning, Jerusalem itself would experience the radioactive rain. And even if he were slightly off, and the winds shifted south, it would be the Saudis who would pay, and their oil fields that would be disrupted for months.

He sat patiently in his chair, drinking his last cup of Egyptian coffee. By noon, he would be in Paradise.

Chicago

Those are sirens in the distance. Randy Elton was close to his target.

Do not panic. They are not coming for you. No one knows about you.

Just a block away, the Sears Tower was in view, looming above the other nearby buildings. He maintained his measured pace, but the sirens drew nearer.

They could not have found out!

Now the wail was almost on top of him as he crossed Franklin Street and he quickened his pace. A taxi and a gasoline truck patiently waited their turn at the light, and he entered the crosswalk directly in front of them, while behind him, the sound was now piercing. He looked over his shoulder, only to see a black SUV with heavily tinted windows screech around the corner and head down Franklin. In hot pursuit were no fewer than three Chicago police cars. For a few brief seconds, Randy Elton was relieved, knowing that he was not the object of the sirens.

Then it dawned on him that the SUV was out of control . . . and headed straight for him. He froze right in the crosswalk, in front of the big gas truck.

Cashbox Gilliam was frantic, already knowing he'd made the biggest mistake of his life by running. Police closed in on him, and he swerved around onto Franklin, three cop cars close behind. He kept looking in his mirror, and as he made the turn, the SUV rocked wildly back and forth until it tipped completely on its side in a shower of sparks, sliding at over 50 miles per hour, heading straight for an intersection where Randy Elton stood in front of a gas truck.

Before either man could so much as scream, the SUV smashed into Elton, crushing him and smashing the vials inside his suitcase, and in a few milliseconds, as the sparks hit the SUV's gas tank, it exploded. The driver in the gas truck leaped out, his own truck ignited in a giant fireball. Cars on both sides were blown over as metal shards flew like shrapnel in every direction. In the now-charred hand of Randy Elton was a smashed suitcase, whose contents were instantaneously seared into impotence. Cashbox Gilliam's six kilos of cocaine and Randal el-Tahlon's VX gas all evaporated in a thunderous explosion.

In the coming days, several people would report runny noses, abdominal cramps, flu-like symptoms, diarrhea, and minor convulsions. Most local doctors chalked it up to the Asian Flu. The truck driver, who had been closest to the suitcase just after impact, died of mysterious convulsions.

Western Pakistan

Mick had Palmer on the radio, but the reception was horrible in this tiny tunnel. "Got 'em. I can see on of them, about 20 meters ahead . . . ." then it became unintelligible.

"Palmer," Mick said firmly in his microphone, "do you copy? Palmer!"

Mick crawled as fast as he could, but he knew that Palmer was in even better shape and would stay ahead of him. Then he heard gunfire.

"I've got an exit here . . . I've . . . ." and more gunfire.

"Palmer, what's the situation. You're breaking up."

"There's a road down there . . . . I can see . . . . Get some gunfire on that vehicle, but shoot the tires. We can't kill bin Laden . . . yet!" Palmer's voice was interspersed with static.

Mick finally saw the gathering light through the hole Palmer referred to. He popped through the opening, seeing the Ranger behind some rocks, below and to his left, leaping from rock to rock, blasting away with his pistol at the two fleeing figures. A pickup had appeared on the road at the base of the hill, a good 50 meters from where Palmer was. Somehow, bin Laden and Zawahiri had called for help, and here was their ride. If they got to the pickup, it was over.

"Mick!" Palmer screamed. "Gimme covering fire!"

There was no time to argue. Mick was much better with a rifle than a pistol, but he began to unload clip after clip at the vehicle as the men crawled into the back of the pickup. Mick's rounds snapped all around them. Then Palmer, within feet of the truck, lunged at the side, grabbing it just as Mick fired at the back tire. Mick swore he had aimed low enough, but Palmer lost his grip and fell, shifting him right into Mick's line of fire.

"NOOO!" Mick screamed, bolting down the rocks to Palmer's body. The moment he got a close look, Mick knew his rounds had killed another American.

By then, other Rangers had emerged from the tunnel. They carried the body back to the huts, where Camel sat staring blankly at a cell phone. He looked up as the Rangers lay Palmer's body on a cot and covered him.

"I shot him. It was my rounds. I was aiming lower, but he fell. I hit him. He almost had them, too. He was climbing into their pickup, and I killed him." Mick slumped to a wooden chair.

"*Esse*," Chico said quietly, consoling his friend, "we make mistakes, man. He did a brave thing. *You* did a brave thing. You were trying to protect him, man." But Chico knew that it would take a lot more than words to rescue Mick.

Camel and Lt. Schwelling stood together. "I hate to tell you, but this op was a total screw-up from the get-go. Bin Laden got away, and we killed our informant here," pointing at Malid's body, which lay in a puddle of blood. "He was the only one with the code phrase. Throw in our Ranger, there, and we're oh-for-three."

"Meaning, exactly, what?" asked Schwelling, as Chico joined them.

"Meaning that there is an operation under way that we cannot possibly stop. All he told me was that this was a two-pronged operation, in two parts of the world---one was the U.S.---and that it would be many times more devastating than 9/11."

"Oh my God," moaned Mick, head in his hands.

A Ranger radioman tapped the lieutenant on the shoulder. "We've got more problems. A recon plane sighted some Pakistani forces moving into this area."

Chico looked at Camel. "No doubt bin Laden called some of his flunkies in the Pakistani army, and now we are officially trespassing."

Camel nodded, and the lieutenant barked, "We have to get out of here, *now*. This cannot become an international incident. *Move*."

Chico grabbed Mick and shook him. "Come on, esse. This ain't the time." Mick looked up, still stunned, but grabbed his weapon and said, "Rogers, Scaransky, help me with Palmer's body." The Rangers lifted their dead comrade and moved rapidly out of the area.

It took several hours, but their lead on the Pakistani forces was sufficient that by mid-day they had crossed the Afghan border. Only then did they sit and take out their canteens. Lieutenant Schwelling gathered everyone around. "It should be obvious that we've been on a mission that did not happen, and there was no gunfire on the Pakistani side of the border." They all looked somberly at Palmer's covered body as the lieutenant took his M-16 and fired several rounds. "There *was* a firefight on this side of the border with some al-Qaeda." He fired more rounds. "They got away."

"Do you understand me?" he asked.

"Hoo-aaah," came the unenthusiastic reply. The lieutenant laid down the weapon.

"There was *no* indication that Osama bin Laden was with these men."

"Do you understand me?"

"Hoo---ahhh."

"We took a friendly-fire casualty." He looked at Mick. "Sorry, Sergeant, but it has to be this way. The medics can tell the difference between our pistols and AK-47 wounds. We can't lie about that one and get away with it."

Mick nodded, as if it was what he deserved.

"We lost a good Ranger. He did not die in vain. We continue the war. Do you copy?"

"Hooo-aaah."

"Let me be clear: this is a potential international incident---a violation of an ally's border. There is to be no discussion of this--- *none*---not even to each other---after we return to base. Am I clear."

The "hooo-aaahh" was barely audible this time, accompanied by grim looks, tempered by the loss of one of their own.

"Now, let's get back to base."

Cairo

Jaleel carried his package to the top of the tallest minaret in Cairo, again taking care not to be noticed by the mosque staff. His last message had only been a "go" order for "Allah's Wind." He was told that only a phone call from the same cell phone, with a precise code phrase, could abort the mission. So far, he had not received such a call. His only other directions involved taking care that the wind was blowing northeast or southeast.

And so it was today. What Zawahiri did not know when Jaleel was recruited was that he was a simple man, and had enough trouble picking up today's weather report, let alone the intricacies of wind patterns.

And, indeed, when he left for the minaret, the wind was blowing northeast---toward Israel.

Nor did Jaleel know much about his "delivery," except that it contained a large amount of explosives---how much, he did not know---and radioactive junk, including sand packed inside, although he did not know that. It had a simple timer that he activated with a small button. He had no idea where the device came from. If he had, he would have learned that Saddam Hussein had financed the acquisition of a Russian warhead that was part of the original plan, but during Iraqi Freedom, that had been sent to Syria. Now, Jaleel was dealing with a much smaller-scale "suitcase" nuke than bin Laden hoped. Worse, they had been limited by the weight of the device, and it was even smaller than Zawahiri originally thought.

Much smaller.

Nor did Jaleel know that he was half of what was originally a bold plan to strike simultaneously at Israel and/or the Saudi Royal family and America, in both cases using air currents to be the angel of death.

Least of all, Jaleel could not have guessed that at that half of "Allah's Wind" had been incinerated in a Chicago fireball, or that bin

Laden and Zawahiri were at that moment literally running for their lives.

Jaleel only knew that today he would strike a blow against Zionists or the heretical house of Saud, and that the explosion that took his life would be so massive and quick that he would not know that it had happened. In truth, there was a great deal Jaleel did not know.

Reaching the top of the minaret, he set down the heavy suitcase---*sand is not light!*---and scouted for anyone who might interfere. He was alone. Moving the suitcase to the edge near the guard wall, he pressed the button, and said a final prayer.

Within 10 seconds, a blinding flash and monstrous explosion rocked the mosque, as though artillery had cleaned off the top of the minaret. A thick, black cloud rose into the air as fine particles of radioactive sand rode the wind. Dozens were already dead from the explosion, but thousands in Cairo would be exposed to serious (and some lethal) doses of radioactivity.

The cloud drifted, for miles, northeast, exactly as planned, but dissipating. Then, slowly, steadily, the wind shifted to the north, then the northwest. Just as the trailing edge of the cloud crossed over Sinai, it began to head out into the Mediterranean. By tomorrow morning, the only people outside of Cairo seriously exposed to the radiation were some Turkish sailors unfortunate enough to pass through its wake.

Indeed, had it maintained its potency, it might have posed a threat to the Italian boot and, ironically, the French Riviera. But, of course, it was completely dissipated by then.

331

Epilogue

September 11, 2004, Memorial Service at Ground Zero

"Here we are, C-23-24," Connie said to Jan, pointing down the row. Even though they had arrived early, they still had to excuse themselves to get past a couple and their two teenage sons. "Pardon us. Sorry."

"No problem," replied the man, who gave his wife a smile of warm affection.

The man looked vaguely familiar, but Connie couldn't place him. "Excuse me, but did you lose someone close? On 9/11, I mean?"

The couple glanced at each other again, and he smiled gently. "No family members, but a bunch of fellow firefighters. That's why we're here. I mean, I'm a fireman, and our unit---the whole FDNY--- lost people. But we come here in part to give thanks. I got out, only by the grace of God." He squeezed Shannon's hand tightly as the two boys looked on, bored. "I'm sorry," he extended his hand. "Michael Callahan. This is my wife Shannon and those are my boys Patrick and Sean." Connie could see the boys give a slight uptilt of their heads before shifting their attention.

"Constantine . . . Cataris . . . and my wife, Jan."

"So," Callahan prodded, "why are you here? Brother? Sister?"

A brother? Yeah, you might say that. "His name won't be on the list, and it won't ever appear on a wall. But he's a hero."

"What is his name?" asked Callahan.

"Jake." Connie's eyes misted over, then he regained his composure. "Jake Cleland. Helluva kid." Then, after a pause, Connie lifted his head. "Helluva kid," he repeated.

"I think I know what you mean. We got a lot of heroes at FDNY."

"Fireman Callahan, I'm sure you do. In fact, America has a lot of them. Are you sure we haven't met?"

CNN Report

"Continuing earlier reports out of New York, the turmoil at the United Nations regarding the resignation of Idi Kofar continues. Although Mr. Kofar has admitted to nothing, documents obtained by CNN reveal that money from the Iraqi Oil for Food program funded the 9/11 hijackers. There are allegations that funds also went to support the suicide bombers in Israel as part of the 'intifada' and to pay families of suicide bombers in Iraq.

Along with the surprise resignation of Mr. Kofar, the governments of France, Germany, and Russia have today all introduced a proposal to move the United Nations to Paris. None of the Security Council members voiced any objections, and it appears the General Assembly will confirm the decision. The United States has said it will support the decision of the majority.

Further ramifications of this involve a resolution that appears to have enough votes to pass, that would have the United Nations pay reparations to Israelis for the Oil for Food/suicide bomber scandal. This resolution picked up surprising support from several Muslim countries, including Egypt, which is still recovering from a terrorist "dirty bomb" attack . . . "

Tempe, Arizona

Two Army Rangers in full dress uniforms stood at the front door of the Palmer house. When Ann Palmer opened the door, Chico and Mick came to attention. Mick shifted a little, then began, "Ma'am, we're here unofficially on behalf of the United States government. We have something to tell you---more than you know---about your son's . . . ah, your son's death."

She paused a moment, mustered a brave smile, then opened the door. "Would you like some lemonade? Even in September, Arizona can be hot for out-of-towners, especially in those uniforms."

"Yes, ma'am. That would be nice, ma'am."

"All you Rangers are heroes, you know," she said, grabbing a pitcher of lemonade out of the refrigerator.

Mick grew more uncomfortable by the moment, and knew he couldn't wait. "Ma'am, I have to tell you something. We're here unofficially because you have not been told the truth of your son's death---because he was on a secret mission, and even now we can't tell you the details of it. But I can tell you this . . ." and Mick paused as guilt washed over him ". . . I . . . I was responsible for your son's death." *No, that's not exactly right, is it.* "No, I killed your son. There was a gun battle with, shall we say, a *very* important enemy combatant, and your son . . . it . . . it was an accident, but he got in the line of fire while single-handedly trying to stop this ene . . . ."

Tears formed in Ann's eyes, yet a gentle smile crossed her face. "That's just like Tom. Trying to save the world by himself." Then she noticed the Ranger was weeping too. She set down the lemonade and gathered herself.

"Now, you stop that!" she instructed. "You're a RANGER. You were doing your duty, and I know Tom was doing his. We don't know why our loved ones die---why some live and some don't. Look at the Twin Towers. Do you think only the unjust and unrighteous people died there? Don't you think some good people were trapped, while some evil ones escaped? It doesn't matter to me the details of how my son died. I know, however it was, that he was serving his country with *honor*, the way you do, Sergeant. And you too!" she added, jabbing her finger at Chico.

She dabbed her eyes one last time, then straightened up and managed a smile.

"Now, I'm going to pour some lemonade, and we are first going to toast the heroism of my brave son, then we are going to toast the U.S. Army Rangers, then you two are going to get back to saving the world." Fighting back tears, they managed a smile and they took the lemonade.

"God knows you're going to have to work harder now that my Tom isn't there to help you out!" Then Ann Palmer hoisted her glass.

"To Tom," she said.

"To Tom," they replied quietly.

Then Chico added, "Rangers lead the way!"

THE END

About the Author

Larry Schweikart, former rock musician, has been a professor of history at the University of Dayton for more than 20 years, producing more than 20 academic books and 50 articles.

More recently, his book, co-authored with Michael Allen, *A Patriot's History of the United States* (Sentinel, 2004) has sold more than 42,000 copies and is in its fourth printing in less than a year. His newest non-fiction, *America's Victories: Why Americans Win Wars, and Will Win the War on Terror*, will appear from Sentinel in May 2006.

Printed in the United States
44286LVS00003B/10

9 780974 761084